MONTREAL STORIES

Universitas Press

Montreal

www.universitaspress.com

Canadian Classics Series Editor: Cristina Artenie

Cover illustration: Victoria Square, Montreal, 1870.

First published in November 2024

Library and Archives Canada Cataloguing in Publication

Title: Montreal stories / John Arthur Phillips ; edited by
Henry M. Wallace.
Names: Phillips, J. A. (John Arthur), 1842-1907, author. |
Wallace, Henry M., 1970- editor
Identifiers: Canadiana (print) 20240505735 | Canadiana
(ebook) 20240505808 | ISBN 9781998579013
   (hardcover) | ISBN 9781988963716 (softcover) | ISBN
9781998579020 (EPUB)
Subjects: LCGFT: Short stories.
Classification: LCC PS8481.H55 M66 2024 | DDC
C813/.4—dc23

John Arthur Phillips

MONTREAL STORIES

Edited with an introduction and notes by Henry M. Wallace

Universitas Press
Montreal

John Arthur Phillips in 1897

J. A. PHILLIPS.
President, Parliamentary
Press Gallery.

TABLE OF CONTENTS

Introduction

There is no entry about John Arthur Phillips in the *Dictionary of Canadian Biography*. His name appears in a list in Carl F. Klinck's *Literary History of Canada* about the Montreal publisher John Lovell, in the chapter on "Publishing before 1900," written by H. Pearson Gundy: "Over a period of some fifty years he [Lovell] sought to bring before Canadian readers short stories, novels, and verse by Canadians. A dozen or more writers of fiction and a score of poets and poetasters appeared under the Lovell imprint. The very names of most of them are now forgotten—J. A. Phillips, A. L. Spedon, G. B. Chapin, H. S. Caswell, Frank Johnson, Augusta Baldwin, H. F. Darnell, Mrs. J. P. Grant, Henry Patterson, Kate Douglas Ramage and others. The more successful Canadian writers of fiction at the popular level, such as James De Mille and May Agnes Fleming, published all their work in the United States" (Gundy 196). In fact, in the first edition (1965) of Klinck's *Literary History* there were no names; they were added in the second edition from 1976. Of the ten names listed by Gundy, the last five are actually poets; two or three of the fiction writers are not really Canadian. Lovell's publishing business had a branch in Rouses Point, New York (close to the Canadian border), set up in order to circumvent Canadian copyright laws. As a result, he often had books authored by Canadians printed in Rouses Point and books authored by Americans printed in Montreal. From Gundy's list, Frank Johnson (who published both poetry and fiction with Lovell) was an Englishman who had lived in New Zealand and was back in England after a brief sojourn in Canada. Caswell has not been definitively identified but may have been an American author. Chapin was a young American author from Ogdensburg, New York. Apart from Phillips, the only other truly Canadian fiction writer is Andrew Learmont Spedon (born in Scotland and buried in Bermuda) but, while he remains obscure, he is not entirely forgotten: his name has often been mentioned in recent decades, though mostly thanks to his travelogues.[1] Phillips's name is not mentioned in William H. New's 1989 *A History of Canadian Literature* or in David Staines's recent *A History of Canadian Fiction* (2021).

---

[1] One of Spedon's stories ("The Highlandmen's Hunt; or, The Tale of the Black Hog," which first appeared in his 1866 *Canadian Summer Evening Tales* published by Lovell) was included in our anthology *A Dark Conspiracy and Other 19th-Century Canadian Short Stories in English* (158-165).

Some of the most important pieces of information about John Arthur Phillips come from himself, via Henry James Morgan, the editor of *The Canadian Men and Women of the Time* (1898). Morgan (1842-1913) had been a clerk employed by the federal government and had been for a long time in charge of keeping the country's state records. When he was only 20 years old, he published his first biographical companion, *Sketches of Celebrated Canadians* (1862), which was followed by several editions of the *Canadian Parliamentary Companion* and the *Bibliotheca Canadensis* (1867). A year before his death, he published a second edition of *The Canadian Men and Women*. For all his biographies, Morgan used a questionnaire to which his respondents gave very precise bits of information, beginning with date and place of birth, education, career, etc., and ending with political affiliation, marital status, and address. Morgan also inserted, from time to time, at the end of some of his entries, a blurb from contemporary newspapers (there is one at the end of his entry on Phillips). The entry deserves to be quoted in full, as this will help us compare it with any other information we can add on Phillips (abbreviations have been spelled out):

"PHILLIPS, John Arthur, author and journalist, is the s[on] of Arthur Phillips, Barbadoes, W[est] I[ndies], by Mary Ann Griffith, his wife, and was b[orn] in Liverpool, Eng[land], Feb[ruary] 25, 1842. Ed[ucated] in Barbadoes, he was engaged in business there for several y[ea]rs. He commenced his journalistic career in N[ew] Y[ork], Jan[uary], 1865, under Cha[rle]s Graham Halpin ('Miles O'Reilly'), then publishing the *Citizen*, a weekly literary paper. Coming to Can[ada], 1870, he joined the Montreal *Star*. Later, he ed[ited] the *Hearthstone* and *Favorite*, both weekly literary papers, published by the late G. R. Desbarats. In 1873 he returned to the *Star*, with which he remained until 1875. He then became city ed[itor] of the *Sun*. In 1877 he joined C. R. Tuttle in preparing for publication his 'Illustrated History of the Dom[inion],' and was engaged in this work for over 4 y[ear]rs, writing nearly the whole of the 2 quarto volumes. In 1878 he removed to Ottawa in connection with this enterprise, and has remained a resident of the Federal Capital up to the present time. He was for some time ed[itor] of the Ottawa *Daily Citizen*, and for 14 y[ea]rs he has been Ottawa correspondent of the Montreal *Gazette*. He is also the regular resident correspondent of several other Can[adian] newspapers. Mr. P[hillips] excels as a writer of short stories. Among his published works are: 'Thompson's Turkey, and other Christmas Tales' (1873); 'Hard to Beat' (1877); 'Bad to Worse' (1877); 'The Ghost of a Dog' (1885); 'Out of the Snow, and other Stories' (1886). He has likewise written the patriotic song, 'The Flag for Me.' In 1896 he was elected Presd[iden]t of the Ottawa Press

Gallery. Politically, he is a Con[servative]. He m[arried] 1875, Miss Ivy Sarah Parson.—*78 O'Connor St., Ottawa.* 'Has clearly talent for picturesque and vivid sketches.'—Ottawa Journal." (Morgan 819) This was repeated almost verbatim in William Stewart Wallace's *Encyclopedia of Canada* (V: 153) many decades later.

From Barbados to New York

Phillips was born in Liverpool, but his family must have been native Barbadians. In fact, in an autobiographical essay from 1872 he wrote that "My parents were Barbadians, and indeed our family had been settled on the island over one hundred and fifty years, and I had cousins and other relations without number" ("How I Smashed" 8).[2] There were a lot of people with his last name in Bridgetown in the nineteenth century. He may have been related, for example, to a certain Tobias Phillips, who published a *Barbados Almanac* from 1828 to 1858. He grew up there, which explains why he had such intimate knowledge of the island, its inhabitants, its landmarks, and why he once had a Montrealer (in the story "Out of the Gutter") use the term "frighten-Friday," which actually belongs in Barbadian English (Allsopp 245). He put this knowledge to use especially in his novella "Hard to Beat," which he first serialized in 1873 and later published in a volume with Lovell in 1877, as well as in the story "A Terrible Christmas," included in the same volume and later reprinted in his last collection, *Out of the Snow*, in 1886. In the autobiographical essay "How I Smashed a Ghost" (1872), he also reminisces about an event in his life that had occurred "[a]bout a dozen years ago when I was just getting out of my teens, and trying hard to persuade a sickly little moustache to grow so that I might be taken for a man . . . on the island of Barbadoes in the West Indies, where I spent nearly all my boyish days" (8). The only character who has a line in the essay is his mother, who calls him "Arthur."

One of the most vivid memories of John Arthur Phillips's "boyish days" must have been the 1854 cholera epidemic. The entire world was struck by cholera from 1846 to 1860 and millions of people died during that period. 1854 was probably the worst year and, in English-language sources, it remains associated especially with the London epidemic and with the personality of Dr. John Snow, who identified contaminated water as the way through which cholera was transmitted. Less known is the fact that the West Indies was also hit by the pandemic and that

[2] Also, his obituary states that "As a child he removed to Barbadoes, *the home of his father*" ("Old Newspaperman" 2; my italics).

more than 20,700 people died in Barbados (Sheller 168), out of a population of around 136,000. The novella "Hard to Beat" starts off on 19 May 1854 in the churchyard of St. Leonard's, an Anglican parish in Bridgetown, where cholera victims are summarily buried. The church was actually consecrated on 4 February 1854 and Phillips, who must have witnessed its construction, describes it as "the most peculiar in the West Indies, where buildings are usually low, broad, and flat-roofed; and it would seem strangely familiar to a Canadian. It is long, narrow, high, and has a singularly steep roof, framed expressly to throw off the snow—an unknown luxury in the region where the little chapel stands. It was in fact built after the model of a church near Quebec of which a nephew of the Bishop of Barbadoes was pastor at the time St. Leonard's was built" ("Hard to Beat" 9-10). In 1854, the three main characters of the novella are all teenagers. All three end up in Montreal. Harry Griffith, who turns out to be the villain of the story (and who shares a last name with Phillips's mother), goes to "that El Dorado of his imagination, Canada" (22) and remains with an uncle in Toronto for three years, that is, until 1857. However, "Canada quickly proved too slow for his fiery energy and yearning for rapid success; and so, having a small amount of money, he went to New York to seek his fortune; for the next four years he had varying success, but, on the breaking out of war, he was lucky enough to be engaged in the office of a broker who was well informed [and] he made a rapid fortune" (42). Many years later, on the verge of bankruptcy, Griffith came to Montreal and, in 1870, when the story begins, he is a doctor on Beaver Hall Hill.

In "A Terrible Christmas," one narrator is a Barbadian who comes to Montreal seeking revenge, while the second narrator, a Montrealer raised in upstate New York makes the reverse trip and, on 15 June 1866, travels from Montreal to Barbados, an opportunity for Phillips to show himself well acquainted with the capital of Bridgetown and with other places on the island. In Phillips's other stories, the Barbadian connection is missing, but characters still have both a British and an American past. In "From Bad to Worse," Arthur Austin (who shares a first name with Phillips) is "an Englishman, whose father had emigrated to the States while he was quite a boy . . . he had been in business with his father in New York . . . the father died; the son came to Canada." Father and son were worth "nearly one million" towards the end of the Civil War, but their company went bankrupt six months later when "the close of the war paralysed Wall Street for a time." Arthur Austin then went to Chicago to work as a clerk and from there came to Montreal, where he was hired by Mr. Lubbuck, who had also "started from his home in England at the age of sixteen, and came to Canada, where, after several years roughing it, he settled down in Montreal." Mr. Lubbuck even had a sister whom "he had left behind in Liverpool" before bringing her to Canada.

Like so many of his characters, Phillips must have started out in business (as Morgan's dictionary entry indicates), first in Barbados, then maybe even in New York—he seems to know quite well the world of Wall Street and Broad Street and the stock market of the 1860s, as he mentions the "risings and failings of the value of gold during 1863-4," "the collapse in Mariposa" (1865), "the big rise in Central" (1868) and "Black Friday" (1869)—but, like Thompson in "Thompson's Turkey," he "thought he would turn his talents to account [in] the American papers." In January 1865, according to his answer to Morgan's questionnaire, he started working for the New York *Citizen*, described as "a weekly literary paper." The *Citizen* was a publication of the Citizens' Association of New York, founded with the express purpose of combatting local corruption. Since 1864, its editor was Charles Graham Halpine (or Halpin), born in 1829 in Ireland (he was the son of a Church of Ireland clergyman). Halpine came to the United States in 1851 and he soon became a famous journalist, especially after he followed William Walker's 1855-1856 filibustering expedition to Nicaragua as a correspondent for the recently founded *New York Times*. In 1861, Halpine enlisted in the Union Army and rose to the rank of colonel, being finally promoted to brigadier-general upon discharge. Throughout the war, he published humorous poems, essays, and speeches attributed to an Irish private named "Miles O'Reilly," which became his better-known pseudonym. A critic of the Democratic stronghold of Tammany Hall, Halpine was mostly in favor of a reform movement and pulled no punches when he found fault with certain policies, paying no heed to the party which had originated them. For *The Citizen*, he continued to write both articles and poems, many of which attacked the corruption of various city officials. The young John Arthur Phillips probably found in Halpine a model for the humorous essays about Montreal, which he wrote in the early 1870s under the pseudonym "James Bumpus," as well as for the occasional verse that earned the praise of his contemporaries.

Phillips also had the opportunity to get to know New York City, especially the boroughs of Manhattan and Brooklyn. In many of his stories, he talks admiringly of New York City's theatres, hotels, restaurants, and parks. He even names local celebrities, such as Gus Hamilton, "that prince of ticket speculators" (as he calls him in "From Bad to Worse"), a well-known Broadway scalper. He turns Captain Young, a famous New York City detective, into a secondary character in the same story (and seems to know very well how much money was necessary to buy the officer's allegiance). Phillips's apprenticeship under Halpine lasted only until 3 August 1868, when the editor of the *Citizen* unexpectedly died from an overdose of chloroform (which he used to combat headaches and insomnia). The newspaper came under the editorship (and ownership) of Robert B. Roosevelt (1829-1906), a Democratic politician and sportsman, and continued its run until 1873. Phillips may have stayed on until 1870, as he told Morgan, or he may have contributed to some of the many other New York publications. The only New York newspaper he later mentions in his stories is the *Clipper*, which published news from the entertainment industry. The city, however, shows up in many of his writings, from the first stories he ever published in Montreal ("My Reporter," in which two characters elope to New York, and "S. E. B. H.," set entirely in New York) to his last novella, "The Ghost of a Dog" (which is set mainly in Georgia). In "The Ghost of a Dog," the narrator is a Canadian soldier in the Union Army who took part in "Sherman's March to the Sea" and Phillips would have had the chance to get a host of details from Halpine, who had personally met General Sherman.

Montreal

After 1870, Phillips continued his journalistic career in Montreal, writing for the *Star*. The Montreal *Evening Star*, as it was originally called, had recently been founded (in January 1869) by two young journalists, Hugh Graham and George T. Lanigan. The *Star* was a one-cent ("one copper") daily, which published a lot of sensational news and covered miscellaneous events. It is very possible that the 28-year-old Phillips started as a reporter covering the police beat, since many of his stories feature policemen, magistrates, petty criminals, and murderers. In "The Ghost of a Coat," probably the last short story he ever wrote, Phillips has an alter-ego narrator (a journalist named "Art") investigate the murder of his room-mate, Donnelly, a reporter with a fictional Montreal newspaper who was covering the police beat. After Donnelly's death, Art takes over his friend's beat. Policemen, police detectives, and amateur detectives populate many of his other stories, such as "From Bad to Worse," "Thompson's Turkey" or "The Policeman's Christmas." Most of this early fiction was first published in *The Hearthstone* and its successor *The Favorite*.

The *Hearthstone* was a literary weekly, of which seven numbers had been issued in May-June 1870, after which it became a monthly until September of that year, when it was bought by a certain Thomas H. Churchill, who lowered the subscription cost from $2.50 per year to only $1 and offered a set of teaspoons to each subscriber. Over fifteen thousand people paid for the annual subscription but Churchill absconded to the US with the money.[3] The paper was then taken over by George-Édouard Desbarats (1838-1893), a renowned printer and inventor, who was also the publisher of the *Canadian Illustrated News*. According to his own account, Desbarats kept *The Hearthstone* afloat for a while, despite the bad reputation it had acquired under Churchill (Desbarats 4), by serializing best-selling British fiction (by the likes of Wilkie Collins, Charles Kingsley and Mary Elizabeth Braddon) or even translations from French authors (for example, Émile Gaboriau) and by reproducing articles from British and American literary magazines. Some time in January 1872, Desbarats enlisted the help of John Arthur Phillips, who became the editor of *The Hearthstone*. Very soon, under Phillips's editorship, *The Hearthstone* started looking more and more like a Canadian publication and like a publication based in Montreal. He probably had two short stories ready for print when he joined the weekly, because the 3 February 1872 issue had on its front page his first ever signed contribution, "My Reporter. A Story of an Elopement" (set in Montreal), and the following issue (10 February 1872) started with "S. E. B. H. A Story of a Secret Society" (set in New York).

During the first half of 1872, Phillips published six satirical essays about the city of Montreal, in a series entitled "Bumptown Papers" (from 23 March to 27 April), one more short story ("A Perfect Fraud") on 20 April, as well as his first novella, "From Bad to Worse. A Tale of Montreal Life," which was serialized from 4 May to 29 June 1872. The only other Canadian author of fiction was Isabella Valancy Crawford, who published in *The Hearthstone* her very first short stories, "The Hospital Gondola" (13 April 1872) and "Windale's Souvenir" (1 and 8 June 1872), as well as her first two poems. In the 29 June 1872 issue of the journal, which included the last instalment of his novella, Phillips[4]

---

[3] Churchill was a real confidence man of the publishing industry. South of the border, he managed to swindle a famous American occultist, P. B. Randolph (1825-1875), taking his money with the promise of distributing his books and then disappearing (see Clymer 38, 107).

[4] We cannot know for sure that Phillips himself penned this advertisement; however, we know that the stories were received and read by the editor and many later notices regarding the competition mention the editor. As William Henry Atherton writes in his 1914 history of the city of Montreal, "the editorial work of The Hearthstone was performed by J. A. Phillips" (III, 471). Atherton's words should be understood quite literally: it is very likely that the entire editorial work was the responsibility of a single person.

(undoubtedly with Desbarats's blessing), inserted an advertisement "To the Literary Men and Women of Canada" offering monetary prizes for novels ($500 for first place; $300 for second place) that could be serialized in *The Hearthstone*; for novellas ($250 for first place; $150 for second place); and short stories "complete in one number" ($50 for first place; $25 for second place). The editor announced a very bold objective: "We want to have an essentially Canadian paper, and gradually to dispense with selections and foreign contributions, &c." ("Wanted!!" 4). Here is the editor's patriotic exhortation:

"We want to become acquainted with you!

We want to unearth the hidden talent, now buried in our cities and hamlets, inland farms and seaside dwellings, primeval forests and storm-tossed barks.

We crave narratives, novels, sketches penned by vigorous Canadian hands, welling out from fresh and fertile Canadian brains, thrilling with the adventures by sea and land, of Canadian heroes; redolent with the perfume of Canadian fields and forests, soft as our sunshine, noble as our landscapes, grand as our inland seas and foam-girt shores.

What inexhaustible fields in the realms of fact and fancy lie open to your industry and genius, women and men of Canada! What oceans of romance! What worlds of poesy! Why then do we see so little worthy of note brought forth in literature by our countrymen and countrywomen? Merely for want of material support and encouragement! That is all.

Now we open a tournament to native talent, and invite all to enter the lists. We ask for novels and stories founded on Canadian history, experience and incident—illustrative of back wood life, fishing, lumbering, farming; taking the reader through our industrious cities, floating palaces, steam-driven factories, ship-building yards, lumbering shanties, fishing smacks, &c." ("Wanted!" 4)

In the following number, Phillips inserted a note explaining exactly how "Canadian" the stories and the authors had to be:

"1st. A story *will* do with the scenes laid partly in Canada and partly in another country; but the choice will be given to a purely Canadian story; the more Canadian it is in plot, incident and feeling, the more likely it is to be accepted. 2nd. By 'native talent' we do not mean to exclude all but born Canadians; any resident of Canada is eligible to compete, and the subject of birth or nationality will not be taken into consideration at all as long as the writer is a resident of Canada." ("Our Prize Stories" 4)

Until the end of the year, Phillips serialized one Canadian short novel, Rosanna Leprohon's "The Dead Witness; or, Lilian's Peril"

(3 August-5 October 1872),[5] and then (at the end of September) announced that *The Hearthstone* would accept Christmas stories: "Let the stories be about Christmas *in Canada*, we can get plenty of stories about other places, but we don't want them; we desire to have a Canadian paper, with Canadian authors, writing tales of Canadian life. We will pay our highest rates for Christmas stories, if they are good" ("Christmas Stories" 4). At the beginning of November, the editor was asking the authors that had submitted stories for patience; in early December, a short notice announced that "In consequence of the serious illness of the Editor there will be some unavoidable delay in deciding upon the merits of the many stories sent in competition for the prizes offered by the Proprietor of the HEARTHSTONE" ("The Hearthstone Prize Stories" 4). One week later, Phillips announced that he was "resuming control of the paper, after an illness of five weeks" and he was "offering his most sincere thanks to Frank Krauss, Esq., Editor of the *Canadian Illustrated News*, and to W. Topless, Esq., Sub-Editor of the *Montreal Herald*, for their valuable services in conducting the paper for him while he was unable to attend to it himself" ("Returning Thanks" 4). Finally, on 28 December 1872, Desbarats announced that *The Hearthstone* would be replaced by *The Favorite*, a new weekly paper, "one-fourth larger" and without "the bad odium attached to" the paper's previous name ("To Our Subscribers" 4). While Phillips's illness had probably been genuine (hence his acknowledgement of the help received from colleagues), the delay in announcing the fiction prizes had clearly been caused by the owner's decision to discontinue *The Hearthstone*. Moreover, Desbarats's message to subscribers contradicted Phillips's promise of Canadianizing the paper and announced that *The Favorite* "will contain the productions of the very best Canadian, English, and American writers" (4).

   The Favorite began with an extra Christmas number (which subscribers to *The Hearthstone* received for free) on 28 December 1872, which included stories by Isabella Valancy Crawford and her sister Emma Naomi Crawford.[6] John Arthur Phillips was present with a short story ("The Christmas Anthem," set in the Eastern Townships),

[5] Rosanna Leprohon (1829-1879), the author of *Antoinette de Mirecourt* (1864) was perhaps the best-known English-language fiction writer in Montreal. Interestingly, her husband, Dr. Leprohon, was often mentioned in newspapers as being summoned to the Montreal Central Police Station to treat various patients (both victims and perpetrators) and he could have met Phillips while the latter was a reporter for the *Montreal Star*.
[6] Emma Naomi Crawford (1852-1876) published a few other stories in *The Favorite*. One of them ("Buggins' Mare") was collected in our anthology *A Dark Conspiracy and Other 19th-Century Canadian Short Stories in English* (197-203).

a satirical essay ("Our Christmas Dinner") and the autobiographical fragment mentioned above ("How I Smashed a Ghost"). In the 11 January 1873 issue (with "Vol. I—No. 1" on its frontispiece), two longer fictions debuted: Phillips's "Hard to Beat" and Crawford's "Winona; or The Foster-Sisters." Crawford's fiction had won the prize competition supervised by Phillips.[7] Other stories by Canadian authors published by *The Favorite* in 1873 had probably been awarded smaller prizes. Phillips's "Hard to Beat" (set in Barbados, Montreal and Longueuil, with a backstory in New York) ran until 5 April 1873. He also published three poems and four satirical essays, the last of which was "A Dream of Life. An Allegory," which appeared on 28 June 1873. It seems quite clear that some time in the summer of 1873 John Arthur Phillips ceased his collaboration with *The Favorite* and Desbarats. He returned to the *Star*, which was becoming more and more popular and whose Saturday edition (*The Family Herald and Weekly Star*) had reached a circulation of 14,000 (Rowell 243). In December 1873, Phillips also published his first volume: *Thompson's Turkey and Other Christmas Tales; Poems, &c* (Montreal: John Lovell), a collection of seven short stories (five of which are set in Montreal) and ten poems. Only one of the stories had appeared in *The Favorite*, which suggests that Phillips had originally prepared them for publication in the weekly he was editing but, after quitting his position there, he decided to have them printed in book form. He remained at *The Star* until 1875 and the next couple of years of his life are a little bit of a mystery.

Toronto and Ottawa

In his answers to Morgan's questionnaire, Phillips indicated that he had worked as city editor of the (Toronto) *Sun* in or after 1875. The otherwise well-informed *Ottawa Citizen* obituary says nothing about Phillips's (probably brief) stint in Toronto. Established in 1872 by W. H. Barrett as an evening paper, the *Sun* (no relation with the well-known paper founded in 1971) did not exceed a circulation of 2,000 (Rowell 241) and was but "a short-lived venture" (Bone 170). Morgan's encyclopedia entry gets the years wrong in saying that Phillips started working for C. R. Tuttle only in 1877 (Tuttle's first volume was published that year and the work clearly required a couple of years of research). The obituary gives another, cleaner, narrative, skipping the *Sun* entirely

[7] Crawford had to sue Desbarats because, although Phillips had selected her story for the $500 prize, the proprietor of the journal seemed reluctant to pay. She won the case ("Reports" 320).

and having Phillips work for Tuttle as early as 1875 "in the preparation of a two-volume history of Canada" ("Old Newspaperman" 2).

Charles Richard Tuttle (1848-1918), born in Nova Scotia, was first a journalist in Boston and elsewhere in the United States, where he prepared historical volumes on Michigan and Wisconsin. Back in Canada, he published an illustrated *Popular History of the Dominion of Canada*, the first volume of which appeared in 1877 and did not mention Phillips. The second volume (covering the period "from the Confederation of 1867 to the close of 1878" and bearing the slightly different title of *The Comprehensive History of the Dominion of Canada*) appeared in 1879; Phillips's contribution is acknowledged in the preface: "The Editor would not fail to mention the name of Mr. John A. Phillips, a gentleman who has been connected with the newspaper press in Montreal, Toronto and Ottawa, and who has assisted in the compilation of *both the first and second volumes* of this work; and whose labors, the writer is free to acknowledge, have been not only faithful and arduous, but very productive. It is the hope and expectation of the Editor, that Mr. Phillips's labors will also be associated with those of the writer in the preparation of the future volumes of this work" (Tuttle 18; my italics). There were no other volumes, however; the same year, Tuttle moved to Winnipeg and became a prominent Manitoban, founding the *Winnipeg Daily Times* and entering provincial politics until 1885, when he moved to Chicago and turned his attention to American history. Tuttle's brief notice (in a preface dated "Ottawa, 1879"), does, however, confirm Phillips's presence in Toronto in the mid-1870s; it also suggests he had found work as a journalist in Ottawa after 1875. Both Morgan's entry and the obituary say that Phillips only came to Ottawa in 1878 and give different reasons for the move: that he came to work for Tuttle's *History* (according to Morgan); and to enter the civil service as assistant secretary to the department of public works (as reported by the obituary). Nevertheless, Tuttle is probably right and, while he compiled the *History of the Dominion of Canada* from 1875 to 1878, Phillips must have found work as a journalist, first in Toronto (for the *Sun* and maybe other publications) and then in Ottawa, where he ended up in government employ.

We do know that Phillips was one of the contributors to the very first issue of *Belford's Monthly Magazine. A Magazine of Literature and Art* (December 1876), published by the Belford Brothers of Toronto. His name appears in this issue attached to a story ("A Familiar Fiend") and a poem ("In the Fire"). The poem also mentions the place of composition as "Montreal," whereas the story does not and the narrator identifies himself only as the inhabitant of a "large city." However, it is very likely that the story was either written in Montreal or about Montreal. In 1877, Phillips brought out a second collection of fiction, again with the Montreal publisher John Lovell, which included his two novellas from 1872-1873 ("From Bad to Worse," first published in *The Hearthstone*, and "Hard to Beat" from *The Favorite*) and a short story ("A Terrible Christmas"), set in Montreal and Barbados. He did not publish any fiction again until the mid-1880s. On 5 July 1878, a "double acrostic" appeared with his signature in the *Listowel Standard*, on the anticipated departure of the Marquess of Dufferin, governor-general of Canada between 1872 and 1878. The poem is dated "Ottawa, 6th June, 1878." In *The Canadian Illustrated News* (published in Montreal by George Desbarats) of 30 November 1878, Phillips published another poem, "A Welcome to Canada" (dated "Ottawa, 23rd November, 1878") dedicated to the Marquess of Lorne (the new governor-general) and his wife Louise (one of Queen Victoria's daughters). Although the obituary hesitates about the time when Phillips left civil service and returned to journalism (and Morgan's entry does not say), it is clear that he was already a journalist as early as 1880 (much sooner than what the obituary suggests), working as correspondent in the capital for the Winnipeg *Times* (edited by his friend C. R. Tuttle) ("Pencillings" 151). In the beginning of the following year he is mentioned as the Ottawa correspondent of a different newspaper: the *Quebec Chronicle* ("The Press Gallery" 1). In June 1881, a brief note in *Grip*, the Toronto satirical magazine, quotes another acrostic by Phillips (originally published in the *Montreal Gazette* but dated "Ottawa, 24th May 1881"), this time about Hector-Louis Langevin (1826-1906), one of the Fathers of the Confederation, who had just been knighted. The article says that Phillips's "post office address is Ottawa, and he writes—what shall we say?—well, he writes acrostics. Others have written acrostics, too, but none so brilliantly as Phillips . . . in the annals of Canadian poetry" ("Phillips 7).

For the last quarter of a century of his life, John Arthur Phillips lived in Ottawa and was known as a correspondent for various Canadian newspapers who wrote occasional poetry. At times, he was sending correspondences from Parliament Hill to two or even three newspapers simultaneously: in early 1882, he is mentioned as the correspondent for the Hamilton *Spectator*, the London *Free Press*, and the Quebec *Chronicle* ("Gallery Notes" 2). He probably sent dispatches, as Morgan's entry says, mostly for the *Montreal Gazette*; but he contributed to various other newspapers, from the Toronto *World* (in 1892) to the *Calgary Herald* (in 1894). Apart from correspondences, he also worked on the editorial staff of some local publications, such as the Ottawa *Citizen* (in 1890-

1891) or *Le Temps* (1906-1907). In January 1896, he was elected vice-president of the Press Gallery of Ottawa ("The Press Gallery for 1896" 2) and in 1897 he became its president (and his picture appeared in *Massey's Magazine*). In 1898, he was mentioned in a short list of notable Canadian journalists in *Canada: An Encyclopaedia of the Country* (Hopkins 230). In March 1897 he was elected vice-president of the Ottawa chapter of the philanthropic St George's Society; he became president in 1901. In December 1895, in *The People's Almanac 1896* (a supplement of the *Montreal Gazette*), he published a poem for which he was still remembered at the time of his death: "The Flag for Me" (dated "Ottawa, 21 October 1895") about the Union Jack. His wife died on 10 November 1899 (their only child had died in infancy). "Captain" Phillips (as he was known to his friends) died on 8 January 1907 in Ottawa, in the press room of the House of Commons ("on [the] scene of his labors," as the *Ottawa Journal* reported). According to the story published the following day in the *Ottawa Citizen*, his last words were addressed to John Cooney, night chief operator of the C. P. R. telegraph, and were "Good-bye, Jack; this is the end" ("Old Newspaperman" 2).

Phillips made two more attempts, both in the mid-1880s, to revive his career as a fiction writer. First, in 1885, he published *The Ghost of a Dog* (Ottawa: A. S. Woodburn) which, apart from the titular novella (set mostly in the American South at the end of the Civil War), includes a short story, "How I Was Mesmerised," set in the Canadian capital. One year later, he published *Out of the Snow and Other Stories and Sketches* (Ottawa: Free Press), a collection of seven short stories, six of which written in the 1870s, and a new fiction ("The Ghost of a Coat") set in Montreal. Almost half a century later, one of the young apprentices in the printing shop of the Free Press (a "printer's devil," as the contemporary term was) recollected his impressions of John Arthur Phillips, "coming to, and going from, the job room. Mr. Phillips at the time was a stout, middle-aged man. He had rooms over Hay's hardware store. . . . To help out in the cost of publication, Mr. Phillips' book carried a number of advertisements of local merchants, many of whom have long been out of business" ("John A Phillips" 2).[8] The two volumes got a few (short) reviews, but they failed to attract too much attention (perhaps the best—and longest—review was that of *The Ghost of a Dog* from the *Montreal Gazette* of 18 December 1885). Phillips's name reappeared in a few publications throughout Canada during the First World War, as his poem "The Flag for Me" resurfaced in people's memory.

[8] George Hay (1822-1910) was a well-known businessman and philanthropist in Ottawa. In the 1880s, he was also a director of the Bank of Ottawa.

Canadian Realism

Commentators of Canadian fiction at the end of the 19th century were usually wary of too much realism to the detriment of the "higher" goal of improving the morals and molding a virtuous nation. The influential John George Bourinot[9] spoke for many when he said, in an 1893 speech before the Royal Society of Canada, that his hope was that "Canadians [would] not bring the Canadian fiction of the future to that low level to which the school of realism in France, and in a minor degree in England and the United States, would degrade the novel and story of every-day life" (Bourinot 20). Like so many of his peers, Bourinot, who had penned a novel himself, preferred romantic fiction, especially a tale of improbable adventure in picturesque settings like remote Canadian forests, all ending with the reward of a wholesome love story. On the other hand, a large number of Canadian authors (especially those practising the art of the short fiction) had embraced first satirical realism and then the "fact-based" plot. The latter did not prevent some fiction writers from veering towards romanticism (even Bourinot claimed that his novel was "founded on facts"), but many authors held onto their realistic designs, whether because "the facts" were borrowed from their own lives (like in the case of Susanna Moodie) or because their heroes were simple men and women that the author had met (see, for example, the case of Mary Katzmann). In the nineteenth century, in fact (as I have argued elsewhere), "the most typically Canadian fictional form [was] the fact-based short story" (Wallace viii).

Phillips, too, used his own personal experiences in Barbados, New York, and Montreal, but he also put to work his "reportorial experiences" ("John A Phillips" 2). His fictions are always set either in the year when they were published or a few years before—and Phillips is always careful with the chronology of events. For example, in "From Bad to Worse," we find out that Arthur married Effie "six years ago," i.e., in 1867; that she faked her death two years later (1869), when a financial panic also started on Wall Street (Black Friday). He is also very careful with the geography of the city, clearly delineated by his characters cruising down the numerous streets of Old Montreal. Like other realists with journalistic roots, Phillips brings up in his stories various news items that contemporary society remembered too well (for example, the tragedy of Tabb's Yard, mentioned in "Out of the Gutter").

[9] Bourinot (1836-1902) was honorary secretary of the Royal Society of Canada since its inception in 1882 and was later elected vice-president and president.

However, Phillips goes so far as to *name* many of the real-life characters that appear in his fiction. In "From Bad to Worse," Arthur and Jessie get married in Christ Church Cathedral in downtown Montreal—and, as this is a real church and the year is 1873, Phillips writes that "the happy pair" were united by "the Rev. Canon Baldwin," since Maurice Baldwin was then canon of Christ Church Cathedral. A police detective in the same story mentions the Police Magistrate and, because there was only one such person in the city of Montreal, Phillips names him: "Mr. Brehaut." Charlie Brydon, towards the end of the story, is under the observation of two police officers, and Phillips again gives their names: High Constable Bissonette and Constable Lafontaine. Both are names of real-life contemporary Montreal policemen. Bissonette and Brehaut, the Police Magistrate, had actually been involved in a cause célèbre in 1866, when a French police inspector arrived in Montreal seeking the extradition of a fugitive called Lamirande. Later, Bissonette was also involved in the capture of some famous criminals, like Charles Worms and Donald Morrison, "the Megantic Outlaw."

Phillips's habit of naming the real-life characters used in his fictions turns truly spectacular when he gives them lines and has them really take part in the story. (He must have received at least some kind of verbal agreement from them.) One of the most famous Montrealers that get lines in "From Bad to Worse" is Charles McKiernan, known as "Joe Beef" (1835-1889), a popular restaurateur and philanthropist. McKiernan appears grumpy, but generous, witty and assertive. Another Montrealer who gets lines but then also becomes a secondary character is Detective Andrew Cullen. In "From Bad to Worse," Cullen is hired by Arthur Austin to do investigative work in New York and Savannah. Later, Cullen arrests Austin before he realizes the real culprit was Brydon. In real life, Andrew Cullen was indeed a detective in Montreal (he would later become Chief Detective of the Montreal Police Force) and also a kind of national celebrity. In Phillips's novella, the detective speaks with "just 'the least bit of a brogue,'" a transparent allusion to Cullen's Irish roots. In fact, Andrew Cullen spoke Gaelic and, in 1868, during the trial of Patrick James Whelan, the presumptive assassin of Thomas D'Arcy McGee, he went undercover in the cell next to Whelan's and heard him confess. Cullen's testimony was then crucial in Whelan's indictment (see Wilson 55). Another policeman that gets a speaking part in "From Bad to Worse" is Captain John Young, formerly with the NYPD. Young was well known both for his efficiency and for his lack of scruples in money matters. In Phillips's story, he appears calm and very practical (the money he asks for in exchange for his services is ten times what Cullen of Montreal had received). In the 1873 short story "A Policeman's Christmas" the narrator/character is an altruistic constable called Barnes. A real-life Sub-Constable Barnes is mentioned in Montreal papers in the early 1870s. In 1872, he saved the life of a man who tried to commit suicide by jumping off McGee's Bridge ("City Items" 5),[10] not far from Wellington Bridge (which is part of Barnes's city beat in Phillips's story). At the end of "The Ghost of a Dog" (his 1885 novella), Phillips inserted a fictional note from the *Ottawa Times*, in which a "Sub-Constable Barnes" is mentioned, suggesting that, in the late 1860s (when the novella is set) Barnes was working in Ottawa. In "A Policeman's Christmas," the fictionalized Sub-Constable Barnes decides to quit the police. Finally, Phillips inserted himself in some of the stories, through alter-ego characters named "Art" or "Arthur" and especially through the narrator in "Thompson's Turkey," an amateur sleuth named "Phillips."

Phillips's Montreal

In "From Bad to Worse," Detective Cullen is once described as "feeling more and more uncomfortable about the case he was engaged in. He *is* a tender-hearted man, and there *is* a soft sport under the left side of his waistcoat" (my italics). The use of the present simple is a rare case in which Phillips seems to acknowledge directly and to signal to the reader that the character is a real person, who also exists outside the page. In the same story, and within the same paragraph, Effie "announced her intention of spending the summer *here*" and Arthur was driven crazy at the "risk he was running through her being *here*" (my italics). The use of "here" instead of the usual "there," whether voluntary or not, shows the scene through the perspective of a bona fide Montrealer. Phillips was clearly very attached to the idea of representing Montreal in all its misery and glory, with all its diverse humanity. He started doing that in a series of essays called "The Bumptown Papers" (the first of which appeared on 23 March 1872 in *The Hearthstone*), in which he pretended to talk about a different city called Bumptown: "Bumptown does not differ in many particulars from your own Montreal. It has long streets not half as wide as they ought to be; its streets are as ill-paved, as dirty and as dusty; its sidewalks are as rotten and as dangerous; its gas is as bad, and its Gas Company is as impudent and extortionate, as in Montreal. Its sidewalks are as slippery in the winter and as hot and dusty in the summer as in your own city. Its water-works are as uncertain

---

[10] Today better known as Pont des Seigneurs.

and their Superintendent as indolent and careless as your own; its City Passenger Company is as careless of the comforts of the public, and runs the same kind of ice boxes as in Montreal. It has a big debt and is very anxious to make it bigger, just like Montreal."

However well described, Phillips's Montreal is a smaller version of the real city: the reader is never taken farther east than St Claude Street and the Bonsecours Market; farther west than Guy Street; farther north than Sherbrooke Street; or farther south than Rue de la Commune and the harbour. His characters move around what we call today Old Montreal and Griffintown, and the center of this limited version of Montreal seems to be Place d'Armes and perhaps the area occupied today by the Palais des Congrès, where the Theatre Royal used to stand. Phillips was clearly a theatregoer (and he wrote about theatre actors in the story "Christmas in the Flies") and it is here that he probably saw *The French Spy* (which is featured prominently in "From Bad to Worse"), with Marietta Ravel (1832-1898) in a triple role. Ravel was in Montreal with the show during the first week of August 1870 (Graham 193) and again starting on 20th May 1872 (205). Phillips's characters are either working class or middle class, with the richest being businessmen whose houses on Sherbrooke Street (but never farther into the "New Town," later known as the Golden Square Mile) are mentioned but rarely seen. Phillips chooses to ignore Montreal's genuine "elite" of (relatively) old money and pretends that the city's most successful businessmen are upstarts like Lubbuck (in "From Bad to Worse") and Dumsic (in "Thompson's Turkey"). Lubbuck is worth $200,000 and is described as "one of the richest men in Montreal." By way of comparison, Sir Hugh Allan, the actual richest man in Montreal at the time, was worth more than 50 million dollars.

One of the social problems that recur in Phillips's Montreal is alcoholism (see, for example, "The Policeman's Christmas" and "From Bad to Worse"), which should not surprise. According to the 1871 Canadian Census, the city of Montreal had about 130,000 inhabitants, and its metropolitan area a population of about 174,000 (both numbers would nearly double over the following two decades). At the same time, in the 1860s and 1870s, the Recorder's Court (which dealt with minor cases and is featured quite prominently in Phillips's Montreal stories) received around 20 people arrested for drunkenness every single day. The highest number on record was, in fact, 1873, when Phillips wrote many of his stories and when 8,558 people were arrested for being "drunk and vagrant" (Borthwick 270). The number took a sharp decline in 1876 and it went as low as 2,190 in 1879, suggesting the temperance movement, which was very active in society and in the press (and to which Phillips contributed in his fiction) had been quite successful. Despite his genuine love for the city, Phillips very subtly likes to point out some objectionable aspects of Montreal's recent history. The villains in both "From Bad to Worse" (Brydon and Effie) and "A Terrible Christmas" (Bergen) stay at the same Montreal hotel: St. Lawrence Hall. Only a few years before, during the American Civil War, so had a host of Confederate spies, including John Wilkes Booth, Lincoln's assassin (who stayed there in October 1864) and John Surrat, Booth's co-conspirator. To make the connection clear, Phillips has Brydon stay at Spottswood House in Richmond, Virginia, before coming to Montreal. John Surrat also stayed at Spottswood House right before travelling north and ending up in Montreal at the end of March, beginning of April 1865 (*Trial* II, 789). In fact, Robert E. Lee had accepted command of the Confederate Army in front of the Spottswood House (Sheehan-Dean I, 5). In "The Policeman's Christmas," the villains try to run to St. Albans, Vermont, at a time when the St. Albans Raid, conducted from Canada into Vermont by Confederate soldiers in 1864 was still fresh in people's minds (as was the fact that the raiders had been arrested in Montreal, but subsequently released).

Phillips was an early practitioner of the detective story, although he preferred, as he always did in his fiction, to give it a satirical twist. He was always concerned with mixing genres (stories and novellas are sometimes presented as plays and divided into acts and scenes) and telling a story from different perspectives, by allowing different characters to show their own version. He was an exponent of that other very specifically Canadian narrative form of the third quarter of the 19th century: the "medley," in which "the narrator/character becomes intimate with the hero of the account, which may or may not be a love story (parodied or not); this account is interrupted by humorous character sketches; dialectal speech is carefully reproduced; there are several scenes in which people of various social strata interact; naturally, it is set in a city or town and cityscapes play an important part" (Wallace viii). It may seem surprising that his name has remained completely forgotten in the last 150 years (and even in the last 50 years since Gundy's account in the *Literary History of Canada*). However, there are two reasons that are quite obvious. First, Phillips made the crucial mistake of never trying to have his fiction published in England and/or the United States. Every single nineteenth-century Canadian author that managed to escape the oblivion pronounced by Gundy had published all or most of their fiction outside Canada and had reached at least some kind of nominal fame. Second, despite the initial reluctance towards realism and towards more "experimental" fiction, both were embraced in the 1960s and 1970s in Canada, but they were only "discovered" in 20th-century literature. When 19th-century fiction writers are resurrected and even studied in English-literature courses, it is because of their "nation-building" efforts in their novels that include a so-called "marriage metaphor," in which an English-speaking man marries a French-speaking woman (or vice versa), sometimes with the help of the benevolent daughter of a First Nations chief. The urban realism of 19th-century Canada is yet to be discovered. Despite the alarm sounded by Robert Lecker almost 35 years ago about the hurried birth of a rigid Canadian literary canon, there are still many authors that do not deserve their obscurity. One of them is John Arthur Phillips.

WORKS CITED

Allsopp, Richard, Ed. *Dictionary of Caribbean English Usage*. Kingston: University of the West Indies Press, 2003.

Atherton, William Henry. *History of Montreal*. Montreal: S. J. Clarke, 1914.

Bone, John, Joseph T. Clarke, A. H. U. Colquhoun, and John F. Mackay, Eds. *A History of Canadian Journalism*. Toronto: The Canadian Press Association, 1908.

Borthwick, J. Douglas. *History of the Montreal Prison from A. D. 1784 to A. D. 1886*. Montreal: A. Periard, 1886.

Bourinot, John George. "Our Intellectual Strength and Weakness: A Short Review of Literature, Education and Art in Canada." *Proceedings and Transactions of the Royal Society of Canada for the Year 1893*. Vol. 11, Section II: English Literature, History, Archaeology. Ottawa: John Durie; Montreal: W. Foster Brown, 1894. 3-54.

"Christmas Stories." *The Hearthstone* 3: 39 (28 September 1872), 4.

"City Items." *Montreal Daily Witness* 4 July 1872. 5.

Clymer, R. Swinburne. *The Rose Cross Order*. Allentown, PA: The Philosophical Publishing Co., 1916.

Desbarats, G-É. "To Our Subscribers." *The Hearthstone* 3: 52 (28 December 1872), 4.

"Died on Scene of His Labors." *Ottawa Journal* 9 January 1907, 8.

"Gallery Notes." *Ottawa Daily Citizen* 14: 34 (10 February 1882), 2.

Graham, Franklin. *Histrionic Montreal. Annals of the Montreal Stage with Biographical and Critical Notices of the Plays and Players of a Century.* Second edition. Montreal: John Lovell, 1902.

Gundy, H. Pearson. "Literary Publishing." *Literary History of Canada. Canadian Literature in English.* Ed. Carl F. Kinck. Second Edition. Vol. I. Toronto: University of Toronto Press, 1976. 188-202.

Hopkins, J. Castell. *An Historical Sketch of Canadian Literature and Journalism.* Reprinted from *Canada: An Encyclopaedia of the Country.* Toronto: Linscott, 1898.

"John A Phillips Was Writer of Short Stories, Eighties." *The [Ottawa] Evening Citizen* 90: 72 (10 September 1932). 2.

Lecker, Robert. "The Canonization of Canadian Literature: An Inquiry into Value." *Critical Inquiry* 16: 3 (Spring 1990), 656-671.

Morgan, Henry James, Ed. *The Canadian Men and Women of the Time: A Hand-Book of Canadian Biography.* Toronto: William Briggs, 1898.

New, William H. *A History of Canadian Literature.* London: Macmillan, 1989.

"Old Newspaperman." *The [Ottawa] Evening Citizen* 63: 19 (9 January 1907), 2.

"Our Prize Stories." *The Hearthstone* 3: 27 (6 July 1872), 4.

"Pencillings from the Press Gallery." *The Printer's Miscellany* 4: 10 (April 1880), 151.

"Phillips." *Grip* 17: 4 (11 June 1881), 7.

Phillips, J. A. "Bumptown Papers. Paper I. Our Town." *The Hearthstone* 3: 12 (23 March 1872), 4.

Phillips, J. A. "Hard to Beat." *From Bad to Worse, Hard to Beat and A Terrible Christmas. Three Stories of Montreal Life.* Montreal: Lovell, 1877. 9-150.

"Reports of the 1873 Autumn Assizes, Peterborough, Ontario." Isabella Valancy Crawford. *Winona; or, The Foster-Sisters.* Ed. Len Early and Michael Peterman. Peterborough: Broadview, 2007. 320-321.

"Returning Thanks." *The Hearthstone* 3: 50 (14 December 1872), 4.

Rowell, George Presbury, Ed. *American Newspaper Directory.* Seventh Edition. New York: Geo. P. Rowell & Co., 1875.

Sentilles, Renée M. *Performing Menken. Adah Isaacs Menken and the Birth of American Celebrity.* Cambridge: Cambridge University Press, 2003.

Sheehan-Dean, Aaron, Ed. *A Companion to the U.S. Civil War.* Vol. I-II. Hoboken: Wiley-Blackwell, 2014.

Staines, David. *A History of Canadian Fiction.* Cambridge: Cambridge University Press, 2021.

"The Hearthstone Prize Stories." *The Hearthstone* 3: 49 (7 December 1872), 4.

"The Press Gallery." *Ottawa Free Press* 21 February 1881, 1.

"The Press Gallery for 1896." *The Canadian Printer & Publisher* 5: 1 (January 1896), 2.

Trial of John H. Surratt in the Criminal Court for the District of Columbia. Washington: Government Printing Office, 1867.

Tuttle, Charles Richard, Ed. *The Comprehensive History of the Dominion of Canada.* Montreal: H. B. Bigney, 1879.

Wallace, Henry M. "Introduction." *A Dark Conspiracy and other 19th-century Canadian Short Stories in English.* Ed. Henry M. Wallace. Montreal: Universitas Press, 2023. vii-xii.

Wallace, William Stewart, Ed. *The Encyclopedia of Canada.* Vol. I-VI. Toronto: University Associates of Canada, 1935-1937.

"Wanted!!" *The Hearthstone* 3: 26 (29 June 1872), 4.

Wilson, David A. "Was Patrick James Whelan a Fenian and Did He Assassinate Thomas D'Arcy McGee?" *Irish Nationalism in Canada.* Ed. David A. Wilson. Montreal: McGill-Queen's University Press, 2009. 52-82.

WORKS CITED IN THE FOOTNOTES

Annual Report of the Chief of Police. Montreal: Louis Perrault, 1882.

Chisholm, C[olin]. R[emigius]., Ed. *Chisholm's Stranger's Guide to Montreal.* Montreal: C. R. Chisholm & Bros, 1873.

Mysteries of Crime, as Shown in Remarkable Capital Trials. By Members of the Massachusetts Bar. Boston: Samuel Walker & Co., 1870.

Redfield's Traveler's Guide to the City of New York. New York: J. S. Redfield, 1871.

Seagrave, Kerry. *Ticket Scalping. An American History, 1850-2005.* Jefferson, NC: McFarland, 2007.

Sheller, Mimi. *Consuming the Caribbean. From Arawaks to Zombies.* London: Routledge, 2003.

Stranger's Illustrated Guide to the City of Montreal. Montreal: The Montreal Printing & Publishing Company, 1868.

Warner, Charles Dudley. *My Summer in a Garden.* Boston and New York: Houghton, Mifflin, 1870.

NOTE ON THE TEXT

The text of the stories in this volume follows closely that of their first edition in book form, i.e., in *Thompson's Turkey and Other Christmas Tales, Poems, &c* (Montreal: John Lovell, 1873); *From Bad to Worse; Hard to Beat; and a Terrible Christmas. Three Stories of Montreal Life* (Montreal: Lovell, 1877); and *Out of the Snow and Other Stories and Sketches* (Ottawa: Free Press, 1886). Some words that appear in archaic spelling (e.g., putrifying, mould, ricketty, dishevelled, instil, illgotten) have been kept unchanged, provided that this is the only spelling used by the author. Some words appear in both British and American spelling ("honor" and "honour"), even within the body of the same story (and once in the same sentence), but we have preserved that as it is a sign of the hesitation of 19th-century Canadian typesetters. We have also kept the variant "altho'," which appears a few times instead and alongside "although," because the author uses it only in the speech of some characters (or in the narrator's free indirect speech to match certain characters). However, we have made uniform the spelling of other words, when the hesitation has nothing to do with national versions but rather with older and newer versions of the same word (e.g., "shew," which appears twice alongside "show;" "ancle," which appears once instead of "ankle," present elsewhere; "trowsers" instead of "trousers," etc.); even the name of one character (usually "Bergen" but also "Bergin"). Punctuation is also the same, except for a few obvious errors and a few semicolons which have replaced the original commas. The word "street" which sometimes appears without a capital initial in the names of streets has been spelled "Street" throughout. The use of hyphens in compound adjectives (which are sometimes used and sometimes left out in the original text) has been made consistent here.

FROM BAD TO WORSE.

CHAPTER I.

OUT OF THE STREET.

It was a cold, windy morning in December, about eight years ago. The snow which had fallen during the night was drifting about in blinding clouds, rendering travel exceedingly unpleasant, and making those indoors very loth to quit their warm rooms to face the chilling blast. Perhaps it was the desire to get a little warmth into their half-frozen limbs which caused the crowd filling the gallery of the Recorder's Court, Montreal,[1] on this particular morning to be so great; but, far more likely, it was that curious and depraved taste which delights in witnessing the punishment of others, which so large a number of Montrealers, especially amongst the lower orders, seem to have.

It is a curious thing to sit and watch this gallery in the Recorder's Court; to see the men and boys who day after day frequent it, and stand patiently (there are no seats) for hours listening with infinite relish to the dull monotony of the "drunks and disorderlies," and the stereotyped sentence "One dollar, or Eight days" fall from the lips of the Recorder.

I have often sat and watched the gallery—when I was forced to attend the Court daily—and wondered what possible pleasure these people could find in visiting the Court so often and hearing the same old story told over and over again. It isn't funny work. Once in a great while a little bit of humor will get into a case, or His Honor will say something funny, and all the policemen, as in duty bound, will laugh a quiet, decorous laugh, just sufficient to show that they "see the point," which they generally don't, but as a general thing it is dreary work; and how anybody can attend the Court with any idea of deriving pleasure from it I cannot discover.

I remember one old man whose silvery locks gave him a grave and venerable appearance, and who seemed to be rather above the ordinary run of visitors to the gallery in station, who actually attended during the

---

[1] In Montreal, a Recorder's Court (the recorder is a magistrate) was established in 1851. The court had jurisdiction over infractions of the city's bylaws, civil matters, vagrants and disorderly persons, assault and battery.

whole sitting of the Court for seventeen consecutive days and seemed really to enjoy it. I got quite accustomed to seeing his white head in the crowd, and felt quite disappointed on the eighteenth day when he failed to appear. I am afraid he is dead, or has left the city, for I have not seen him since; and I scarcely think he could have withstood the pleasure it afforded him to attend the Court if he was in town.

This gallery is not an inviting place. It is the very concentration of filth, although the officers of the Court try manfully to make it presentable; but no amount of soap and water and scrubbing can possibly get much of a start on the constant stream of tobacco juice which is squirted on the floor, and on the little platform which runs in front of the gallery. The smell is almost insufferable, and the normal condition of the walls is dirt.

On the morning in question the Court was more than ordinarily crowded, for it was Monday, and, as is usual on that morning, the number of cases was large. The Court was a little late in opening, and practised observers expressed an opinion that the delinquents would "catch it heavy," as the Recorder[2] came in with a dark frown on his generally good-natured, jolly countenance. Evidently something had disturbed the usual serenity of his temper, and "the quality of mercy" was not at all likely to be strained that morning.

There was very little of interest in the first dozen cases or so, they all coming under the denomination of "simple drunks." The next case, however, caused the Recorder to smile as he read the name "John Smith."

"What is his real name?" asked His Honor, leaning over his desk and speaking to the Sergeant who was in charge.

"I don't know," replied the Sergeant. "I never saw him before. He was very drunk when he was brought in, and refused to give any other name."

"John Smith!" shouted the Sergeant, and John Smith stepped in the dock.

He was quite different in appearance to the "hard cases who had preceded him. He was apparently about twenty-five years of age, tall, dark complexioned, with long, straight black hair, and bright, piercing black eyes. His carriage was easy and graceful, and the hand which grasped the rail of the dock was small and shapely as a woman's. His dress was shabby, but looked like the miserable remains of a once elegant

[2] The City Recorder remains unnamed (here and in another story, "The Policeman's Christmas"). Between 1859 and 1880, the recorder was John Ponsonby Sexton (1808-1880), an Irish-Canadian attorney, Queen's Counsel since 28 February 1873.

suit. But for the sodden, bloated appearance which drink had stamped upon his countenance, he would have been a remarkably handsome young man; but in his present condition he looked like a fair sample of that miserable state of existence known as "shabby genteel."[3] He seemed greatly ashamed, and hung his head as if to hide his features as much as possible from sight.

"What is your name?" asked His Honor.

"John Smith."

"I know that is the name you have given, sir; but what is your real name?" said His Honor, very severely.

No answer.

"I will not have persons giving false names here," continued His Honor; "for all that I know John Smith may be a very respectable citizen, and it may injure him to have his name appear in the list of delinquents before this Court. Poor John Smith," he half soliloquized, "he must be a very great drunkard indeed if we are to believe all the statements persons make, for there is scarcely a day but what his name is given, but generally by a different person. Come, sir, what is your name, now? I know it isn't John Smith. "

"Arthur Austin," this was said very low, and the sound scarcely reached half way across the Court.

"What? Speak up man, open your mouth and let me hear what you have to say."

No answer.

"Sergeant, bring him round here, I cannot hear what he says," said His Honor, and the prisoner was placed in the small iron enclosure immediately in front of the Recorder.

"Now, what is your real name?"

"Arthur Austin." The reply was made in a very low voice, as if the owner of it was ashamed to hear it in such a place.

"Arthur Austin," repeated His Honor, writing the name over that of John Smith on the sheet before him. "It is really a pity," he continued, indulging in one of his little lectures, "to see so young and respectable looking a man as you given over to the demon of drink. With your appearance of intelligence you ought to be filling some responsible and lucrative position, instead of which you stand here a miserable object picked up drunk in a gutter, where you ought to be thankful you were not left to freeze to death and to be hurried into the presence of your Maker in a state of intoxication. What is the case, Sergeant? Call the policeman who arrested him."

---

[3] "Shabby genteel" (keeping up the appearance of gentility, despite being poor) was a term very popular in Victorian England (though coined earlier). One of W. M. Thackeray's early writings is *A Shabby Genteel Story*.

A venerable policeman, with a large development of under lip, and who, probably, had had many such cases to deal with during his long career in the force, stepped into the witness box and began in the usual stereotyped style:

"Between eight and nine o'clock last night, your Honor, as I was coming down Craig Street[4] I seen—"

"In the city of Montreal?" asked the clerk of the Court, who is very exact and particular.[5]

"In the City of Montreal," repeated the policeman in a deprecatory tone, as if he had intended to say it if he had been given a fair chance, "I see this man—"

"Do you mean the prisoner at the bar?" interrupted the precise clerk.

"When I see the prisoner at the bar," said the policeman, allowing the correction, "lying on the sidewalk near St. Lambert's Hill.[6] He was very drunk, so I arrested him, and took him to the station."

"What station?" sharply demanded the clerk, as if he felt sure of catching the policeman tripping this time.

"The Central Station."

"In the City of Montreal?"

"In the City of Montreal," admitted the policeman, and the clerk leaned back in his chair, rested his head on his hand, and gazed before him, with the calm conviction of a man who has performed a great and trying duty, and, if the prisoner escaped justice now, it was through no fault of his.

"Did he make any resistance?" asked His Honor of the policeman.

'No, your Honor."

"Had he no money about him?" asked the Recorder of the Sergeant.

"Only five cents, Your Honor."

"One dollar, or eight days," and Arthur Austin was taken down stairs, either to pay his fine or go to jail.

There was a very respectable, well-dressed, pleasant-looking old gentleman sitting in one of the seats appropriated for witnesses, or the

[4] The eastern portion of Saint-Antoine Street (east of Victoria Square) was called Craig Street at the time.

[5] The clerk of the Recorder's Court was Henry J. Ibbotson (Chisholm 67).He was apparently a bit of an author himself: he published a sketch ("Policeman X") in the British American Magazine (August 1863).

[6] Known as St Lambert's Hill or Street (and later just Lambert Street), this was a short stretch of what is now St Laurent Boulevard (between Notre-Dame Street and the eastern portion of Saint-Antoine Street—then named Craig Street), which was yet to be expanded all the way to Rue de la Commune.

better class of visitors, who had watched the young man while he was in the dock, and seemed greatly interested in him. He took off his gold-rimmed spectacles, carefully wiped them, replaced them on his nose, and, turning to the person sitting next to him, asked,

"Will he be sent to jail if he does not pay that dollar?"

Of course he will, for eight days," was the answer.

"It is a great pity," said the old gentleman, sadly, "a great pity, to see so respectable a young man in such a condition. Could any one pay the fine for him?" he continued, after a moment's pause.

"Certainly; perhaps his friends will, if he has any."

"Where is the money paid?."

"Down stairs, to the sergeant in charge."

The old gentleman said no more, but sat quietly until the case in which he was interested was called. It was a very simple one; his nephew, a boy of about ten, had been coasting down Guy Street,[7] and a bobby, blessed with long legs, had arrested him, after a brief but exciting chase.

It took a long time to get at the facts of the case, for the policeman was not very consecutive in his evidence, and he was so often interrupted and kept to the point by the exact clerk, that his testimony was considerably mixed, and it appeared extremely doubtful whether it was the boy who was coasting in a bob-sleigh and knocked down the policeman, or the policeman who was coasting and knocked down the boy, or the bob-sleigh which knocked down both; all that was very clear was that there was a policeman, a boy and a bob-sleigh, and that they got considerably mixed. At last the policeman made out a pretty fair case against the boy, which was to the effect that he was crossing Guy Street, on St. Antoine,[8] when two boys came down the hill on a bobsleigh and knocked him down, that he chased the boys and arrested one of them, the prisoner at the bar.

His Honor cleared his throat and prepared to administer a little "good advice" to the boy, before fining him. "It is wonderful," he said,

[7] Coasting (or sledding or tobogganing) on a public road in Montreal is often mentioned in contemporary newspapers and magazines as the boys' favorite pastime in winter, even though it was, of course, forbidden. Guy Street runs north-south from Sherbrooke Street (see note 11) to William Street (see note 111). Phillips is usually very careful with small details, but (as it sometimes happen when a story is serialized in a newspaper) he will soon forget about this nephew and his first chapter cameo. It will soon turn out that the old gentleman intends to leave half of his fortune to each of his two nieces. It is very unlikely that he would leave nothing to the nephew.
[8] Saint-Antoine Street, which runs east-west between Old Montreal and what is now Downtown Montreal, had this name only west of Victoria Square (see note 10). East of Victoria Square, it was still called Craig Street (see note 3).

"to think how little regard for their own or other people's lives many of the boys in large cities have. Every winter there are numerous accidents, caused by boys sliding and coasting on the streets and sidewalks, and the only wonder is that all of them are not run over and killed by sleighs and taken home dead to their parents."

Here he looked very hard at the boy, who seemed greatly impressed by the idea of his own sudden death, for he stuck his tongue very hard into one cheek and looked intently at the floor, while he traced the shape of a coffin with the toe of his boot.

"It is to a great extent the fault of parents," continued His Honor, looking very hard at the old gentleman in the gold spectacles, "who allow their children to run about the streets when they ought to be at home or at Sunday school."

Here he looked so hard at the old gentleman in gold spectacles that that individual grew very red in the face and rose as if with the intention of addressing the Court, but was forced to sit down again rather suddenly on account of a vigorous pull at his coat tail, administered by a policeman who whispered something in his ear.

"I am determined to make a few examples," continued His Honor, with another look at the old gentleman, "and if parents or guardians choose to allow their children to desecrate the Lord's day and annoy, and possibly injure, people going to or coming from church, they must be made to pay for it, and I hope the boys will get good whippings when they get home. Fifty cents or four hours' imprisonment."

The latter part of this speech had made a great impression on the small boy, and he appeared, to a casual observer, to be moved to tears, for his face was almost buried in his hands and his frame shook with emotion; but a close examination would have shown that the thumb of his left hand was suspiciously near his nose, and the expressive wink he gave at another small boy accused of the same heinous offence was not very suggestive of fear or veneration for the majesty of the law.

When the case was over the old gentleman went down stairs, and received from the Sergeant the difference between the amount at which the boy had been bailed—two dollars and a half—and the amount of the fine.

"Has Arthur Austin's fine been paid?" he asked.

"No, nor not likely to be. He says he has no friends in the city to whom he could apply for help."

"Could I see him, and talk to him for a few minutes?"

Certainly," said the Sergeant politely, "just step this way, please."

The old gentleman followed the Sergeant, and was soon seated in the inner portion of the Station, talking to Arthur Austin.

The young man's story was very simple, and very common. He was an Englishman, whose father had emigrated to the States while he was quite a boy; he had been in business with his father in New York and had been very rich. A financial panic occurred and the firm failed; the father died; the son came to Canada to seek employment as a clerk; he had succeeded at first, but the mania for drink, which had grown on him since his misfortunes, had caused his discharge about three weeks before the opening of my story, and he was now without a friend or a dollar. This was about the substance of Arthur Austin's story. He told it simply, did not attempt to offer any excuse for his dissipation, and seemed heartily ashamed of it.

The old gentleman looked at him quietly for a little while before he spoke, then he asked, suddenly:

"Were you ever locked up before?"

"Never," he said, with a shudder, "and if I ever get out I'll take precious good care I never get in again."

"Then you must give up the use of intoxicating drinks."

"I have done so; I have had my last drop of intoxicating drink for my whole life."

"Good!" said the old gentleman, patting him on the back, "stick to that vow and you will be all right."

"I have made no vow, and need to make none; the memory of the misery I suffered in that cell and in the prisoner's dock this morning is stronger than all the vows I could make."

The old gentleman talked to him for some time and at last paid his fine, gave him a dollar to buy something to eat, and told him to call at his office at two o'clock. On the card which he gave the young man was printed "Lubbuck, Lownds & Co., Produce and Commission merchants, Common Street."[9] The old gentleman was Mr. Stephen Lubbuck, the head of the firm.

*   *   *   *   *   *   *

That visit of Arthur Austin to Mr. Lubbuck proved the turning point in his life, and opened to him a new and honorable career. The old gentleman had taken quite a fancy to the young man, one of those curious freaks of a generous nature which sometimes occur with elderly gentlemen towards those whom they look on as young enough to be their sons. The quiet, gentlemanly manner, and plain straightforward

[9] Rue de la Commune (named after a 17th-century commons), which runs mostly along the St Lawrence River in Old Montreal.

answers of the young man, increased this feeling, and it was, therefore, not surprising that before the interview was over Arthur Austin found himself engaged at a fair salary as assistant bookkeeper to the firm of Lubbuck, Lownds & Co. He had several letters of introduction from New York and Boston houses; and the firm by whom he had been employed here gave him an excellent character for everything except temperance. That point Mr. Lubbuck determined to risk, feeling confident that Arthur would not return to his old habit again.

Arthur Austin's conduct for the next four months fully justified Mr. Lubbuck's good opinion of him, and the old gentleman congratulated himself on having secured a treasure. Early and late Arthur was at his post, and performed his duties better than any clerk Mr. Lubbuck had ever had. Quick, attentive, fully acquainted with his business, Arthur Austin not only gained the confidence of his employer but of his fellow clerks, whom he was always ready and willing to assist in their duties.

Arthur Austin had now a career of honor and usefulness opened to him, and seemed determined to profit by his opportunity. He left the boarding house he had been in, so as to remove himself from his old jolly companions, and went to one in a better and quieter neighborhood. He avoided all his old haunts, in order more securely to guard himself against temptation, joined a temperance association, and devoted his spare time almost entirely to reading.

As the spring gradually advanced and navigation opened, Arthur Austin proved himself of still greater service to his employers. He was acquainted with many of the leading produce and commission houses in Boston, New York and Chicago, and speedily gained several new and valuable correspondents for Lubbuck, Lownds & Co., whose business was greatly increased thereby, and Arthur rose still higher in his employers' estimation.

It was his custom on leaving the office to walk up St. James Street and through Victoria Square[10] on his way home, and one evening, as he was crossing the square, he noticed a young lady standing by the fountain, with the tip of her parasol resting on the low wall surrounding it. She was gazing in an abstracted, preoccupied manner into the water, and only presented a profile view; but as Arthur first caught a glimpse of that outline he thought he had never seen anything half so beautiful

[10] St James Street (rue Saint-Jacques) is a long street running between Saint-Antoine and Notre-Dame. At the time, the name was used only for the portion located in Old Montreal, which was the city's financial district. Victoria Square (an old public space that got its new name in 1860) is in downtown Montreal and is bordered to the south by St James Street. The statue of Queen Victoria had recently been unveiled (in November 1872).

in his life. Just as he stepped close behind her she started suddenly and looked up, and in the action of surprise loosed her hold of her parasol, and it immediately tumbled into the water.

It was the work of a moment for him to step forward, rescue the parasol, and return it to its owner, with a few words of apology for having unintentionally startled her.

"Oh, don't apologize," she said, turning on him the full battery of the sweetest pair of blue eyes he had ever encountered, while a smile rippled for a moment across the rosiest and most kissable lips he had ever seen, "it was my fault; I stood dreaming while I waited for Frank, and your step startled me, that was all."

Arthur stood for a moment, gazing at her in admiration, and wondering whether he might, with propriety, endeavor to improve the chance acquaintance, or simply raise his hat and pass on. "Who was Frank?" he thought, and somehow a feeling of deadly animosity to that unknown individual stole over him, and he would have very much liked to have had "Frank" there, and have had it out with him on the spot.

CHAPTER II.

OUT OF THE SQUARE.

Mr. Stephen Lubbuck was an old bachelor, and lived in a pleasant little villa of his own on Sherbrooke Street,[11] where his widowed sister and her two daughters, and the little boy we have already seen figuring in the Recorder's Court, lived with him. Mr. Lubbuck was an easy-going, quiet old gentleman who had drifted through life very pleasantly, having met with few misfortunes other than those incidental to any young man struggling to make his way in the world. He started from his home in England at the age of sixteen, and came to Canada, where, after several years roughing it, he settled down in Montreal as a clerk in a produce house. His progress was slow, but sure; and, at the age of thirty-five, he found himself admitted as a junior partner, and in a fair way to competency, if not great wealth. He had been too busy, heretofore, to

[11] Sherbrooke Street is now one of the longest streets in Montreal, but in the 19th century it was much shorter. The Golden Square Mile, a neighborhood of mansions built by the richest Montrealers, was located mostly north of Sherbrooke Street.

think of matrimony, but now he began to think how pleasant it would be to have a home of his own and a bright, loving face to grace it.

He was a careful, prudent man, however, was Stephen Lubbuck, and he thought he would get the cage first and then catch the canary that was to inhabit it. But it took him a year or two to get a cage to suit him, and then he looked about for several years more before he found any one to suit him; and he was still looking about him when he received intelligence of the death of his brother-in-law, Herbert Williams, and he thought of the bright little sister of ten he had left behind in Liverpool twenty-five years before, and who was now a widow, almost destitute, and with three children, two girls, aged eight and nine respectively, and a little baby boy of four months. He thought of his bright boyish days and his fond sister's love, and he thought he had found his canary—or canaries—and so he sent for and installed them in the cage.

Very happily and pleasantly did the little family live together for the next ten years, and many and many a time did Mr. Lubbuck congratulate himself on the canaries he had finally put in his cage after so many years waiting.

The two girls grew up to budding womanhood, but, as they grew older, they became more and more dissimilar, both in appearance and temperament. Frances, the elder, was a tall, robust girl, with big bones, and a general appearance of having been lately polished with an exceedingly rough towel. Her hair was an uncertain black, and her eyes of a waterish grey, quite the reverse of beautiful; her nose was undoubtedly and defiantly a "snub," and her wide mouth displayed a formidable array of grinders, unquestionably highly useful in the masticatory department, but quite a failure as regarded beauty. There was no question about it, Frances was a very plain-looking girl, and had a decidedly masculine appearance. She was slightly masculine in tastes, too. When a little girl, she could run, jump, climb trees, and play marbles, or peg top with any boy in the neighborhood. As she got older she affected muscular exercises, could pull a good oar, use dumb-bells, etc., and managed to develop a vast quantity of bone and a good proportion of muscle; indeed she had more than once remarked, "I could take half these whipper-snapper things called young men, and break them across my knee without any trouble," and she certainly looked as if she could do it. She not only preferred boyish games and exercises, but also masculine studies. She learned Latin, Greek, mathematics, etc., and studied hard at medicine, for the practice of which she acquired a great taste; and it was only by the greatest persuasion that her uncle could induce her to forego her pet idea of going to college, receiving a diploma and entering on general practice. In her early days she had killed four dogs, experimenting on them, and she totally destroyed the digestive organs of three promising young cats, and made them lead miserable lives until she had worried the whole twenty-seven lives out of them. Now she experimented on the servants, but in a mild manner, and did not make more than one a month dangerously ill, which was better than some doctors could do.

You must not think I am describing a wild, uneducated burlesque on femininity; poor Frank, as she was usually called, was as good and warm-hearted a girl as could be found in Montreal, quiet and unpresuming in manner, talented beyond the average, and generous to a fault. Her great drawback was that she looked like a man, thought like a man, had the tastes and feelings of a man, and was a woman.

It would have been hard in all Montreal to find a greater contrast to Frances Williams than in her sister Jessie. Short, slight, *petite*, with great masses of wavy golden hair, bright sky-blue eyes, a clear pink and white complexion, a rosebud of a mouth, and pearls for teeth, Jessie Williams was the fairest, sweetest little vision one could wish to dawn upon him. Made all for sunshine, and joy, and pleasure, she flew about like a beautiful butterfly, carrying warmth and light wherever she went.

In temper, as in appearance, the sisters were equally dissimilar. While Frances was quiet, slightly reserved and self-sustained, Jessie was all impulse, poetry and sensibility. It is almost useless to say that Jessie was the pet of the family, in fact, almost a spoiled child. She had had a first-class superficial education; could play the piano well, sing passably, dance exquisitely, had a smattering of French, and had acquired an immense stock of romance, gathered principally from sensation novels and the American weekly papers. A girl of tender loving qualities, capable of being a good, useful wife and mother, or a heartless flirt and coquette, according to the circumstances into which she was thrown.

*   *   *   *   *   *   *

Arthur Austin's dilemma did not last long. While he was debating with himself whether he should simply bow and pass on, or endeavor to take advantage of the slight opportunity offered him to improve a pleasant chance acquaintance, his doubts were suddenly simplified by his companion exclaiming:

"Here's Frank!"

Arthur turned and saw approaching them a severe and not very prepossessing female, who struck him very much at first as being a man

in disguise. Miss Frances Williams—for, of course, she was "Frank"—
advanced rather quickly, and threw an inquiring glance from her sister
to the strange gentleman she found her with.

"Oh, Frank," said Jessie, before her sister could speak, "I got so
tired waiting for you that I began to have a day-dream by the fountain,
and I dropped my parasol into the water; and—and—this gentleman,"
with a sly look at Arthur from under her eyelashes, which set his blood
boiling, "was kind enough to fish it out for me."

"I am very much obliged to you, sir, for saving my sister's parasol
from drowning," said Frank, very demurely. "I hope you did not hurt
yourself much by the exertion."

"Oh, no! I assure you—very much pleased—allow me—"
stammered Arthur, so much surprised at the quiet, self-possessed tone
of the masculine feminine[12] he was addressing that he did not know
what he was saying.

"Come, Jessie, let us go home," said Frank, turning to her sister, "I
am sorry I kept you so long waiting," and she quietly walked off with
Jessie without looking at Arthur Austin again. But Jessie turned as she
passed the fountain, and shot back one bright glance and a half smile
at Arthur, and he went home feeling lighter at heart and treading more
elastically than he had done for many a long day. All the evening he
thought of that brilliant vision he had seen beside the fountain, and at
night he dreamed of a mass of golden hair, and a pair of sky-blue eyes,
and heard a soft, sympathetic voice saying, "And this gentleman was
kind enough to fish it out for me."

*   *   *   *   *   *   *

Arthur Austin thought a good deal about "the lady by the fountain,"
as he styled her, during the next few days; and the memory of the
handsome young gentleman who had so gallantly rescued her parasol
and ruined his shirt cuff in so doing, was not quite absent from the mind
of Jessie. Perhaps, you do not believe in love at first sight? Well, I do
not altogether, in the abstract, and such passions are usually evanescent,
yet they do sometimes occur, and both these young people who had
met so casually felt the magnetic influence of each other's presence;
and, without being "in love" with each other, still very sincerely desired

---

[12] This formula, which (like its opposite, "feminine masculine")
appears in a few 19th-century publications, can be traced back to the
anonymous "proto-feminist" Jacobean play *Swetnam the Woman-Hater* (published in
1620 and first staged a year or two before).

that this accidental meeting should not be their last. Fortune did not favor Arthur Austin for some days, for, although he almost "haunted" Victoria Square, he saw no more of "the lady by the fountain." About a week had elapsed, when one evening as he was walking home with a friend they met the object of Arthur's thoughts, accompanied by her sister.

As she approached Jessie averted her eyes, but took a sly glance out under the lashes. Arthur timidly and half hesitatingly raised his hat, and then she turned towards him for a second, and acknowledged his salutation by a slight bow and a bewitching little smile. Frank elevated her snub nose a trifle higher than usual, and was passing on when she noticed Arthur's companion, who was bowing very politely, and then her features relaxed into a smile, and she returned his salutation with the air of an old friend. Jessie, also, gave him a kindly smile and bow, and so the two couples passed each other.

"You know them?" said Arthur.

"Certainly," returned Charlie Benson, his companion. "Frank and her sister are old friends of mine. You know them also, do you not? I thought you bowed."

"Yes, after a fashion. Who are they?"

"Frank Williams and her sister. Where did you meet them that you do not know their names?"

Then Arthur told of his little adventure by the fountain, and his friend laughed at it.

"Case of love at first sight, I suppose; struck dead and all that sort of thing, eh? Well, a little harmless passion does not do a boy any harm."

Benson was about thirty and Austin about twenty-five, so the former thought he could affect a few seniorial airs.

"You did not tell me the name of the youngest lady?"

"Jessie."

"Jessie; that is a very pretty name," said Arthur.

"Yes; and a pretty little doll of a girl," replied his companion.

"Are you very intimate with them?"

"Yes, tolerably well so; know them for about five years. Oh, don't be bashful, I know what you want to say, you want me to introduce you; well, I will display the natural generosity of my disposition and promise to do so without being asked. Want to hear a little family history? Here it is. Girls' father is dead, they and their mother live with their uncle, a rich old bachelor who will leave them all his money. There is a chance for you. I don't mind confessing I feel a little spooney on Frank myself sometimes, only she is so fond of practising medicine I am half afraid she would dose me to death in a year. Say, seriously, old boy, Jessie would not be a bad spec[13] for you," and he smiled a quiet, peculiar smile which Arthur remembered afterwards. "Ta, ta, I'm at home: the next time we meet them I will claim the privilege of an old friend, stop them, and introduce you."

*　　　*　　　*　　　*　　　*　　　*　　　*

Arthur Austin was duly introduced. Frank turned up her nose again, but Jessie smiled very sweetly, and, as the quartette walked away together, Mr. Benson went a little ahead with Frank, and gave Arthur and Jessie an opportunity to pleasantly bring up the rear. The conversation was very commonplace, but Jessie had a charming way of saying nothing as if it meant something, and smiling and looking up with those bright blue eyes of hers, which was very bewitching; and Mr. Arthur Austin felt himself momentarily falling deeper and deeper into that unfathomable abyss called love. He knew he was falling, but he liked it and wanted to fall more.

After that first afternoon Benson and Austin managed to meet the girls several times, and Arthur's acquaintance progressed rapidly and pleasantly. There were no direct words of love spoken, few compliments and fewer "pretty speeches;" but Jessie could scarcely fail to understand the warmth of his manner; and she liked it. As for Arthur, he was alternately hot or cold as Jessie smiled on him, or smiled at some chance acquaintance they met. I am afraid Miss Jessie was a bit of a flirt, and liked, as all flirts do, to torment her victim a little, and then pacify him by a little extra graciousness; just as a playful child will swing a pet kitten by the tail preparatory to giving it a saucerful of milk.

One day about twelve o'clock Arthur was crossing Victoria Square, when he saw Jessie coming towards him alone. It was the first time he had met her alone since that memorable afternoon when he had saved her parasol for her, and his pulse beat a little quicker as she approached. They met at nearly the old spot, and after a few formal sentences they got into closer conversation.

They were standing talking earnestly together when Mr. Stephen Lubbuck, coming up one of the side paths, saw them, and stopped in amazement at finding his pet niece and his confidential clerk in such close converse. The old gentleman took off his gold spectacles, wiped them, put them on again, took another look, satisfied himself that he

---

[13] Short for "speculation," very common at the time in financial lingo, but also, by extension, as a slang term for a someone you could pursue as a possible spouse.

had not labored under an optical illusion, and then retired the way he had come, without having been noticed by the pair; but there was a sterner and more angry expression on his face than was usually to be found on that serene countenance.

*   *   *   *   *   *   *

Arthur Austin's acquaintance with Jessie was rather a peculiar one. He knew her personally; he knew that she was an old friend of Benson's, and that she was the sweetest little lady he had ever met, but he did not know where she lived or who her relations were—except her sister; or in fact scarcely anything about her, except that he was deeply in love with her. At that last meeting by the fountain she had been kinder than usual, and, after accepting a pretty little bouquet which Arthur had ventured to present her with, had pulled a forget-me-not from it and fastened it in his button hole, promising that if he and his friend Benson chanced to be walking down Sherbrooke Street about four o'clock the next afternoon they should meet two young ladies they knew.

Arthur Austin completed his errand and returned to the office. To his surprise he found Mr. Lubbuck still there. The old gentleman usually went home about half-past four, and it was long after that hour. As soon as Arthur entered Mr. Lubbuck said, very gravely,

"Mr. Austin, I should like to see you in my private office for a few minutes."

Arthur followed the old gentleman into that sanctum sanctorum of business houses, the "Private Office," and stood before his employer awaiting developments.

"Mr. Austin," said Mr. Lubbuck very gravely, and Arthur felt hurt that he should address him so formally, for lately he had always called him by his Christian name, "how long have you known my niece?"

"Your niece, sir! I know you have two nieces, but I have not the pleasure of being acquainted with them, nor have I ever seen them, to my knowledge."

"I am very sorry, Mr. Austin," said Mr. Lubbuck, severely, "that you should think it necessary to tell me a lie. I have been a good friend to you, have lifted you to a good position, and I regret, for the first time, to find that you are untruthful. You say you do not know my niece, yet I saw you talking to her not an hour ago."

"Do you mean in Victoria Square?" asked Arthur, beginning to understand the facts of the case.

"Yes."

"Then Miss Williams is your niece?"

"Most undoubtedly."

"I assure you, sir, I was not aware of the fact. If you had asked me if I knew Miss Williams I should have admitted at once that I not only know her but greatly admire her; but I was not aware of the fact that she was your niece."

"Is this true?"

"I hope you will not doubt me, sir, when I pledge my word of honor as a gentleman to the truth of my assertion."

"No, no, I do not doubt you in the least, I will speak to you again on this subject. Good evening."

"Good evening, sir."

Arthur Austin left the room; and Mr. Lubbuck put on his hat, pulled it well down over his eyes and started for home, thinking deeply on what he should say to his favorite niece about the strange acquaintance he had discovered that she had made.

CHAPTER III.

OUT OF THE CHURCH.

"Jessie, how long have you known Mr. Austin?"

Jessie looked up at her uncle with a quick inquiring glance, and answered promptly "about a month."

"Do you think it right or proper for a young lady to have clandestine meetings with a man she has only known a month, and whose acquaintance with her is at least a doubtful one? Where did you first meet him?"

"I met him in—in—" stammered poor Jessie, getting quite confused and growing uncomfortably red in the face. Before she could finish the sentence, however, Frank came to her assistance in her usual prompt manner, by saying, "Charlie Benson introduced Mr. Austin to us one afternoon when we were out walking."

"Oh! you know him too!"

"Certainly, and I think him a very pleasant fellow," said Frank, anxious to give Jessie a little time to recover. Mr. Lubbuck stood a little in awe of his masculine niece, and in very wholesome dread of her doses and decoctions in the medical line; besides, he knew and liked Charlie Benson; and he had, moreover, a high regard for Arthur Austin; he was not, therefore, disposed to view the matter very severely. Still, he did not like to be too lenient all of a sudden, so he preserved his grave manner and said, addressing Jessie, "I do not approve of young ladies meeting young gentlemen in public places, and standing talking confidentially to them; it does not look well, and frequently gives occasion for unkind and unpleasant remarks. How did it happen that you met Mr. Austin alone?"

"I—I—don't know," faltered poor Jessie, feeling very much like a naughty child who feared punishment, "I was only—"

"Uncle," said Frank, cutting in suddenly, and speaking in her prompt, determined way, "it seems to me you are speaking very harshly to Jessie about a very simple matter; one would think that Jessie had been meeting Mr. Austin clandestinely, and by appointment; now I have been with her every time she has seen him and it has only been three or four times, and then only for a few minutes walk—and she happened to be alone with him in the square because—because—" Frank hesitated a moment, blushed a little and continued—"because I left her in the square for two or three minutes while I did an errand at Morgan's[14] for Mamma."

Frank omitted to state that it was on a former, and not the present, occasion she had so left Jessie.

"Oh! Frank," exclaimed Jessie.

"Don't be a fool," said the brusque Frank *sotto voce*.

"You misunderstand me, Frank," said Mr. Lubbuck rather overcome by his niece's volubility, "I do not object to a proper acquaintance between Mr. Austin and yourselves; I only took exception to the manner in which that acquaintance had been formed; but don't let us say any more about it; you girls are young and giddy, and I daresay no harm was intended on either side. I might say," continued Mr. Lubbuck, willing to make a little concession, "that I esteem Mr. Austin very highly; he is an exceedingly clever young man, steady, and undoubtedly a gentleman; I scarcely think you can derive any harm from an acquaintance with him, provided it is properly conducted and not allowed to go too far."

---

[14] Morgan's was a department store in Montreal, in Victoria Square, on the north side of St. James Street. In 1891, it moved to a new location on Saint Catherine Street. This was bought by Hudson's Bay Company in 1960 and is today the well-known Bay Building in downtown Montreal.

"So you know him, too!" exclaimed Frank.

"Certainly, my dear, he is my bookkeeper and confidential clerk, a very clever young man."

"Then, Uncle," said matter-of-fact Frank, determined to make the most of the advantage she had gained, "if he is such a clever young man and you like him so much, why don't you ask him to. come and see you? I'm very democratic in some things, you know, and I believe in employer and employee knowing each other socially as well as in business."

"Yes, my dear, but—"

"Oh! you need not be afraid of me, I like men's society,—I wish I was a man, instead of a poor helpless woman, but you need not fancy I shall fall in love with his handsome face and fine moustache; and as for Jessie, if such a foolish notion gets into her head I'll give her a seidlitz powder,[15] and bleed her. So, Uncle, ask Mr. Austin and Charlie Benson to dinner on Sunday."

"Oh! it's Charlie? is it?"

"Don't be a silly old goose, but ask them like a good old fellow as you are."

*   *   *   *   *   *   *

"Mrs. Williams presents her compliments to Mr. Arthur Austin and requests the pleasure of his company to dinner on Sunday next at six o'clock."

It was a stiff, formal little note, but in Arthur Austin's eyes it was very precious, for he felt that Mrs. Williams never traced those fairy characters, and it was as much as he could do to restrain himself from pressing the writing, which he felt sure was Jessie's, to his lips. He did not do any thing so ridiculous, however, but, after a few moments' thought, walked into Mr. Lubbuck's private office, and, handing the note to him, said:

"I found that on my desk, a few minutes since, sir."

"Yes. I put it there myself, and I beg to add my own request to that of Mrs. Williams, that you will dine with us on Sunday."

"I shall be very happy, I assure you, sir. I—"

"Mr. Austin," said Mr. Lubbuck, gravely, "I have already told you, and have given you tangible proofs of my sincerity, that I have been highly pleased with your conduct since you have been with me. Our

---

[15] Seidlitz powders were a popular digestive in the 19th century.

business arrangements have been highly satisfactory, but I feel, as my niece Frank expresses it, that 'employer and employee should know each other socially as well as in business.' I think men get at each other's inner natures better over their dinners, and a glass of wine. Oh! I ask your pardon, I forgot you do not take wine, and quite right too—than in a year's business transactions together. I do not mind confessing that I desire to know you more thoroughly than I have done during the six months you have been with me, as I contemplate some business changes this fall which may render it necessary for me to be able to trust implicitly in you. I, therefore, hope to see you frequently at my house in future, and hope that our social relations may prove as satisfactory as our business ones have done. I wish, however, to be perfectly frank with you; you will of course be frequently thrown into the society of my nieces, whose acquaintance you have already made; now I do not object to an acquaintance, or even a friendship springing up between you, but there must be no idea of its ever being anything more. Frank, I'm not afraid of, she's able to take care of herself, and is more than a match for any man, unless he can stand unlimited experiments in medicine, and has the constitution of a horse; but my little pet Jessie is scarcely more than a child, and I won't have any one trying to stuff her head with nonsense for these many years to come. I am plain with you, because I want no misunderstanding in this matter. If you want to fall in love with anybody try Frank, she'll soon bleed and blister you out of the idea. I have been so candid with you because you said you not only knew but admired my niece; now get any such foolish notion out of your head at once, or it will lead to a disruption of all our relations, business and otherwise. That will do; bring me the morning paper and the letters."

*   *   *   *   *   *   *

Arthur Austin soon became a constant and welcome visitor at Mr. Lubbuck's, and grew steadily in favor not only with the old gentleman, but with the whole family. Even Frank—who, although she liked the society of men, generally declared that the young men of the present day had no brains and were decidedly "flat"—declared that Arthur was "a brick,"[16] which was a great compliment from Miss Frank, and that he was "a fellow who knew something."

In fact Arthur was "a fellow who knew something;" he had received a first-class education, had travelled a great deal, was naturally

---

[16] 19th-century slang word for a loyal, dependable person.

observant, and possessed that rare faculty of talking just enough to please and interest, but not enough to bore. He could sing tolerably well, possessing a fair voice, which he managed cleverly. He fairly captured Frank by his knowledge of medicine, and when he showed that young lady an experiment in electricity and very nearly resuscitated a defunct tom-cat which had been poisoned while experimenting on him the day before, Miss Frank's admiration knew no bounds, and she almost threw her arms round him and killed him for joy, but contented herself with slapping him on the back and saying, "that's first rate, old fellow!"

Arthur was certainly very attentive to Frank, and, strange to say, Mr. Lubbuck seemed to like it. Arthur and Frank used to have a great many arguments on medical and other topics—Frank was every inch a man in her love of argument—and the old man would sit and listen, nodding approval, and occasionally putting in a word. At first he used to keep Jessie by him, but Arthur tried hard to keep his implied promise to Mr. Lubbuck, and scarcely spoke to that young lady, except the most commonplace civilities. After a little while Frank discovered that Arthur played chess, and claimed him frequently for a game, while Jessie either sat quietly by, pretending to do some fancy work[17] or would steal off to the piano and play over old-fashioned airs softly to herself. Although they met frequently now, Jessie and Arthur had really less opportunity of speaking to each other than when he and Charlie Benson used to meet Frank and Jessie for little pleasant walks; each seemed to avoid the other, for Jessie felt hurt that Arthur did not pay her more attention, and Arthur was very careful to remember, if possible, Mr. Lubbuck's warning. Try as he would, however, it was no use; the mere fact of her presence, a turn of her head, a glance of her eye, would attract his whole attention at once; when he was playing chess with Frank at one end of the room and Jessie was singing at the other, he would bend all his attention to catch the lowest murmur of her voice, or the softest note she touched. Often Miss Frank would take him to task for his absent-mindedness; and numerous were the pennies that young lady offered for his thoughts without having her stock of pocket-money reduced.

About six weeks after Arthur had paid his first visit to Mr. Lubbuck's he was sitting one evening playing chess with Frank, with Mr. Lubbuck looking on and Jessie singing softly to herself. Mrs. Williams was not very well, and had excused herself after dinner. Presently a servant came to speak to Mr. Lubbuck about one of the horses having gone lame, and he went out to consult with the groom. Jessie had been singing very softly, so softly that Arthur had been unable to catch a word, but as

[17] Decorative embroidery (usually spelled "fancywork").

her uncle left the room she raised her voice a little and sang clearly and distinctly a scrap of a simple little ballad:

"Have you forgotten the stroll by the fountain;
Have you forgotten the path o'er the lea;
Have you forgotten those days on the mountain;
Have you forgotten them all, with them me?"

Arthur sat silently listening while the simple strain lasted, foolishly holding his queen in his hand, and at last making the very worst move on the board, putting it immediately in the way of Frank's queen. That young lady promptly captured the unlucky queen, and crying "Checkmate," rose from the table, saying:

"Mr. Austin, you don't seem to care about playing chess tonight, and I want to read; make yourself useful by turning over Jessie's music for her."

She threw herself into an easy chair and took up a book, but she did not read; the book was only intended as a blind, under the cover of which she might observe what was going on at the other end of the room. The fact is Miss Frank had noticed Arthur's absent manner, his wrapt attention to Jessie's singing, and his eager watching of her every movement, and she made a pretty good guess as to the state of his feelings. Don't suppose Frank felt the least bit jealous, she liked Arthur Austin very much, he was a sensible fellow, could talk well, and had many tastes and pursuits in common with her, but Miss Frank never for one moment fancied herself in love with him; in fact she was more in love than she cared to confess with some one else, and it was as much to pique that some one else as anything that she had thrown herself in Arthur's way so much. So she quietly watched behind her book and awaited developments. Arthur sauntered as unconcernedly as he could up to the piano, and, leaning over Jessie, said:

"Will you please sing that 'Have you forgotten' again, it is so sweet?"

"I'm sorry I interrupted your game of chess, Mr. Austin, pray do not let me disturb you."

"I was only too glad to be interrupted so pleasantly, Miss Jessie; won't you, please, repeat that song?"

"Frank will expect you to finish your game," said Jessie, rather spitefully.

"Miss Frank herself gave up playing, and desired me to come and turn over your music."

"Have you quarrelled with Frank?"

"Certainly not; what could make you think so?"

"When people who are so fond of each other, and are so much together, suddenly separate, it looks—it looks," continued Jessie, as if she doubted whether to say the next words or not, "as if they had had a lovers' quarrel." She finished, desperately, savagely intoning the "lovers."

"Lovers' quarrel! Why, Miss Jessie, what on earth can you mean?"

"Why, you and Frank are so much together and so much—that everybody—well, it looks as if—" said Jessie, with a rising sensation in her throat, and tears almost starting into her eyes.

"You never thought so, Miss Jessie, did you?" said Arthur, bending earnestly over her.

"Why, of course, I——I——."

"Jessie, darling, how could you fancy such a thing. I admire your sister, of course, but you must have seen, must know, although I have never told you so in words, that I love, never can love any one but you. I know I have acted strangely of late, but I was forced to it by a feeling of respect to the wishes of your uncle, who almost made me promise to avoid you. I tried, tried hard to tear you from my heart, darling—but it was impossible, the more I tried the more I loved you. Jessie, I am only a clerk, and shall lose my best chance of advancement by this step, but I have health and strength, and, with the hope of your smile to cheer me on, I will succeed. Will you give me one word of hope, one smile to show me I am not wholly indifferent to you?"

"And you don't love Frank?" said Jessie, bending over the piano until her glowing face was almost hidden by her falling hair.

"No one but you, darling. Oh! Jessie, will you give me one word, one look. Will you promise one day to be my wife?" Jessie said nothing, but raised her eyes, swimming with happy tears, to his, her cheeks glowing with burning blushes and a bright smile playing around her lips. She half rose from the piano stool, and in another moment Arthur had clasped her to his heart and imprinted a burning kiss on her glowing lips.

"Hallo!" exclaimed Miss Frank, bringing her book down on the table with a bang which caused the lovers to spring apart, and Jessie to run over to her sister and hide her face on her shoulder—"this is more than I bargained for; I did not think matters had gone so far as that."

"Oh! Frank," half sobbed Jessie, "I'm so sorry—and I'm so happy—and Arthur didn't mean——"

"I hope, Miss Frank," said Arthur, "that my conduct of late has not deceived you; I know it was wrong, but I promised your uncle to avoid Jessie, and I hope—"

"That I have not fallen in love with you; make your mind easy on that score. I like you very well, you're a sensible fellow, and will make a first-rate brother-in-law. I think you are just suited for Jessie, and I give my consent."

"But your uncle?"

"Oh, he's very fond of Jessie and won't want to part with her, but he'll get over it. I'll manage him, if I have to give him a dose of physic to make him sick."

*　　*　　*　　*　　*　　*　　*

Frank was as good as her word, and succeeded much easier than she had expected. Mr. Lubbuck held out for a little while, and required, as conditions to his consent, that Jessie should not leave him, but Arthur come and live with them; and, also, that the wedding should not take place for a year; to both of which proposals Frank unconditionally surrendered. Before Mr. Lubbuck finally gave his consent to Jessie's marriage, he wrote on to New York to an old confidential friend, and had private inquiries instituted as to Arthur Austin's antecedents, for he did not intend to give his pet niece to a man he had picked out of the Recorder's Court, without taking good care to know who he was and all about him. The information he received was highly satisfactory. He found that Arthur had come to New York about ten years before with his father, who was sent out as travelling clerk for an English banking-house, but who soon gave up that and went into business for himself as a gold broker, in Broad Street,[18] and was highly successful, amassing a large fortune in a short time. Arthur joined him in the business, and, by lucky speculations, managed to make a great deal of money; his speculations were bold and daring, and at the time of his coming of age, and being admitted as a partner in his father's business, he was judged to be worth nearly one million of dollars. Six months after the tide of speculation turned, the close of the war paralysed Wall Street for a time, and Austin & Son were one of the firms which hopelessly failed. Overspeculation had done its work, and both father and son were ruined. The shock so affected Arthur's father that he had an attack of brain fever, from the effects of which he died. Arthur, not wishing to begin at the bottom of the ladder in a place where he had once held so high a position, resolved to go to Chicago and re-commence life as a clerk. About this time he began to acquire habits of intemperance, which had clung to him till he came to Montreal. Nothing whatever was known against his character or morals, except his intemperance, and, as Mr. Lubbuck was quite satisfied on that head now, he gave his consent.

---

[18] A street in Lower Manhattan (in the Financial District), going from South Street to Wall Street (after which it becomes Nassau Street).

When two young hearts are anxious to be mated, and are aided and abetted by a masculine feminine of a medical turn of mind, it must be a very obdurate old gentleman, indeed, who could long resist. Mr. Lubbuck was not obdurate, and, consequently, he soon agreed to waive the provision in his consent, by which the young people had to wait a year; indeed, he had changed his mind entirely on that point, for he insisted that they should be united as soon as the necessary arrangements could be made.

Of course he had a motive for this; staid old gentlemen don't change their minds so suddenly and completely without some good reason, and this was Mr. Lubbuck's reason: The firm of Lubbuck, Lownds & Co. was a branch of an English house, Lowry, Lubbuck & Lownds, the said Lownds being a young man, son of the former head of the house, and also partner in the firm of Lubbuck, Lownds & Co. One fine morning it got into old Mr. Lowry's head that he wanted to die, and so he died right off, leaving Stephen Lubbuck his executor, and bequeathing to him the bulk of his large fortune.

Mr. Lowry, like his partner, was a bachelor; and he had no near relative that he cared about. When Mr. Lubbuck received information of his partner's death, he saw that he must at once go to England to settle up his affairs, and, probably, to make arrangements for residing there permanently, as head of the firm. A few mornings after he received the intelligence he called Arthur Austin into his private office, and said:—

"Arthur, I have received news of the death of my old friend Lowry; he has left me his executor, and I shall be obliged to go to England for some time, probably for several months. I shall sail on 13th November, you must be married on 29th October, and must return from your wedding tour before I leave. I shall give you a power of attorney to represent the firm during my absence, and you will, of course, take charge of my house while I'm away. Mr. Lownds may perhaps come out to take charge during the winter, but he will not remain long. I shall return in the spring, and then we shall see about re-constructing the firm. How do you think Lubbuck, Austin & Co. would sound, eh?"

*　　*　　*　　*　　*　　*　　*

The wedding took place in Christ Church Cathedral,[19] and was a very grand affair; Frank was chief bridesmaid, and looked supremely

[19] The seat of the Anglican Diocese of Montreal, located on Saint Catherine Street, between Robert Bourassa Boulevard and Union Avenue (that is, between today's Hudson's Bay Company and Eaton Centre).

uncomfortable, as she did not know whether or not to be exceedingly happy or perfectly miserable. Charlie Benson was groomsman, and took such a deep interest in the service that one might think he was rehearsing for his own benefit. A wedding is a stupid thing to describe, so I shall simply say that the Rev. Canon Baldwin[20] united the happy pair, and the ceremony proceeded in the usual way.

As the wedding party was about entering the church, a seedy looking individual, who was apparently sauntering purposeless down St. Catherine Street, approached, evidently attracted by curiosity only. He was a peculiar looking individual; his hair was red, and he wore it very long, but it was brushed to the most exasperating degree of smoothness, and, indeed, appeared to have been literally "plastered" to his head and then pressed down with a hot iron, so smooth and glossy did it appear; his red whiskers were very luxuriant, and were brushed as carefully as his hair; his dress was seedy in the extreme, and his thread-bare coat was buttoned close up to his throat as if to hide any want of clean linen, but every garment was shining from the effect of frequent brushing, and not one speck of dirt could be noticed on him. His dilapidated old hat was tipped jauntily on one side, and he carried a mean looking scrubby little cane with the air of a swell.[21] He was quite close to the wedding party when Arthur Austin got out of his carriage, and as soon as the dilapidated individual saw him he gave so natural and unexpected a start that the jaunty hat very nearly tumbled into the gutter, "Saints alive, can it be possible? Arthur Austin, as I'm a living sinner! Evidently in clover too, dear boy, and about to be spliced to a very charming young lady. How well the dear boy is looking too, and dressed in such unexceptionable togs.[22] I must do myself the honor of witnessing the nuptial ceremony."

He entered the church, and keeping well behind one of the pillars to escape observation, watched the ceremony to its conclusion. Waiting until the happy party had departed, he strolled leisurely up to the sexton and began conversing with him:

"An exceedingly nice affair, and most excellently conducted, thanks to your admirable arrangements. May I inquire who are the happy parties?"

---

[20] Toronto-born Maurice Baldwin (1836-1904) had become canon in 1871. He was appointed Dean in 1879, but was later elected Bishop of Huron (with the seat in London, Ontario) and left Montreal in 1883.
[21] "Swell" was a term applied to either a dandy or a member of the upper class.
[22] A series of 19th-century slang terms: "togs" means clothes; "spliced" means married (and "splice" was another word for "wife"); "in clover" means in great comfort or luxury.

"Mr. Arthur Austin and Miss Jessie Williams. A very nice young gentleman," continued the sexton, thinking of the liberal fee Arthur had slipped into his hand.

"Undoubtedly so; and rich seemingly."

"Bless you, no! He is only her uncle's clerk, but her uncle is enormously rich, and very fond of the young man."

"Dear me, how interesting! And the uncle is?—"

"Mr. Stephen Lubbuck, one of the richest men in Montreal; they say he is worth over two hundred thousand dollars."

"Is he? Then he has two hundred thousand additional claims to my esteem. The happy pair go on a wedding tour, I suppose?"

"They go to New York by this afternoon's train, but won't stay long, as Mr. Lubbuck goes to England shortly, and Mr. Austin must return before then. Excuse me, sir, I must close the church."

"Certainly, my dear sir, certainly; business before pleasure, as we say in the classics. Allow me to wish you a good day, and to thank you for your kindness."

"Two hundred thousand dollars!" soliloquized the seedy stranger as he stood in the porch of the church, "here's a windfall! Mr. Robert Brydon allow me to congratulate you;" and he shook hands with himself. "Very lucky thing for you, Bob; things were getting to a very low ebb, but now the tide has turned with a vengeance. You always were a lucky fellow, Bob, but this beats all. How surprised the dear boy will be. Well, Montreal is a nice place, rather dull for a man of fashion like myself, but it will do. I shall hang my hat," he continued, taking off his dilapidated head covering and looking at it, "no, not this hat, but a new one I mean to buy, and prepare to spend the rest of my natural days in Montreal, and lead a virtuous, happy and peaceful life. Mr. Austin, I shall do myself the honor of calling on you as soon as you return from your pleasant trip."

He tucked the scrubby-looking cane affectionately under his arm, tipped the dilapidated hat the least bit over his right eye, and walked jauntily away.

CHAPTER IV.

OUT OF THE CANTEEN.

The wedding trip of Arthur and Jessie was a short but a very happy one. Once in a while a shadow of an old sorrow would flit across the brain of Arthur, but one glance at the bright, joyous face by his side would quickly dispel the vision, and he would be gay and happy again. As for Jessie, all the warm impassioned love of her nature thawed naturally and quietly out under the influence of the sun of her adoration. Their holiday was brief—scarce two weeks—but they thoroughly enjoyed it. There is scarcely any city, except, perhaps, Paris, when Paris was at her zenith, where two weeks can be more thoroughly enjoyed by persons who have no business but pleasure than they can be in New York. The splendid vistas of streets, the magnificent buildings, the teeming population, all so earnest and busy; the glories of Central Park, the calm quiet repose of Greenwood,[23] the flash and glow of the theatres, the splendors of the opera, the roar and bustle of Broadway, the vivid vitality of the whole place, tends to make up a picture of fascination which it is difficult to rival. Jessie had never been in any larger city than Montreal, and the glories of the opera and the wonders of the theatre were all new pleasures to her, and she drank them in with avidity, and turned from them with regret when the brief holiday had passed away and they were obliged to return. Although her life had been a happy one yet it seemed to her she had never known what true happiness was until within these two weeks. Still she was not sorry to return to Montreal, as she pictured quieter domestic joys which would more than compensate for the giddy round of pleasure she was experiencing.

Mr. Lubbuck sailed for England at the time specified and left Arthur Austin in full charge of the business, unless Mr. Lownds should take a fancy to visit Canada. Mr. Lubbuck expected to be absent about a year, and Arthur was duly installed as master of his house during his absence. The old gentleman had taken care to raise Arthur's salary to a liberal figure, so that he might not feel dependent on his wife, whose settlement had been a very liberal one, securing her $2,000 a year during

---

[23] Greenwood (also, Green-Wood) Cemetery in Brooklyn. Built in 1838 as both a cemetery and a public park, it was such a popular destination that it inspired the construction of Central Park two decades later.

her uncle's lifetime and one-half of his fortune at his death. It was about a week after Mr. Lubbuck had sailed that Arthur was walking up Jacques Cartier Square[24] when he felt a hand laid lightly on his shoulder, and a voice which sounded familiar saluted him with:

"Dear boy, how magnificently you are looking; allow me to congratulate you on your improved appearance and also on your improved prospects. I had the pleasure of witnessing that interesting little ceremony at the Cathedral a couple of weeks ago, and I assure you it affected me deeply."

"Why, Bob, old fellow, I am astonished to see you, and should certainly never have recognized you, your appearance has so much changed, you look so—so——"

"Seedy, dear boy, don't be delicate about expressions! Confoundedly seedy, if you feel in a humor for using adjectives. I confess the fact, dear boy; luck has run dead against me, and I believe I am the most impecunious and seedy individual in Montreal."

"I am really sorry to hear that, and you know, old fellow, you have only to call on me for any help you need, but where have you been these last two years that I have never heard from you; and how did you come to Montreal?"

"Dear boy, one question at a time; the story is long, and standing here is not pleasant, let us adjourn to a quiet retreat I know in the neighbourhood where we can obtain food for the body as well as the mind, and where we will not be disturbed."

They walked down Notre Dame Street to Claude, and down that almost to St. Paul, when Brydon stopped in front of Joe Beef's canteen.[25]

"Let us enter," he said, "the exterior is not inviting, and the interior is very little more so, but it is cheap, very cheap, and, as a natural

---

[24] Called Place Jacques-Cartier in French, it is a wide pedestrian thoroughfare going down from the City Hall (on Notre-Dame Street) to rue de la Commune. Nelson's Column, Montreal's oldest monument (dedicated in 1808 to the memory of Horatio Nelson) stands at the top of the square.

[25] Saint Claude is a street connecting Notre-Dame Street and Saint-Paul Street (both of which run east-west in Old Montreal, the latter being closer to the river), one block east of Jacques-Cartier Square (see note 24). Charles McKiernan (1835-1889), known as "Joe Beef," was an Irish-born former quartermaster in a British artillery regiment. After his discharge in 1864, he opened his famous "Canteen" on Saint-Claude but, in 1875, when the street was widened, he moved on the corner of Rue de la Commune and Rue de Callière. He was well known for never refusing a meal to someone who could not pay for it.

consequence, extremely acceptable to a man whose finances are in a chronic state of consumption; the fare is simple, but nutritious, and wonderfully filling,—a little of it goes a long way. Let us enter."

"No," said Arthur, "I do not believe in visiting saloons; and I don't like the appearance of this one."

"Mere prejudice, dear boy. Enter and refresh your drooping spirits with the bounding cocktail, or the foaming tankard. Besides," he added in more serious tones, I have something very particular to say to you,"

"You have certainly selected a very curious place," said Arthur, "but it makes little difference to me."

They entered, not the saloon where two rotten cheeses, a heap of ham knuckles, and piles of flat-looking bread, bountifully displayed on the counter, were the pervading features, but a side room which bore over its entrance door the pretentious sign, "Oyster saloon, meals, etc."

It was a low, dark, mean-looking room, furnished with a few heavy square tables and some benches and chairs, in one corner stood a platform which looked as if it had been used for a piano, if the place had ever been a music hall, and the walls were ornamented with a few rude pictures on sporting subjects. Mr. Brydon led the way to a side table, and sat with the air of a man who "had been there before." Arthur sat opposite him, and awaited with some impatience the communication which Brydon said he had to make to him.

Mr. Brydon settled the seedy-looking hat firmly on his head, dived into one pocket and produced an old clay pipe, black with age; into another, and brought out a handful of tobacco, filled the pipe, and carefully returned the few grains left in his hand to his pocket. He then dived into another pocket and, producing a match, lighted his pipe and took two or three contemplative whiffs.

Arthur Austin had known Robert Brydon for many years, they had been school-mates together, and Brydon had been for some time in the office of Arthur's father when Arthur himself was a clerk there. He had left the office under rather suspicious circumstances, a cheque had been forged for a small sum, and suspicion had for some time been thrown on Arthur Austin, but a thorough investigation showed Mr. Brydon as the probable culprit, the case was not very clear against him, and Mr. Austin contented himself with simply discharging him. Brydon took the discharge in the light of an injustice, and tried hard to throw the guilt on Arthur, but Mr. Austin so scouted[26] the idea that he quickly changed his tactics, and tried to conciliate the friend he had

---

[26] To scout (of a different origin than the better-known identical word) means to reject with contempt.

endeavored to abuse. Arthur was of an easy, forgiving disposition and soon forgot the injustice and wrong Brydon had tried to do him. At that time Arthur was rather wild—as young men with plenty of money generally will be—and Brydon soon established himself as his boon companion. They had numerous "sprees" together, and Brydon was closely connected in a transaction which Arthur had every desire to blot from his memory, and every wish to keep concealed from the rest of the world. Brydon after he left Mr. Austin, had for a while run a faro bank on the Bowery;[27] but some ugly tales had been told to the police, and one night a descent was made on it, and the proprietor and inmates arrested. It does not take much trouble or ingenuity—but generally a good deal of money—for the keeper of a New York faro bank to escape from the clutches of a New York Judge, and so Robert Brydon suffered nothing more than a heavy fine, and the confiscation of his "lay out," "checks, &c."[28] He remained about New York for a few months after this, figuring conspicuously as a "sport," attending the races, driving a fast team in the Park, wearing a big diamond pin in his shirt bosom, and otherwise playing the heavy swell. Then he disappeared, and Arthur Austin had seen or heard nothing of him for over two years, when they suddenly met in Jacques Cartier Square. When Brydon left New York Arthur Austin was at the height of his success, and reputed to be enormously wealthy. In a few months more a collapse had come, and he was reduced to almost beggary. What Brydon had been doing in these two years and a half, and what had reduced him from the gay cavalier to the seedy individual he now was, were matters of conjecture to Arthur Austin.

"Sit down, dear boy, and refresh," said Mr. Brydon. "Allow me to recommend the beer; the presence of water is plainly recognizable, but it retains some of its ancient flavor and is not bad, all things considered. Mr. Beef," continued he, as that personage entered the room, "will you oblige me with one of your excellent steaks and a tankard of mulled ale. My friend will take——"

"Nothing, thanks," said Arthur. "I do not need any lunch, and I never take any intoxicating liquor."

"Phew," whistled Mr. Beef, "you're a cold water customer, are you? Well, I shouldn't wonder if you were," he continued, with a supercilious glance, "you look like it."

---

[27] Faro was a popular gambling game using cards; a game of faro was known as a "faro bank." The Bowery is a street as well as neighborhood in Lower Manhattan.
[28] In faro, each player bets on one or more of the 13 cards of the original "layout." "Checks" are the chips bought from the house.

"Dear boy, dear boy," said Mr. Brydon, "you don't mean to say that you have come the cold water dodge![29] Sorry to hear it, very; it ruins the coating of the stomach, and brings a man to an early and uncomfortable grave. You won't take anything? then I must drink alone. Mr. Beef would you oblige me by seeing that that steak is fat and of fair proportion, I feel slightly peckish."

"Yes, you generally do feel 'peckish' when you come in here," responded Mr. Beef, as he went into the bar-room to execute the order. Before leaving the room, however, he took the poker out of the coal-scuttle, gave it a preliminary wipe with his handkerchief and put it in the stove.

"Brydon, what is it you want to say to me, and why did you come here to say it?" asked Arthur Austin, as soon as they were alone.

"Dear boy, what a trick you have of asking two or three questions at once. One at a time will last much longer, and give me so much more of your company,"

"I have no time to wait, what do you want? Do you want money?"

"Dear boy, your last remark is the most sensible one you have made yet. I have for some time past been in a chronic condition of wanting money."

"Well, you know, Bob, you have only to tell me how much you want, and if it is possible for me to accommodate you I will do so."

"Dear boy, your kindness overpowers me. Suppose we say 'a tenner' to begin with. I have a most unexceptionable suit of togs, for which I paid—no, I mean *owe*—Brooks Brothers[30] fifty-five dollars; and an obliging relative of mine in Montreal—in fact, my uncle—was considerate enough to lend me three dollars and a half on them. With those released, and a new pair of boots, 'Richard will be himself again.'[31] No, stop, not quite himself. I promised myself a new hat to hang up in Montreal, perhaps you wouldn't mind adding another V[32] so that I may keep my promise."

Arthur Austin took out his pocket book and counted out four five dollar bills which he handed to Brydon, saying, "Bob, you know I have

[29] Dodge was a slang term for "line of work," "pursuit," or "vow."
[30] Founded in 1818 in Manhattan as a family business, Brooks Brothers (the name dates from 1850) became a household name during the American Civil War, when they made uniforms for Union soldiers and suits for dignitaries such as Abraham Lincoln.
[31] The phrase (indicating a return to normal) originated in Colley Cibber's 1700 play *Richard III* (an adaptation of Shakespeare's eponymous play), in which it appears as "Richard's himself again."
[32] Old American slang term for a five-dollar bill, which, in the mid-19th century, featured on its reverse both the word "five" and (more prominently) the Roman numeral "V."

been under pretty heavy expense lately, and my funds are running low. I will let you have all I can spare, twenty dollars, and if I can be of any further use to you, you can command me. I will be wanted at the office, so I must leave you."

"Dear boy, you are generosity itself, but do not go just yet. I have something to tell you which it is important for you to hear."

Further conversation was interrupted by the entrance of Mr. Beef, artistically arrayed in his shirt sleeves, bearing a pewter mug of ale in one hand and a red herring suspended by the tail in the other. He placed the mug on the table, took a plate from a cupboard and skilfully "slung" it along the table until it stopped in front of Mr. Brydon. He then proceeded to the stove and drawing out the poker, returned to the table and said:

"Here's your two-eyed beefsteak and your mulled ale," at the same time bringing the herring down with a smart slap on the plate, and plunging the poker into the ale, which foamed and hissed tremendously.

"And very excellent they appear to be, good Mr. Beef," said Mr. Brydon. May I trouble you for a cracker and the mustard ?"

"Here's a cracker, there ain't any mustard. I'll trouble you for five cents."

"He's too civil a chap by half," muttered Mr. Beef to himself as he went back to the bar, "and I don't like the looks of him, though he has been here pretty often the last two weeks, and always paid his way like a man."

"Now, Brydon, what is it you want to say to me?"

"Dear boy, don't be impetuous, this herring is excellent, and so is my appetite; the beer is thin, but; I am thirsty: allow me to refresh."

Arthur sat silently thinking for a few minutes whilst Brydon "refreshed." He was thinking over his friend's manner which did not impress him favorably. He knew Robert Brydon thoroughly, and although he would lend him money for "Auld lang syne," or do him a good turn if he could, he would not trust him. He was aware of one or two dark spots in Mr. Brydon's career, and he placed little confidence in him. He also remembered that Brydon was fully acquainted with an unpleasant episode in his own career, which he wished to forget but could not, and, spite of himself, the man's presence in Montreal gave him an unpleasant, anxious feeling. What had brought him to Canada? Perhaps some sort of misconduct in the States, but what could it be that he wanted to say to him?

"Brydon," said Arthur, at last, "you have very nearly finished that herring, and my time is precious, what is it you have to tell me?"

"Excellent refreshment, and filling at the price," said Mr. Brydon, quite imperturbably, "but rather dry and needing more fluid to wash it down. Mr. Beef, will you oblige me with another mug of beer, cold this time, the poker imparted rather a greasy flavor to the last lot. Now, dear boy," he continued, after his mug had been replenished and he had taken a good pull at it, "pardon my keeping you in suspense, but what I have to say is serious, and I prefer entering upon a serious subject on a full stomach, it gives one more confidence. Dear boy, that was a very pleasant ceremony I witnessed the other day, and I congratulate you on your good taste; Mrs. Austin No. 2 is certainly a very charming little lady, and I do not wonder at your susceptible heart being captured by her beauty, without taking into account the ulterior attraction of her uncle's fortune."

"I do not see what my wife's personal appearance has to do with the matter," said Arthur very stiffly, "pray come to the point."

"Dear boy, that's just what I am coming to, but the point very nearly concerns Mrs. Austin No. 2, and, therefore, I am forced to mention her."

"What do you mean by calling my wife Mrs. Austin No. 2.?"

"Simply, dear boy, that there is a Mrs. Austin No. 1."

"*Was* you mean, not *is*; there is no use dragging up that old story of my folly and its punishment. I will save you the trouble of repeating the tale of how a beardless boy, not twenty, became enamored of a pretty ballet dancer, with a well-turned ankle and captivating black eyes; of how he followed her in his infatuation to a small village in Pennsylvania, and, in a moment of madness, married her; of his awaking from his wild dream to find that she was wicked, abandoned, vile, all that a woman should not be, and that he was tied to her for life; of the year of misery that he passed. No, there is no need for you to repeat that old story, I remember it only too well; it is only too deeply engraved on my heart, and is the one dark memory of my life. But, thank God! it is only a memory, death has closed that page of my life and I do not desire to have it re-opened."

"Not the least doubt of it, dear boy, and quite proper on your part, but I fail to understand your allusion to death."

"My wretched wife died four years ago, just about the time of the failure of Austin & Son. Oh! don't look incredulous, I have a letter from the doctor who attended her and the undertaker who buried her; the letter enclosed bills which I paid; but although the gentlemen were prompt enough to send me their bills, they were never polite to forward receipts for the money. I also saw an announcement of my wife's death in a Savannah paper, in which place she was playing at the time. Besides, you know, I was allowing my wife $2,000 a year at that time, and her quarterly allowance has not since been claimed, not that I could have paid it, because our failure left me without the means to do so, but because there was no one to pay it to."

"What a wonderful memory the dear boy has," said Mr. Brydon rather mockingly, "but incorrect as to facts. Miss Effie Barron, or, to speak more correctly, Mrs. Austin No. 1, must be a very remarkable person to die in Savannah four years ago, and to have been alive and well in New York two months ago when I had the pleasure of seeing her."

"Alive!" shouted Arthur Austin, starting from his chair.

"Not the least doubt of it, dear boy, alive and kicking, absolutely kicking, for I saw her kick a bell-boy at the St. Charles Hotel[33] because he refused to furnish a couple of brandies and soda without payment in advance."

"It's a lie."

"Perfectly true, dear boy, perfectly true; the doctor's and the undertaker's letters and bills were ingenious forgeries, very neatly executed by a friend of yours who desired to relieve your mind of a load of grief. Your first wife is alive and very anxious to find you, as she is confoundedly hard up and would like her allowance renewed. The pleasant little ceremony I witnessed at the Cathedral was, no doubt, very enjoyable to you; but it was a sad mistake for you, dear boy; it is an awkward thing to commit bigamy."

"Bigamy! Oh Heavens! Poor Jessie, poor Jessie!" exclaimed Arthur, clasping his head in his hands and leaning forward on the table; "My poor little darling!"

"Yes, yes, it is rather hard on the little lady with the golden hair; but it is rather harder on the other lady, Mrs. Austin No. 1."

"Robert Brydon," said Arthur rising, and looking at his companion with a vengeful, dangerous look, "I know you to be a scoundrel, a thief, a liar, and an unprincipled adventurer."

"Don't be complimentary, dear boy, please don't, or you will make me blush."

"You will remember," continued Arthur, "that I induced my father to spare you once when you forged his name. I have always been your friend in good repute and evil repute. I would even be your friend now, for we played together as children, and grew up almost as brothers; but, by Heaven, if you are hatching any of your infernal plots against me I will hound you to death like a dog. You are trying to raise the phantom of my past misery to blight the happiness of the present, but have a care! I know enough of your past life to send you to prison, and I will do it if you try to annoy me."

[33] The Saint Charles was a hotel that used to stand on the corner of Broadway and Leonard Street.

"Don't, dear boy, don't, I have been there, and I can't say I like it; the grub is meagre, and their drink is bad,—only water, and poor at that. I have resided in Sing Sing[34] two years and have no desire to return there, besides, dear boy, you forget I am quite safe in Canada, although I might be in danger in the States."

"What does your story mean?" said Arthur, restraining himself with an effort, and again taking his seat. "Is it an attempt to extort money from me?'

"Extort money," said Mr. Brydon, suddenly changing his manner, and rising and speaking with great force and emphasis, totally different from his former quiet, bantering style. "To extort money? yes; but it is more than that, Arthur Austin, it is to pay off an old score. I have had a debt of hate against you for a long time and I mean to pay it, Arthur Austin. You have crossed my path three times in my life, and I mean to lie down across yours for the rest of your or my existence, so that you cannot get rid of me. Excuse me, dear boy," he continued, suddenly changing his manner again and resuming his seat, "I am afraid I was a little excited; I hope you will pardon me, and allow me to tell you a little story. Can you remember twelve years ago, Arthur Austin, when we were at school together? Can you remember how you bullied me? I can. Do you remember thrashing me? I do. Do you think I have ever forgotten those days, no, no, I remember well every blow you gave me, every cross or hard word you used, and I swore then that when I came to manhood I would return you 'blow for blow' and I mean to keep my oath. Oh! I kept on good terms with you, was always your good friend, but it was only because the nearer I was to you, the deeper I could strike. My first blow failed. You remarked just now that I forged your father's name. I did, yes, I forged his name and tried to throw the guilt on you. I failed, and was discharged,—that was the second time you crossed my path. I still kept on good terms with you and bided my time. One night I was fool enough to introduce to you the girl on whom I had set my heart, and who I believed loved me. Your baby face, your smooth, plausible manner and your wealth, won her from me. You married her. Well, Effie Barron never was a good lot, and you found that out very shortly after your marriage, when the scales had dropped from your eyes. You tried to get divorced from her, but Miss Effie was too clever to have committed any act *since* her marriage which gave you any legal claim to cast her off. Oh, no! virago, devil, as she was, she was too clever to give you the power to throw her aside when you discovered what she had been. Bad as she was—and none knew better than I how bad—I

[34] Sing Sing Correctional Facility (on the east bank of the Hudson River, in New York State) was built between 1824 and 1828.

loved her wildly, passionately, loved her then, love her now, and shall always love her." He had spoken fiercely, his voice gaining depth and passion, although it was only slightly raised. He paused now, overcome by genuine emotion, his voice almost choked by the thick quick sobs which rose to his throat. Any one looking at him now would scarcely have recognized the easy-going self-possessed cynical individual who had been speaking a few minutes before. After a short pause he continued: "When she first told me she was going to marry you, I meant to shoot you. I waited for you one whole night outside her house but you did not visit her. I dogged your footsteps for three whole days, watching for an opportunity to murder you, and finding none. Then I changed my mind. Death was too quick a punishment for you. I would wait and seek some more lasting means of torturing you as you tortured me. You will remember, dear boy," he continued, again changing to his light, playful manner, "that I assisted at that little ceremony at which Miss Effie Barron became Mrs. Austin No. 1; I assisted at one or two of the amusing little matrimonial squabbles in which you indulged; I assisted in furnishing you information about your wife's former character; I assisted in defeating your application for divorce, and I assisted at some thing else which you did not suspect—your wife's funeral which never took place." He was speaking earnestly and bitterly again, and the wicked, devilish look was on his face. "After your separation from your wife she returned to the stage—she could scarcely be said to have ever left it—and I met her. I had some money then, and I could afford to pay for a whim. I thought that if death relieved you of your wife, or, to speak more correctly, if you supposed death had relieved you, you would probably marry again. I proposed a scheme to Effie,—she loved you none too well, and joined with me readily. I wrote the letters and bills you received. I prepared the advertisement for the Savannah papers, which, by the way, was contradicted next day, although you did not see that. I laid my plan carefully, and then I came North and was with you in New York when you received the letters which had been posted by Effie herself. I remember well your joy at their receipt, and I expected to see you a married man in less than a year, but your confounded failure drove you from New York and spoiled your chance of marrying again for some time. I thought I was foiled again, but fortune has favored me at last. You are married now—married well and wealthily; and I hold the dagger in my hand which can fall and destroy your happiness and commit you to prison whenever I please; and I please to keep the dagger suspended above you."

Brydon had risen to his feet, and his voice had grown in intensity and power, although only slightly raised, but it contained all the concentrated force of long pent-up feeling. As he stood bending over Arthur Austin, whose head had drooped on his crossed arms on the table, with his right arm uplifted, he seemed as if he really fancied he held a dagger in his hand, and only hesitated a moment before plunging it into his companion's heart. He recovered himself quickly, however, and, resuming his seat, said in more quiet accents: "I have been a little violent, excuse me; you seem slightly overpowered, will you take something to steady your nerves?"

"Brandy!" said Arthur in so hoarse and unnatural a voice that Mr. Brydon involuntarily started.

"Mr. Beef," Brydon called, "will you oblige me with a glass of your best brandy, and another glass of beer?"

The drinks were brought and Arthur tossed the brandy down at one gulp, and ordered his glass filled again. When the second glass had been swallowed in the same manner, he turned to Brydon and said:

"What do you mean by what you have told me? what do you want? you did not lay so clever and diabolical a plan for nothing."

"Quite right, dear boy, quite right, it is wonderful how the brandy has cleared your powers of perception." The man had entirely recovered his equanimity again, and spoke in his usual bantering style: "I certainly did not expend so much time, money and ingenuity without some definite plan of remuneration. One motive I have already told you, the other I will now explain, and I shall do it in the fewest possible words: I want to be provided for."

"Provided for?"

"That is exactly the idea, dear boy, I see you understand it perfectly."

"You are mistaken if you suppose I can support you in idleness; I am only a clerk working for a fair but not large salary. My wife—"

"Mrs. Austin No. 2," interrupted Mr. Brydon.

"My wife," continued Arthur Austin speaking very quietly, "has an allowance until her uncle's death, and will then receive one half of his fortune; but not one penny of that money shall you ever touch."

"Certainly not, dear boy, certainly not; your sentiment does you infinite honor; you are doubtless thinking of the necessary provision to be made for a prospective group of charming little Austins, all with their mother's golden hair and bright blue eyes."

"Cease speaking in your sneering way of my wife, or I dare you to do your worst."

"Sneering! You mistake, dear boy, I greatly respect your charming lady."

"Your proposition is nonsensical, I am unable to support you in idleness."

"Idleness! dear boy, you labor under a delusion. I never said anything about idleness. I proposed that you should provide for me; but, of course, I intended that you should do so in some easy, pleasant way. Do I look like an idle man? I flatter myself I look like an energetic man. I only want some nice quiet place where there is little or nothing to do, and good pay for doing it. Surely you can assist me to some such place. Get me a contract with the Corporation,[35] or a good fat berth under Government where there will be nothing to do but draw my pay."

"I cannot assist you in that way, I have no influence. Brydon, I may as well speak plainly with you."

"Do, dear boy, I admire candor, and always practise it myself."

"I do not believe this story of yours. I regard it all as a base fabrication invented to wring money from my fears. I shall sift this matter thoroughly, and if I find you have told me the truth I will be forced, I suppose, to—to—"

"Make terms, dear boy, make terms, that is the correct expression."

"Make terms; yes, I suppose so, for I cannot give Jessie up."

"Nothing further from my wishes, dear boy; don't think for a minute of giving her up."

"But if I find you have attempted to play on my feelings, and extort money from me, I shall hunt you down as I would any other mean, contemptible cur."

"Don't use bad words, dear boy, you hurt my feelings. You doubt my word also, that hurts my feelings again; perhaps you can believe your own eye-sight. You think your first wife is dead, here is a letter written by her to me about three months ago; excuse the calligraphy and orthography, dear boy; and also a few ornate embellishments, in the way of oaths, etc., for which I am in no way responsible, they are the exclusive property of Mrs. Austin No. 1."

Arthur took the letter, glanced at it, and his cheek blanched, there was scarcely any mistaking that struggling hand, and that supreme disregard of Lindley Murray.[36] It brought back unpleasant memories, and seemed to him like a message from the dead. He read it through twice; the first time with a dead feeling of fear and misery at his heart, the second with a slight flush on his cheek and a bright sparkle in his eye. As he read the letter a second time, hope whispered to him that there was a way out of his difficult and dangerous position which he could accomplish without the aid of Mr. Robert Brydon. That gentleman

[35] The Corporation of the City of Montreal, the official name of the local governing body of the city at the time.
[36] Lindley Murray (1745-1826) was the author of several English grammar books.

watched him keenly, and, as Arthur handed him back the letter with a smile, he said:

"Amusing, dear boy, isn't it? I could not help smiling myself when I read the affectionate terms in which Mrs. Austin No. 1 writes of you. You seem elated too, dear boy; you think you have found a way to untie the Gordian knot; don't have any such fancy. I can tell you what you have been thinking. You have noticed one or two expressions in that letter which lead you to believe that you can renew that pleasant little divorce suit with a better chance of success by making your humble servant co-respondent;[37] quite an error, dear boy. Even if you could prove that Mrs. Austin No. 1 had been unfaithful, that would not improve the position of Mrs. Austin No. 2; you would still have committed bigamy by marrying her before you were divorced from Mrs. Austin No. 1. And again, the moment you institute proceedings for divorce that moment my dagger falls, and Mrs. Austin No. 2 is made aware of the fact that she is not married at all. You see the position, dear boy; I am prepared for any emergency."

"What can I do?"

"What I have already proposed to you; provide for me."

"I cannot."

"You must."

"Brydon, I shall begin to-morrow to inquire into the truth of what you have been telling me. It will take a week or ten days to find out whether it is true or not; meanwhile, I will supply you with what money I can spare. What guarantee do you give me that you will keep faith with me?"

"My word of honor, dear boy, my word of honor."

"Your word of honor; that is worth a great deal, isn't it?"

"Don't be cynical, dear boy; well my personal advantage then, for if the cat jumps out of the bag, my supplies are cut off, don't you see; and, therefore, it is my best policy to keep a still tongue and quietly bleed you."

"And Effie?"

"Shall receive a letter from your humble servant, dated from New Orleans, informing her that I have traced you to that city only to find that you had gone to Rio Janeiro, or Buenos Ayres, or Hong Kong, or Honolulu, or any other place you might prefer; and if she chooses to follow you there she will have a long search, that is all."

"Very well," said Arthur rising, "I must go now; I shall be wanted at the office."

---

[37] In a petition for divorce at the time, a co-respondent (i.e., "co-defendant") was the man charged by the husband of having committed adultery with his wife.

"One moment, dear boy; that word office gives me an idea. You are in charge now that Mr. Lubbuck is away, and you must find your duties rather arduous. You want a bookkeeper; the position will suit me exactly, you can do the work and I will draw the pay; equal division of labor, you see."

"You in Mr. Lubbuck's office! No, no, I don't care to have so much of your company."

"But if I insist."

"We will see about it."

The two men left the canteen together, but separated at the door.

CHAPTER V.

OUT OF THE SOBER PATH.

Arthur Austin did not go directly to his office, in fact he did not go there for quite a long while. On leaving Brydon he went first to the "Terrapin"[38] and had another drink, then lighted a cigar, walked down to Viger Garden[39] and sat for a long time thinking and smoking. The terrible calamity which had fallen on him had quite unnerved him, and he could scarcely collect his thoughts. Although he affected to, he did not really disbelieve the strange story Brydon had told him. He knew Brydon to be utterly unprincipled and capable of almost any wickedness; and he knew his former wife to be low, cunning and vicious. He remembered her rage and threats when he first discovered her true character, and tried to thrust her from the proud position she had expected to occupy as his wife. After the first shock, therefore, he was not surprised to hear that she had joined Brydon in a scheme of revenge and blackmail on himself. Her ceasing to draw her quarterly allowance had completely fooled him—no doubt Brydon, who was well to do at the time, had

[38] An elegant restaurant on Saint Catherine Street, part of the Crystal Block, proprietor Joseph Carlisle.
[39] The garden had been a public park since 1860. Today, the same area is covered by Viger Square.

made that up to her; for Arthur Austin had seen, what Brydon did not think he had seen, the contradiction in the Savannah papers of the report of Effie Barron's death. It was scarcely a contradiction, merely a line or two saying that they had been misinformed as to her death; but that she was most dangerously ill and not expected to recover. The letters from the doctor and undertaker, added to the fact of her not drawing her quarterly allowance, completely deceived him, and he fully and honestly believed himself free until Brydon had laid bare to him the diabolical plot to which he had been made a victim.

He sat for a long while thinking it over. At first he thought he would make a clean breast of it to Jessie, separate from her for a time, and endeavor again to get a divorce from his wife; but then the publicity, the disgrace, the pain and grief to Jessie, the chance of a criminal prosecution of himself, all rose in terrible array before his vision, and he had not the moral courage to face the dangers that threatened him. He would compromise, he would conciliate Brydon and endeavor to keep him quiet. He by no means, however, intended to accept Brydon's statement without examination; and after duly considering the matter he decided to apply to one of the detectives and get him to test the truth of Brydon's story, by making minute inquiries in both New York and Savannah. With this resolution he rose and started at once for the Central Station; on his way, however, he stopped at the first tavern he came to and took another drink.

From the moment Brydon had told him of the crime he had unconsciously committed he appeared to have become an altered man; he forgot, in one moment, his vow and the pleasure he had experienced since he had taken the pledge, he forgot his duty to the woman he had sworn to love, honor and cherish, and remembered only that he had a dull, heavy feeling at the heart, and that the old craving for drink was on him again. It was during the excitement and worry of his failure that Arthur Austin had first sought consolation from the bottle; and when trouble again overtook him he turned again to his old enemy and destroyer, and, without a thought, without a struggle, gave himself up to the power of the liquid demon.

It is one of the most dangerous, and, at the same time, the most incongruous, features of the power of drink, that men instinctively turn to it at the very moment they should most shun it. When the mind is most enervated by some gigantic calamity; when the brain is temporarily prostrated by some sudden and unexpected blow; when the physical system is shaken by some great shock; when the shadow of some dire misfortune throws its pall over mind and body, and mind and body are least able to withstand the attack of the enemy, it is then, above all other times, that men instinctively turn to the arch destroyer who is always lying in wait for them. They drink under the idea that the temporary stupefaction of the brain is relief, and wake from their slumbers only to find their brain on fire, their throats parched, and the grief or sorrow heavier to bear than before. At the very time a man needs all his intellect, all his force of mind, all his moral and physical strength to fight against some great disaster, at that very moment he voluntarily enlists another enemy against him—the most dangerous he can have, for it strengthens all the others.

So it was with Arthur Austin. At the very time he ought to have kept his mind clearest, in order to combat the well-laid schemes of his enemy, he quietly and without a single effort to save himself, gave way to the domination of drink. Had he looked his trouble in the face like a man, met and combatted it like a man, with a firm faith and trust in God, he could easily have extricated himself from the difficulties in which he was placed; but he enlisted the devil on his side, and from that moment his course was downward, downward to destruction.

It was past five o'clock when Arthur reached the Central Station, and none of the detectives happened to be in. He was told that Cullen would be on duty at night and would be in any time after eight. He then returned to the office where he had not been since one o'clock.

"Mrs. Austin is in the private office," said one of his fellow clerks as he entered.

Arthur went into the office and found Jessie sitting in the large office chair swinging about in it, and tapping her little foot impatiently on the carpet.

"Why, Arthur," she exclaimed starting up, "where have you been so long? I've been waiting for you nearly an hour," and she looked at the little clock over the desk as if to corroborate her statement.

"I have been very busy, darling. I am sorry to have kept you waiting but I could not help it. I will be ready to go with you in a few minutes."

"Is anything the matter, Arthur?" she asked as she came to him and laid her hand on his shoulder, "you do not look well."

"I don't feel very well to-day, darling; I have been worried a good deal about some unpleasant business." He stooped over her and kissed her. Jessie half started from his arms and gave a little cry as she looked suddenly into his flushed face and said, "Oh, Arthur."

"What is it, little one?"

"Oh, Arthur, you've—you've been drinking," she half sobbed as she hid her face on his shoulder.

Arthur paused for a moment and his face flushed with shame, as he thought, for the first time, how weak and culpable he had been.

"Not much, darling; I have been very unwell to-day and I took a little brandy medicinally," he added after a little hesitation and a blush at the falsehood he was telling.

"Well, don't do so anymore, Hubby; I don't like people who drink, and I love my Hubby so much and am so proud of him, I don't want him to do anything which will lower him in the estimation of others."

She said this so sweetly, and clung to him with such a tender, loving clasp, that Arthur groaned in spirit, and had to support himself by holding on to the table to prevent himself from falling. In one moment he felt all the bitterness which he would suffer at being parted from Jessie and all the misery he owed Robert Brydon for his diabolical plot, and if that easy-going individual had been there at the moment, Arthur could have killed him without the slightest compunction.

"Let us go home," he muttered, and they left the office together.

*   *   *   *   *   *   *

When Mr. Robert Brydon left the canteen he walked up to the corner of Notre Dame Street and soliloquized thus:

"Robert, my boy, allow me to congratulate you; you have opened the campaign nobly, and a great career lies before you. Nothing to do, and well paid for doing it. I like the programme, but I scarcely think I shall stick to it, I am so fond of doing something. The people here seem green and confiding; I should like to introduce them to some of the mysteries of Faro, or Poker, perhaps it would not be a bad idea to open a bank. I'll think about it. Meanwhile, Bob, my boy, you look seedy, confoundedly seedy, and you need a thorough renovation; the trouble is you need so thorough a renovation that it is difficult to determine where it is best to begin. I think it would be best to begin with the shirt. It is so long since I have indulged in the luxury of a clean shirt that I really think I must begin with that."

He purchased a shirt, with a flashy set of cheap jewellery, a pair of boots, a rakish white hat, with a black band around it, a pair of gloves and a cheap cane. He then proceeded to the pawnbroker's where his clothes were pledged, and, having redeemed them, took all his treasures to a house in Bonaventure Street where he was living.[40] He decked himself out in gorgeous array,[41] and then consulted the three square inches of dimmed glass which did duty with him as a mirror.

[40] The name given at the time to a part of St James Street (see note 10), between McGill Street and Place Saint-Henri.
[41] A phrase often used sarcastically in the 19th century. Its origin is in a line from Edmund Spenser's *The Faerie Queene* (1590-1596).

"The get up is pretty good," he said complacently looking down at his pantaloons, and affectionately regarding his well-fitting frock coat; it is a pity, a thousand pities, that I should be deprived of the services of so thorough an artist as the cutter at Brooks Bros., New York, and such confiding people as they are. Ah, well, well, Bob, you can't expect to have everything exactly as you desire it, you must cultivate some Montreal tailor and do the best you can with him. The get up is good," he continued after a pause, again looking in the glass, "but the aid of the tonsorial artist is sadly needed. I must take a stroll as far as the Hall[42] and indulge in the luxury of a shave."

He put on the new white hat, drew on his gloves, gave the new cane a gentle twirl in the air and went out. He strolled leisurely up to the Hall, and, entering the barber shop, placed himself in the hands of Charlie.

"My sable friend,[43] I would like you to take off all the superfluous hirsute appendages you can, leaving me only a modest moustache, and a fair allowance of hair."

"You want to be shaved?" inquired Charlie.

"That is my humble wish, my most noble knight of the lather and razor."

Charlie went to work industriously with a pair of scissors, and in a few seconds Mr. Brydon's ample whiskers and beard lay in a little heap on the floor.

"Do you want a close shave, sir?"

"Take off everything but the skin. Leave that, if possible, uncut."

"Yah, yah! You bet I don't take none of that off."

Mr. Brydon's shaving, hair cutting and hair dressing being completed, he had his hair and moustache dyed a glossy black, and arose from the chair a new man, scarcely recognizable as the seedy, unkempt individual of the morning. He surveyed himself with great satisfaction in the glass and muttered, "That will do. I think it would puzzle a Philadelphia lawyer to identify Richard Cranston, of Richmond celebrity in the past, with Robert Brydon of the present. I have wanted to make this change for some time, but waited until I could make it complete; now it is complete, and Brydon is himself again."

He walked jauntily out of the barber shop, stepped into the barroom, took a drink and a cigar, and then went for a pleasant stroll. It was quite

---

[42] Mentioned later by its full name of St Lawrence Hall. It was a famous hotel, on Saint James Street (see note 10), on the corner of Saint-François-Xavier, opened in 1851. It was torn down in 1910 to make room for a new building, still standing, known as the Dominion Express (an office building at 215, rue Saint-Jacques).

[43] "Sable" is an archaic term for black or dark-skinned.

dark when he got tired of walking about, and, being reminded by certain inward cravings that his lunch had been light, he proceeded towards the Terrapin, determined that his dinner should be heavy, and that he would drink to his own good health in a pint of champagne.

*   *   *   *   *   *   *

It was more difficult for Arthur Austin to keep his self-imposed appointment at the Central Station than he had supposed. With true womanly instinct Jessie knew that something very serious had happened to annoy him; and, although she forbore questioning him, she fluttered around him all the evening, giving him now a gentle caress, now a fond look, now a bright smile. She sang for him, and tried all a woman's loving wiles to cheer him and win him from the gloom which seemed to weigh him down. But it was in vain. The more Jessie caressed him, the greater the weight grew at his heart; and, although he tried hard, the gloom would deepen on his brow as he thought how soon he may be debarred from enjoying those caresses. At last he rose to leave the room, and said he was going for a short walk, but would be back in half an hour.

"Let me go with you," said Jessie. "I have been indoors. nearly all day and a walk will do me good."

"No, darling. I am going to meet a gentleman on business and it would not do for you to go with me. To-morrow night we will take a nice long walk together."

Jessie pouted the least bit, and a tear sprang to her eye; it was the first request Arthur had ever refused her; and she, spoiled child as she was, felt it more keenly than others would a more serious matter.

"Don't fret, pet," said Arthur, kissing her; "I won't be long, and Frank will keep you company until I return."

"I shall wait up for you, Arthur, so come back as soon as you can."

"Wait up for me! Why, I shall be back before ten."

"Are you quite sure?"

"Quite."

It was a little after nine when Arthur Austin reached the Central Station. In answer to his inquiry for Cullen he was directed to the detective's room up-stairs, where he found the detective in conversation with an eccentric-looking individual who, he afterwards discovered, was a newspaper reporter. Cullen was evidently giving him an "item," and the reporter seemed greatly pleased thereat, for he laughed heartily as he made notes in his memorandum book of what Cullen was telling him.

Arthur stood in the background and quietly watched the detective. Somehow he gained comfort from looking at him. The face was that of a thoughtful, intelligent, honest man. Mild, quiet eyes, with a slightly meditative look in them; a strong fine-cut mouth, giving indication of strength of purpose and determination; a well-knit frame, of good size and proportion; large hands with strong wrists, giving indications of great physical strength: altogether he was a man to prepossess you at first sight—a man you instinctively felt it would be safe to trust a secret with, and who would do his work quietly and unobtrusively, but do it well. He was smoking an ancient meerschaum pipe in quite an enjoyable sort of way.

There is quite an art in smoking a pipe. Do not think that smoking consists simply in putting the end of a pipe in your mouth, violently inhaling a quantity of smoke and then as rapidly exhaling it again. That is not enjoying a smoke. That is only burning tobacco. I like to see a man smoke calmly, slowly and deliberately; to draw in the smoke quietly and easily and hold it in his mouth a moment as if he enjoyed the taste of it. I like to see him emit the smoke carefully, a little at a time, in curling little puffs, and let it twine about his face as he inhales the rich aroma of the weed. A man who smokes in this way has not, as a general thing, "a sweet-smelling savor" to the non-smoker, but he thoroughly and entirely enjoys a smoke as nobody else does. His pipe is to him a friend and companion, tobacco smoke a sort of ether in which his fancy roams at will, and pictures beautiful and fantastic shapes in the clouds of eddying vapor as they rise.

Cullen smoked a pipe in a comfortable sort of way, and Arthur Austin, who was a great smoker, felt his confidence increase in the man who knew how to smoke a pipe well. In a corresponding degree his opinion of the reporter fell as he noticed that he sat with his knees doubled up, the heels of his boots caught in the rung of the chair, and puffed away in short quick jerks, like the action of a steam tug, at a dirty-looking briar pipe;[44] so short and quick were the puffs that it did not need a great stretch of the imagination to fancy that he heard the panting of the engine.

Cullen rose as soon as Arthur entered, and advancing to him said, with just "the least bit of a brogue," which made his voice sound even fuller and sweeter[45] than it naturally was,

---

[44] Briar pipes are made from the wood of the briar plant (also known as tree heath) native to southern Europe and eastern Africa.

[45] Cullen is (as the brogue in his voice suggests) an Irish surname. Andrew Cullen had been a Montreal detective since November 1867 (see *Mysteries* 321). He was later promoted Chief Detective of the City of Montreal.

"What can I do for you, sir?"

"I want to see Detective Cullen. I suppose I am addressing him."

"You are. Take a seat, sir, I will be disengaged in one minute."

Then turning to the reporter, he continued, "I got a cab at the depot and brought him up to the Central Station, and he will appear before Mr. Brehaut[46] to-morrow morning."

"All right," said the reporter, making a few mild-looking hieroglyphics which passed current with him for notes. "Anything else to-night?"

"Only one little case of a girl stealing some clothes. Lafon[47] can tell you about it, I do not know the particulars, or, perhaps, the sergeant in charge can tell you. Now, sir," he continued, turning to Arthur as the reporter left the room, still puffing away vigorously at the dirty-looking pipe, "what can I do for you?"

"Sit down, Sergeant, I wish to have a long talk with you if you please. Don't put your pipe aside, I like smoke, and perhaps you will allow me to light a cigar. Can I offer you one?"

"No, thank you, sir: I prefer a pipe."

Cullen filled and lighted his pipe, and Arthur lit his cigar, and both men took a few whiffs in silence; then Arthur said:

"What I wish to consult you about is a very delicate and private matter, and requires great care and caution. I need scarcely tell you that the utmost secrecy is expected."

"Quite unnecessary, sir; all our affairs are secret. If we were even to begin to talk, our work would be done, and we would never find out anything."

"Good. Now I want to know if you could go to the States for a week or ten days, to prosecute some private business for me? Of course you shall be handsomely rewarded."

"I might be able to go, but I should have to get orders from the Chief.[48] I could not go without his order."

"Then it will be necessary for the Chief to know the errand you go on?"

"Certainly."

Another to be taken into his confidence; another aware of his guilt, if he was guilty; another who would hold in his hands the power to

---

[46] William Henry Bréhaut (1809-1880) had the title of Police Magistrate for the district of Montreal.

[47] Vincent Lafon was a detective of the Montreal Police (*Annual Report* 8). He and Cullen were both detectives and police sergeants.

[48] Chief of Police for the City of Montreal since 1865 was Frederick Walter Long Penton (1826-1879).

dash the cup of happiness from his lips. The thought was a bitter one to Arthur, but there was no alternative; he must find out the truth or falsehood of Brydon's assertions, and there was no way so sure, so silent and so speedy as this. He paused for a moment and then said:

"A friend of mine has suddenly and unexpectedly found himself in a very curious position; in fact he has every reason to fear that he has, unintentionally, committed a great crime."

"Murder?"

"No; not quite so bad as that, but bad enough—bigamy."

"Phew," whistled Cullen in a sympathetic sort of way, "I never could find what some people want with so many wives; one gives trouble enough as a general thing, but two or three always make mischief. What are the circumstances, sir?"

Arthur narrated the circumstances of his first and second marriage, just as I have already told them, only he concealed names. He explained Brydon's plot, and said that he thought the woman was in New York, where he wanted inquiries first made to ascertain whether she really was alive; he also wanted inquiries made in Savannah where her death was reported to have occurred. When he had finished, Cullen paused for a few moments, thinking over the case; he then said, "I don't see anything difficult about the case; if she is alive, I can easily find her; she is an actress and I can get her address from the *Clipper*[49] or from one of the Dramatic Agencies, I should think. She goes, I suppose, by the name she bore before her marriage?"

"I do not know. When she returned to the stage after her separation from her husband she resumed her maiden name, but if she was cunning enough to sham death she would be cunning enough to change her name."

"Most likely. What was her maiden name?"

"Effie Barron."

"What was the name of the gentleman she married?"

"Arthur Austin."

Cullen carefully noted the two names down in his pocketbook, and then asked for a general description of her appearance, age, etc. This was given with great exactness and minuteness by Arthur Austin, indeed so minute that, when he mentioned a mole on the left shoulder which was quite hidden except when she wore a very low dress, and a small bright red mark behind her right ear, Cullen looked up very sharply at him as if he had just conceived an idea.

[49] The *New York Clipper* was a weekly newspaper devoted to the entertainment industry. Founded in 1853, it was acquired by its rival *Variety* in 1922 and ceased publication in 1924.

"I have her photograph, taken some five years ago, if that will be of any use to you," said Arthur, in conclusion.

"It might be, at all events it won't do any harm to let me see it."

"I will bring it with me to-morrow morning when I come down to see the Chief. I am much obliged to you, and, if you can bring me information of that woman's death, I will give you one hundred dollars."

"I can't bring you the information unless she is dead, but I think I can find out the truth of the matter at all events."

"Get me the truth, and you shall have the reward all the same; of course, I pay all your expenses.. When will you be ready to start?"

"By to-morrow afternoon's train, if the Chief will let me go."

"Very well, good night."

"Wait one moment, sir, please, you did not give me your name and address."

"Is that necessary?"

"Certainly, we must know who we are working for, or we don't know how to proceed."

Arthur paused for a moment, and then handed Cullen one of his business cards.

"I thought so," said Cullen as soon as he had read the name and address. "I thought from the start that this was your own case, Mr. Austin, but it makes no difference, sir, you might have trusted me at first. I know your uncle, Mr. Lubbuck, well; he's a fine old gentleman, and I shall do my best to find out all I can for you. Good night, sir!"

"Good night!"

*   *   *   *   *   *   *

It was only half-past nine when Arthur left the police station and he sauntered leisurely up Notre Dame Street. His interview with Cullen had excited him considerably, and again the tempter whispered in his ear that he needed some stimulants to strengthen his nerves. When he got opposite the Terrapin he paused for a few seconds, and finally, deciding in favor of the devil, went in and ordered a glass of brandy and water. After he had drank it, it occurred to him that he had eaten no lunch and very little dinner, and that he felt rather hungry; he, therefore, ordered some oysters and went into the inner room to wait for them being cooked.

"Ah, dear boy, (hic) glad to see you," said the voice of Mr. Robert Brydon as he entered, and turning he saw that worthy, evidently a little

49

the worse of liquor, sitting at one of the tables, eating nuts and raisins and drinking champagne. The change in the man's appearance surprised him, but it made him look more like the Robert Brydon he had known in other days and under other circumstances. His first impulse was to pass on and take the most distant table he could find, or leave the room altogether; but, on second thought, fatal second thought! he fancied that he would pretend to be very friendly with Brydon, and so disarm any suspicion he might have that any investigation was being made; besides, he thought, in his present condition, Brydon might be talkative and perhaps drop some information which would be of service to him; he, therefore, patted Brydon on the shoulder and said familiarly,

"Why, Bob, old boy, you are completely metamorphosed; allow me to congratulate you on your improved personal appearance, you look something like your old self."

"Don't flatter, dear boy, you will make me blush. Sit down, and try some of this 'Moet and Chandon.'[50] Capital, upon my word, and you know I used to be considered quite a good judge."

Arthur took a chair and the proffered glass, and these two men who had once been friends, and who now hated each other with a deep and bitter hatred, drank each other's "good health" with seeming cordiality. This is the democracy of drink. Arthur set himself to work to get Brydon drunk so as to make him even more talkative than usual, but, like many another man who has started out with the intention of making a friend drunk, he unfortunately took too much and got drunk himself. They sat drinking and talking until midnight, when they adjourned to another tavern and kept up the carouse until nearly two o'clock, when the proprietor sent for a cab and ordered them to be taken home.

*　　*　　*　　*　　*　　*　　*

Jessie sat silently thinking for a long time after Arthur had left her; Arthur's curious behavior, and the fact that he had been drinking, worried her greatly. Her young life had been so free from care, so much one unbroken chain of joys linked together by loving hands, that the

[50] Usually spelled "Moët & Chandon," it has been one of the world's best-selling champagnes since its founding in 1743. It is known today for labels like Dom Pérignon and Brut Impérial, but in the early 1870s the name "Moet and Chandon" appeared in many songs and there was even a "Moet and Chandon Waltz" (1871) by George T. Evans, who in 1874 wrote the music for the famous temperance song "The Lips That Touch Liquor Will Never Touch Mine."

least thing fell with blighting force on her sensitive nature, and she already fancied that she saw the shadow of some great sorrow looming up in the distance. She pondered and pondered, but could find no solution for Arthur's anxious, abstracted manner, and Frank found her in a brown study,[51] in the parlor where Arthur had left her, still thinking, thinking, what could be the pressing business which had called Arthur away from her side for the first time since they had been married.

"Did Arthur go out?" said Miss Frank, "I thought I heard him in the hall."

"Yes, he is gone, and oh! Frank, I am so anxious, there's some horrid business Arthur is keeping from me, and I feel miserable."

"Pooh, pooh; you haven't got over your honeymoon yet, and, of course, you expect Arthur to be tied to your apron strings. Women always make that mistake when they are first married; they think the man marries them, on the contrary they marry the man, and that makes the difference. Arthur won't run away, Jessie, don't be afraid of that. Come and play something for me."

"I can't play, Frank, didn't you notice how strange Arthur appeared to-night?"

"Yes, he seemed to me to be troubled with bile, and I shall recommend him to take a blue pill in the morning. Come, play something for me."

Jessie obliged her sister for half an hour or so, and then began to weary of playing, and finally went off to her room about ten o'clock and waited for Arthur's return. Miss Frank waited in the parlor for half an hour, picked out a few airs on the piano, sang "Champagne Charlie" for her own edification,[52] and finally decided to go to bed and read her brother-in-law a small lecture in the morning. By eleven o'clock the house was perfectly quiet, and there was only one anxious, loving heart, waiting in breathless expectancy, and listening with fervent earnestness to every sound, longing, fearing, hoping for the coming of the one it loved. Eleven—twelve—one—two o'clock struck and still Jessie sat at the window, anxiously waiting for Arthur's return; all sorts of fancies flitted across her brain, the most fearful disasters which might possibly have befallen her darling appeared as possible as the most ordinary every-day occurrence. At last she heard the sound of approaching wheels, and a cab stopped before the house; the cabman descended, and with great difficulty assisted a limp and helpless figure to the ground and managed to guide it as far as the door. The moment Jessie saw that

[51] Daydreaming, with a vacant stare, in a melancholy mood (obsolete).
[52] A music hall song introduced in 1866, with lyrics by George Leybourne (1842-1884), who wrote another hit in 1867 ("The Daring Young Man on the Flying Trapeze").

figure she recognized it, and she ran down stairs at once, and opened the door before the cabman could ring the bell. The cabman assisted the figure—it could scarcely be called a man—to the staircase and then left it clinging blindly to the bannister. The door was closed, the cabman had departed, when poor Jessie, almost broken-hearted, approached the swaying, uncertain figure, and, clasping it tenderly but firmly around the waist, said:

"Arthur, darling, come to bed."

Slowly and with great difficulty the helpless figure was assisted up-stairs by the frail girl, and when their room was reached the figure sank heavily on the bed and in a few seconds was in a fast, deep sleep. His gentle, loving wife—the girl of but yesterday—hung over him with tender care, loosened his collar, opened his shirt, with almost superhuman effort placed him easily and comfortably in bed, and then sank on her knees by the bedside and prayed long and earnestly. Poor Jessie! the great grief of her life had come; the sorrow which she had, almost unconsciously, dreaded all night had fallen on her; the man she loved and honoured with fervent, passionate adoration, lay before her an inanimate mass of humanity, sodden and stupefied from the effects of drink; the idol of her adoration was abased, and she cried in bitterness of spirit at the great sorrow which had fallen upon her.

CHAPTER VI.

OUT OF THE THEATRE.

Mr. Robert Brydon did not return to his boarding-house after he parted with Arthur, but went to the St. Lawrence Hall and took a room for the night, or rather morning. He was very drunk, but not nearly as bad as Arthur, and he awoke about ten o'clock the next morning, with just a slight headache, and feeling as he expressed it "rather seedy." He was too old a campaigner to care much for that, so he took a good cold bath, ordered a "John Collins,"[53] imbibed it with evident relish, and started for a long walk. He walked his headache off, then had breakfast, and afterwards called at the office of Lubbuck, Lownds & Co., to see if Arthur had come down. The clerk in charge told him that Arthur had not been at the office that morning, and, while they were talking together, Jessie and Frank came in to say that Arthur was not very well, and would not be at the office all day. Jessie looked very pale and worn, and her eyes showed signs of recent tears. Mr. Brydon politely raised his hat, and Frank elevated her aspiring nose, and quietly looked him down. Mr. Brydon had a very fair share of assurance, but the calm, quiet, unflinching stare of Frank's clear grey eyes took all his impudence out of him, and he actually tried as hard as he knew how to blush, as he put his hat on again and turned away. The girls did not stay long, and, as soon as they were gone, Mr. Brydon addressed himself to the clerk again, saying carelessly,

"Mrs. Austin, I presume?"

"Yes."

"And the lady with her?"

"Her sister, Miss Frank."

"Ah! thanks. Please tell Mr. Austin that Mr. Brydon will call on him at eleven to-morrow morning. Good day."

"Her sister, Miss Frank," soliloquized Mr. Brydon—"that reduces matters a little—two into two hundred thousand goes one hundred thousand times. Very neat, very neat, indeed; and worth looking after. Miss Frank is a fine-looking girl, too, plenty of bone and lots of muscle, not much beauty to boast of, but a good, healthy-looking girl, and I don't care much about beauty. I must make Austin introduce me; the spec would not be a bad one, and I mean to go in for it. I must think of other matters though. I must not neglect business, and my business, at present, lies in the epistolatory line."

He strolled back towards the Hall, and on the way stopped at a stationer's, and bought a packet of envelopes and a quire of note paper. He then went into the reading-room at the Hall and addressed himself to his task. The letter seemed to be a very particular one, for he thrice tore it up and re-wrote it; at last he seemed satisfied with his efforts; he read the letter over carefully, sealed and directed it, and then went over to the Post Office and mailed it for the States.

---

[53] The original version of the Tom Collins cocktail (gin, lemon juice, sugar, and club soda), which had suddenly become extremely popular in the late 1860s. The name was changed, presumably, because the original recipe called for the Old Tom Gin (an old type of gin that is sweeter than London Dry).

*   *   *   *   *   *   *

Arthur Austin passed a miserable day. Jessie uttered no word of complaint, but her pale face and sad expression reproached him more than any words of hers could have done. He fully realized how foolish and cruel he had been, and firmly determined that he would never yield to temptation again. He attempted no explanation with Jessie, but was even more tender and loving to her all day than usual, as if to offer some sort of mute apology for the pain and sorrow he had caused her the previous night. He went to business the following morning, not feeling very well yet, but sufficiently recovered to attend to his duties. Punctual to his appointment arrived Mr. Brydon, looking as fresh and bright and as scrupulously clean and polished as usual.

"Ah, dear boy, charmed to see you again. Quite recovered, I hope, from the effects of Wednesday night?"

"Nearly so, but not quite. Come into the private office, I want to speak to you."

They entered the private office, and Arthur carefully closed the door. He stood by the table for a few seconds, watching his companion, who had seated himself in the large easy chair and was quietly surveying the room, and then said:

"Brydon, we must come to terms."

"Exactly, dear boy, nothing will suit me better."

"I have told you I have very little means of my own. I can make you a small allowance, and I am willing to do it if you will keep my secret until I can find some means to get out of the terrible difficulty I am in. My present salary is eighteen hundred dollars a year. I am willing to allow you fifteen dollars a week, which is as much as I can afford, and is more than you could work for in Montreal."

"Very liberal, dear boy, very liberal; but I really don't like to accept. You see I asked you to provide for me, but I don't exactly like the idea of being pensioned off. I like to make a show of doing something, even if I don't do it; but, 'pon my word, I feel such a desire for hard work coming over me that I really think I should do something if I had the chance."

"I know of no place that would suit you."

"I do."

"Where?"

"Here, Lubbuck, Lownds & Co. want a book-keeper, behold an excellent one who wants the place; double or single entry, sterling or currency, it's all the same to me. You know, dear boy, that I am competent, and, if the duties are too arduous, you can help me. As for salary, give me what you yourself received before the late happy little event, and if it does not suffice for my modest bachelor wants, I can borrow from you what I may require. Consider the thing done, dear boy, consider it done."

"I do not like the idea," said Arthur. "I scarcely have the right to employ any additional help during Mr. Lubbuck's absence, especially in the dull season, when I can easily do all the work. Besides, to tell the truth, Brydon, if I have got to buy your silence, as I suppose I must, I don't care to see any more of you than I cannot avoid."

"That's unkind, dear boy; don't let your mind be prejudiced against me. I want to do the square thing; you're up, I'm down; you've got a rich wife, I haven't a red cent to bless myself with; you've got a secret, I know it; let us pull together. Two heads are better than one, and perhaps together we may find a way of disposing of Mrs. Austin No. 1. Better let me be your friend, dear boy, as I have been since boyhood; think it over well before you decide. I have a special reason for becoming connected, even in an humble way, with the eminent house of Lubbuck, Lownds & Co., and I hope you will not thwart my whim. It gives a man an air of respectability, you know, to be attached to a great house, and I sadly need a little respectability in Montreal."

Arthur sat for a minute or two, thinking. He did not wish to have Brydon in the office with him, but then it may only be for a short time. Cullen must be back in two or three weeks at the latest, and he would then know the truth or falsehood of Brydon's story; if it was false he would simply have to dismiss him; if it was true, he felt sure he could hit on some way by which he could make sufficient of a case against Miss Effie Barron to obtain a divorce from her, and then he would marry Jessie over again.

He thought it would be better to have Brydon under his eye, even to be friendly with him, as he may, perhaps, gain from him Effie's present address, or the name under which she acted. He had the power, if he pleased to exercise it, of employing or discharging anyone in the office during Mr. Lubbuck's absence, and so, after a slight pause, he said: "Brydon, I agree with you, it is better that we should be friends. You can take the position of book-keeper in the firm as soon as you please."

"To-morrow morning, dear boy, to-morrow morning."

"Very well; your salary will be eight hundred dollars. I shall expect you, of course, to keep the regular office hours—nine to five—and to make a show of doing your work, even if you are not competent to do it."

"Not competent, dear boy, not competent! I can keep a set of books backwards. Not competent, indeed; it must be a queer set of books Lubbuck, Lownds & Co. keep if I am not competent to keep them."

"Very well then, old fellow, you shall keep them. Everything else satisfactory?"

"Everything, except one trifling matter, which is scarcely worth mentioning. I should like to be introduced to your charming little wife, and her particularly masculine looking sister. Nothing like cultivating the domestic virtues, dear boy, and you know I always was fond of ladies' society."

"I see no advantage to be gained from your having an acquaintance with my wife."

"But I see considerable advantage to be gained from an acquaintance with her charming sister."

"What have you designs on Frank? Why, Brydon, you are the most extraordinary chap I ever met. So you want an opportunity to win Miss Frank and her hundred thousand dollars; well, I don't think there is the least chance for you, but you may try."

"Thanks, dear boy; as to the chance I am somewhat egotistical, and think that when a kindred soul like hers becomes acquainted with a kindred soul like mine, it will be a case of 'veni, vidi, vici,' as we say in the classics."

"Which in your case will mean, I came, I saw, I got kicked out."

* * * * * * *

Leave for Cullen to go to New York was easily obtained from the Chief, and the detective accordingly started on his voyage of investigation. He was away for three weeks, during which time he did not write, and Arthur became very anxious to know something of his success. At last one morning he walked into the office very quietly and gave his report. He had been successful and unsuccessful; he had established beyond a doubt that Miss Effie Barron did not die at Savannah at the time her death was reported to have taken place. He had visited Savannah and discovered that there were no such persons as the doctor and undertaker from whom Arthur had received letters; he had made inquiries and found that Miss Barron had been ill—or had pretended to be—but had recovered and left Savannah, it was thought for Charleston, he had gone to Charleston but could find no trace of her. He next tried New York; the Dramatic Agencies knew nothing of her; she had never been of much importance in the profession, and very little importance was paid to where she might be. One agent thought she was dead, another that she was married and had left the stage. He had inquired at the St. Charles hotel, where Brydon said he had seen her, but no one knew her by name, or recognised her photograph or description; the proprietor said the photograph resembled a Mrs. Cranston who had boarded at the hotel some two or three months previously, but it could not be her, as her husband was with her, and she was much stouter than the photograph appeared to be. Application to the police evolved nothing, and a pathetic advertisement in the *Herald*,[54] inviting Effie Barron to communicate with "an old admirer and hear of something to her advantage," brought forth no response. Cullen was, therefore, obliged to return very little wiser than he went, except that he had established the truth of Brydon's assertion that Effie Barron bad not died at Savannah at the time Arthur Austin supposed she had.

This news was not very satisfactory to Arthur, but he was compelled to be content with it; Cullen had evidently done all in his power, and he must now trust to finding out something from Brydon. That gentleman developed a new quality—he got fond of work; he actually set himself zealously to work, keeping the books and accounts of Lubbuck, Lownds & Co., and, being a good accountant, he soon got them well in hand and managed to make himself tolerably well acquainted with the position, financial standing, resources, etc., of the house. He found out that a large amount of money was kept in the Banks during the winter season, when trade was almost at a stand-still, and that a still larger sum was temporarily invested in stocks and other easily convertible securities. He found, without much trouble, that the amount so invested reached the sum of something like seventy-five thousand dollars, and he used frequently to lie awake at nights, thinking about these "available funds," as he used to call them. He was steady and attentive to business, and really assisted Arthur a good deal. They got on very well together. Arthur trying to disarm any suspicion Brydon might have of him, and Brydon endeavouring to dispel any feelings of resentment which Arthur might have against him on account of the rascally trick which had been played on him. The constant strain on Arthur's nerves, the incessant dread of discovery, the fear of Brydon's treachery at any moment, and the uncertainty of his position operated on him terribly. Never accustomed to exert much self-control, and not naturally possessed of a very strong

[54] The *New York Herald*, at the time the most widely distributed daily newspaper in the United States. Founded in 1835, it merged with another paper in 1924 to become the *New York Herald Tribune*, which folded in 1966.

will, he lately gave way to temptation again, and sought from the use of stimulants to fortify his courage or deaden his sensibilities to the danger of his position. Many and many a night Jessie would wait up for him and, although he seldom came home in as beastly condition as he was on the first night he met Brydon, still he never came home sober. He became slovenly and untidy in his dress, let his beard grow, and took no pains with himself. In his carouses Mr. Brydon was his constant companion, but what was poison to Arthur Austin seemed meat to him, and except an occasional headache and, once in a while, a little flush in the face, or eyes a trifle blood-shot, he showed no signs of his dissipation, and did his work as well as if he had kept perfectly sober. To be sure he did not drink nearly as hard as Arthur, who drank with the reckless avidity of a man who wants to drink himself drunk, but still he drank a great deal, and nothing but the excellence of his constitution could have borne it so well. Nothing more was said by him about being introduced to Jessie and Frank, and Arthur thought he had given up the idea, when one evening, about a week after Cullen's return, the sisters called at the office for Arthur, and went into the private office with him.

They had not been in there more than two or three minutes when Mr. Brydon wrote on a slip of paper "introduce me," and entering the private office, under a pretence of getting a letter signed for the mail, handed it to Arthur, who, after a moment's hesitation, complied, and introduced Mr. Robert Brydon to his wife and sister-in-law. Mr. Brydon did not stay long in the room; he exchanged a few commonplace remarks with Frank, paid Jessie a little compliment about how pleased he was to see his old friend so happily married, excused himself on the plea of business, and bowed himself out. He had accomplished what he wanted, the ice was broken, and he could cultivate the acquaintance at his leisure. He could be very pleasant and affable if he pleased, and his easy, rattling style had made him quite a favorite amongst the ladies at one time of his life, and he had no doubt he had enough of the old fascination left to interest Miss Frank. To be sure that independent young lady had not seemed much impressed at first sight, and had slightly elevated her nose—she had a trick of doing it when anything did not please her—but Mr. Brydon did not take that very seriously to heart— his self-conceit being more than sufficient to make him believe that he could easily overcome any little prejudice about "first impressions."

"I did not know you had a new clerk, Arthur," said Jessie, when Brydon left the room; "he seems very gentlemanly, too," she added, as the memory of the compliment Brydon had paid her recurred to her. Jessie had only been married a short while, and any compliment about her marriage still made her blush and feel very happy.

"He's a snob," said blunt Frank, "and I don't like him."

"Oh! Frank, I am sure he seemed very polite and quite a gentle man. Who is he, Arthur?"

"I told you his name, darling, Robert Brydon. For the rest he was a schoolmate of mine and is an old friend."

"There, Frank," said Jessie, triumphantly, "he is an old friend of Arthur's. How could you call him a snob?"

"Because Arthur isn't a snob it doesn't prove that all his schoolfellows or acquaintances are not," said the persistent Frank. "Mr. Brydon may be a very nice gentleman, but I should never accuse him of it, judging from present appearances. But never mind him; come, Arthur, let us go home; dinner will be waiting."

*   *   *   *   *   *   *

Three months slipped quietly away, and brought nothing very momentous with them. Mr. Brydon showed Arthur a letter dated and postmarked "Paterson, N. J.," which was evidently written by Effie Barron and addressed to Mr. Brydon, New Orleans, that ingenious gentleman having contrived, through the medium of a friend, to write a letter from New Orleans, and receive an answer there while he quietly remained in Montreal. The letter was a mixture of bad grammar, bad spelling and bad temper; it was written in answer to one from Brydon informing Effie that he had traced Arthur to New Orleans only to find that he had accepted a five years' engagement in the Figi Islands, and that he had left for his new home about a month before he, Brydon, had reached the Crescent city.[55]

Miss Effie wrote in a very bad humor, abused her "scamp of a husband," as she called Arthur, very liberally, and concluded with a threat which he sincerely hoped she would carry out, namely, that she intended to apply for a divorce on the ground of desertion and infidelity. This letter reassured Arthur a little, and made him feel somewhat more at ease, but still he could not overcome entirely his uneasiness with regard to Brydon, and the fear was ever before him that that gentleman was only playing with him as a cat does with a mouse, in order to prolong his torture and make his ruin more complete. Then the anomalous position in which Jessie was placed was a constant misery to him; a wife in the eyes of the world, and about to become a mother and yet not married to

[55] Figi is an old spelling for Fiji. Crescent City is a nickname for New Orleans (a reference to the course of the Mississippi).

him. Again and again he tried to tell her, and again and again his courage failed him. Then he thought of writing to Mr. Lubbuck, explaining all and asking him to return or to get Mr. Lownds to come to Montreal to take charge of the business, and allow him, Arthur, to take Jessie to England, where he thought he could leave her with less scandal than he could do here. But he never wrote the letter; when it came to the point of doing so he always put it off and allowed himself to drift on, trusting to chance to shield him from discovery and disgrace before Mr. Lubbuck's return.

During those three months Mr. Brydon had been propriety itself. Wonderful to relate, he had not exceeded his salary, had "borrowed" nothing from Arthur, and had attended closely to business. He lived quietly and indulged in no excesses—at least none that were known—except his periodical sprees with Arthur, and altogether behaved himself exceedingly well. His sprees grew less frequent, and he even attempted to dissuade Arthur from his habits of intemperance, which had grown terribly strong on him, and really did influence him a little; but the habit had become too strong, and nothing but the greatest effort of self-control could stop it now. Mr. Brydon had become a regular and frequent visitor at Mr. Lubbuck's, and, singular to relate, appeared to have made a favorable impression on Miss Frank. She did not call him a snob any more, but confessed that, although he was not very refined, he was exceedingly polite and highly entertaining and amusing. He was full of anecdotes and stories, had read a good deal of the light literature of the day, and was rather an agreeable companion. He sympathized deeply with Frank in her medical studies, and actually studied medicine a little, on the sly, to be able to converse with her. He escorted her to church every Sunday evening, and sang the hymns in a very loud voice, very much out of tune. To be sure, he used to go to a well known French restaurant afterward and indulge in a game of euchre with any one who was not aware of his extraordinary luck in holding bowers and aces,[56] and drink a good deal of brandy and water "to wash the taste out of his mouth," as he called it; but nobody but himself knew of that, and he passed as a very quiet, respectable, steady young man.

Miss Frank had not assumed her liking for Brydon at first; in fact, she quietly snubbed and ignored him for about a month, but gradually she had changed her manner towards him, and now treated him politely, and, indeed, sometimes very kindly, as if he was an old friend. Mr. Brydon ascribed this change to his own personal powers and agreeable

[56] In euchre (a card game that had become extremely popular in mid-19th-century North America), jacks or knaves are called "bowers."

manner, and would have been greatly chagrined had he known the real cause of her altered demeanor towards him. That penetrative young lady had very quickly discovered that there was some private understanding between that talkative young man and her brother-in-law. She noticed that Brydon exercised some sort of authority over Arthur. She knew it was not that authorized by old friendship, for she was convinced Arthur did not really like Brydon, and would have kicked that insinuating young gentleman out of the house had he dared to do so. What, then, was the secret that bound them together? That there was a secret of some kind Miss Frank was certain, and as she had a natural antipathy to mysteries, she resolved to ferret this one out. She noticed that Arthur's habit of intemperance had commenced only after his acquaintance with Brydon, and also that his whole nature seemed to have changed since his intercourse with that worthy. Frank had not more than the average curiosity of women, but she felt there was something wrong about the secret between Arthur and Brydon; she mistrusted that glib individual, and determined to set her woman's wit to work against him, and in favor of her brother-in-law whom she really liked and sincerely respected. This was the secret of Miss Frank's changed manner towards Mr. Brydon, but that gentleman being totally unconscious of it prided himself on an easy conquest, and already felt that the hundred thousand dollars was secured to him.

Matters went on smoothly for three months, when Mr. Brydon, led away by his self-conceit, made trouble for himself by formally proposing for her hand and hundred thousand dollars.

Frank was thoroughly astonished, and Mr. Brydon had kissed her hand and attempted to press her to his breast before she had recovered her presence of mind enough to snatch her hand away and tell him not to make a fool of himself.

"Mr. Brydon," she said, "you have perfectly astonished me. What could ever have put into your head a notion that I ever cared for you? I have treated you as Arthur's friend, but nothing more, and any other construction you may have put upon my conduct has been the result of your own self-conceit. I trust you will never recur to this subject again." She bowed haughtily, and left the room.

Mr. Brydon in his turn was thoroughly astonished. He had expected an easy victory, and had suffered instead an ignominious defeat. He saw all his brilliant project of getting one hundred thousand dollars vanish in a moment, and his disappointment was very bitter. He appealed to Arthur to interfere, but this Arthur peremptorily declined to do.

"I told you you would have no chance with Frank," he said. "You have tried and failed, and I do not intend to interfere. Besides, Frank is her own mistress, and what I could say would probably have very little weight with her. You must manage your own affairs without any assistance from me."

"Very well, my dear boy, I will try, and perhaps I shall succeed."

Although Mr. Brydon tried to speak lightly, he felt his disappointment keenly. He had taken quite a little fancy to Frank and quite a large fancy to her prospective hundred thousand dollars. In fact, the possession of that had become quite a morbid fancy with him; and he felt as if he had actually been defrauded by Frank out of what properly belonged to him. He was not a man, however, to be defeated by one rebuff, and he set himself to work to find out a way to recover what he considered his lost fortune, and, to a man of such great resources for evil as he was, it did not take long for him to devise a plan which he thought would answer his purpose. His plan took an epistolatory form, and again he addressed himself to his correspondent in the States. A few days after he made his first application to Arthur for money he said he wanted two hundred and fifty dollars for a few days, when he would return it. Arthur gave him the money, but had no idea it would ever be returned.

*   *   *   *   *   *   *

It was now the early part of March, and the theatre had been closed for several months, when suddenly every dead wall in the city was covered with flaming placards announcing in glaring letters of immense size that Mdlle. Seraphine, the great pantomimic and burlesque actress would give six performances, commencing on the following Monday in the great sensation drama of the "French Spy."[57] Arthur was a great admirer of the drama, and although he did not like plays of the French Spy order, as a general thing, still it was so long since he had any opportunity of attending the theatre that he determined to go. He therefore engaged a box for the opening night, and asked Jessie and Frank to accompany him. On the evening of the performance, however, Miss Frank excused herself on the plea of a headache and remained at home, and Jessie and Arthur went to the theatre together. The house was crowded in every part, and the piece proceeded smoothly until near the

[57] *The French Spy* was a pantomimic drama (a play in which speaking parts are much reduced and the storytelling is done in large part by music and choreography) by British author John Thomas Haines (1799-1843), first staged in 1831. The same actress is supposed to play three characters, including two cross-dressing parts: the heroine, Mathilde; an Arab boy; and the titular French spy.

middle of the first act when Mdlle. Seraphine made her *entrée* as Henri St. Almi,[58] a French soldier. She was a fine looking woman, coarse, but of great physical development, and her handsome tight-fitting uniform displayed her ample figure to great advantage. She came on with the easy self-possession of an actress who feels assured that she will be well received by her audience, and she was not disappointed; ringing plaudits greeted her from every part of the audience, and she paused near the centre of the stage and, raising her cap, bowed low in acknowledgment of the compliment. As the applause subsided she raised her head and looked with a steady unflinching gaze into the private box where Arthur and Jessie sat. One look at her sent every drop of blood in Arthur's body chilling back to his heart; he sat like one suddenly turned to stone, gazing with a fixed rigid look and blanched terror-stricken countenance as one suddenly spell-bound, and unable to remove his eyes from the young French soldier.

Husband and wife looked into each other's faces.

Mdlle. Seraphine paused only for a second, and then with a scornful, bitter smile she barely touched the brim of her cap, bowing very slightly, and turning to the actors went on with the piece. No one had noticed the acting of this small drama, "not set down in the bills," and all were now too intent on the business of the scene to pay any attention to the pallid, horror-stricken face in the private box, watching with glaring, wild-looking eyes every movement of the voluptuous figure on whom the attention of all were now centered. Even Jessie did not notice the strange glance exchanged by the actress and Arthur, and it was not for some time that she turned to him to make some remark about the play, and noticed his deadly paleness.

"Arthur, darling, what is the matter, are you ill?" she said, laying her hand on his arm. He started as she spoke, and shrunk from her touch as if it stung him.

"No, no," he said in a hoarse, pained voice, "I am not very well, I want some fresh air; I will be back directly." He rose hastily and moved towards the door of the box.

"Let us go home, darling, if you are not well; I don't care to stay."

"No, no, you remain here, I will be back presently." He staggered out like a drunken man, and had to support himself by the backs of the seats as he passed out to the entrance door.

He did not return until the second act was nearly completed, and Jessie saw with pain, by his flushed face and unsteady manner, that he had been drinking heavily. He took his seat without a word, and sat

[58] Actually, Henri St-Alme. The actress playing this part is supposed to wear the uniform of an officer in the French army in the early 1830s.

sullenly looking at the stage. Mdlle. Seraphine noted his return, and a strange hard bitter smile hovered for a moment about her lips and then passed away. She was just coming to one of her most effective "points," and she appeared nerving herself for a great effort.

It may be remembered by some of my readers that one of the most dramatic situations in the "French Spy" occurs in the second act when the heroine, disguised as the Arab boy Hamet, shoots a burning arrow over the walls of Algiers to the French forces without. All actresses take great pains with this part of the business and execute it carefully; and Mdlle. Seraphine acted the pantomime with more spirit than she had hitherto displayed. She affixed the paper on the arrow, lighted it at the old sergeant's torch, as is always done, and then advancing to the footlights fitted the arrow to the string, knelt for a moment on one knee as if silently engaged in prayer, and reverently kissed the haft of the arrow. But instead of rising, going to the back of the stage and shooting the arrow off, as all actresses do, she simply turned on one side facing the box Arthur was in, and, with a look of deadly hatred on her face, raised her bow, and aimed the point of the arrow directly at Arthur's head.

"Bravo! Bravo!" shouted Mr. Brydon from a front seat in the pit, bringing his hands together with a mighty clap like a young cannon: "never saw anything finer, splendid! splendid!"

Mdlle. Seraphine started at the sudden noise, her hands trembled, and the arrow, unconsciously released, buried itself harmlessly in the wainscoting of the proscenium. She stifled a half uttered curse, and turned angrily up the stage. In a moment however, she recovered her self-possession and drawing the arrow from its position she continued the business of the piece, apparently suffering only from the interference of Mr. Brydon. That gentleman did not find his position a comfortable one, the audience evidently looked on him as an evil-disposed person, who had maliciously spoiled a very fine situation and there were many friendly suggestions to "punch his head," "put him out," etc., but Mr. Brydon saved anybody the trouble of putting him out by quietly leaving the theatre and going round to the stage entrance. As he went up the narrow dark alley leading to the dressing-room he thought to himself:

"A near squeak, by Jove! One second more and that she-devil would have driven that arrow through the dear boy's head, and I should have lost my fortune. No, no, Miss Effie, I am very fond of you, and you can have the pleasure of shooting the dear boy if you particularly desire it, but not until I have done with him, and provided the necessary funds for both of us to spend the remainder of our days in virtuous ease and comfort."

He went behind the scenes like one accustomed to the place, and having the right of entree, and waited at the wing until Mdlle. Seraphine had finished her "grand broad-sword combat," and the act was over; he then followed that young lady to her dressing-room and, carefully closing the door, had a long and earnest conversation with her.

Arthur scarcely noticed the pointing of the arrow at him, in fact he was too drunk to notice anything, and, even if he had, he would have wished that the arrow had sped on its way, and he had been relieved of all his difficulties by death. Jessie, however, noticed the strange action of the actress, and the wonderfully vengeful expression which came over her face at the moment she levelled the arrow, and she was greatly terrified; she thought the actress was mad, and Arthur had in some unknown manner excited her resentment—no suspicion of the truth occurred to her, and her first thought was to get Arthur away before the next act commenced. Arthur, however, refused to go, and they sat while the orchestra was playing, Jessie trying to get Arthur away and he obstinately refusing to go, he could not tell why. There was a long wait, and the orchestra had to fill in another piece; the audience was getting impatient and expressed its displeasure freely; there was considerable excitement behind the scenes, the actors were all ready, the scene all set, but the "star" was still in her dressing room and the prompter could not induce her to come out and continue the piece. A very stormy scene was being enacted in that dressing room between Mdlle. Seraphine and Mr. Brydon, but Mr. Brydon won, and the result of his victory was that before the orchestra had finished the "Overture to Zampa"[59] for the second time Mdlle. Seraphine had written a note and despatched the call-boy to the front with it. The note was addressed to Arthur Austin, and this is what it contained:

"ARTHUR AUSTIN,—Your legal wife wants to see you to-night after the performance, you will find her in room — St. Lawrence Hall. Mind you come, or look out for trouble.
"EFFIE."

The audience was at last appeased, the curtain commenced to rise, and almost at the same time the note was delivered to Arthur; he glanced at it—intuitively guessing its import—and then said hurriedly to Jessie: "Let us go home. I am sick of this trash, I am sure you must be."

Jessie was only too glad to go and get her husband home before he would have an opportunity to drink any more; they thereupon left the

---

[59] *Zampa* (first performed in 1831) is a French "opéra comique" (an opera that contains spoken dialogue) by Ferdinand Hérold.

box at once, and when Mdlle. Seraphine made her first appearance in the third act she found the box empty. When Arthur reached home he simply opened the door for Jessie to enter and told her to go in, that he had to meet Brydon on some business and would be back in an hour. She tried hard to get him to remain at home and not go out again at that late hour, but he was obstinate, and slamming the door behind her, went back to his cab and ordered the driver to take him to the St. Lawrence Hall.

*   *   *   *   *   *   *

Miss Frank had her own peculiar reason for having a headache and not being able to go to the theatre, and the following note, written by her, might elucidate matters a little:

"DEAR CHARLIE,—Come and see me about eight, or half-past to-night, *sure*;[60] something special to say to you.
"Frank."

It might be as well to recall to my reader's memory the fact of the existence of such a person as Mr. Charles Benson, to whom the above note was addressed, and who had quite a sneaking kindness for Miss Frank; but Mr. Benson had been suffering a great deal during the last few months; all the jealousy, ill-will, malice prepense,[61] etc., etc.—it wasn't much with him—had been stirred up by the "scandalous way Frank was carrying on with that fellow Brydon,"—I quote his own words—and he had openly cut Frank, and he was ready at any moment to "punch Mr. Brydon's nose"—his words again—at the slightest provocation. The receipt of Miss Frank's note pleased him greatly, but he was wary and careful; he really loved Frank—he had only found that out since Brydon's appearance on the scene—and he meant to win her if he could, but he did not like to exhibit any signs of haste, and therefore he waited until almost nine o'clock before he replied in person to Frank's note.

"You're a pretty fellow!"[62] said Miss Frank, as soon as he entered; "here I have waited half an hour for you, why didn't you come at the proper time?"

---

[60] An obsolete adverbial use of "sure," with the meaning of "without fail."
[61] A (mostly) legal term, better known as "malice aforethought." It refers to the act of premeditating a crime or, like here, to the act of planning a crime, going over it in one's head, without actually committing it.
[62] In the 18th and 19th centuries, this was an expression of contempt.

"I was afraid I might interrupt a pleasant *tête-à-tête*," Mr. Benson said this with what he considered a cuttingly sarcastic intonation, but Miss Frank did not seem to be at all impressed by it, she simply shook her head and said:

"Oh, Charlie! I did want some one with brains so much, and I am *so* sorry to find you are such a fool!"

"That's very complimentary, but really I did not wish to intrude on your—well your—your *friend*, Mr. Brydon, by coming too early."

This was another attempt at sarcasm, but somehow Mr. Benson felt he was not succeeding at sarcasm on this occasion. Frank rose very quietly, and laying her hand on Mr. Benson's arm, said:

"Charlie, you and I have been friends almost from childhood. I am in a trouble, and I thought you would help me; but, if you talk that way there is no use my telling you what I want you to do."

"What do you want me to do, Frank?"

"I want you to watch Robert Brydon; I want you to haunt him like his shadow. I want you to find out what secret there is between him and Arthur, and to know something of the man's past life."

Her manner had grown very earnest, and she clutched his arm with convulsive force as she finished.

"Well, that's cool, Frank; you press me rather too hard when you ask me to watch your lover, and find out something of his past life for you."

"My what?"

"Your lover."

"Charlie Benson, I never thought you were such a fool; what! that thing Brydon! he a lover of mine; you ought to be ashamed of yourself."

"But don't you——"

"No, I don't. I have tried to get into this man's confidence because I suspected he had some secret power over Arthur, and I wanted to find out what it was, so that I might protect Arthur from a bad man, but you men are all fools. Brydon must needs think I was in love with him, and he has proposed and I have rejected him; and, of course, I cannot watch him myself now, so I want you to do it for me."

"You have rejected him?"

"Yes, I didn't mean to tell you, but as I have said it I suppose there is no great harm done."

Mr. Benson made no answer in words, but he indulged in the most extraordinary action he had ever ventured on with Miss Frank; he had known her for several years, but had always kept at a respectful distance; now he suddenly caught her in his arms and once or twice kissed her— three or four times. I am almost ashamed to say that Miss Frank seemed to like it, and didn't struggle a bit. The next half hour was passed in that imbecile condition which lovers always think indispensable to a first confession of their mutual love. Miss Frank was the first to recover her self-possession and come back to the matter she had been discussing.

"So you see, Charlie dear, I want you to get intimate with Brydon, to find out who he associates with, and if possible solve the mystery which binds him so strongly to Arthur."

"Well, Frank, I'll try; but 'pon my word I'd rather punch the fellow's head than shake hands with him; but as you wish it, and it is for Arthur's sake, I shall cultivate Mr. Brydon very extensively; and he had better look out for himself."

CHAPTER VII.

OUT OF THE HONEST WAY.

"Has Mdlle. Seraphine returned from the Theatre yet?" asked Arthur Austin of the polite clerk of the St. Lawrence Hall.

"Yes, sir, she just came in a moment ago; here Jim, show this gentleman to No.—"

Arthur was shown Mdlle. Seraphine's room, and, in answer to his knock, received a rough invitation to "come in," which he accepted and found his wife half reclining on a sofa with a large tumbler of gin and water, which she was in the act of imbibing, momentarily suspended in her right hand. She looked for a moment at her visitor, finished the spirits, and then said,

"So you have come, you villain; I supposed you would, you knew it would be best for you."

Arthur paused for a moment and looked intently at her before replying; drunk as he was he could not but be struck at the great change to her appearance from what it had been four years before. On the stage he had not noticed it, but now, face to face, the false color of the rouge glowing on her cheek only lent intensity to the yellow, unhealthy color of the flabby skin; the fine lines of India ink under the eye-lashes, intended to impart brilliancy to the eyes, only served to show the dark circles under them, and to throw up in strong relief the glassy, filmish expression of the eyes themselves. The finely rounded form lost all its symmetry when released from its tight bracing, and showed only an unsightly mass of bloated humanity. The rich, sensuous lips, which looked so lovely and kissable from the front of the theatre, were smeared with vermilion, and the pungent odor of gin drove away all ideas of grace or beauty from them. Arthur saw her as she was, a drunken, besotted creature, without one spark of true womanhood about her, given over to the demon of drink and abandoning herself freely to all evil passions; he saw her, and even to his drunken mind came a feeling of repugnance, and he wondered if it could be possible that he had ever loved this creature. He did not pause long, but, advancing one step nearer to her, said: "What do you want with me?"

"That's a pretty question for a husband to ask the wife he has deserted for four years. What do I want with you? I want you to support me as your wife, as you ought to do; I want you to put away that baby-faced doll you had with you to-night; I want you go back to the States with me, and live with me as my husband—I love you so much." She said this with great passion, and she threw all the bitterest contempt and scorn she was capable of into the last few words: "I would have you know, Arthur Austin, that I claim you as my husband, and I don't mean to allow any woman to take my place, unless I please that she should, and I don't please that yellow-haired child should do it."

"I thought you were dead, Effie."

"And was glad to think so, no doubt ?"

"God only knows how thankful I was at my supposed release."

"No doubt; but you're not released, and I don't mean that you shall be yet awhile. I shall live a long time, you may depend on it. I mean to, just to spite you."

"Why did you send for me?"

"I want to make arrangements with you."

"What arrangements? God knows," he cried in the bitterness of his spirit, "the miserable plot of Brydon and yourself has borne enough wretched fruit already. The pair of you laid a very pretty snare for me; I unconsciously walked into it; I am caught. Now I know both of you well enough to know that you did not go to so much trouble and pains without hope of ultimate gain; how much do you want?"

"I want my old allowance renewed, and the same right you have taken yourself to marry whoever I please."

"I cannot pay you the money; I am not able to afford it."

"Mr. Arthur Austin, I close my engagement here on Saturday night. Unless I have my first quarter's allowance, five hundred dollars, paid me before three o'clock on Friday, I will have you arrested for bigamy before ten o'clock on Saturday. Do as you please,—what I say I mean."

"Suppose I comply with your demands, what guarantee have I that they will suffice, and that you will cease to annoy me?'

"No guarantee but my word; you ought to know that I can keep it when I please. Do you remember when you tried to shake me off by claiming a divorce? Do you remember that I swore then to be even with you? I am even with you now. You had better accept the terms I offer you, and these are the terms: if you pay me two thousand dollars a year for five years, quarterly in advance, payable at any place I please to name, I will swear not to molest you in any way for that time: I to enjoy myself any way I please, and you to possess your tow-headed darling.[63] At the end of that time I shall do as I please. Accept or refuse as you see fit, it is six of one and half a dozen of the other to me."

"Suppose I accept, what guarantee have I against Brydon ?"

"Bob will go with me!"

"What?"

"I will take care," said Miss Effie, guarding her speech more closely, "that Mr. Brydon does not annoy you."

"You speak very confidently about Mr. Brydon."

"I do. I know more of his secrets. You may depend on it that I can make him do what I promise he will do. Do you accept my terms?"

"Give me a few days to think them over."

"I will give you until twelve o'clock Wednesday. Will that suit you?"

"Yes."

"Good night."

*   *   *   *   *   *   *

Mr. Brydon did not sleep the sleep of the model young man he pretended to be that night; in fact, he tossed about for a long time without sleeping at all. He "reviewed the whole position," as he called it, and came to the conclusion that he had made a mistake when he selected Montreal as a good place to hang up his hat. In his present mood he would have greatly preferred Paris, or some quiet German watering-place where there are no unpleasant questions asked as long as a man can pay his way. Miss Effie's exhibition of temper and passion

---

[63] Tow-headed means blond (from "tow," another word for flax).

in the theatre had greatly discomposed him, and his estimation of that lady had fallen considerably. He had no wish or intention that she should so suddenly kill the goose which he expected to lay so many golden eggs; and he made up his mind that he would in future play his little game alone. He had concocted a very neat little scheme in his own mind of how he would "get square" with Miss Frank for refusing him, by gradually drawing most of her fortune away through Arthur, helped out by the presence of Effie in Montreal; but her sudden passion had shown him that she was a very unreliable agent to work with, and he tried hard to find some way to make a "big haul," that's what he called it—and leave Canada. There was one vision that constantly recurred to him as he lay tossing on his bed, and that was a vision of seventy-five thousand dollars of "available funds," and, after much thought, he believed he had solved the problem of how the available funds of Lubbuck, Lownds & Co. were to be appropriated to the personal use of Mr. Robert Brydon, and then he turned over, went to sleep, and slept happily and comfortably.

$$* \qquad * \qquad * \qquad * \qquad * \qquad * \qquad *$$

Arthur Austin hesitated for some time before accepting the terms his wife offered him. He knew he would be utterly unable to carry out the agreement for any length of time, as he had simply promised to pay her more money than he was working for; but in the miserable hope of "something turning up" to free him from his difficulty, he decided to temporize, and accordingly paid Miss Effie five hundred dollars, and agreed to pay her a like sum every three months. Of course he expected that she would leave Montreal at the close of her engagement at the theatre, but to his surprise she remained at the Hall day after day and week after week, and announced her intention of spending the summer here. For this result he was indebted to the influence of Mr. Brydon, that gentleman having made up his mind that he needed Miss Effie's presence for a short time in order to assist him in carrying out his plans with regard to the "big haul" he contemplated. Mr. Brydon studiously avoided her, at least he appeared to do so, but he managed to meet her nearly every day in private, and he kept her well informed of Arthur's movements, and so it happened that Miss Effie was constantly meeting Arthur in the most "accidental" manner. In his drives with Jessie he was almost certain to encounter Miss Effie, and she would smile so sweetly and bow so kindly that poor little Jessie began to be quite jealous of the bold-looking, handsome actress, who seemed so intimate with her husband. Arthur had told her that Effie was a friend of Brydon's and that he (Arthur) had only a very slight acquaintance with her; but as the meetings continued, and the bowing and smiling grew more and more marked, Jessie began to be seriously grieved, and had many a hearty cry at what she considered Arthur's faithlessness to her. Arthur, for his part, was driven almost crazy by the continued presence of Effie, and the daily, almost momentary, risk he was running through her being here. He abandoned himself more than ever to drink, and, for days at a time, scarcely knew what it was to be once thoroughly sober. He was ably assisted in his drunken orgies by Mr. Brydon, who, however, took good care not to get very drunk himself, and managed to be always able to attend to business, so that he was gradually getting the affairs of Lubbuck, Lownds & Co. under his own control. There was one person who had long ago suspected that Brydon was trying to worm himself into the secrets of Lubbuck, Lownds & Co. for some purpose of his own, and that person was Miss Frank. To think and to act was synonymous with that energetic young lady, and she, therefore, wrote a long letter to her uncle, telling what habits Arthur had fallen into, and begging him to come home at once, as she feared matters were not going well at the office.

Mr. Lubbuck found it was impossible for him to leave England at the time he received Frank's letter. The winding up of his old partner's affairs proved more complicated than he had expected, and he found it would be necessary to remain in England some months longer. The news he received from Frank about Arthur affected him deeply; he felt hurt, grieved and angry at Arthur's conduct, and resolved to read him a severe lesson. He wrote to him, expressing himself very severely, and informing him that Mr. Lownds would leave England at once to take charge of the house during his, Mr. Lubbuck's, absence.

This letter sobered Arthur a little, and he really made an effort to break his habits of intemperance, but in vain. Mr. Brydon was constantly at his elbow, and Miss Effie was too regular in her annoying attentions to leave his mind very easy, and, as he became troubled again, he again fell into his bad habits.

*   *   *   *   *   *   *

Mr. Lownds arrived about ten days after the letter. He was a small, wiry, active man of about two or three and thirty, close and sharp in business matters, fond of hard work, attentive to business, and having few pleasures outside of the office. Moderate and abstemious in all things himself, he was little disposed to view Arthur's excesses leniently, and he felt slightly prejudiced against him before he had seen him. Acquaintance, unfortunately, did not very much alter the first impression. Arthur sobered up for a few days, but in the course of a week had fallen back into his old habits, and sunk proportionately in Mr. Lownds' estimation. Mr. Lownds at once took the general management into his own hands; but Arthur still acted as cashier, although his power of attorney to sign for the firm had been cancelled, and Mr. Lownds signed all cheques, etc., himself.

Mr. Brydon was in high feather; he took the pledge[64]—so he said—the day of Mr. Lownds' arrival, and he was so attentive to business, and knew so much of the affairs of the firm, that he created quite a favorable impression on that gentleman. Mr. Brydon had not, however, forgotten "the available funds," and, as it was now getting near the opening of navigation, when the available funds would be actively employed, he bestowed more thought on them, and finally had everything arranged in his own mind to his entire satisfaction.

One morning, about a month after Mr. Lownds' arrival, Arthur was sent to Lachine[65] on business which would probably detain him all day. It so happened that on that very day Mr. Lownds needed ten thousand dollars to send to Chicago as an advance on some grain he expected from there as soon as the river was open; he, therefore, gave Mr. Brydon a cheque on the Merchants' Bank,[66] where the firm had a balance of about twelve thousand dollars, and told him to get a draft on Chicago for the ten thousand dollars. Mr. Brydon speedily returned with the startling intelligence that there was only about two thousand dollars to the credit of Lubbuck, Lownds & Co., and that a cheque for ten thousand dollars had been paid to Mr. Austin a few days previously. Mr. Lownds was very much astonished; he knew Arthur as a drunkard, but never once suspected him of being a thief. He went to the Bank and examined the cheque; it was apparently filled up by Arthur, and signed with the signature of the firm. There seemed no doubt at all about it, and Mr. Lownds at once consulted the Chief of Police. The case was

---

[64] In high feather means in high spirits; to take the pledge meant to promise to abstain from alcohol.
[65] Today a borough of Montreal, it had just become a town in 1872. It is located on the southwestern portion of the island of Montreal.
[66] The Merchants' Bank of Canada (formed in 1868 through the merger of the Merchants' Bank of Montreal and the Commercial Bank of Canada). It was absorbed by the Bank of Montreal in 1921.

given to Cullen, who immediately formed his own conclusions, but said nothing about them, based on what he knew about Arthur, and Mr. Lownds did not, viz., that he had two wives, and Cullen could see, what Mr. Lownds could not, a motive for the robbery. He had very little doubt that Arthur had left the city, but took all proper measures to ascertain the correctness of his suspicion. He found that Arthur had gone to Lachine, and following him there discovered, to his surprise, that he had returned to Montreal. Cullen was puzzled at this. It looked curious that Arthur should not take advantage of so good an opportunity to get across the line,[67] and he thought that, perhaps, there may be a mistake somewhere and Arthur may not be guilty. He returned to the city and went to Mr. Lubbuck's house; Arthur had not been home. It was now evening, and Cullen thought the only thing he could do was to put a man at the depot[68] to see that Arthur did not escape that way, and watch the house himself on the chance of Arthur's returning there. About eight o'clock he accidentally met Arthur in the street. He was very drunk, and staggered from side to side. Cullen went up to him and, laying his hand on Arthur's shoulder, said:

"I am very sorry for it, Mr. Austin, but I have orders to arrest you. You are my prisoner."

"Arrested," said Arthur, a terrible fear coming over him that the worst must now be known; "what for?"

"Forgery," said Cullen, very quietly.

"It's a lie," exclaimed Arthur, greatly relieved to find that he was arrested on a charge of which he was innocent. "Who says I have committed a forgery?"

"You had better not talk much, Mr. Austin," said Cullen, kindly, "I might have to use what you say as evidence against you. Mr. Lownds has made an affidavit that you have forged the name of the firm to a cheque for ten thousand dollars; you will learn all the particulars before the Police Magistrate to-morrow morning, you must go to the station with me now."

"Must I be locked up all night?" asked Arthur, after a moment's pause. "Cannot I give bail for my appearance to-morrow morning?"

"Not to-night, sir."

"But I must see Jessie, I must tell her—poor girl, poor girl;" and he broke down entirely; the hot tears starting to his eyes, and his whole frame trembling with emotion as he thought of the shock this would be to Jessie in her present delicate condition.

[67] "Across the line" is a Canadian expression (still in use) meaning "across the border," i.e., in(to) the USA.
[68] In the old sense of railway station.

"You won't be able to see Mrs. Austin to-night," said Cullen, "but," he added kindly, "I will go and see her for you, if you like, and break it to her as easy as I can. Don't get down-hearted, perhaps you will be able to show it's all right to-morrow morning;" he said this more to cheer him up than anything else. The charge was very strong, and the proof seemed pretty clear; still the fact of Arthur's returning to the city and his honest appearance of innocence weighed a good deal with the detective, and he felt by no means certain that Arthur was guilty.

Arthur was locked up in the Central Station for the night, and Cullen executed his unpleasant task of informing Jessie of what had occurred. She took it much quieter than he had expected. Did not go into hysterics, nor make any great exhibition of her feelings; but the deadly pallor of her face, the short, quick catching of her breath, her painfully-constrained manner and unnatural quiet, showed how deeply the blow had struck, and it was all the more deadly because she bore it, and made no sign. Not for one moment did she believe him guilty, never for an instant did she doubt his integrity; she loved him, trusted him, believed in him too fondly, too implicitly, too truly for that, but there came over her a terrible fear, a nameless dread of something unseen, unknown, and undefined, which loomed up in fearful indistinctness behind this ridiculous charge, and terrified her more than she could express. Yet she kept seemingly calm, and asked Cullen the particulars of the case with an amount of quietness that surprised him, and caused his admiration of the delicate, fair-haired little creature, who bore up so nobly under misfortune, to increase considerably. She had asked him several questions with forced self-control, when Frank entered the room, then Jessie's courage suddenly gave way and she threw herself into her sister's arms, sobbing hysterically, "Oh Frank! Frank! Arthur is arrested, and I shall never be his wife again."

"Arthur arrested! What for; for drunkenness?"

"No, Miss," said Cullen, "I wish it was for that; but it's a good deal more serious."

"What is it for?"

"Forgery."

"It's a—it's not true," indignantly shouted Miss Frank, almost forgetting herself in the sudden heat of her indignation. "What would Arthur want to commit a forgery for?"

"That I don't know, Miss," replied Cullen, "but a cheque of Lubbuck, Lownds & Co.'s for $10,000 has been forged on the Merchants' Bank. Mr. Lownds is very certain that the writing in the body of the cheque is Mr. Austin's, and the signature looks something like his writing; the teller says he paid the money to Mr. Austin."

"What does Arthur say?"

"He says, of course, that he's not guilty, and, to tell the truth, he don't act or look as if he was."

Miss Frank tenderly laid Jessie, who was still sobbing hysterically, on the sofa, and bending over her, and kissing her with more tenderness and gentleness than her usual manner seemed capable of, she whispered, "don't cry and make yourself ill, Jessie dear, or you will only add to my difficulties in helping Arthur, by getting sick on my hands, and then I shall have to nurse you. Try and bear up as well as possible. You don't believe Arthur guilty, nor do I. I know he is a great fool, for he has had some trouble on his mind for a long time, and has not told you what it is, as he ought to have done; but he isn't a thief. I know it, and, please God, I'll prove it!"

"You will, Frank! Oh! bless you for that," and Jessie threw her arms around her sister and wept again, but they were calmer, almost happy, tears now. She had been accustomed from childhood to look up to Frank as some one who could never be wrong, and who could do almost everything. The force and strength of that young lady's character had always exercised a great control over Jessie's weaker, but more affectionate nature, and Frank's bold assertion of Arthur's innocence, and her announcement of her determination to stand by him, greatly re-assured Jessie, and she felt almost as if Arthur was free already.

Cullen stood in the centre of the room, silently watching the pair, and feeling more and more uncomfortable about the case he was engaged in. He is a tender-hearted man, and there is a soft spot under the left side of his waistcoat; and so it was no discredit to him that he found his handkerchief come into requisition once or twice, and experienced a sensation in the throat as if he was trying to swallow something which absolutely refused to go down. Frank did not keep him waiting very long; she left Jessie on the sofa, and, placing herself in front of Cullen, took a good look at him and then said:

"You look like a sensible man. Who are you?"

"I am Cullen, the detective."

"Very well, I'm glad of that. I want to see whether you are a good detective or not. Now who do you suspect of having committed this forgery?"

"Mr. Austin is the only person suspected; and the evidence against him——"

"Fiddlesticks for your evidence," said Frank, contemptuously snapping her fingers; "you're a nice defective[69] not to see that this

---

[69] This well-known pun was already being circulated. It was used a couple of times in the London *Punch* in the 1860s.

is a plot to throw the guilt on Arthur and shield the real culprit. You detectives are all alike, you never find out anything unless it is rubbed under your nose."

"Well," replied Cullen, meditatively rubbing his nasal appendage, and rather nettled at Miss Frank's sharp attack, "if I did suspect anybody, it would not show me to be a smart detective if I told you who I suspected."

"That's true; and as you are afraid to tell me what you suspect, I will tell you what I am sure of; and that is, that this forgery was committed by that born devil, Brydon, who has managed in some way to throw the blame on Arthur."

"Whew!" whistled Mr. Cullen in astonishment; this new view of the case struck him so suddenly and unexpectedly that he momentarily forgot his usual politeness, and could not avoid giving vent to a slight whistle. Up to this moment he had never had any very serious doubts of Arthur's guilt; he wavered occasionally, but it seemed so clear to him that Arthur, goaded by the presence of his first wife in Montreal—he knew that, for Arthur had taken him fully into his confidence and set him to watch Effie,—and driven to despair at the danger constantly hanging over his head, had determined to leave the city, either with one of his wives or alone, and try and find peace elsewhere; and what more natural than that he should take advantage of his position to appropriate some funds to be used in commencing life in a new world? But now the few earnest words of Miss Frank had let in a flood of light on his mind; he was well acquainted with the peculiar part Mr. Brydon had played in the supposed death of Miss Effie Barron; Arthur had also told him that Mr. Brydon had been in love with Miss Effie, and it did not take the astute detective more than a few seconds "to take in the whole position" from his new standpoint. He saw in a moment how Mr. Brydon could at once satisfy his love, his revenge, and his cupidity by stealing the money himself, throwing the blame on Arthur and then quietly eloping with Miss Effie and his illgotten gains. It was easy enough to see it, but he knew it would be a very hard matter to prove. He looked with more respect at Frank, and at last said: "You may be right, Miss Williams, but it will be a terribly hard case to prove. I know something of Mr. Brydon, and I know he's a bad one, and not likely to try such a game unless he was pretty sure to win. Mr. Austin will have a hard matter to get out of his clutches, now he has got him."

"Ah! you know what the secret is between them?"

"I didn't say anything about a secret," said Cullen, hastily, rather surprised at Miss Frank's quickness.

"Don't tell a story now, I can see you are not accustomed to it; you blushed as much as your whiskers would let you, and a man who blushes never makes a good liar. I know there is a secret and I mean to find it out, so you might as well tell me, for I have a man now on Robert Brydon's track, and he will hunt him to death, but he will find out the cause of Brydon's influence over Arthur."

"Who is the man? perhaps he might help me in this case."

"He might; we will go and see him together. Tell me what it is you know about Brydon?"

"Well, I'm not sure but what I ought to tell you now, but—" he paused, and cast a meaning glance at Jessie, who was still lying on the sofa, in response to which glance Miss Frank bestowed on him a knowing wink—she was not at all afraid of winking when she thought it would be more expressive than words—and crossing to Jessie, knelt by the sofa and laid her hand softly on her sister's head:

"Jessie, darling, I have been talking to Mr. Cullen, and I think there is no doubt we can prove Arthur as innocent as we know he is, so don't cry and make yourself miserable. You had better go to your room and try to get a little sleep; I am going to see Charlie Benson, I think he can help us."

"What! at this time of night, Frank? it is nearly nine o'clock."

"What difference does that make; I am able to take care of myself, and if I wasn't I have a big detective who is going with me to take care of me. Mr. Cullen," she continued, turning towards him, "I shall be ready in two minutes to go with you. Can I offer you a glass of wine, or anything else, while you wait for me?"

"No, I thank you, Miss, I never drink anything strong; but, if you'll excuse me, as I haven't had any dinner or supper, and I don't know how long this job will last, I wouldn't mind having something to eat."

"No supper! come down stairs at once. I don't believe in people working on empty stomachs, it breeds indigestion."

Miss Frank only occupied a few minutes in making her preparations, and joined Cullen in the dining-room before he had quite finished a hasty supper.

"Now, Mr. Cullen, we are alone, and you can tell me what you know about Brydon."

"I am doubtful whether I ought to tell you at all, as I promised Mr. Austin to say nothing about it; but it might be useful now to use against Mr. Brydon, and I suppose it must be known some day."

"Promised Mr. Austin? Why, does Arthur' know you are acquainted with the secret?"

"He told it to me himself when I went to New York and Savannah to make some inquiries for him."

"Inquiries! What about?"

"About his first wife."

"His first wife! Why, man, you are crazy. Arthur was never married until he married Jessie."

"He was married about six years ago to Miss Effie Barron in Wilkesbarre, Pennsylvania."[70]

"It is singular that Arthur never mentioned it to any of us; he never said he was a widower."

"He is not a widower."

"What! man, man, what do you mean?"

"That his first wife is alive, and is in this city now."

"Oh, Heavens!" exclaimed Frank, springing to her feet as the whole truth flashed upon her, and then sinking back again nearly fainting, while she muttered, "Poor Jessie, poor Jessie, it will kill her."

Frank did not faint, however, she was too strong-minded for that; she poured out and drank a glass of water, and after a slight pause to recover herself, said in a low, husky voice, "Tell me all about it."

Cullen told her all he knew of Arthur's marriage to Effie Barron, of her supposed death, of Mr. Brydon's appearance on the scene, of his own exertions in the case, and finally of Miss Effie's appearance in Montreal as Mdlle. Seraphine, and of the watch he had kept on her, by which he had discovered that she met Brydon frequently, and that there was, no doubt, a perfect understanding between them.

Frank sat quietly watching him until he finished, then she thought a little while, and at last said, "I fully believe Arthur thought she was dead; it is a diabolical plot between this woman and Brydon, but I'll defeat it yet as sure as my name is Frank Williams."

She brought her hand down on the table with a mighty smack that made Cullen jump, and as he looked into her calm grey eye ablaze with passion, her face slightly flushed, and her mouth firmly set, he thought Mr. Brydon would be very likely to discover before long that he had met his match at last.

---

[70] Wilkes-Barre, Pennsylvania. With a population of a little over 10,000 in 1870 and over 23,000 in 1880, it had a booming economy based on coal mining.

CHAPTER VIII.

OUT OF THE COURT.

Mr. Charles Benson had been having an alternately very uncomfortable and very ecstatic existence for the past few weeks. He had not previously had the slightest idea how much he loved Frank, and he was perfectly happy while he was in her company, nor had he known how cordially he disliked Mr. Brydon, and he was proportionately uncomfortable when he was in that gentleman's company; for he made it a point of honor to "cultivate" him as he had promised Frank he would; but the more he cultivated him the less he liked him, and his reward in the way of information obtained from Brydon scarcely repaid him for his trouble. Indeed he found out nothing about Brydon except that he was very, very intimate with Mdlle. Seraphine, and met her frequently, but generally at some out-of-the-way place around the mountain,[71] and seldom visited her room at the Hall. Of course he was ignorant of the relation in which Mdlle. Seraphine stood to Arthur, and her intimacy with Brydon did not specially attract his attention.

He had written to Captain John Young of the New York detective force,[72] but received no information from him, except that Brydon had been discharged by Austin & Son some years ago, and it was supposed there was something wrong, and that he afterwards kept a faro bank in the Bowery, and had been pulled by the police. He had been absent from New York for three or four years, and nothing was known of him. This by no means satisfied Mr. Benson, and he sat on the evening of Arthur's

[71] Mount Royal, in the middle of the island of Montreal. Phillips must be referring to its eastern and southeastern slopes, close to downtown Montreal.

[72] Captain John Young had until recently been chief of the New York Police Detective Force, but he had opened his private detective agency. Even while employed by the city of New York, Young was allowed (like Cullen) to do private work. He was often accused in the press of being corrupt and he was sued by police commissioners for not sharing the profits of his private work while in charge of the detective bureau.

arrest, in his boarding house in Bleury Street,[73] with his feet resting on the stove, meditatively smoking a pipe, and thinking he would go and tell Frank that it was no use trying any longer to pump Mr. Brydon, as he absolutely refused to be pumped. It was rather late for a call, being after eight; and, Frank being always particular about his coming early, he thought he would postpone his visit until the next evening, and make one more endeavor to "cultivate" Mr. Brydon, by passing the evening playing billiards with him,—although that gentleman's wonderful skill with the cue made it rather an expensive luxury, even if nothing more than the game, drinks and cigars were played for. He was disappointed, however, for, when he reached Mr. Brydon's boarding-house, he found that gentleman had not been to supper, and had not come in since. Mr. Benson felt rather surprised at this. Mr. Brydon was a man who so constantly and persistently got the best of his fellow-men in everything that Mr. Benson thought it somewhat suspicious that he should allow the landlady to gain one supper on him, and he went home slowly, trying to guess what could have occupied Mr. Brydon's evening. On reaching home he was rather surprised when he opened the door to find Miss Frank seated in front of the fire, and Cullen leaning against the mantelpiece talking to her.

"Frank! Why, darling, what has happened? What brings you here?" he exclaimed, seizing Miss Frank in his arms and kissing her, without the slightest regard for Cullen's presence.

"Charlie, a terrible thing has happened—Arthur has been arrested for forgery."

"For what?"

"Forgery! but oh! Charlie, you can't be fool enough to think he is guilty?"

"I'll be—well, I don't think he is."

Mr. Benson was considerably surprised, but he had got accustomed in the last half-hour to being surprised, and, therefore, he quickly got over his astonishment, and quietly thought the matter over while Cullen was finishing his statement of what he knew of Arthur's first marriage.

"It's all stuff and nonsense," said Mr. Benson when Cullen had finished. "I begin to understand this fellow Brydon now; it's as clear as crystal; he was in love with this actress and has been trying to revenge himself on Arthur for cutting him out. As to the question of bigamy, no sane jury would convict Arthur on that charge, while the conspiracy between Brydon and Effie Barron could be proved. What I am afraid of

[73] A street running north-south between Sherbrooke Street (see note 11) and Saint-Antoine Street (see note 8).

is that Brydon has been more careful in this forgery business, and that Arthur may be found guilty of the very crime of which he is innocent."

"How can he be found guilty?" said Frank, "he never committed this forgery."

"My dear girl," replied Mr. Benson "when you know as much of law and lawyers as I do, you will find that the more innocent a man is, and the less he has done, the more likely he is to suffer heavily when he gets under the power of the law. Steal a pocket-handkerchief and you will be sent to prison for a year; knock a man's brains out with a stick of wood and the jury will bring you in innocent of even a common assault. If Arthur had committed a forgery I feel confident he would be acquitted, but, as he is innocent, I am afraid we will have great difficulty in clearing him.

"If this forgery was committed by Brydon," said Cullen, "and, he got the ten thousand dollars, he won't keep it here; he will send it somewhere where it will be safe."

"Perfectly correct," said Mr. Benson, "and the probability is largely in favor of his sending it to New York. I am pretty well acquainted with the brokers in New York, having been in a Wall Street office for two years, and I mean to start for New York to-morrow morning."

"You had better engage a lawyer for Mr. Austin before you go, sir," said Cullen.

"Right again; I will engage two, and if they can't pull him through, then I am afraid there is no way of getting him clear."

$$* \qquad * \qquad * \qquad * \qquad * \qquad * \qquad *$$

Arthur Austin was brought before the Police Magistrate next morning, and, after a preliminary examination, was fully committed for trial at Queen's Bench.[74]

The case against him was very strong, and a new and alarming fact was disclosed by Mr. Lownds' affidavit that, not only had a cheque been forged on the Merchants' Bank, but all the available funds—amounting to some sixty thousand dollars, in bonds, etc., had been abstracted from the safe where they were kept, and to which safe no one but Arthur and Mr. Lownds had a key. With regard to the forgery, the teller testified to having paid the money to Arthur, but said that Arthur was so drunk at

---

[74] The Court of Queen's (or King's) Bench of Quebec had jurisdiction over criminal cases. While the jurisdiction was later transferred to the Superior Court of Quebec, the Queen's Bench became today's Quebec Court of Appeal.

the time he (the teller) thought it was scarcely safe to trust him with that amount and advised him not to take it. The handwriting in the cheque was identified by the clerks in the office as being probably Arthur's, but none of them, except Mr. Brydon, could swear positively to it; it looked like Arthur's writing, but there was a little difference. Mr. Brydon's testimony—given with a great deal of pretended reluctance—was very damnatory. He swore positively to the writing in the cheque, and produced a $100 bill, which the teller of the Bank had sworn was one he had given to Arthur, and which Mr. Brydon swore Arthur had lent him the day after the cheque was forged, and an I O U of Mr. Brydon's for a like amount, bearing the same date, was found in Arthur's pocket. He also swore that he had seen Arthur send a package by express the same day the forgery occurred, and that the parcel was addressed to New York, and appeared to contain money. The books of the Express Company[75] showed that such a package had been sent on that day, but the clerk could not identify Arthur as the man who sent it. Two lawyers appeared for the prisoner, and, by their advice, he simply put in a plea of "not guilty," and reserved all attempts at defense until the trial took place, which would be in about three weeks' time. Charlie Benson had explained the whole case to them, and they came to the conclusion that it would be better that Mr. Brydon should not think he was suspected, and that the time intervening between the commitment and the trial would afford ample time to make any inquiries as to any attempts which might have been made to dispose of the stolen funds. It was agreed that Mr. Benson should go to New York and endeavor to find out if any of the bonds had been offered to the brokers there, and the lawyers were to institute the same inquiries in Montreal. Mr. Benson left by the afternoon train and nothing was heard of him for some time, and the lawyers began to despair of his success.

*   *   *   *   *   *   *

The change which came over Arthur from the moment of his arrest was something remarkable. He grew strangely calm and cool; he refused to be admitted to bail—which could have been easily obtained, as he had numerous influential and wealthy friends—and preferred to be committed to jail for trial. He stoutly asserted his innocence; but

---

[75] The National Express Company, incorporated in 1855, a messenger service between New York and Montreal, as well as throughout New England.

was forced to confess that, on the day of the forgery, he was so drunk for the greater part of the day that he had no recollection of what he had done, and that he might have drawn the money from the bank without being conscious of it. He was certain, however, that he could not have filled up the cheque, as when he was drunk he was unable to write legibly, although he could walk and talk tolerably well. His lawyers spoke to him about his first marriage. He was, of course, surprised that they should know of it, but gave them a full account of the whole affair, and explained his connection with Brydon and Mdlle. Seraphine since he had been in Montreal in a way which gave the lawyers hope that they might pull him through in spite of the hard facts against him.

Jessie visited him in prison.[76] Frank did not come with her the first time, and they met alone, thanks to the courtesy of the Governor of the jail, who allowed the interview to take place in his own parlor instead of the general ward for untried prisoners in which Arthur was confined. It was a long and painful interview, for Arthur told her everything; the time for concealment was past, and Jessie learnt the terrible fact that she was about to become a mother, and yet was no wife. She bore up bravely, more bravely than could have been expected of her under the circumstances, and clung to her love with all a true woman's fondness and devotion.

"Arthur," she said, "you were wrong to hide this thing from me, you ought to have told me as soon as you knew it; but it is too late for reproaches now. In the sight of God and man, I am your wife; I love you as truly now as I ever did, and I shall never cease to love you in this world or the next."

*   *   *   *   *   *   *

The trial took place at the regular sitting of the Court of Queen's Bench. The evidence was very strong against Arthur. Mr. Lownds testified to the forgery, and the Bank teller identified Arthur as the person to whom he had paid the money. The cross-examination of these witnesses was very slight, the lawyers for the defence appearing to be reserving their forces for something which was to come.

It was in the afternoon when the case was called, and it was nearly four o'clock when Mr. Robert Brydon stepped into the box.

---

[76] The Pied-du-Courant Prison, today a museum, operated between 1836 and 1912. It is located on the corner of Notre-Dame Street and De Lorimier Avenue, close to the Jacques-Cartier Bridge.

Both counsel for the prisoner gave their gowns an extra pull up at the shoulder—lawyer's gowns somehow always will slip down a little at the shoulder—as if the "something" they had been waiting for had come, and both began to take copious notes of the evidence as it progressed. It was in substance very much the same as he had given before the Police Magistrate, but had evidently been very carefully prepared.

While his evidence was being given a boy came into the Court with a telegram for Miss Frank, which that lady read with great interest and immediately had it passed to Arthur's counsel, who perused it with great attention. The two lawyers then laid their heads together and conversed in an animated whisper for some moments; the taking of notes was suspended and their attention was entirely diverted from the case, until the prosecuting Attorney, in the course of his examination of the witness, said:

"Mr. Brydon, you have known the prisoner for a long time; has he always borne a good character?"

"Yes."

"Do you know of any reason why he should so suddenly have changed his nature and committed this robbery?"

"I know one reason," said Mr. Brydon, speaking with assumed reluctance, "and that is that Arthur Austin had a wife living at the time of his marriage with Miss Williams; his first wife is now in Montreal, and is, I believe, about to enter proceedings against him for bigamy. Austin knew this, and he may, perhaps, have thought it best for him to take all the available funds he could lay his hands on, and leave the city."

There was dead silence in the Court for nearly a minute after this announcement, and then the Prosecuting Attorney turned to the prisoner's counsel and said:

"Gentlemen, the witness is yours."

The leading counsel for Arthur rose, but instead of beginning the cross-examination of the witness he addressed himself to the Court as follows:

"Your Honor, it is now nearly five o'clock, and I would respectfully ask that the cross-examination of this witness be postponed until to-morrow morning. It is impossible to finish the case to-night, and I have just received a very important telegram from New York, informing me that some witnesses who are very essential to the case will be here to-morrow morning. I would also ask that the witness be detained as it is very important that he should be here when the Court opens."

"Have you any objection to showing me the telegram?" asked the Judge.

"None, I will read it." He looked straight at Brydon to watch the effect of the telegram on him, and read as follows:

New York, 2 o'clock.
"Miss F. Williams, Montreal,—Have found out enough to clear Arthur of both charges. Evidence complete. Leave with witnesses to-day. Keep an eye on Brydon, he will be wanted.
"Charlie Benson."

CHAPTER IX.

OUT OF THE DETECTIVE'S OFFICE.

Mr. Benson did not find his task in New York an easy one. He did not find so many of his old friends in Wall Street as he expected. "Black Friday," "the collapse in Mariposa," "the big rise in Central,"[77] and other prominent events in that speculative locality had taken place during Mr. Benson's absence from the home of American gambling, and many of his friends had been "on the wrong side," and had been squeezed dry by the bulls and bears,[78] and had retired sadder and wiser men, but infinitely poorer ones also. Wall Street brokers are not, as a rule, communicative men; if they are very anxious and willing to give you "a point," you may be pretty sure "the point" is the wrong way; and it is not at all likely that brokers to whom he was partially unknown would tell Mr. Benson that they were dealing in bonds or securities which were known to have

[77] Black Friday is a huge financial panic that began on 24 September 1869. The Mariposa Company, which held gold mines in California, went bankrupt in 1865. The stocks of the Central Pacific Railroad rose then dropped dramatically in 1868.
[78] "Bulls" and "bears" refer to market trends: the former represents rising stock prices as well as earnings, low inflation and low interest rates; the latter, to falling stock prices as well as earnings, rising inflation and rising interest rates. By extension, investors expecting one trend or another are identified as "bullish" or "bearish."

been stolen, or inform him which of them had received ten thousand dollars which were known to have been obtained on a forged cheque. His only way of gaining the information he wanted was through his old fellow-clerks; but most of them had developed into full-blown brokers, or had speculated, got ruined, and "left the street." The two or three that he found in their old positions either knew nothing of either bonds or money, or knew too much to say anything, and Mr. Benson found that his acquaintance in Wall Street availed him nothing. It took him a week to arrive at this conclusion, and when he had arrived at it he felt rather discouraged; he had counted surely on being able to trace some of the bonds or securities by their numbers. He had obtained a list of numbers, etc., of the securities from Mr. Lownds, who had found it in Arthur's desk;—but his efforts were unavailing, and, although he left a printed description of the various securities with every broker, nothing was known of them, and he began to fear that they had either not been placed upon the market or had been sent elsewhere than New York. He applied to Captain Young of the detective force, and offered him five thousand dollars for the recovery of the securities—it is no use trying to get a detective in New York to do anything unless you offer him a big reward—but nothing came of it. Day after day, Mr. Benson's spirits fell more and more, and when the first of June came, and he had discovered nothing, his spirits fell to zero, and he very nearly abandoned his task as hopeless. Captain Young told him the same story every time he called on him; the bonds had not been offered on the market, and nothing was known of Mr. Brydon. On the fourth of June Mr. Benson sat in his room at the Hoffman House after dinner,[79] ruminating on his failure, and thinking himself the most miserable fellow in New York. Again and again he read over the following telegram received a few minutes before from Miss Frank: "What are you about? Why don't you find out something at once? Arthur is to be tried to-morrow and will be convicted unless you do something. Please do something." And the more he read it, the more convinced he became that he could not "do something." At last, in sheer desperation, he put on his hat and started for the police headquarters to see Captain Young, and find out if he could "do something." He strolled leisurely down Broadway, puffing at a very doubtful cigar, for which he had been charged a quarter, and which obstinately refuse to "draw," and thinking whether it would not be better for him to telegraph Arthur's counsel that he had "done something," and that he must get the trial postponed until the next term. The idea

---

[79] One of the most elegant hotels in New York, on Broadway between 24th and 25th Streets. It had opened in 1864. Rooms were "$2 per day and upwards" (Redfield's 21).

did not strike him as very brilliant, but he thought postponement would be better than nothing, and he had almost decided to send the telegram when just as he was passing Wallack's theatre,[80] that prince of ticket speculators, Gus. Hamilton,[81] accosted him with, "Want a ticket, sir? Good seats in the orchestra or dress circle.[82] House very full. Can't get any seats at the box office." Mr. Benson paused for a moment, and, looking at the posters on the side of the entry way, saw advertized, "Last night of the season. Last appearance of Mr. Lester Wallack in Rosedale."[83] He was a great admirer of Lester Wallack, and as he had not seen him act for some time he thought he would go in "for an hour or so;" he, therefore, invested to the extent of a dollar and a half with the obliging Mr. Hamilton, and got a pretty good seat in the dress circle. When a man goes to Wallack's to see "Rosedale" "for an hour or so," he generally stays until the performance is over, and it was a quarter past eleven when Mr. Benson left the theatre. It was too late then, he thought, to see Captain Young, and he walked down Fourteenth Street to Delmonico's to get some supper,[84] his dinner having been rather light, and nature reminded him that she needed support. He entered that fashionable restaurant, and was making his way to a vacant table near a window opening on Fifth Avenue, when a gentleman who was sitting at one of the centre tables with a couple of young ladies, suddenly rose and came towards him, exclaiming,

"Why, Charlie, old boy, where did you drop from?"

"Fred, old fellow, I'm delighted to see you. I've been wondering several times that I have not met you. I called at Clarke, Dodge & Co.'s, but the boy in the office at the time told me you had left, and did not know where you were."

"Yes, I left them over a year ago. I am with Frank Worth & Co. now.[85] Come over to our table and take supper with us. I'll introduce you to some nice girls."

---

[80] The new Wallack's Theatre, which was at 844 Broadway on the corner of 13th Street between 1861 and 1881, often described as the best theatre in the country.
[81] Gus Hamilton was, indeed, a scalper who was active in front of Wallack's (see Segrave 34).
[82] The dress circle (also, "grand circle") is the first level of balconies (or "galleries").
[83] Lester Wallack (1820-1888) was an actor and manager of the second Wallack's Theatre (see note 80). One of his greatest successes was as Elliot Grey in his own play Rosedale; or, The Rifle Ball (which had premiered in 1864).
[84] At the time, this (East 14th Street and 5th Avenue) was one of the four locations of the famous "Delmonico's."
[85] Clarke, Dodge & Co" were registered as bankers at 51 Wall Street. Frank Worth was a prominent New York City banker.

Mr. Benson went, was duly introduced to the "nice girls," and chatted for a quarter of an hour on unimportant topics, varying his conversation with a spirited attack on an excellent chicken salad—you can't get chicken salad in perfection anywhere but at Delmonico's—and an occasional sip of champagne. His friend, Mr. Fred Parsons, and his party had been to Niblo's and the young ladies were rather ecstatic about the scenery of the "Black Crook," and the wonderful dancing of the beautiful young ladies in very scant clothing.[86] After the salad had been finished, and theatrical matters pretty well discussed, conversation flagged a little, and Mr. Parsons found time to ask Benson something about his own affairs.

"Well, Charlie," he said, after rather an awkward pause, "where have you been, and what have you been doing, the last two years?"

"I've been in my native city, Montreal; you know I left New York to go there to my father, who is in business there, and I have been with him ever since."

"And what brings you to New York?"

"Well," replied Mr. Benson, rather hesitatingly, "partly business, partly pleasure;" he did not want to tell Mr. Parsons exactly what business he was on, and how miserably he had failed.

"Oh, yes! I know you Montreal chaps seem to be lucky. You've come on to invest, I suppose. By-the-bye, do you remember Brydon who used to be with Austin & Son some five years ago? Of course you don't—that was before your time in Wall Street. Well, he seems to have hit a fat thing in Montreal. I hope you were in with him."

"No, I wasn't," half gasped Mr. Benson. "I know Brydon; what fat thing has he been into? I never heard of it in Montreal."

"No! Why, he sent us on a lot of bonds and other things three or four weeks ago, and ordered them all to be sold and invested in New York Central and Erie;[87] he knows what he is about, both stocks are sure to rise."

"Oh, yes! he knows—that is, I know—how much did he send?" said Mr. Benson, in such a strange, excited manner that his friend, instead of replying, asked:

"Charlie, old boy, what's the matter? You don't look well."

"I'm all right; how much? Tell me quickly how much?

[86] Niblo's Garden was a theatre on Broadway and Crosby Street between 1823 and 1895. *The Black Crook* (which premiered in 1866) is considered the first ever musical. It had a revival in 1870 and another one in August 1873 produced by the Kiralfy Brothers. One of the highlights of their production was the dancing numbers performed by their three Kiralfy sisters.
[87] The New York Central Railroad (controlled by Cornelius Vanderbilt) and the Erie Railroad.

"I don't know—something like fifty thousand, I think."

"I've got him," half shouted Mr. Benson, "D——n him, I've got him, and I've done something after all; he was so much excited that he brought his hand down with a sudden slap on the table—mistaking it, no doubt, for Mr. Brydon's head. The ladies screamed a little, and the polite waiter, almost strangled in a white tie, slid deferentially up to the table to see if the gentleman had not been taking too much wine.

"What is the matter, Charlie?" said Mr. Parsons, a little alarmed about his friend's sanity. "Are you ill?"

"All right, old fellow," said Mr. Benson, regaining his composure, "I'm all right now. Excuse me, ladies," he continued, bowing to them, "you can have no idea of the importance of the information Fred has given me, or you would forgive my apparent rudeness; let me hope you will forgive me any way, and I will not offend again." The ladies, of course, bowed forgiveness, but looked uncomfortable, and the one to whom Mr. Parsons seemed devoted gave that gentleman a very meaning nod, and pushed her chair back a little, intimating that it was time to go. Mr. Parsons was greatly astonished at Mr. Benson's warmth of manner; but he managed to stammer out:

"My information, old boy, what do you mean?"

"Nothing," said Mr. Benson, who had quite recovered his composure; "I was a little astonished at something you said, but this is not the place to talk about it. Can you call at the Hoffman tonight for half an hour? You will do me a great favor, and the matter is urgent and important!"

"All right, old fellow, I will be there in about—" he hesitated, looked at his young lady, she shook her head, he sighed, and then added, "in half an hour."

The party left the restaurant, Mr. Parsons to escort the two young ladies home, and Mr. Benson to rush up Fifth Avenue to the Hoffman House, as though his life depended on his being there before Mr. Parsons. Once arrived at the hotel he stationed himself at the entrance, and impatiently awaited Mr. Parsons—that gentleman was late; he found that he had more "last words" to say to his young lady than he had thought of, and many times he had to stop her as she was going from the door to tell her something very important, and to—well, never mind, most of us, I suppose, know how a fellow feels when he is talking nonsense (he thinks it sound, common sense) to the girl he loves, or thinks he loves, at the door of her house, late at night, when he knows he ought to go away at once, but doesn't want to, and generally doesn't under an hour.

Mr. Benson got awfully impatient, and stamped up and down the pavement in the most restless manner, but that did not hurry Mr. Parsons, and it was nearly one o'clock before he arrived at the Hoffman House.

Mr. Benson at once took Mr. Parsons up to his room, and explained fully to him the nature of his business in New York, and how the information of Brydon's having sent a large amount of bonds, &c., from Montreal, immediately after the robbery would affect the case.

Mr. Parsons had known Arthur Austin when he was one of the luminaries of Wall Street and it was an honor to know him, and he was ready and willing to help him now. He told Mr. Benson that, some three or four weeks since, the firm by whom he was employed had received a letter from Brydon, who was an old customer of theirs, enclosing a large amount of United States bonds and other securities, with orders to sell them, and make other investments. They had received no gold or notes. Mr. Parsons did not know the numbers of the bonds, &c., but promised to get a list next morning, and offered to accompany Mr. Benson to Montreal.

*   *   *   *   *   *   *

Mr. Benson slept happily and contentedly that night, although he dreamt a little; but his dreams only added to his happiness, for he dreamt only two dreams, in one of which he saw Mr. Brydon hung up by the neck; and in the other he (Mr. Benson) was leading Miss Frank to the altar. He dreamt these dreams over and over again, and awoke in the morning in a great state of ecstacy, feeling that he was much more than a match for Mr. Brydon, and very confident that he would soon prove it to the great dissatisfaction of that gentleman. He met Mr. Parsons at the time agreed on; but was greatly disappointed to find that the bonds and securities sent on by Brydon did not agree in any particular with the list found in Arthur's desk. Mr. Parsons was quite sure about the numbers, denominations, &c., of the securities received, and Mr. Benson felt thoroughly nonplussed. At last he thought he would call on Captain Young, and see if that clearheaded detective could throw any light on the subject.

They found Captain Young in his office, talking to a rather dilapidated-looking individual, who rose on their entrance, and, turning himself out of the room, said he would call again in an hour.

The Captain heard Mr. Benson's story, paused for a moment to consider, and then said:

"Mr. Benson, your case is as good as finished; the list of securities you have is a forged one, put in the drawer it was found in by Brydon to throw suspicion on the wrong track. We have been trying hard to find bonds and other securities which either don't exist, or are out of the market, while the stolen bonds have been quietly disposed of through one of the most respectable firms on Broad Street. It was a clever dodge of Brydon's; he must be a mighty sharp customer, and it is some credit to get square with him, but the game can be spoiled easy enough now. You want to take Mr. Parsons and, if possible, another witness, on to Montreal with Brydon's letter; you also want a good expert to compare the letter with Brydon's writing in the books of the firm with the forged cheque. It is just about as easy a case as I ever saw, and it is almost dead sure to be all right. I wish I could say as much for another case I am engaged in, but that is a tough one."

"What is it?" said Mr. Benson, not feeling the least interest, but simply because the detective seemed interested in it, and appeared anxious to tell the story.

"Well, you see it is a case of mistaken identity, and has led to some queer developments. Something like six months ago a man calling himself Richard Cranston went to Richmond, Va., put up at Spottswood House,[88] and cut quite a swell for a few days. He opened an account in the First National Bank of Richmond,[89] depositing a couple of thousand dollars in bills, and got very much liked about the hotel on account of his easy, pleasant way, and the strong Southern principles he advocated. After about a week he went into a tobacco speculation, and bought several hundred cases to be shipped to New York. It was a pretty big purchase, amounting to between six and seven thousand dollars, and he paid in a cheque of the cashier of the National Bank of Commerce, New York,[90] for five thousand dollars, and drew against it. The cashier of the First National Bank, Richmond, was a little doubtful about this cheque, so he telegraphed to New York and found that it was a forgery. Of course, payment was stopped, the tobacco not shipped, and a warrant issued for Mr. Cranston's arrest; but he had, somehow or other, got wind of the affair, had disappeared, has not

[88] Spottswood House was the most elegant hotel in Richmond, Virginia. It survived a devastating fire in 1870.
[89] The largest bank in Virginia at the time, chartered in 1865.
[90] Established in 1839 as the Bank of Commerce, it was the largest bank in the country in the 1860s. Immediately after the Civil War, it was converted into the National Bank of Commerce, through the National Banking Acts of 1863 and 1864. The First National Bank of Richmond was also a national bank (i.e., a private bank which is required to be a member of the Federal Reserve System).

since been found. A few days after he left it was discovered that the bills he had paid in when opening his account were counterfeits, and the Bank determined to make an effort to secure Mr. Cranston, although they had not lost very much by him. You see, this sort of thing has been tried several times in Richmond and 'an example' was wanted. The Bank offered $1,000 reward for Cranston's arrest, and Brownson, of the Richmond force, came on here and applied to me, as it was thought that Cranston had come to New York—somehow, people *will* think that all the rascals in the world come to New York; but, between you and I, I think that New York exports more thieves, burglars, and rascals generally than she imports. Brownson and I worked up the case together, and we traced Mr. Cranston to the St. Charles Hotel, where we found that he and his wife had been staying for a few days. They had left; and we could not get any trace of Cranston until about ten days ago, when, by chance, I discovered that Richard Cranston was living out at Flatbush.[91] Now comes in the funny part. I arrested Cranston, and telegraphed for Brownson and the cashier of the First National Bank of Richmond, both of whom knew Cranston well by sight, to come on and identify him. They came on and did identify him; but Cranston pleaded ignorance of the charge, and proved beyond the shadow of a doubt that he could not have committed the crime with which he was charged. He showed by numerous respectable witnesses that he had not been out of Brooklyn for more than a day or two at a time, for over two years; and on the very day the forged cheque was presented in Richmond he was in the Second Precinct Station House, arrested for drunkenness. It was the clearest *alibi* I ever saw; but still it would have been hard for him to get off, only that the story he told, and the way he told it, was so plausible that we were forced to believe that he was not the Richard Cranston that we wanted. This Cranston is a peculiar looking man—you saw him here when you entered—with long shaggy red hair and whiskers, and rather marked features. Now it seems that there is another man who looks as much like Cranston as his own brother could—only Cranston hasn't got a brother, so he don't exactly know how he would look. The only material difference is that the other man's hair is black, but a bottle of hair dye would soon set that all right; and Cranston says that if they were both dressed alike he could scarcely tell which was himself, and which the other fellow. You see, Cranston—who turns out to be a very respectable man, although not well off, and addicted to going on a spree once in a while—owes this

---

[91] Today a neighborhood in central Brooklyn. An independent town at the time, it was absorbed by Brooklyn in 1894.

Bill Gangley, as he calls himself—although, I suppose, that is not his real name—a grudge on an old score, and wants to get square with him. It appears that some six or seven years ago, Cranston married a ballet girl and she turned out a bad one, they often do, and ran away from him, and took up with Gangley. Cranston does not care much about her; but it isn't pleasant for a man to have another man run away with his wife, and then steal his name and commit forgery under it, and so Cranston wants to get square."

"I hope he will," said Mr. Benson in an absent way, feeling rather bored, and not more than half understanding the story; "and I hope he will find his wife."

"Oh! he don't care much about her; it isn't likely he would be very anxious to find such a bad lot as Effie Barron."

"Who?" shouted Mr. Benson, now fully interested. "Who did you say?"

'Why, his wife, Effie Barron."

"I've got it," exclaimed Mr. Benson, throwing his arms in his excitement around the astonished Captain. "I've done something now, and no mistake. It's all right, hurrah!"

"You've got me, certainly," said Young, somewhat surprised, "but what else have you got?"

"Why, don't you see? Of course you can't see—you don't know—I didn't tell you—can't you understand? No, I don't suppose you can."

"Most certainly I cannot understand what you have just said. What do you mean?"

"I mean this," said Mr. Benson, making an effort to be calm, "that if Effie Barron married Richard Cranston six or seven years ago, she was a married woman when she committed bigamy by marrying Arthur Austin; and Robert Brydon and Richard Cranston No. 2 are one and the same person, and—and—I've done something; hurrah!"

"I wish," said Young, quietly, "you would compose yourself and explain what you mean so that I can understand it."

Mr. Benson rapidly collected himself and told Captain Young the whole story, so far as he knew it, of Arthur's marriage, etc. The Captain sat quietly listening until Mr. Benson had finished, and then said, "I can straighten this thing out."

"I am sure you can," said Mr. Benson, rather too confidently.

"What is the reward?" asked practical Captain Young.

"You get $1,000 reward for Brydon's arrest from the Richmond Bank," answered Mr. Benson, "and I will give you the same amount if you can take Cranston to Montreal and prove that he was married to Effie Barron before she married Arthur Austin."

"Make it $2,500 and expenses paid, and I'll fix the thing all right in Montreal to-morrow," said practical Captain Young.

"All right," said Mr. Benson, "consider it a bargain."

"Put it there," said Captain Young, extending a large, hard, brawny hand and holding it palm upwards.

Mr. Benson "put it there" by bringing his right hand down heartily into the open palm of the Captain, and the two men shook hands on the agreement.

A short while afterwards Mr. Benson sent to Montreal the telegram which closed the last chapter.

CHAPTER X.

OUT OF THE WORLD.

It was not a very difficult matter to get Arthur's trial postponed until the next morning, and Mr. Brydon found himself a sort of honorary prisoner in the hands of High Constable Bissonette,[92] who was exceedingly civil, polite and accommodating to him, but by his vigilance debarred Mr. Brydon's one great hope now, that of effecting a bolt. Finding there was no chance of escape Mr. Brydon became affable; he had plenty of money about him and he proposed a little supper and a cigar; Bissonette refused supper, as the bosom of his family was waiting for him to repose on it for the evening meal, but he did not mind taking a cigar to smoke after supper. Cigars were obtained and under the influence of a gentle whiff Mr. Brydon obtained permission to walk as far as his boarding house, accompanied by Constable Lafontaine, and obtain a clean shirt, collar, etc., which he declared he was greatly in need of. He was only a few minutes in his room and the Constable was with

---

[92] Both High Constable Bissonette and Constable Lafontaine (whose name appears a few lines below) were members of the Montreal Police and were often mentioned in contemporary newspapers.

him all the time, yet he managed to take something out of the bureau and put it in his pocket, and he seemed greatly pleased at what he had done.

Mr. Benson and his witnesses arrived next morning, the case was continued, and did not occupy a great deal of time. A genuine list of the bonds, etc., was found in a private drawer of the safe, where no one had thought of looking for it—it being said that the list had been found in Arthur's desk—and the evidence of Mr. Parsons and the experts fully cleared Arthur, and after a very short trial the Judge instructed the jury to dismiss the complaint which was accordingly done. Arthur's counsel then formally moved for the discharge of the prisoner, which was granted, and Arthur Austin came from the prisoner's dock to the floor of the Court a free man and received the hearty congratulations of his friends. But there was one whose congratulations he valued more than all and that was the one he had always loved, and whom he now knew was really and truly his lawful wife. There was quite a pause when Arthur came out of the dock and his friends crowded around him, and the Judge good-naturedly waited a few minutes for the excitement to subside before the next case was called.

There was one person who did not feel particularly elated at Arthur's acquittal, and he, of course, was Mr. Brydon. That gentleman had not as yet been formally arrested and was still a sort of honorary prisoner, seemingly not under control, but really watched constantly by two or three constables, and as he had been brought up for cross-examination at the opening of the trial, but dismissed to make way for more important witnesses, he was still in court and was standing in front of the reporter's desk when Mr. Austin was formally discharged. Arthur passed quite close to him as he crossed the court to speak to Jessie, and Mr. Brydon's lips twitched convulsively, and his right hand stole quietly into the breast pocket of his coat. He controlled himself, however, and while Jessie was still in Arthur's arms he advanced towards the pair and said:

"So glad, dear boy, to see you acquitted; allow me to congratulate you on your triumph—but it will not be for long," he continued savagely, suddenly changing his tone and manner, "not for long, Arthur Austin; you have won against me all the time, but I'll trump your last trick or my name is not Robert Brydon!"

Quick as thought he withdrew his right hand from his coat pocket, a bright shining barrel gleamed for one moment in the air, then came a sharp ringing report, a loud scream of agony, and Arthur Austin fell on the floor of the Court a dead man. There was scarcely a quiver of the flesh, hardly a movement of the muscles, the bullet went straight to the heart and death was instantaneous. Ere the horrified spectators could attempt to seize him Mr. Brydon had placed the barrel of the pistol in his own mouth and pulled the trigger.

*   *   *   *   *   *   *

My story is almost done. The report of Mr. Brydon's pistol evoked an expression of terror from almost all the astonished spectators, but above all rose one scream, one outburst of heart agony, as Jessie threw herself on the lifeless form of her murdered husband. For a moment all was wild terror and confusion; but the Judge quickly recovered his equanimity and restored order and quiet by his prompt and self-possessed action. It was at once discovered that Arthur was dead, there was no question about that; and it was feared that Jessie's spirit had followed that of the one she loved to the shadow land. Medical help was speedily obtained, and Jessie, in a state of unconsciousness, was removed to her home closely attended by Miss Frank, whose medical knowledge had proved of some account, as her quick and effective treatment of Jessie showed. No one seemed to consider Mr. Brydon, and he lay on the floor a mangled mass of humanity, until a carriage was obtained to take Jessie home; then Miss Frank turned to His Honor the Judge, as she was leaving the Court, and said:

"That wretch Brydon is not dead. Take good care of him and get him well, for I mean to see him hanged."

Miss Frank was right. Mr. Brydon was not dead; the bullet he had meant to penetrate his brain had been misdirected, and had passed through the back of his neck, inflicting a dangerous, but not of necessity mortal, wound. He had ample attendance, and was conveyed as soon as practicable to the General Hospital, where he was well cared for. But Mr. Brydon had no desire to be hung—he knew that was inevitable,—and as soon as he recovered strength sufficiently to lift his waistcoat from the chair by his side, on which it had been laid, he took a little rough-looking paper ball out of the fob pocket and deliberately chewed it up and swallowed it. It was a preparation which Mr. Brydon had carefully made up many months ago, and its efficacy was fully proved now, for the nurse who attended him reported about two hours after that he was dead.

The Coroner, of course, held an inquest, and the medical testimony showed that Mr. Brydon had died from poison; the intelligent jury, after much deliberation brought in a verdict of suicide, and Mr. Brydon's career was closed.

Jessie was taken home insensible and lingered for a couple of days, and then she quietly and peacefully passed away to join the one she loved. The long strain on her nervous system, consequent on Arthur's arrest, and the sudden shock of his death, brought on premature child-birth, and she was too weak to survive its pangs. She remained unconscious, and knew not of the advent of a little girl, who only opened her eyes on this world to close them again for ever; and in three days after Arthur's murder his body and his wife's and child's were laid side by side in the cold earth.

There is little more left to tell. Of course Frank married Mr. Benson, and they are living happily together. There are several little Franks, and their maternal parent takes good care of them as far as medical matters are concerned, and her first son, whom she called Arthur, after her brother-in-law, bids fair to become a travelling drug store; but he bears up bravely under it, and will no doubt become some day a fine man. Miss Frank and her husband are happy, and live tranquilly and pleasantly together, but there will sometimes come over them a feeling of sadness, and a spirit of gloom when they think of the two who were so suddenly snatched away from them, and how much brighter and happier they might have been if Arthur had possessed sufficient moral courage to grapple with his trouble like a man, and not give himself over to the demon of drink as he did, from which moment his course was downwards to destruction.

THE END.

THOMPSON'S TURKEY

CHAPTER I.

How Thompson Got the Turkey

It wasn't Thompson's fault.

I take this the earliest possible opportunity, to give it as my free, candid and disinterested opinion that it wasn't Thompson's fault. I am quite well aware of the fact that there were people before the time who said it was Thompson's fault; I am quite well aware of the fact that there were people at the time who said it was Thompson's fault; I am quite well aware of the fact that there were people after the time who said it was Thompson's fault; I am quite well aware of the fact that there are people who even at the present day maintain that it was Thompson's fault; but I never did believe it was Thompson's fault, and I never will.

The fact is Thompson couldn't help it.

I know very well there were people at the time who said that Thompson could have helped it; I know very well that there were people after the time who said Thompson could have helped it; I know very well there are people now who still assert that Thompson could have helped it; but I never did believe Thompson could help it, and I never will.

And, after all, what was it that people said was Thompson fault; and what was it that people said Thompson could have helped doing?

Why, getting married; that was all!

I never could see, and I never will see that it was Thompson's fault to get married; other people do it, why shouldn't Thompson? I never could see, and I never will see that Thompson could have helped it; other people can't help it, and why should Thompson?

And then everybody wanted to marry Winnie Dumsic, why shouldn't Thompson? But, Winnie—her name was Winnetta, but we always called her Winnie for short—didn't want to marry everybody; she didn't even want to marry me, although I was ready and willing to marry her several times over if necessary; she didn't want to marry old Flailflax, the wealthy linen draper, although he did own a big house on the mountain side,[93] and was reported to have so much money in the bank, that an extra vault had had to be built on purpose to hold it all; she didn't want to marry young Grunter, the pork packer, although he was always as sleek and smooth as if just freshly rubbed with some of his own grease, and his father was said to have left him enough money to pack every pig in Canada, himself included; she didn't want to marry the Rev. Mr. Maypole, the new curate of St. Fashionable's, although he was so upright, and dressed so nicely, and read prayers "beautifully"— so the other girls said—and gave the old women snuff to brace up their nerves—the girls all said that was "so charitable"—and did a thousand and one things which always made unmarried curates so agreeable to the female portion of the congregation of St. Fashionable's; the fact is Winnie wanted to marry Thompson, and she did it.

Young ladies sometimes will do such things, whether their parents like it or not; and, therefore, as Winnie had made up her mind to marry Thompson, she did marry him, and I say it wasn't Thompson's fault, and he couldn't help it.

There were other reasons why Thompson couldn't help it. Winnie Dumsic was one of the sweetest, most lovable little bits of femininity that ever set a poor male mortal crazy; she was so rosy, so joyous, so artless, so natural, so piquant, so winning that nobody could help loving her; I couldn't, how could Thompson?

Then she and Thompson had grown up together from childhood; even when she was a little thing in short frocks and frills round her pantalets nobody could help stealing apples, and cakes, and sweetmeats, and other things for her, and tearing their clothes climbing for flowers to please her, and fighting each other on her account, and wanting to kiss her and being too bashful to do it; I couldn't, and how could Thompson?

She always looked to me like a lump of sugar, and I was not at all astonished when Thompson put her in his cup of life to sweeten it for all time; I wasn't astonished, but everybody else was.

You see this was the way of it. Winnie was rich; old Dumsic, her father, was a large dealer in small-wares, pins and needles and such things, and a good deal of money had stuck to old Dumsic's fingers

---

[93] In other words, a house situated in the Golden Square Mile, on or above Sherbrooke Street (see note 11).

by the aid of pins and needles and such things. He was a proud man, was old Dumsic; very fond of his only child, and very fond of talking of his "connections in the old country"—Rumor said he had been a pot-boy[94] in Dublin in his youthful days, but Rumor might have lied as she very often does; and everybody knows that every Irishman, out of Ireland, is either an Irish king, or the descendant of one. It has often struck me that kings in Ireland must have been very plentiful at some time, and that they must have been amongst the earliest immigrants, which would, of course, account for so many of their descendants being found on this side of the Atlantic; be that as it may, Dumsic was the lineal descendant of an Irish king, so he said, and had a right to be proud, which he was, whether he had the right or not.

Being proud, Dumsic, of course, would not hear of Thompson for a son-in-law, for Thompson was poor; in fact, Thompson was only a clerk in old Dumsic's store, and although Dumsic and Thompson's father had been great friends, and Dumsic himself had been very kind to Thompson since his father's death, still he would not have dreamed of giving Winnie to him.

Nor was poverty his only objection to Thompson; no, that might have been overcome; but it was Thompson's name, that could not be overcome.

You see old Dumsic had studied genealogies and derivations very deeply—that was how he found out that he was the descendant of an Irish king—and he informed Thompson that his name was very plebeian: in fact, old Dumsic went so far as to say that there was no such thing as a Thompson with a p. He argued, and with considerable show of correctness, that the name, as a surname, was derived from the Christian name Thomas, and had been originally written Thomas' son, and applied to a younger member of the family as indicating that he was a son of the original Thomas; that on the general adoption of surnames the apostrophe and one s were dropped, and the name written Thomason, which in due course of time had become changed to Thomson, or Tomson; but Thompson—with a p—he looked on as a base impostor of a name, and triumphantly asked "how did the p get in?"

Of course, Thompson did not like to hear his name abused, and retaliated on Dumsic by telling him that his, Dumsic's, name was originally Drumstick, and that the r, t and k had been knocked out of the name at various stages of its transmission from the Irish king to the present owner; but that only made Dumsic mad, and when Thompson

---

[94] A waiter; a boy carrying pots of ale in a public house.

told him that he loved Winnie, and asked his consent to their union when he was able to support her—for he was a proud fellow, was Thompson, and didn't want to marry Winnie for her money, but because he loved her—old Dumsic poured out all the vials of his wrath, and vowed that if she married Thompson he would cut her off with a farthing, so that the p in her name should not even stand for a penny.

That was a terrible time for Thompson; of course he lost his place in old Dumsic's store; and, of course, old Dumsic forbid his seeing or speaking to Winnie again; and, of course, Winnie and Thompson used to meet each other on the sly and vow eternal constancy and all that sort of thing; and, of course, they used to write to each other every day, and I used to deliver the notes without old Dumsic suspecting me—for he rather liked me and thought I was going to marry Winnie, but Winnie didn't love me and did love Thompson, and although I liked Thompson very well, I didn't care to marry a girl who loved him and didn't love me.

Thompson soon got another place, but it was not as good as the one he had lost, and the chances of matrimony seemed further off than ever; but things are often nearest to us when they seem furthest off. It was summer when old Dumsic discharged Thompson, and the lovers agreed to wait five years for each other; but, somehow as the cold weather came on, and it was not so pleasant waiting in Viger Garden, or Victoria Square[95] to meet each other, both parties suddenly changed their minds, and one morning early in December Thompson entered my office in a very excited manner and asked me to come and see him married.

Thompson and I were always very friendly, although we did love the same girl; it wasn't his fault if Winnie cared for him and not for me, so I couldn't blame Thompson, could I? So I went to see them married, and gave away the bride, I did, and I kissed her next after Thompson, I did; and it made me feel as if a frozen poker had been run down my back when I thought it was the last time I would ever kiss her. But I didn't let them see that I felt it, and offered to take Winnie's note to her father asking for forgiveness and deliver it in person.

It was as great a refresher to me as a shower bath to see old Dumsic get mad when I told him what had happened; he turned so red in the

[95] Both are in the southern part of Downtown Montreal, though almost a mile apart. Victoria Square, a long public space on the western edge of Old Montreal, looks today (despite the addition of high-rises) quite similar to the way it looked in the mid-1870s. On the other hand, the Viger Garden, famous in the 19th century for its greenhouses and its musical concerts, has been replaced by Viger Square, on the concrete roof of an expressway. The project of its redevelopment has been on the books for a long time (see also note 39).

face I thought he would go off in a fit of apoplexy, and I half wished he would, for I knew he had made a will leaving Winnie his heiress, and if he died right off he would not have time to alter it; but he didn't know enough to die decently, he must live to make himself disagreeable, and so, after a while he recovered himself, and the first things he said was:

"Phillips, you're a fool."

I told him that possibly he might be correct, but I did not think it polite to state it quite so plainly. He did not mind that at all, but repeated the obnoxious expression prefacing the word fool with a very objectionable adjective which made me so angry that for a moment a desperate desire to seize him by the throat, choke him to death, and say he died of apoplexy on hearing the news, came over me; but I thought of the marks I should leave on the neck, of the coroner's jury, of a trial for murder, of a rope and other unpleasant things, and stifling my indignation contented myself with saying "you're another."

But if I stifled my wrath old Dumsic didn't stifle his; he raved terribly, and used shocking bad language for so old a man; he swore he would never forgive Winnie, that he would drive Thompson to despair, and so many more dreadful things, that I was forced to leave him, and the old fool made a new will that same day and took himself off on an express train that night no one knew whither.

Poor Thompson had a hard time of it at first; his salary was small, and Winnie had been accustomed to so many luxuries that it seemed a shame to deprive her of. But they both put their shoulders bravely to the wheel, and it was astonishing how well they got on. Winnie would not hear of boarding, and determined to keep house herself. They got the upper part of a house in a cheap and quiet by-street and it was surprising how nicely and cosily they fitted it up, considering their limited means. Thompson always used to say that he could never have done it but for the timely aid of a kind friend; but Thompson, although a good fellow, is rather foolish on some subjects, and sometimes talks about things that he ought not to speak of to everybody.

How happy they were; how much they loved each other, and how they cheered and helped each other nobody knows better than I; and nobody felt it more than I did the first evening I spent with them and sat by the fire crying, half with pleasure, half with pain, like the great fool that I am, and swearing all the time that it was a splinter from the crackling wood which had flown into my eye and made it water. Very happy and very contented they were, and very hard Thompson worked to sustain his humble home.

He wasn't a fool, wasn't Thompson; far from it, he was a clever sort of chap, and could do lots of things besides wait behind a counter and sell ribbons and things to young ladies. He was a well educated fellow, was Thompson, and could write poetry so nicely that the girls were always wanting him to write in their Albums; and so, when old Dumsic discharged him, Thompson thought he would turn his talents to account and he sent some of his writings to the American papers, for the Canadian papers were willing enough to publish, but very unwilling to pay, and as Thompson was writing for bread and butter he could not afford that kind of business.

Very nice stories did Thompson write, and his *nom de plume* of "Phontoms"—anagram of Thompson, for he would stick to his name—soon got to be well known and liked. But at first he got very little pay for his productions, and what he did get, added to his salary, was scarce enough to keep Winnie and himself, even with the exercise of great economy.

It was about three weeks before Christmas that they were married and commenced housekeeping, and Winnie had set her heart on giving a "party" at Christmas and asking some of her old friends to come and witness her triumphs of housekeeping; but it was a great undertaking, and had to be calmly considered and gone about in a serious manner.

Dinners are expensive things, and economical as she tried to be, Winnie found that the plainest fare she could afford to set before the half dozen friends she had invited would make a deep hole in her scanty purse; and very little would be left to provide refreshments for those who had been asked to come after dinner and spend the evening.

"I don't see how I can manage it," said Winnie, pushing back her hair and looking up from a little red book, in which she had been making some entries, at her husband who was busy writing at the centre table; "Do you think we could do without any dessert, Charlie, dear!" I forgot to mention before that Thompson's other name was Charles, but I suppose it don't make much difference.

"Do without dessert, darling? well, it wouldn't look very well for Christmas; but you know best, if we can't afford it, don't do it. I have given you all the money I have, and I won't run in debt; a man in debt never belongs to himself, and I mean to belong to myself if nothing else does."

"Nothing else?" inquired an arch voice, as a pair of loving arms were wound round his neck and a dainty little form threw itself into his lap with an impetuous rush which sent all the papers flying.

"Well nothing worth speaking about; of course, you don't count now, you are part of me, and the law does not recognize you as a good and chattel."

"But do you recognize me as a good? I don't like to be called a chattel."

"The best good in the world to me;" and then there was a little joyous squeeze, and a great deal of nonsense was said, and the ink bottle escaped being overturned on the new table cover by a miracle before common-sense conversation was resumed. They were very nonsensical people, were Thompson and his young wife, and they were not yet through their honeymoon you must remember.

"But about the dinner, Charlie," resumed Winnie presently. "I've stretched the money as far as it will go and if I have dessert there won't be enough for the turkey; we ought to have a turkey, oughtn't we?"

"I suppose so; people do generally have a turkey for Christmas dinner; but if we can't afford it we must do without it. I wish we had the one I have described in that Christmas story I sent to Harpers."[96]

"We can't eat a turkey out of a Christmas story," said Winnie, sententiously. "We might as well try an entire banquet out of 'The Arabian Nights' at once."

"Then Phil"—Winnie always would abbreviate my name somehow—"and the others must be content with roast beef and plum pudding; I'm going to make a plum pudding, Charlie, for it wouldn't be Christmas without it."

"Say you are going to try to make one, puss, but don't expect me to eat any of it; I have too much respect for my digestive organs."

"Then you shan't have a bit of it, sir, for your impudence, and Phil shall have the whole of it."

"Poor Phil, I pity him," sighed Thompson with mock concern for which he got the tiniest possible slap on the ear and the sweetest possible kiss on the lips.

"Now then, puss, jump down and let me go on with my writing," and so the turkey was dropped for the time being.

But Thompson did not forget it; he thought of it several times the next day, and determined to stretch a point, if possible, and get a turkey if only to surprise and please Winnie.

Luck favored Thompson, and two days before Christmas he received a polite note from Harpers enclosing a cheque for twenty-five dollars for the accepted Christmas story, and offering to purchase more of his productions.

---

[96] The publisher Harper & Brothers (started by James Harper in 1817 in New York City) oversaw three periodicals: *Harper's New Monthly Magazine* (founded in 1850), *Harper's Weekly* (1857) and *Harper's Bazar* (1867; a second "a" was added to this name in 1930). It was common practice to refer simply to the name of the publishing company when it owned several magazines. Many Canadian authors contributed stories to all three publications of Harper & Brothers.

This was the largest sum he had ever received for an article, and a proud man was Thompson as he walked into a neighboring broker's office and got his cheque cashed. "One ten and the rest in ones, if you please," said Thompson, thinking how he would surprise Winnie by presenting her with the turkey, and then raining one-dollar bills on her afterwards. The broker gave him the money, and smiled quite pleasantly as he said,

"Making your fortune fast now, eh, Thompson, my boy? That's right. A merry Christmas to you," and Thompson felt himself grow half an inch taller as he walked out.

It was a busy day at the store that day, and it was quite late when Thompson took down his overcoat to start for home where he knew tea was ready and Winnie anxiously expecting him; he was a little late already, and, besides, he had the turkey to buy.

"Wait a minute, Thompson," called out the junior partner as Thompson passed the office, "I have something to say to you before you go."

And so he had to wait another five minutes; but the "something" proved very pleasant to hear, for the junior partner told him that the head of the firm—who was the junior partner's father—was very much pleased with the way he had conducted himself since he had been in the employ of the firm, and presented him with a cheque for fifty dollars, and promised him an increase of one hundred dollars salary next year.

Happy Thompson! He almost kissed the junior partner on the spot, and with difficulty restrained himself from executing a little impromptu dance of joy; but he managed to stammer out a few words of thanks and reserved his terpsichorean performance until he should have reached home.

"That's right," said the junior partner approvingly to what Thompson had said, "you always take an interest in your employers' business, and be sure they will take an interest in you. Here," he continued to a cash-boy who was passing, "take that to the cashier and ask him to give me small bills, ones or twos, for it. I am going off to Toronto to-night, Thompson," he went on as the boy departed on his errand. "I shall eat my Christmas dinner there, and be away three or four days; look after the store for me a bit while I am gone."

"The cashier says he aint got no small bills, sir," said the cash-boy returning and holding out a ten-dollar bill to the junior partner.

"That's very provoking," said that gentleman, "I have nothing but tens and twenties and I want to buy some car tickets. Do you happen to have any small bills, Thompson?"

Of course Thompson had, and he handed ten of them to the junior partner, buttoned up the ten-dollar bill with the cheque and his other money, and went on his way rejoicing to buy the turkey.

CHAPTER II.

How the Turkey Got Thompson

It was a hard turkey to buy, and took some time to select. Thompson had never done any marketing before, and had an idea that it was a very easy matter to walk into the market, select a turkey, pay for it and carry it off with him; but when he got there he saw so many turkeys it was quite distracting to make a selection, and the clatter of the poultry vendors so confused him that he had nearly invested in a scraggy looking goose when he was touched on the shoulder and a laughing voice said at his elbow,

"Ha, ha, Mr. Married Man, doing your own marketing already; where is the gude wife?"

"Oh, Mrs. Westerville, I am so glad to see you. I was just—that is I want to—well I was trying to buy a turkey."

"And very nearly purchased a goose. O you men are not fit to be trusted marketing by yourselves; why didn't Winnie come with you?"

"You see I intend this for a surprise."

"And you would have surprised her I have no doubt, if you had taken her home a goose and called it a turkey. Let me make your purchases for you."

"Oh, thank you. I am afraid I shall make a mess of it if I try it alone."

"Of course you will; men always do. And how is Winnie? I haven't seen her since your marriage. Oh what naughty people you were to get married on the sly, and not even send me a piece of wedding cake."

"Winnie is quite well, thanks, and will be glad to see you if you don't mind calling in rather queer quarters. We are not very rich, you know, and poor people can't be very particular where they live."

"Never mind your 'queer quarters,' Mr. Poor Man, I'll come and see you if you will give me your address. There, will that turkey do?" holding out a large plump bird which she had poked in the breast, and pinched in the back, and pulled by the legs, and squeezed by the bill, and satisfied herself was young and tender.

"That will do very nicely indeed, thank you. What is the price?" to the stall keeper.

"Seven and sixpence."

"A dollar and a half!" cried Mrs. Westerville in pretended astonishment.[97] "It's downright robbery. I paid a dollar for one only yesterday; these market people always take advantage of you men, they see you know nothing about it, and cheat you in the most barefaced manner."

After a little haggling the turkey was purchased for a dollar and a quarter, and Thompson having bought some vegetables which he thought Winnie might want for dinner, and some grapes which he intended for her own special eating, changed one of his ten-dollar bills so as to get plenty of small change again, and having loaded himself up like a pack horse trotted homeward happy.

Very much delighted was Winnie, and very sceptical about the quality of the turkey until told that Mrs. Westerville had bought it, and then she suddenly subsided before the superior wisdom of that matron of nearly a year's standing. Very much delighted was Winnie, and a very pleasant, happy evening they passed, she sitting on his lap eating grapes and occasionally holding one between her rosy lips and making him take it from them with his—I told you they were a very silly couple; and very animated was Winnie with her details of the grand preparations— in a small way—which she had made for the eventful Christmas; very merry and joyous she was, and a little inquisitive too, for she asked Thompson more than once where he had got all the money from to buy "turkeys"—she said turkeys, although there was but one—"and grapes, and vegetables and all manner of things."

But he was a dark and mysterious Thompson that night, and for the first time in his life deceived his darling a little; for he was a plotting and a scheming Thompson also, and was laying a deep plan for surprising his little wife the next night; and so he answered evasively that he had "found that he had more money than he expected, and could afford a little extra expenses," and so put her off with a kiss. Very happy and very merry were they, and many a little joke was cracked about the turkey.

Next morning Thompson was up bright and early and off to business with a light heart; and several times during the day he caught himself whistling snatches of gay little songs as he attended on the

[97] According to the Currency Act of 1853, pounds, shillings, and pence, as well as dollars and cents, were recognized as Canadian currency. The exchange rate varied from one province to another, but the price of this particular turkey (seven shillings and sixpence) indicates that, in 1873 in Montreal, one pound was worth exactly 4 dollars; one shilling (one twentieth of a pound) was worth 20 cents; and sixpence (half a shilling) was the equivalent of 10 cents.

customers who thronged the store. A little before dinner time he got his cheque changed by the cashier, receiving as many small bills as that gentleman could spare—it was wonderful how much Thompson seemed to want small bills—and four tens.

As soon as the clock struck twelve he ran out ostensibly to dinner, but that was surely only an excuse, for he had told Winnie he would be too busy to come home and that he would get something to eat down town. Nowhere near home, nor any restaurant did Thompson go, but right to old Dumsic's store in Notre Dame Street, and entered it as large as life just as if he was going to buy the whole store and pay for it on the spot.

But he didn't want the whole store, he only wanted a very small portion of some of the goods in the store; for be it known that amongst the "small wares" in which old Dumsic dealt were sundry articles of jewellery, and one of these articles, a dead gold[98] brooch with a small amethyst in it, Thompson had set his heart on possessing and presenting to Winnie as a Christmas present. Very glad were his old fellow clerks to see him, and many a merry little joke was passed about his "changed appearance since he became a double man," and other kindred pleasantries; and when he pulled out two ten-dollar bills to pay for the brooch—the price was twelve dollars and a half—one of the clerks began to chaff him and asked if he had "struck a mine," or "robbed a bank," or "made them himself," and such like playful questions. And when he went to the cashier's desk to get his change there sat old Dumsic himself, who had returned suddenly that morning from nobody knew where, looking as cross as he could, and he never said a word to Thompson, or as much as look at him; but he put on his spectacles and peered very suspiciously at the bills as if he thought they were bad, and he grunted in a disappointed sort of way as he threw them into the drawer and counted out the change. Very cross and savage indeed did old Dumsic look, but Thompson never heeded him, his heart was too full of joy for him to mind how old Dumsic looked; and he went whistling gailyn out of the shop and turned into a tobacconist's, where he was known, and enquired the price of a handsome little meerschaum cigar holder which he wished to present to a stupid, blundering, foolish sort of a friend of his whom he was pleased to think himself under some sort of obligation to.

He changed another ten-dollar bill at the tobacconist's, and after he had received the change counted out twenty-five dollars in one-dollar

[98] "Dead gold" refers to the unburnished surface of gold, also called "matte gold."

bills and put that away carefully in one pocket, and laughed slily as he did so, did that artful Thompson, and put the remaining twenty-two dollars—two tens, and a two—into another pocket; then he went back to business, and every now and then during the afternoon he chuckled to himself in a satisfied sort of way.

As Thompson had not gone home to dinner he was allowed an hour and a half for supper, and he went off sharp at six whistling all the way and in the best possible humor with himself. But all the good spirits in which he had been all day were as nothing to his uproarious hilarity when he heard Winnie's little shriek of delight at the production of the brooch, and saw her look of wonder when he pelted the one-dollar bills at her, one at a time to make them last longer; and then she climbed on his lap and made him tell her all about it; and beautiful castles in the air they built of the great things which they were to do when Thompson had become a world renowned author and made an immense fortune— authors always do make immense fortunes, in books you know, although they very seldom do in real life.

Very merrily and gaily they chatted away without thinking of supper, and Thompson's hour and a half was almost all gone when he suddenly remembered that he was very hungry and fell to with a good appetite.

But Thompson was not destined to enjoy his supper that night, for he had scarcely taken two bites out of the round of toast when there was a great knocking at the door, and on Winnie's opening it three men pushed past her and entered the room.

Thompson knew them in a moment, and rose in astonishment; they were old Dumsic, a detective—whom Thompson knew by sight— and a policeman in uniform.

"What does this intrusion mean?" asked Thompson looking with surprise at the intruders, while Winnie, with that instinctive feeling which women have that one they love is in danger, came to his side and put her arm around him as if to shield him.

"There he is," said old Dumsic savagely, "catch him before he runs away."

"I'm very sorry, Mr. Thompson," said the detective, who was a mild-eyed, gentlemanly-looking man, "will you step outside for a minute?" and he glanced at Winnie.

"No, he won't," she interrupted, before Thompson could speak: "Whatever you have to say you can say before me. What is it?"

"There is a little trouble about some one passing counterfeit bills," said the detective, "and he's wanted down at the Station;" somehow he didn't like to tell that brave-looking little woman that a charge of passing counterfeit bills had been made against her husband.

"Tell the truth," said old Dumsic sharply, "he's arrested for passing counterfeit notes; the woman he bought a turkey from last night has made a charge against him, and he passed two on me to-day. I'll make an affidavit to-morrow. The rascal to steal my daughter and then try to rob me; he ought to be hung."

"It's all a confounded lie," shouted Thompson taking a step towards old Dumsic in so fierce a manner as to make that gentleman skip nimbly behind the policeman. "I know nothing about any counterfeit bills; all the money I have had for the last two days I got from Mr. Stamps, the broker, and from the cashier of our store."

"Well, perhaps you'll be able to make it all right, sir," said the detective kindly; "but if you'd take my advice you wouldn't say much now. I may have to use it as evidence against you."

"Use whatever you please," said Thompson savagely. "I've got nothing to conceal in the matter. Take me anywhere you please at once and let me explain this matter."

"Oh, yes," said old Dumsic peeping cautiously from behind the policeman, "he can explain, of course! He can explain where he got the money to buy turkeys"—*he* said turkeys too, although there was but one—"and give dinner parties, and buy brooches, and throw bank notes about like this," and he pointed to the heap of dollar bills which Winnie had left on the table.

"I will explain nothing, except before the proper authorities," said Thompson calmly: "I am ready to go at once. I scarcely thought, Mr. Dumsic," he continued, turning to that gentleman, "that your spite against me would have carried you as far as this. May God forgive you the injustice you do me, and the pain you cause your own flesh and blood."

"It isn't him," said the detective, "it's the poultry dealer who made the complaint; she found out this morning that the bill was bad, and I went to the store to find you. The cashier told me you were here, and as I was coming along I met Mr. Dumsic who told me you had passed two counterfeits on him; he hasn't made any charge yet."

"Yes, I have," cried old Dumsic, "I make it now, and I will swear to it to-morrow morning."

"Let us go," said Thompson reaching for his hat. "I want to get this thing settled at once. Cheer up darling," he continued to Winnie, "it is nothing serious, I will be back soon."

"Do you think I am going to let you go alone? No, Charlie; I'm your wife, and wherever you go I go with you. I know this is a base, wicked calumny, a plot to separate us, but it shan't; no matter where they take you, they must take me too."

Her face was very pale, but her lip never trembled, and her eyes shone bright and trusting up to Thompson's.

"Stay where you are," said old Dumsic speaking to Winnie, and looking at her for the first time. "I am your father, I will take care of you, you shan't go to prison with this fellow."

"Father, I always tried to be a good dutiful daughter to you; I loved you dearly until you endeavored to make my life miserable and forced me to an act of disobedience; I am happy now in the love of the man who loves me, and I cannot and will not leave him."

She disengaged herself from Thompson's arms and quickly put on her bonnet and cloak.

"Come, we are ready now. Can you go round by St. Urbain's Street?"[99] she asked the detective. "I have a friend there I should like to consult."

"All right, ma'am," replied the detective, "we can make it in the way."

"You'll go quietly, sir?" he inquired of Thompson.

"Certainly."

"Come along then," he said, and walked out of the room followed by Thompson and Winnie, which conduct so astonished the policeman who was a Frenchman, and had understood nothing of what had passed and who had come to assist at arresting somebody, that he seized old Dumsic by the collar and led him off in triumph.

CHAPTER III.

HOW THE TURKEY GOT EATEN

I do like to enjoy a good smoke. I don't know anything more calculated to make a man feel at peace with his washerwoman and the rest of mankind than to lie in an easy chair, with one's slippered feet duly elevated, and slowly and luxuriously inhale peace, comfort and bliss through the medium of a well-seasoned pipe, after having partaken of a good hearty supper. I always did take especial pleasure in my after-supper smoke, and on this particular Christmas Eve of which I have been writing, I derived more than my usual comfort from my

---

[99] A long street, running north-south, east of downtown Montreal and less fashionable.

favorite clay; for it was charged with primest of Latakia,[100] and I had my most particular friend and boon companion, Jack Rainforth, sitting opposite me pulling away industriously at an ancient briar, and varying his occupation occasionally by mixing a little warm brandy and water and telling funny stories.

He was a wonderful fellow, was Jack, and knew a little of everything; he was a bit of a lawyer, and a bit of a doctor, and something of an author, and had been a strolling player, and could tell lots of funny stories about "the profession" as he called it,[101] and was always full of good humor, so that it was quite a treat to have him for a companion. I always considered it a treat to have Jack with me, and thought myself particularly lucky this evening to have him all to myself so that I could enjoy him alone and not have to share him with others. Jack was just telling me a capital story about a dog which belonged to a friend of his when there was a sudden knock at the door, and before I had time to call out "come in," it opened and Thompson, and Winnie, and the detective entered.

I never was more astonished in my life, and sat stupidly staring at them with my feet still on the table, quite forgetting that I had dropped one of my slippers and that there was a great hole in the toe of my sock, until Thompson's voice roused me.

"Phil, old fellow," he said, "I have been arrested for passing counterfeit money, and am on my way to the police station, will you come with me; perhaps I shall want a friend to help me out of the scrape."

"Go with you, old boy, why of course I will," I cried, trying in my excitement to pull on my pipe under the delusion that it was a boot and burning my toe so that it made me jump. "But what do you mean? tell me all about it."

Then Thompson told us what has been related in the last chapter, and we all stood silent for a moment when he had finished, looking at each other; it was Jack who spoke first, and his words made us all start.

"Where is the cashier?" asked Jack fixing his eye on the detective.

"He was at the store half an hour ago," answered the detective looking as blank as a blank cartridge after it has been exploded.

But it wouldn't do, Jack kept his eye on him and saw that he saw that Jack saw that he saw what Jack meant.

---

[100] A type of pipe tobacco, originally produced in Latakia, Syria.
[101] "Strolling players" were members of travelling theatre groups in Elizabethan times, but in the Victorian era the term (as well as the designation of "the profession") was also associated with vaudevilles and the circus.

"You won't find him there now," said Jack. "You gave him warning by calling at the store, and by this time he is on his way to Rouse's Point.[102] You all go down to the Station and wait for me, I will just go round by the store and then join you. Come with me, Phil."

Jack and I went to the store where Thompson was employed, and found one of the other clerks at the cashier's desk.

"Where is Mr. Moyson," that was the cashier's name, I asked.

"He's been gone about half an hour, sir; he said he didn't feel well, and left me in his place for the rest of the evening."

"Did he lock the safe?" asked Jack.

"No," said the clerk, rather surprised at the question, "he counted what money he had taken and put it away, leaving me to lock up when I got through."

"Just look in the safe and see if the money is there," said Jack.

The clerk looked very much astonished, but turned to the safe, and in a minute he came back with a blanched face, and said,

"I think Mr. Moyson has taken it home with him; it isn't there."

"I think he has," replied Jack dryly. "Do you know where he lives?"

"No.——, McGill College Avenue."[103]

"Thank you," and Jack hurried out of the store. "It's just as plain as it can be," he continued, when we were on the street, "this fellow has been planting a lot of bad bills by the aid of his position, and he gave those tens to Thompson; and now, seeing that his game is up he has collared all the cash he can lay his hands on and bolted." Jack used a great deal of slang sometimes, especially when he was excited.

"Perhaps he hasn't gone yet, he might be at his boarding house packing up," said I.

"I intend going there at once," replied Jack hailing a sleigh.

We reached McGill College Avenue, and found a sleigh waiting before Moyson's boarding house.

"All safe," whispered Jack, "now for a touch of diplomacy." As he said this he walked up to the carter who was waiting for Moyson; and after a few words of conversation I saw the man put something Jack gave him into his pocket, get up in his seat and drive off. Jack then gave some instructions to our carter, and we waited for Moyson's appearance.

He did not keep us long but came running down in a great hurry, threw a carpet-bag into the sleigh and was just about jumping in when Jack caught him roughly by the shoulder and said,

---

[102] Rouses Point, New York, is a village located one mile south of the Canada-US border.

[103] A short street in downtown Montreal, running north-south between Sherbrooke and Sainte-Catherine; it was a very recent street, as the area on which it was built had been ceded to the city by McGill University in 1856.

"You're my prisoner!"

He reeled as if he had been struck a heavy blow, and his teeth fairly chattered as he stammered out,

"What do you mean?"

"All right, my tulip," said Jack—it was wonderful to see how naturally Jack played the policeman, that is, the kind of policeman one sees on the stage; "*You* know well enough what I want you for; those flash notes of the Bumptown Bank,[104] you've been shoving lately—it's all right, my beauty, tumble in;" it really was extraordinary how Jack picked up all his slang.

"Who are you, and how dare you stop me?" said Moyson gaining heart a little. "You have no warrant for my arrest."

"Who am I, eh? I am Detective Rocks of the Bumptown force," and he turned back the lappel of his vest and showed a large reporter's badge—for Jack had been a bit of a reporter amongst other things—which Moyston mistook for a detective's shield, "and as for warrants there's half a dozen out for you, here's one if you would like to see it, my buttercup," and he pulled out a large and official looking paper which he flourished before the cashier's eyes; but he never glanced at it, one look at the supposed shield was enough, and he stood perfectly stupefied with fear.

"Now then, look alive, my blooming morning glory" cried Jack pushing him into the sleigh, "we'll make you all comfortable for a few years at government expense, my full blown sunflower." Jack's facility for finding names for him was surprising.

"Wait a minute," cried Moyson as we drove off, "I'll give you"—and he whispered something in Jack's ear.

"Will you?" said Jack. "Honor bright."

"Honor bright," replied Moyson, "I've got the money in my pocket."

"All right," said Jack, "we'll have to go to the station, just for form sake, you know, but I'll get you discharged and then you can go."

"How can you get me discharged if I once am in the station?"

"Oh, the easiest thing in the world; when I see you in the light I say I find I have made a mistake in the dark and arrested the wrong man; you come the indignant dodge, threaten to have me dismissed for arresting an innocent citizen and all that sort of thing; nobody there knows you: I admit that I haven't a warrant for your arrest—you not being the man I want and off you go, don't you see!"

---

[104] "Flash notes" are counterfeit bills; "Bumptown" is Phillips's sobriquet for Montreal, a city he discusses in a series of "Bumptown Papers," signed "James Bumpus" and published in *The Hearthstone* in March-April 1872.

"Yes I see it now, all right."

"All right it is," said Jack *sotto voce*. "I'm glad you see it, for if you had resisted I don't know how I should have got you to the station; I suppose it will be all right when I do get you there, although I don't know but what I have made myself amenable to the law for burglary, or something, passing myself off as a detective and arresting a peaceable citizen; anyhow I'll chance it;" somehow Jack would use slang even when talking to himself.

It was a funny sight when we reached the station; there was the French policeman making a charge against old Dumsic for passing counterfeit money and resisting the police, for old Dumsic had resisted considerably as the damaged condition of the policeman's face showed; and there was old Dumsic tearing and swearing like a wild man, and threatening everybody with destruction if he was not instantly released. But when the Sergeant ordered old Dumsic to be searched and two counterfeit ten-dollar bills were found in his pocket, matters began to look serious, and old Dumsic would probably have been locked up if Jack and I with Moyson had not happened to arrive at the time, just as the detective entered with Thompson and Winnie.

Of course it did not take very long to explain matters to the Sergeant, and Moyson's capture threw an entirely new light on the subject of Thompson's passing the counterfeit bills; for when he was searched a large number of counterfeits were found on him, and seeing there was no chance of escape—for Jack soon undeceived him about his being a detective—he confessed that he had given the bad bills to Thompson, and also that when the junior partner had sent to him for change he had kept the good bill and substituted another.

It was quite evident that there was no ground for a charge against Thompson, but as a warrant had been issued, he had to be taken up to the house of the magistrate, who, on a representation of the case being made, accepted bail for his appearance on the day after Christmas.

Old Dumsic sat on a bench in the Police Station and abused that French policeman for a good half hour, which must have been very entertaining to the man, who did not understand a word of English; and the man fully explained how the mistake of arresting him occurred, in French, which was all a mystery to old Dumsic, who was quite ignorant of that language. At last old Dumsic got tired of that kind of conversation, and, having deposited a sufficient sum as his bail to appear and answer the charge of assault, left the station and went home; but a great change seemed to have come over him, and he appeared to be arguing something over to himself as he went along.

I suppose it is scarcely necessary to say that the Christmas dinner next day was a great success. Of course Jack was there and had a story all ready to tell about a friend of his who had got into a scrape very similar to the one Thompson had got into buying his turkey; and very handsome the turkey looked when it was brought on the table lying helplessly on its back with its legs in the air; and very merry and jolly we all prepared to be.

But the funniest thing of all happened just as Thompson had his knife raised to carve the turkey, for the door suddenly opened, without any previous warning, and in walked old Dumsic looking a little ashamed of himself I thought, but doing his best to smile pleasantly. He walked right up to Thompson and, offering his hand, said,

"Charlie, I've come to the conclusion that I have been in the wrong, and as I can't prevent your marrying Winnie now, I give my consent. Home don't feel like home at all without Winnie, and I want to have her back. Oh, you shall come too," he continued to Thompson. "I'm going to turn over a new leaf to-day and what I can't cure, I'm going to endure, and not make myself a fool about it."

Then Winnie looked at Thompson, and Thompson nodded his head, and she tripped up to her father and gave him a sounding kiss, and Thompson shook hands with him and made him sit down to dinner, and the very first cut of the turkey was given to old Dumsic.

It was quite wonderful to see how old Dumsic thawed, just as quick as an icecream pyramid when a red hot poker is applied to it; and awfully jolly he got too, and he and Jack told stories that kept everybody laughing, and old Dumsic had ordered a basket of wine in, and I am afraid Jack and he drank rather too much, for they vowed eternal friendship after all the others had left the table; and Dumsic told Jack he didn't believe he was the descendant of an Irish king at all, and that he would not be at all surprised if his name had originally been Drumstick as Thompson said, and that a very jolly old Drumstick he felt, which everybody knows Dumsic would never have done if he had been quite sober. And the fun we had after the friends who had been invited for the evening arrived, was too much for me to tell, and there was old Dumsic running about making love to all the girls, and declaring he wanted to get married again.

That was last Christmas, and I am going to dine with Thompson again this year, but he doesn't live in "queer quarters" now, but with old Dumsic, who has given him an interest in the pin-and-needle business; and there is to be something more than a Christmas party for there is to be a christening too, and the young gentleman's name is to be Phil after his godfather, and Dumsic after his grandfather, so I will finish my story by wishing long life and happiness to Philip Dumsic Thompson, Esq.

THE POLICEMAN'S CHRISTMAS.

BY ONE OF THE FORCE.

Perhaps you are one of the people who don't think a policeman ought to want to keep Christmas like other folks; maybe you belong to that class who believe that a policeman ought always to be "on his beat," and that he should never fail to be just on the very spot in that beat— no matter if it be two or three miles long, as it often is—at the very moment that a burglary is being committed, or a fire breaks out, or a child gets run over, or a fight takes place, or a drunken man slips on the sidewalk, or any other accident occurs. Possibly you think, like a great many do, that a policeman hasn't got the same feelings as other people, that, when he puts on his blue coat with brass buttons and sticks his staff in his belt he ceases to be an ordinary man and becomes "a limb of the law," something of a nondescript animal, half man, half locust club. Don't you believe anything of the kind. Long service, getting used to rough life and mixing with the lowest classes; seeing human nature at its worst, and always having to keep a bright look-out for others' failings, don't tend to elevate a man; I admit that; it isn't the sort of work that tends to improve a man's opinion of humanity; it's not the sort of thing to make a man think better of his fellow men; still, I don't believe you can ever make a policeman quite a machine like we are told a soldier can be made—though I have my doubts about that, too.

You see we have to mix too much with the people to get all the man taken out of us and leave nothing but the machine, doing its duty and knowing or caring nothing beyond. It isn't natural to suppose that we can be on the force for any length of time without making a good many acquaintances, and, perhaps, a few friends. We are for the most part pretty nearly always on the same beats; of course, we are changed about every now and then so that we may get well acquainted with the city, but we keep pretty well to one station, and get to know most of the people we meet. It isn't always that we know them to speak to, but just by sight, and many a time on a cold, raw, winter's morning, it has given me a sort of comfortable feel to meet some great gentleman I knew by sight, and to feel that the wind and the snow, and the cold didn't have any more respect for him than it did for the poor policeman who was nearly dead with the three hours' freezing he had got on his beat.

When I say, "get acquainted," I don't mean in the way you read in thrashy novels—written by people who know nothing of the force—about policemen, being always dodging down area ways to spark cooks, and arresting small boys, and never being on their beats when wanted, and running away when they hear a row; that's for the most part all stuff written by people who don't know what they are writing about. I ask you as a sensible person—I suppose you are a sensible person, tho' I may be mistaken,—did you ever see a policeman hanging about area railings making love to the cook or the house maid, either for her own sake, or for the sake of the broken victuals? Did you ever see a policeman arrest a small boy, except those nuisances who will go coasting down steep streets when there's any snow, to the great danger of their own necks and of damage to all passers-by—that sort have to be arrested once in a while just to frighten the rest a bit; but did you every know a policeman who made it a practice of arresting only small boys? I'll bet you never did, and never saw one except on the stage, or in a comic paper. And as for running away from rows—well, if you're green enough to believe that, I'm sorry for you, that's all. No, the sort of acquaintances I mean that a policeman makes is mostly the people he passes and repasses on the street and the people he has to arrest.

Were you ever arrested? Well, you needn't get mad at the question, quite as good men as you have been arrested, and it don't always prove, because a man is arrested that he has done anything wrong; but if you ever should be arrested it might, perhaps, surprise you to find yourself known by some one or more on the force, if not by name at least by sight, altho' you are a very quiet, respectable citizen, "unknown to the police," as the saying is. You might not know a single policeman by sight, but the chances are that some of them know you; why, Lor' bless me! put the police force of Montreal, small as it is, in the middle of Champ the Mars,[105] and let all the grown up men and women—and a good show of the children too—pass round them, and I'll bet my buttons, and that's a good deal for a policeman to bet, that at least a quarter of them could be recognized by some member of the force. You see it's sort of natural—at least it is to me, and I suppose it is to most of the force—to look pretty sharp about us as we go up and down our beats, and from meeting the same people frequently and forming acquaintances with the shop-keepers and such like, who are generally very glad to be acquainted with "the policeman on the beat,"—we get to know pretty nearly everybody who passes along our beat every day or so.

[105] Champ de Mars (sometimes Champ the Mars in English) is a park next to the ramparts that originally enclosed Old Montreal (completely demolished by 1817). It was still used for military parades at the time.

I remember when I first went to the Ottawa Street Station, I was quite a stranger to that part of the city, and knew very little about Griffintown[106] except that it had a bad name, and I didn't feel as if my life was quite safe there at first, but, bless you, a name is all in this world. "Give a dog a bad name and hang him,"[107] you know the old saying; Griffintown isn't really much worse than many other localities where the poor live, but it's got the name and it will stick to it. I used to keep my eye pretty well open, and I soon had to make a good many arrests for drunkenness and corner loafing. Corner loafing is the besetting sin of the youth of Griffintown. Whenever a young fellow can beg, borrow, or steal the time from himself or anybody else, he thinks it the proper thing to "hang on" at one of the corners, Kempt and Ottawa is the most fashionable corner, but Colborne, McCord and other streets get a good share of patronage.[108]

About the first man I arrested was a young fellow who went by the nickname of "Rowdy Ducks," and who had a reputation of being one of the "hardest" cases in Griffintown; his right name was Roderick Duckworth, but he was best known to the police by the *sobriquet* his misconduct had earned for him. He was drunk when I arrested him, and resisted a bit so that I had great trouble in getting him to the station; but I managed it at last, and next morning, he having been up very often of late, the Recorder sent him down for two months.

Rowdy's friends told me to "look out" for myself when he came out, as he never forgot or forgave a policeman who had once arrested him; but I soon found I had nothing to fear, and after a little we got to be quite friendly, and he used to come up to my house some nights when I was off duty to smoke a friendly pipe. He was quite a decent young fellow as long as he would leave drink alone, and quite intelligent. He was a plumber by trade, and a first-rate workman, so that he never wanted long for a job.

---

[106] Ottawa is a street in Griffintown, two blocks east of Notre-Dame Street. There was a police station there and, because of its location in a disreputable area, it was often mentioned in Montreal newspapers in the 1870s. Griffintown is a neighborhood in Montreal, immediately southwest of downtown. Since the early 1800s, it had been inhabited mostly by Irish immigrants.

[107] An old English proverb describing what is sometimes called character assassination.

[108] Kempt Street is now called Young Street; Colborne was the name of Peel Street south of Notre Dame Street; McCord became Mountain Street (rue De La Montagne). A police station (7th precinct) was soon (1875) built on Kempt Street.

He got a little steadier that summer, and was only arrested two or three times for drunkenness, but as he had money he paid his fine and was not sent down.

A couple of nights after his last arrest I was off duty, and he came up to my house, so I took the opportunity of talking to him a bit.

"Look here, Rowdy," I said,—we generally called him Rowdy,— "what is the good of your going on this way; you're a young man and a good workman, and you ought to be ashamed of yourself to go to the dogs the way you are going now; why don't you marry and settle down?"

He flushed up a little when I said this, and tried to laugh it off; but after a while he said, quite serious like:

"I've thought about it Barnes," (my name is Barnes—S. C. Barnes—S. C. stands for Samuel Charles, not Sub Constable, although I am one) "but I don't know exactly how it would do. You see the devil seems to get into me when I have a drop of drink, and I don't know what I am doing. I am half afraid to trust myself, for I should hate myself if I married Mollie and then abused her as I see some men do."

"Oh, ho!" I said, "it's gone as far as that has it; well, Roddy, my man, take a fool's advice, swear off drink, marry Mollie, and settle down for a while out of Griffintown, where you will be away from your old companions and out of the way of temptation. You ought to be too much of a man to let drink get the best of you at your age; if you don't put your foot down like a man and kill your taste for it now, you won't be able to do it in ten years time, if you live so long."

"Well, old man," he answered, "I'll think about it: I've got a good place now, and this would be about as good a time as any for me to turn over a new leaf; perhaps, I'll do it. Good night, old man."

"Good night, my boy, and stick to your good resolution."

I lost sight of Roddy for some time after that, and the winter was nearly gone when I met him again. It was one morning when I was one of the first relief, and had the Wellington Street[109] beat; perhaps, I had better explain here how the men are divided at the stations, as you may possibly understand my story better then.

Every policeman is on duty for twelve hours during one half of the month, and sixteen hours a day for the other half—how is that for work, you eight and nine hour men who grumble at what you have to do, and talk about "the lazy police?" The day men have to be at the station at six o'clock in the morning, and are then divided into two reliefs, first and second; the first relief goes on duty on the beats from six o'clock until

[109] Wellington Street is a long thoroughfare that starts in the borough of Verdun and ends in Old Montreal at McGill Street. The "beat" probably covered only the portion that is now in Old Montreal.

nine, and are then relieved, going on patrol again at twelve o'clock for three hours more; both reliefs remain on duty—either on the beats or at the station—until six o'clock in the evening. The night duty men have to report at the station at two o'clock in the afternoon—except those who make prisoners the night before and have to attend the Recorder's Court, they are generally allowed until five o'clock to report—and remain on duty until six next morning. That is pretty good time it seems to me, and the pay was only a dollar a day then—it's been raised to eight dollars a week now for old hands, and little enough it is at that I say. The night men have to report in the afternoon because they have to do odd jobs, notifying persons who have committed a breach of any of the Corporation By laws, by keeping dogs without paying the tax and such like matters. Every two weeks the day men become the night men, so that we change and change about.

I think that is enough explanation for the present, so I'll get back to my story. I was on the first relief of the day duty men, and just as I walked down Wellington Street, I saw Roddy crossing the bridge—this was before the present railway bridge was built—coming from Point St. Charles way.[110] He was looking better than I ever saw him look before, neat and tidy, and his clothes all nicely brushed, and altogether quite smartened up from what he used to be. He saw me about as quick as I saw him and came across the street, laughing and holding his hand out;

"Well, old man," he said as soon as we had shaken hands, "I've taken your advice. I've got as nice a little girl as you could find in a day's travel, for a wife, and I'm living out at the Point and keeping steady."

"That's right, Duckworth," I said—somehow I didn't like to call him "Rowdy" now he was so much changed for the better, "nobody congratulates you more heartily than I do; stick to your new way of life, and who knows but what you may be Mayor of Montreal one of these days."

"I'm not such a fool as to expect that," replied he, "but I hope in a couple of years to start a shop of my own and begin business on my own hook. I've got to look ahead now a little more than I used to, you know."

It was astonishing how paternal he looked at that moment, anybody might have thought he was the father of a large family.

[110] A long portion of Wellington Street runs parallel to the Lachine Canal (completed in 1824 and passing through the southwestern part of the Island of Montreal), then veers northeast across the canal and this portion is known as the Wellington Bridge. There is still a footbridge connecting Griffintown to Point St. Charles, south of the Lachine Canal. Griffintown and the eastern part of Point St. Charles were both inhabited mostly by Irish immigrants and were both part of St. Ann's Ward.

"Well," I said, laughing, "you are counting your chickens before they are hatched, but there is nothing like looking ahead. And who is the wife, the one you spoke to me about?"

"Yes. I'd like you to see her, Barnes."

"Well, just you bring her up next Sunday evening; I shall be off duty at six, and my old woman will be glad to know her."

"That I will, and thank you, too," he said, and walked off to his business.

You see we poor people can't afford to stand on ceremony like rich folks; there's no need of calling cards, and previous introductions, and formal invitation with us; if we want a man to come and see us we ask him right off, and if he wants to come, he comes; and if he don't want to come he stays away, that's all.

Roddy came on the Sunday night, and brought his wife. She was a very pretty girl, was Mollie Duckworth, almost too pretty I thought, and seemed very fond of Roddy; but somehow, I can't say, I took a fancy to her, and my old woman didn't like her at all.

"She's a wild, flirting thing, that cares for nothing but dress and nonsense," said my old woman after they were gone, "and is no fit wife for a working man like Rowdy. Mark my words," she continued, "he'll be sorry for it before a year is out;" having delivered which opinion she marched off to bed.

I used to see Rowdy pretty often that summer going to work in the morning, and two or three times he came to see us, and one Sunday my old woman and I took tea with him at his house. He had been married near a year then and was still living out at the Point, but talked of coming up to the city in the winter, as he said he was too far from his business. His wife seemed anxious for him to come into town too, declaring she was "moped to death" out there, and although I tried to persuade him not to come back to the old place, I could see he had made up his mind, and I felt pretty sure it would not be long before he was in Griffintown again and, perhaps, up to his old games.

They did not seem to get along well together; he was very fond of her but she appeared careless about him, and rather free for a married woman; still I thought that would wear off, the more so as there was a prospect of there being a little Roddy before very long. We did not spend a very pleasant evening, and my old woman would not go again although they asked us.

Early in the fall they left the Point and came to live in Barré Street,[111] where they had half of a small brick house, and Mollie

[111] Rue Barré, in Griffintown, runs parallel to Notre-Dame Street.

kept house after a fashion; but most of her time was spent gadding about St. Joseph Street and around that portion of the city, instead of minding her duties at home, and I could see that Roddy was not very comfortable with his wife. Still he kept steady for a while and did not go with his old companions; but it did not last long. The baby was born early in November and died in a few days, and after that Mollie was out more than ever, and neglected the house so that Roddy was never quite certain that he would get anything for supper when he came home after work.

This soon brought about the result I expected; finding he could get no comfort at home, Roddy fell back into his old habits, and one night I found him loitering, half drunk, at the corner of Kempt and Ottawa Streets. I did not take him in charge but walked home with him part of the way, giving him a bit of advice.

"I can't help it, Barnes," he said, "Mollie is driving me to it with her careless ways. I never get any peace or comfort in the house, and to-night she never came home to get supper; so I went off with the boys a bit and had a few drinks. I haven't been drinking lately you know, and a little got the best of me. Barnes, old fellow," he went on after a minute, "I wish I never had married; I don't think Mollie cares much about me, and perhaps never did, although I have been a good kind husband to her. She likes any place better than her home, and sometimes I think"—he didn't finish what he thought, but I could hear his teeth grind together in a way that made my flesh creep all over and a little cold shiver run right through me. I never did like to hear people grind their teeth, but I never heard any teeth get such a grinding as Roddy gave his that night.

"Never mind, old fellow," I said, trying to cheer him up a bit, "she's young yet, and when the kids begin to come she will settle down at home never fear. Are you all right now," I asked as we reached his door, "if so, I'll leave you. Go to bed, Roddy, and don't come out again to-night, or you might get into trouble."

"I'm all right, old man," he said as he opened the door. "Good night."

He went in as he spoke, leaving the door partly open, and I could see Mollie sitting by the table reading something which she hastily put in her pocket as she heard Roddy's step in the room. "This is a nice time for you to come home, and a pretty condition you are in," she said, turning on him sharply.

"Where have you been all the afternoon?" he retorted angrily. "Why didn't you come home to get supper?"

I didn't catch any more, but I could hear their voices raised as I walked away, and I knew they were having a row.

After that, Roddy "went to the dogs," as the saying is, faster than ever. He soon was out of work, and spent most of his time loafing at street corners or drinking in the saloons. I saw him drunk several times, but he kept away from me, and as he behaved himself quietly and did not make a row I didn't arrest him, and he managed to keep out of the station house. I knew he and Mollie were getting on worse than ever together, for I heard some of his companions talking about it; but Roddy evidently did not want to speak to me of it, and avoided me as much as possible.

It was two nights before Christmas, and I was resting myself a bit in the station, and thinking whether the old woman would have a turkey or a goose for Christmas dinner, when a boy came running in and said, the police were wanted down in Barré Street, that a man killed his wife there.

It was almost eleven o'clock, and I was pretty well tired out, having been on duty since two o'clock trying to catch some boys who would insist on coasting down Mountain Street, at the imminent risk of their own necks and other people's limbs; and I had also been three hours on patrol, but I jumped up quite fresh and lively the moment the boy spoke, for it flashed across me in a minute that the man was Roddy, so I pulled on my coat and taking another man with me started for Barré Street.

The street was all in a bustle when I got there, and quite a crowd had collected in front of Roddy's, from whence sounds of swearing and a smashing like furniture being broken, and a woman's cries and sobs proceeded.

I pushed my way through the crowd into the house and found everything in confusion. Roddy was standing in the middle of the room with the fragment of a chair in his hand which he had been smashing to pieces, his face was terribly flushed, his eyes flashing, and his whole manner showed that he was laboring under great excitement besides being very drunk; Mollie was in one corner with her hands pressed to her head, sobbing and shrieking out, "Murder," every now and then; the furniture was all knocked about, and looked as if there had been a scuffle in the room. The moment Mollie saw me she ran to me and shouted out: "Save me, Mr. Barnes, he tried to kill me!"

"And I will too," growled Roddy savagely, "You won't carry on your games much longer at my expense, my girl," and he took a step towards her with the piece of broken chair raised above his head, but stopped ashamed like when he saw me.

"It's all right, old man," he said, trying to laugh. "I was only making fun, I wouldn't hurt her."

"He struck me," cried Mollie, "see here," and she took her hand from her face and showed me a great red mark on one side which looked as if she had been struck with an open hand. "He struck me twice and swore he's kill me, and I want him arrested. I'm afraid to trust myself with him. Take him away and lock him up."

"I only gave her a slap, Barnes," said Roddy. "I'm a little drunk and she made me mad; it's all right now, I won't touch her again."

He spoke quite rationally although he was drunk, and his passion was all gone, so I talked the matter over a little with him and quieted him down before I took him to the station, for I could not help arresting him as Mollie continued to make her charge against him. He went very quietly; but I could see how he felt being arrested again after keeping out of the station so long.[112]

It was near twelve o'clock when I got back to the station, and time for me to go on my beat, so Roddy was kept a few minutes until the second relief came in, when some of the men were to take him up to the Chaboillez Square[113] station where all prisoners from Ottawa Street had to be taken in those days, as there were no cells in Ottawa Street.

"Don't swear too hard against me to-morrow morning, old man," said Roddy as I went out. "I didn't mean to hurt the girl, and it is the first time I ever struck her."

When I came off my beat at three o'clock, I heard that the men who were taking Roddy up to Chaboillez Square, had been set upon by a lot of Roddy's friends at the corner of Colborne and William Streets,[114] and a rescue effected; Grigson, one of the officers, had got a bad cut over the eye with a stick, and the other man had been pretty roughly handled. A squad of men had been down to Roddy's house looking for him, but he had not been there. I was sorry Roddy had been rescued, for I knew he would soon be caught again and it would go harder with him then.

Next morning I had to go up to the Recorder's Court about the boys I had been chasing the day before, three of whom we had caught. I was a bit late, for I had overslept myself, and was hurrying along William Street when just about Colborne a gentleman stopped me and asked me a question. It was a bitter cold morning and the wind was blowing right through me, so that I didn't hear him at first. It's no use telling me that

[112] We have added the word "how," which seemed to be missing in this sentence.
[113] Chaboillez Square is today a small park in downtown Montreal, on the edge of Griffintown.
[114] William Street is in Griffintown, north of Ottawa Street, and the intersection with Colborne (today Peel) is one block from Ottawa on the way to Chaboillez Square.

the wind never blows *through* a man but round him, I know better; I've felt it many a time come in at the third button-hole of my coat, just about the pit of my stomach, bore a straight hole clean through me, and go out at the small of my back. It has happened to me frequently, so I ought to know; any way, this morning the wind had stopped up my ears and I had to ask the gentleman to repeat his question. "Can you tell me the way to Barré Street, if you please?"

I gave him the direction, and wondered a bit what a swell like him could want in Barré Street. He was a very fancy sort of a fellow with a handsome seal skin coat, cap and gloves on, and very new pants, I could tell they were very new for the basting thread had not been pulled out on one side, and they didn't bulge out at the knees like old pants do. He was a good looking chap too, with bushy black hair and a big moustache, but there was a wicked look about the eyes I didn't like; however, I had not much time to waste, for it was nearly ten, and I hurried off to the court.

The Recorder was on the bench when I got in and the first case had been called; it was a simple drunk, and soon disposed off, then the Recorder astonished me by calling out "Roderick Duckworth!"

I was thoroughly surprised for I did not know he had been re-arrested, and I hastily arose to go into the box, thinking it was my case.

"Why, it's Rowdy!" exclaimed His Honor, a smile of recognition playing over his good humored countenance as the prisoner stepped into the dock, "so you've come back again Rowdy, eh?"

"My name isn't Rowdy," said Roddy sulkily.

"The more reason for you to be ashamed that your misconduct has gained such a *sobriquet* for you," returned His Honor, taking him up quite sharp. "What is the charge?"

The officers who arrested him stated that he had been found in St. Charles Borromée Street[115] about three o'clock in the morning very drunk, and taken to the Central Station, where it was discovered that he had been arrested in Griffintown and subsequently rescued.

"What was he arrested for, the first time?" asked His Honor.

"He was drunk in his own house, Your Honor," replied the Sergeant, "and beat his wife."

"Oh," said His Honor, looking crossly at Roddy, "you have added that to your other accomplishments, have you. Well, go on with the case; has the woman made a charge against him?"

There was a pause for an instant and I saw Roddy look up and throw an anxious, inquiring glance around the Court to see if Mollie

---

[115] Saint-Charles-Borromée Street is now called Clark.

was there. Not finding her his face cleared, but it clouded over again in an instant as he saw the Clerk of the Court enter with a sheet of paper in his hand, closely followed by Mollie who had a handkerchief ostentatiously tied across her face covering her left eye.

His Honor read the deposition and putting on his sternest look, said, "Duckworth, you are charged with committing a violent assault on your wife, by striking her with your fist in the face inflicting a severe wound. There is no class of men," continued His Honor, settling himself down for a little lecture, "whom I more cordially abhor than the mean, cowardly wretches who raise their hands against weak, defenseless women; there is nothing more cowardly, nothing more ruffianly than the wife-beater, and I often regret that the law does not allow me to condemn them to a number of lashes with the cat-o'-nine-tails, so that they may feel some of that corporal suffering they are so fond of inflicting upon others. You have long been known to this Court as a drunken loafer, and now you have added another crime to the long list already against you, one too, of the worst crimes a man can be guilty of. Here is a young, delicate woman—scarcely more than a girl—whom you have sworn before God's holy altar to cherish and protect, and I find you using brutal violence towards her, such as no man with any feeling would use to a dog. I warn you, sir, that the Court will not be disposed to be any too lenient to you, and unless you amend your way of living, your course will lead you down to—to—perdition," concluded His Honor, rather bothered for a moment for a word; but getting it, started off again. "Yes, to perdition, and, perhaps, will lead you to the gallows, for in a moment of drunken delirium, when your unbridled passions are allowed full sway, you may strike the blow which will place you in the murderer's cell." Having thus comfortably disposed of Roddy, His Honor asked for the evidence and ordered Mollie to be sworn.

"Your Honor," said Roddy, earnestly, "I never raised my hand against her before, and she drove me to it with her flirting ways. I haven't been here for eighteen months, and I would never have come here again but for her."

"That will do, that will do; you will have an opportunity to say what you have to say by and by. Go on with the evidence."

Mollie took her place in the witness-box, and after darting a vindictive glance at Roddy gave her evidence. It was dead against Roddy, and showed him as a regular ruffian who continually illused her,[116] and

---

[116] "Ill used" or "ill-used." The verb was sometimes spelled as one word at the time.

who had walked into the house and without a word of provocation felled her to the ground, giving her, as she expressed it, "an awful cut" on the forehead.

"Poor thing," said His Honor, very compassionately, "it is a mercy he did not kill you in his brutality. Take off the bandage, if you can, and let me see the wound."

"I only struck her with the back of my hand, Your Honor," put in Roddy, "it would not have killed a fly."

"Hold your tongue, sir; you have no legal right to strike her at all. Let me see the injury."

Mollie coquetted a good deal about taking off the handkerchief and began to cry, and said it hurt her too much and a lot more stuff, so His Honor kindly told her not to mind, and Mollie brightened up in a moment and shot a glance of triumph at Roddy; but I wasn't going to see him beaten that way, so I just slipped my thumb under the knot of the handkerchief, gave a pull and brought it away, very nearly pulling off her bonnet in the operation.

His Honor looked for a moment as if he was going to read me a lecture for my officiousness, but his attention was distracted by a suppressed cry from Mollie and he turned to her, so I escaped.

She had flushed up as red as a beet, and looked at me as if she would like to bite me, but I didn't mind that; I was watching His Honor who was looking at her face.

There was not a mark or a scratch on it.

His Honor gazed at her steadily for a moment and a sterner look came over his face. He has a keen sense of humor has His Honor, and I have often seen him laugh at his own jokes; but he has also a keen sense of justice, and an honest, kindly heart beats beneath his judicial waistcoat. Mollie saw that she had gone too far and stammered out:

"He didn't cut me, Your Honor, he stunned me and it hurt awfully."

"Is that the only *mark* you have got?"

Mollie nodded assent, and His Honor continued, "it doesn't seem to be a very dangerous wound; let me hear what the policeman has to say."

My evidence was soon given as well as that of the officer who accompanied me. His Honor paused for a moment, and then asked the Sergeant on duty how long it was since Roddy had been before him.

The Sergeant referred to the book and said it was eighteen months, and I took the chance to put in a good word for him.

"Duckworth," said His Honor, "I find that the charge against you does not seem to be so grave as it appeared at first; your wife's statement is rather vague, and seems to be dictated to some extent by spite, and is not borne out by the policeman's statement. I am glad to hear you have been more steady of late, and hope you will let this be a warning to you not to fall back into your old evil courses. It is really a pity that you and your wife cannot get on more comfortably together, you are both young and should try to live happily together. I shall give you a chance this time; but, mind, if you are brought before me again for the same offense I shall send you down for two months. Five dollars or one month."

Roddy made a sign to me as he left the dock, and I went down stairs to him.

"Get the money from Mollie and pay the fine for me, Barnes," he said, "don't let me be sent down. I have the money at home."

I went to Mollie and asked her to pay the fine; but she tossed her head at me and said, "It would serve him right, if I let him rot in jail, the brute."

I didn't have time to go back to Roddy then, as I had a good many things to look after, and I had promised my old woman to buy the goose—we had decided to have goose—for Christmas dinner, and I had to go on duty again at five o'clock, so Roddy slipped my memory, and I did not think of him again until next morning, when I thought I would go round to his house and wish him a happy Christmas. The house was all shut up and deserted, and one of the neighbors told me Roddy had not been home all night nor the day before either. I tried to rouse Mollie but could not make her hear. As I had nothing very particular to do for an hour or so, I thought I would go to the Central Station and see if Roddy's fine had been paid, or if he had been sent down.

Just as I expected, I found that Mollie had not been near Roddy, and that he had been sent down. Now, I suppose I am rather a foolish policeman, very likely I don't look at things in the way some people might think a right-minded policeman ought to view them, but I told you at the beginning of this story that I was not a machine and never would be, and it did seem to me pretty hard that poor Roddy should spend his Christmas in jail, so I just went home, got five dollars off the old woman—she is the cashier of our firm—went down to the jail and paid Roddy's fine.

"Thank you, kindly, old man," he said. "It was good of you to think of me and not let me spend Christmas in prison; Mollie might have paid the fine, there is more than fifty dollars in the house and she knows it. I'll be round after dinner, old man, and give you the money."

I am partial to goose. I don't know whether it is quite compatible with the dignity of a policeman to make such a confession, but I do like "the bird of folly," and am not ashamed to own it.[117] I have a kind feeling for a goose too, and I think it a gross libel to call it the bird of folly; didn't a flock of geese save Rome, and Romulus and Remus,[118] and Julius Caesar, and Nero, and Rienzi,[119] and all the other noble old Romans? Of course they did, or my Roman History tells a great big— no such thing. And if the geese hadn't saved Rome we couldn't have any Roman candles, or maccaroni, or Coliseum, or old Roman coins— made in Birmingham[120]—now a days, could we? Of course not, so I don't think it fair to abuse the goose; I admire and respect the goose, especially when it is roasted with sage and onions and served up hot with nice rich gravy.

It was a model goose we had for our Christmas dinner, it weighed twelve pounds after it was cleaned and was as plump and fat as a partridge, and my old woman had done it to a turn.[121] I like goose better than turkey, it is so much more filling and has more flavor in one drumstick than a turkey has in its whole body; besides there is a richness about it no turkey can ever have. I stood and looked fondly at that goose, and I felt a little sympathy for him—I suppose a policeman can feel sympathy for a goose without breaking the rules—as I though how suddenly he had been cut off in the prime of his youth and goosehood; and I stood with a knife suspended over him for a moment, while the old woman and the children waited in longing expectation.

But I was not destined to carve that goose. Just as the knife was descending there came a sudden knock at the door, and before I could get to it it was opened, and Roddy burst into the room looking so wild and strange that I involuntarily dropped the knife and fork and exclaimed,

---

[117] Allusion to the old saying "silly as a goose."

[118] The famous story about the geese who warned the Romans that their city was being attacked by the Gauls dates from 390 BC (or a few years later). This means that the geese "saved" Rome and its future (including Julius Caesar and Nero), but not Romulus and Remus, who are the legendary founders of the city in 753 BC.

[119] Rienzi (misspelled in the original as "Reinzi") is the character of a novel (1835) by Bulwer-Lytton and of an opera (1842) by Wagner. However, the protagonist is a 14th-century Italian from the city of Rome, rather than an "old Roman." It is true, however, that the full title of the novel is Rienzi, The Last of the Roman Tribunes.

[120] The fireworks known as "Roman candles" were not invented by the Romans (they were named after an alleged method of torture preferred by Nero). Fake antiquities ("made in Birmingham") were a common object of derision in the British press at the time.

[121] Cooked perfectly (an idiom more common in the 19th century, originating in the practice of roasting on a spit).

"For the Lord's sake, Roddy, what is the matter."

"They've gone," he gasped out. "Gone; come with me, Barnes, come with me and follow them."

"Who has gone?" I asked, "where do you want to go to?"

"Stop and take your dinner first, Roddy, whatever it might be," said my old woman, "I'm sure the goose is beautiful and you look most clammed."

"Mollie," said Roddy, not noticing my old woman's interruption, "Mollie has run away from me, and gone off with some fellow, taking everything they could lay their hands on. Come with me, old man, I must catch *him*."

I didn't like the way he emphasized that word "him," and the look on his face made me afraid to let him go alone. Still I did not like to leave the goose, and to gain time as much as anything else, I said:

"Tell us all about it, Roddy, what has happened?"

He stood silent for a moment as if to collect himself, and then said: "When you left me, Barnes, I went home expecting to find Mollie; she was not at home, as usual, and I began to get things ready for dinner. In moving about the room I noticed that a good many things were gone, and everything seemed to have been tumbled about; I thought somebody had robbed the house while I was away—God knows I did not suspect Mollie then; I knew she was wild and careless, but I didn't think then she was as bad as I know now she is. Then I thought of the money; it was put between two bricks under the stove, and nobody knew where it was but Mollie and myself; the bricks were moved and the money gone. Barnes, old fellow, it came on me like a clap of thunder; she had run away from me!" Poor fellow, he stopped for a minute, and I could see big tears trying to come into his eyes, but sticking in his throat; he gulped them down and went on. "I asked some of the neighbours, and they told me she had gone away about an hour before in a sleigh with a swell-looking fellow in a fur coat and a big black moustache." Roddy was too much excited to be particular in his description, and did not stop to mention the other things the man must have been in. "One of the boys heard the man saying they would be in St. Johns[122] in time for dinner, and then they drove away. Come with me, Barnes, I have a light cutter[123] here and a good horse, we can catch them before they get to St. Albans."[124]

[122] St Johns was the English name of Saint-Jean-sur-Richelieu, a municipality in Quebec, 25 miles (40 km) south of Montreal, on the road to Vermont.
[123] A small, light sleigh, drawn by one horse.
[124] St Albans is a city in northern Vermont, USA.

I took another look at the goose. I like Roddy, and I was willing to do anything I could for him, but I was hungry and the goose looked very tempting. Policemen like good things as well as other people, and I doubt that I should have given up the goose for Roddy's sake if it hadn't been for my old woman.

"Samuel," she said, "you had better go with Roddy." Roddy was a favourite with my old woman, altho' Mollie wasn't. "You may be wanted to arrest that thief and bring him back, for mark my words, he's no gentleman, but some loafer who has stolen some good clothes and run away with Mollie for what little money she could get. Take your dinner with you," she continued as she saw me look again at the goose, "and you and Roddy can eat it on the way," and before I could say a word she had seized the knife, cut both legs off the goose, folded them up in paper with several slices of bread, some butter, a screw of salt,[125] a couple of knives, and stood with my coat all ready for me to put it on.

Of course I went; somehow I generally do what my old woman wants me to, and the last thing I heard as we drove away was my old woman calling out,

"Be sure you bring back the knives."

It was a long cold drive, and we talked very little on the way. We stopped for a minute at St. Lambert's and took our dinner just as we left there, but the goose did not taste nearly as good as I expected, and as for Roddy he scarcely tasted a morsel, but kept lashing at the horse in a vicious kind of way, altho' there was really no occasion to touch him, for he was a good one to go and warmed up to his work first rate.

We heard of them at St. Johns. They had dined there and left about half an hour ahead of us. We made an effort to counterbalance that disadvantage by getting a fresh horse, as we found out they had not changed theirs.

Just as we were getting into the sleigh I made a discovery. Roddy's coat swung open for a moment as the wind caught it, and something hard struck my hand. I recognized the touch in an instant.

It was a pistol.

Then I remembered the queer way Roddy had said "I must catch him," and I gave myself a kind of a shake up as I said to myself: "Now look here, Mr. S. C. Barnes, Sub Constable, just attend to what you are about; if this here man shoots that there man it won't be pleasant for you; if you must go running after men who run away with other men's wives on Christmas Day, instead of staying at home and eating your

---

[125] A "screw" was a bit of greaseproof paper with the top twisted to stop the salt from escaping.

hot goose like a sensible policeman, you must not let anybody get shot; for if you do some of those bothersome newspapers will get hold of it and give you a hauling over the coals about it, and you will find yourself in trouble. So look sharp and get hold of that pistol or look out for squalls."[126]

It did not take me long to make up my mind what to do.

I asked Roddy to have a smoke and pulled out a meerschaum,[127] but in dragging out my coat tail to get at my tobacco pouch I pulled Roddy's coat a little away from his body, and quicker than I ever thought I could have done it, I whipped the pistol out of his pocket and put my pipe case in it. He drew his coat up pretty quick and touched his side with his elbow, but the pipe case felt all right, and he didn't suspect anything.

If I had been asked two minutes before if I could pick a pocket I should have laughed at the idea; but after I had done it I could not help thinking either that pocket picking was a good deal easier than is generally supposed, or that a first-class pickpocket was spoiled when I became a policeman.

We had not got more than about three miles out of St. Johns when we sighted a sleigh just going round a little bend in the road about a hundred yards ahead of us, with three people in it; the driver and a man and woman sitting pretty close together on the back seat.

Roddy gave a start as he saw the sleigh, for he recognized Mollie; and I took that opportunity—the first I had—to give the pistol a push off the seat on to the bottom of the sleigh.

Now I never was partial to pistols; and I have always specially objected to those self-cocking, self-firing off things called revolvers. A good old-fashioned horse-pistol[128] that measures about half a yard or so in length, takes a young steam engine to cock it, and a good strong kick by a full-grown bull to fire it off, I don't so much mind; that gives a man time and warning, so that there is a good square chance to dodge; but these revolving things always go off when they are not expected to, and nothing can persuade them to go off when wanted, if they don't happen to have a mind to.

Now, nobody wanted that pistol of Roddy's to go off when I touched, but off it went. Whether I pulled the trigger without knowing it, or whether it fell on the caps, or whether Roddy or I stepped on it

---

[126] "Look out for squalls" means "be ready for trouble."

[127] A pipe made from "meerschaum" (a soft white clay mineral), popular especially in the first half of the 19th century.

[128] A large pistol (also known as "pistoleer") usually carried by cavalry troops.

and set it off there is no means of knowing now. All I do know is that
two barrels of it *did* go off the minute I pushed it from the seat, and in
another second our old horse had his tail up, the bit in his teeth and was
tearing down that road at a pace that would have astonished Dexter;[129]
while Roddy gave a jump that nearly threw him out of the sleigh, and
let a howl out of him loud enough to scare a whole churchyard. That
miserable revolving machine had sent one ball through the dashboard,
taking about four inches of skin and a handful of hair off the old horse's
tail; and driven the other ball through the calf of Roddy's left leg. Then
I made a grab at the reins, which Roddy had dropped, and moved my
right foot in so doing, and the machine shot off again; but whether it
did any damage or not I never found out, for by that time our horse
had caught up with the sleigh ahead of us and tried to take the shortest
cut out of reach of the shooting machine behind him by going over the
sleigh, occupants and all.

The driver had heard our little bombardment and saw us coming;
he tried all he could to give us room to pass and pulled well over into the
snow bank on the left, but it was no use; the road was too narrow, and
our horse, having nobody to guide him, did just what seemed best to
his misguided fancy, and the last discharge of that miserable revolving
machine had scarcely reverberated in his startled ears before we collided
with the sleigh in front of us.

We struck about midships, as the sailors would say—at least I
should judge so from the fact that our sleigh broke very nearly in half,
and the old horse ran away with the front part while the back part was
left with Roddy and I—but I could not be very certain of anything
more than that we did strike; and that inside of half a second afterwards
five feet nine and half inches of policeman was describing a parabola
through the air, and that just before he disappeared head first beneath
the snow, he had a sort of vague and indistinct vision of a large flock
of petticoats, buffalo robes, men's legs, splinters of sleighs, pieces of
harness and other things, too numerous to mention, flying about in all
directions; while the entire British Army, Volunteers and all, seemed to
be firing a fusillade of joy at the event, such a tremendous noise did that
miserable revolving machine make in letting off its last two shots.

How long it took me to get my head out of the snow, I can't tell; it
felt like an hour, but I don't think it could have been over a minute, for
the snow was soft, and although I went in far I came out easy. When
I got up and looked around the first thing I saw as the tail of our old
horse sticking up like a sign post, while he was tearing down the road

---

[129] Dexter (1858-1888) was at the time a famous American horse, who
dominated harness racing from 1864 to 1868.

like mad with the fragment of the sleigh behind him, and the other horse and sleigh, with two people in it, close after him. Then I looked to the left and saw a pair of legs trying to kick themselves out of the snow, so I got hold of one of them and gave it a good strong pull and brought out a smooth-faced, red-headed man, I did not recognize, and as he sat down to recover himself I looked around for Roddy.

He had fallen under what portion of the sleigh was left us, and was partially stunned by a blow from some piece of the broken sleigh, and that added to the loss of blood from the wound in his leg had made him quite faint, so that it took some little time before I could bandage up his leg with my handkerchief and recover him a bit. He soon came to himself, and as quick as he recovered his senses he asked,

"Where is Mollie?"

I turned and pointed down the road when we could still see the race between our old horse and the other horse and sleigh, ours still having the best of it, and said,

"Gone."

He first looked at me for a second, and then with a great cry he jumped past me, and the next thing I saw was two men rolling over together in the snow, tearing and fighting, and a black curly wig and big black moustache lying in the road.

Of course I got at them at once and tried to separate them, but I should have had a poor chance if the bandage hadn't slipped off Roddy's leg, and it began to bleed again, so that he turned faint and loosed his hold; then I got out a pair of handcuffs I had in my pocket and slipped them on the other man. Why I did it, I couldn't have told, except that I was fighting one to two, but I was glad of it afterwards. When he found himself fast he just gave me a good hearty curse or two, and then sat down on the broken sleigh in a sullen manner and didn't say a word more.

It took me some time to quiet Roddy, and I don't know how I could ever have got them both into St. Johns if a farmer hadn't happened to drive up just then, and I got him to help me and let me use his sleigh.

We managed to hire a sleigh in St. Johns, and after making arrangements for having the horse and the remnants of the cutter sent after us, if our old horse ever allowed himself to be caught, we started for Montreal.

Before leaving, I searched my red-headed friend, who proved, when he had his black wig and moustache one, to be the same man who had spoken to me on William Street the morning before, and found Roddy's watch and fifty-five dollars in money on him, part of which Roddy identified, so I was all safe in taking him back.

It was near midnight when we got to Montreal, and I had my man lodged in the Chaboillez Square Police Station, and then I took Roddy home with me, and my old woman fixed us up a bit of hot supper, and I took a drop of something warm, for I had to go to the Ottawa Station and report for duty as soon as possible; but Roddy wouldn't touch a drop of anything although he must have been pretty cold.

"I've had my last drink, old man," he said, "today's business has sobered me for life. Perhaps Mollie would have proved a better wife to me by and by if I had kept straight, and not taken to drink again. Poor girl, I must go to St. Albans after her to-morrow, Barnes. I can't let her go to the bd this way without making one effort to save her. She can't be all bad yet, and I haven't behaved any too well to her lately. I must see her again."

Poor fellow, he pushed away the plate of hot giblets and other remnants of the goose which my old woman had put before him, without having more than tasted it, and sat with his head on his hands quite sorrowful. Somehow the goose seemed to stick in my throat, and I felt very much like I was going to cry, which would have been very undignified in a policeman, when my old woman cut in with,

"Samuel, you did not bring back the knives. I knew you wouldn't."

It was a fact, and worse than that I had lost my pipe, an old pet meerschaum which had been a good friend to me for years; the case was all safe in Roddy's pocket, but my good old pipe was gone. So was Roddy's shooting machine, but I did not care about that, and felt rather glad than otherwise that it was at a safe distance where it couldn't go off without warning and shoot somebody.

Next morning I was at the Central Station early to make my deposition, and there I made an agreeable discovery. I discovered that I had made a great capture; that my red headed friend was no less a personage than Mr. William Sinclair, alias Dick Smith, alias Augustus Hamilton, against whom three or four warrants had been issued in Toronto and Hamilton, and for whose arrest a reward of $1,000 was offered. It appeared that Sinclair had been clerk in a large business house in Hamilton, and had robbed his employers of several thousand dollars, but had managed it so cleverly that it was some time after he left before it was discovered. Meanwhile he had gone to Toronto, where he passed under the name of Dick Smith, and there forged two cheques for about fifteen hundred dollars on the National Sand Bank of that city; having accomplished which he had run off with the wife of one of the Bank clerks, and had been tracked to the States, where all trace of him was lost, and he was supposed to have gone to California. This was about a year before I saw him; our detectives here had been on the look out for him at the time, and had his description, photograph, &c., but the scent had grown pretty cold, and when Mr. Augustus Hamilton appeared in Montreal as a gentleman "just out from the old country," he was not suspected. What he wanted in Montreal, or whether he had committed any robbery here never transpired, as no charge was made against him, Roddy refusing to prosecute when he found there were already so many more serious crimes for him to answer for. He was transferred to Toronto, where he was tried and condemned to grace the Penitentiary for seven years, and he is still there, his close cropped red head being much admired, and being quite an ornament to the place.

Roddy went to St. Albans as soon as his leg was better, but could not find Mollie, who had gone on to New York. He followed her there, and found her so much worse than he expected that he left her to follow her evil courses and went to California, where he remained for a couple of years.

Two Christmasses came and went, and I made my dinner off that noble bird the goose in peace and comfort, without interruption; and the third one was well on its way to us when one fine night, just as my old woman and I and a large number of small Barneses were siting down to supper, in walked Roddy looking so bronzed and stout that for a moment I hardly knew him.

He told us all his adventures, which were very interesting to us, but would most likely bore you as they were principally an account of hard work, so I shall not repeat them. Enough to say that he had tried gold mining a while, found it didn't pay, and had finally settled down to his old trade in San Francisco, where he could make from four to six dollars a day. But he did not like the place, and had just returned to Montreal, bringing a couple of thousand dollars with him, with the intention of setting up in business for himself.

All the time he was talking I could see that my old woman was itching to ask him a question, I knew what, for there was one name he had never mentioned, and at last she could keep back no longer but blurted it right out:

"Roddy, what has become of Mollie?"

He grew very pale for an instant, but said quite softly and reverently, "Dead. She died six months ago in a brothel in St. Louis. Poor girl, may God be merciful to her for her sin, and forgive me my share in making her what she turned out to be, a drunkard and a prostitute. Yes, old man, a good deal of it was my fault. I ought to have been kinder to her, and checked her flirting ways gently, instead of getting into mad fits of jealousy as I used to. Oh, you never knew half of the quarrels we had, although, thank God, I never struck her but once. Yes, old man, I was some to blame, I was not steady enough to marry such a young girl; she was pretty and fond of admiration, and it was only natural when I made a beast of myself by getting drunk and abusing her, that she should turn to some one else. Poor girl, let us leave her memory in peace, I can't bear to talk much about her."

We didn't say another word, but my old woman got up and went to the cupboard, and very soon came back with something in a glass which smoked and smelled very refreshing, which she put by his side and said,

"Take a drop of something hot, Roddy, it will warm your stomach and cheer you up a bit."

Somehow my old woman has a motion that there is no remedy in the world for any complaint, whether mental or physical, like "a drop of something warm;" and I think if I was taken home some night with my neck broken or my brains knocked out my old woman would administer, "a drop of something warm to cheer me up a bit;" but Roddy pushed the glass from him and said gently, but firmly,

"Thank you kindly, Mrs. Barnes, but since the last night I was in your house, I have not tasted a drop of strong liquor, and with God's help, I never will again. I don't say anything against a man taking a glass if he can control himself, but I can't; if I drink at all I must drink too much, and then I am more like a devil than a man, so the only safe plan for me is to swear off altogether and I have done it. Drink and jealousy together nearly made me commit one murder—you know, old man— and I can't but feel that is partly responsible for Mollie's death. No, I have taken the pledge, and I mean to keep it."

And he has to this day.

You need not ask for Sub-Constable Barnes in the force after New Year's, for I have sent in my resignation; but if you want any plumbing or glazing done just look for the firm of Duckworth & Barnes in the directory and give us a call; and we'll plumb you and glaze you as reasonable as any people in the business. And if you are anywhere in my neighborhood on Christmas Day stay where you are and don't come bothering me for I want to eat my goose in peace, and I don't know but what you may want to run away with my old woman, and then I should have another chase after a runaway couple on Christmas Day. So stay at home like a good fellow, eat your own goose and I'll wish you a good appetite to enjoy it with, and a Merry Christmas and a Happy New Year after.

OUT OF THE GUTTER

CHAPTER I. RUN OVER.

It certainly was not a pleasant Christmas. Even the most joyful observer of that cheerful time could not derive any comfort or encouragement from the dull, leaden, overcast sky; the dripping clouds and the slight flurries of snow which melted to slush as it touched the filthy streets, ankle deep in mud and filth and running streams of dirty water. The trees sighed mournfully and tossed their branches about in the moaning wind with a dismal, despairing action; the sun hid his face as if ashamed of himself that the weather should be unpropitious for Christmas. The bells were ringing out for church, and straggling streams of rain-drenched, limp and draggled figures, fighting manfully with unruly umbrellas, were threading St. Catherine, Dorchester[130] and numerous cross streets on their way to the different churches. Now and again a sleigh would drive by; but, it didn't have the merry, cheery ring which a sleigh ought to have; the horses' hoofs splashed heavily into the sodden street, and the runners cut gratingly through the half frozen snow and muck. No cheerful voices rang out, no gay laugh or light jest broke upon the ear; the driver sat crouched in a heap on his seat with cap drawn over his eyes, and head bent to the drifting sleet; the occupants huddled together as if for warmth, and presented a mingled mass of draggled furs, soaked garments and demoralized umbrellas.[131]

No well-disposed, self-respecting umbrella could sustain itself in an upright, independent way, as if it rather liked to be rained on, on such a day; the downpour of rain, snow, sleet and hail, coming in quick succession, so quick as to appear to come all together, was enough to discourage any umbrella, and none of them made an effort to hold up their heads in a defiant manner, as umbrellas sometimes will on a

---

[130] Dorchester Boulevard is now called René-Lévesque (though two small portions of it, one in Westmount, the other in Montreal-Est, are still called Dorchester), one of the main streets in Montreal, running east-west (one block south of Saint Catherine Street, the main commercial street in downtown Montreal).

[131] The term "demoralized" had recently acquired a special meaning in the language of economics ("demoralized prices," "demoralized market," etc.).

hot day or during a short summer shower. Some sagged limply down between the ribs and poured little streams, like miniature waterfalls, on unprotected passers by or neighboring umbrellas; some displayed broken ribs sticking out in an apologetical sort of way as if to say "I would be very smart and independent of wind and weather, but you see my careless master has broken my pet rib, and what can you expect of an umbrella with a broken rib;" some lacked a ferrule; the seams of others grinned open in a despairing fashion as if they had held on to the silk, or cotton, as long as umbrella nature could stand it, and now were forced to give up from exhaustion; some had great rents in them, and served merely as conduits for plentiful streams of water to pour on the misguided carriers who fondly believed they were being protected; all had a disheartened, discouraged appearance, and seemed to express, as well as umbrellas can express, their opinion that it was not at all what Christmas ought to be.

In all that crowd there was only one umbrella that seemed to have any self-assertion; only one which held its own firmly and bravely against the weather, not in a bragging, boastful manner, but in a resolute, determined way as if it knew it was simply doing its duty and did not intend to allow any sort of wind or weather to prevent it. A dogged-looking sort of an umbrella, not particularly pleasant to look at but withal presenting a very useful appearance; an umbrella that had seen service, as its faded color, and a very perceptible patch, and the well-worn ferrule testified, but one that was still ready to do duty for years, if treated to a new cover, as the strong whalebone ribs, heavy blackthorn stick, and massive buckhorn handle showed. A resolute, serviceable umbrella made for use not show, and in admirable keeping with the man who carried it.

He was a tall, well-built, compact man of forty-five or fifty years of age, with clustering black hair, just tinged with grey, brushed back from his high wide forehead; and trim side-whiskers displaying to advantage a square deep chin and a mouth rather above the average size with firm, but kindly lines about it. His eyes were of that nondescript kind of grey commonly known as "cat's eyes," and their expression was partly hidden by a pair of spectacles. His dress betokened him a clergyman, and his rapid pace showed that he was a little late for service. He hurried along St. Catherine Street and had almost reached the cross street where his church was situated when, suddenly, a loud shout fell on his ears;

"Hi, look out there!"

In another instant a sharp scream of agony pierced the air; there was a vision of a sleigh rapidly disappearing down a cross street, the driver standing up and lashing his horse almost to madness in his anxiety to escape, and of a crushed, moaning, cursing mass of humanity lying in a heap on the street, round which a small crowd had already begun to assemble.

Pushing his way through the wet figures and discouraged umbrellas the clergyman advanced to the figure and bent beside it.

What was it? Was it a small man or a large boy; was it human, or was it some terrible monstrosity bearing the resemblance of man?

The figure was doubled up in agony, and the helpless, awkward manner in which the right leg lay showed that it was broken; a ragged cap had fallen off and revealed an unkempt head of long black hair, matted and dirty and soiled with the mud of the street; half peering out from shaggy eyebrows and the masses of dark hair shone a pair of piercing black eyes, almost glaring with mingled rage and pain as it shook its doubled fist at the retreating sleigh. It was the figure of a boy, with the face of a demon and the garb of a man.

A pair of worn-out top-boots, with holes in the soles and the toes peeping out of the uppers, encased his legs and received into them the bottoms of a pair of pants many sizes too large for the wearer; a rough pilot jacket, out at elbows and in the last stages of decay, generally completed his outer garments, and he seemed to have nothing under but a ragged and dirty cotton shirt, soiled portions of which could be seen through the rents in his coat and pants. He was writhing terribly in his agony, and mingling with his groans, fierce oaths and horrible execrations against the driver of the sleigh which had run over him.

"Cuss you, cuss you," he shouted as he tried to raise himself and fell back exhausted—"Oh, God, my back's broke! Oh! oh! he's killed me, cuss him if I aint dead I'm crippled for life; won't nobody catch the murderin' thief an' hang him; where's the perlese? they's alwers round after poor boys like me when they ain't wanted,——them, where's they now?"

"Where are you hurt, my poor boy?" inquired the clergyman kindly. "Are any bones broken?"

"I'm broken all over," groaned the boy; "Cuss him, he done it a purpose, I see him drive right at me as I was a crossing the street; he's broke me leg an' me back, an' I 'most think me neck's broke."

"Not quite so bad as that, let us hope," rejoined the clergyman mildly, "come, try to get up, let me help you." He placed one arm gently under the boy's shoulders and tried to lift him, but the pain proved too great for the little sufferer and he fell back fainting.

The crowd, which had by this time grown to a considerable size, now began to find their tongues and offered aimless bits of advice, and threw out suggestions of impossible things which ought to be done, in that reckless manner which usually characterizes a crowd hastily drawn together by an accident. Several suggestions to "send for the police" were made but nobody went, everybody seeming to think it was somebody else's business to go; propositions were made to "run after the wretch and stop him" (meaning the carter) but none stirred; one excited little barber, who had darted out of a neighboring shop with a shaving-brush filled with lather in his hand, offered to "give the alarm," but as it was not made clear that the firemen were needed, the suggestion was not acted on; and one lady, whose appearance gave evidence that she ought to have remained at home, declared that it had given her a "turn" from which she did not expect to recover until a certain interesting event had transpired, and then she would not be surprised if "it" was marked with a sleigh and a horse trampling down a boy; which announcement called forth a sigh of commiseration from some of the female by-standers.

The only persons in the crowd who seemed to have their wits about them were the clergyman, who was kneeling in the mud to the utter destruction of his new black pants, supporting the boy's head; and a bare-footed, bonnetless, ragged little crossings-sweeper[132] who had made her way to the front and stood leaning on her broom looking at the injured boy.

"It's jest like them drivers," she said, "they alwers runs over boys an' girls. Why don't they run down fokes as is their own size an' cud take their own part. Shall I run fur a sleigh, sir?" she continued, turning to the clergyman, "there's a stan' near by."

"Yes, if you please, my good girl; make haste, he ought to be taken to the hospital at once."

"All right, boss," cried the girl, and darted round the corner at a run.

"I ain't goin' to no hosspittle," said the boy, in a voice weak from pain, just recovering from his swoon. "I don't want nobody a cuttin' me up, an' I don't want no skilley.[133] I ain't a pauper, an' I wants to be took home to my own house."

"Where is that?" inquired the clergyman.

"Briggs's Yard, off Kempt Street."

"What is your name?"

"Billy the toad."

---

[132] Usually called a "crossing sweeper." This was a street sweeper, very often a child, who swept the streets while asking for tips for the service provided.

[133] "Skilley" was a slang word for the gruel offered at breakfast in workhouses. By extension, it can refer to the workhouse itself.

"What?"

"That's what the boys calls me. Me right name's Billy Taylor. Oh, me back's broke—— ——" and then followed a terrible volley of oaths making the blood run cold in the veins of at least one listener as he heard the horrible imprecations falling from the lips of one so young.

"Hush, hush, my boy; you must not use such fearful words."

"Why mustn't I cuss him; what did he want to run over me fur?"

Further conversation was prevented by the arrival of a sleigh with the little crossings-sweeper hanging on behind, who immediately announced her return by exclaiming,

"Here we are, boss."

The injured boy was with difficulty lifted into the sleigh and covered with buffalo robes, not, however, without his indulging in another volley of oaths until pain again overcame him and he became insensible for the second time.

"Take him to his home, Briggs's Yard, off Kempt Street," said the clergyman to the carter, "it will be better, perhaps, for him to be with his parents; and then take this card to Dr. Homecraft, Beaver Hall Hill,[134] and ask him to attend to the boy at once, it would be best for you to take the doctor to the house, then return to me and I will pay you; here is my address." The carter looked at the card handed him and read "Rev. Charles Chessworth, D. D., LL. D.,[135] No.— St. Catherine Street."

"All right, your honor, I'll see him all safe," said cabby, getting into his seat.

"Can't I go with him, yer rivirince?" asked the little crossings-sweeper. "I knows his fokes." This assertion was a base fabrication, but Mr. Chessworth did not know that and smiled consent while he said,

"Take good care of him my little woman, and tell his parents I will call to-morrow or next day."

"You bet, boss," was the rejoinder, as she clambered into the sleigh, broom and all. "Oh, crickey,[136] ain't this style, oh, no, not at all?"

---

[134] Beaver Hall Hill is a steep street in Montreal, from Victoria Square to Saint Catherine Street (though the portion north of Boulevard René Lévesque is now called Rue du Square Phillips and the portion south of Avenue Viger is called Rue du Square Victoria). It was a very fashionable street and it was known for its several churches.
[135] DD stands for "Doctor Divinitatis" ("Doctor of Divinity"); LL.D. stands for "Legum Doctor" ("Doctor of Laws").
[136] A variant of "crikey," an exclamation of astonishment common in the UK and Commonwealth.

CHAPTER II. BRIGGS'S YARD.

The Reverend Charles Chessworth, for the first time in his life, kept his congregation waiting that morning, and entered hot and flustered with his rapid walk and quick change of garments; but his parishioners all agreed that never before had he preached so eloquently, never before had he gone home so closely to their hearts and wked in them so deep a sense of the thanks they owed to the Almighty for his infinite mercy and goodness; and when he referred to the accident which had detained him, and described in terse but earnest terms the scene he had witnessed, and how the boy had been almost cut off in his sins, with words of profanation on his lips, many an eye grew moist, and many a silent prayer for strength to repent while there was yet time was breathed, and many a mental vow was taken, let us hope, to be firmly kept.

The service was over, and the rector sat in the vestry slowly putting on his gloves preparatory to leaving when the carter he had sent with the boy entered and gave him a note; it ran as follows:

"DEAR CHARLES,

Come and see the boy you sent for me to attend, as soon as possible. I am afraid I can be of little service to him, and he is sadly in need of you. It is a queer case.

Yours,

GEORGE HOMECRAFT."

The rector pulled out his watch and looked at it; it was half-past one, and a little sigh escaped him as he thought of his tempting Christmas dinner which would be ready in an hour, and which he would now, probably, have to postpone. Don't smile at him; rectors are but human, and a light breakfast had tended to make the Rev. Charles hungry, but he stifled the selfish wish, and finishing pulling on his gloves grasped the reliable umbrella in his hand, followed the carter out, and desired him to drive again to Briggs's Yard.

It is an old time-worn saying that "one half of the world does not know how the other half lives," but I am pretty confident that one half of the inhabitants of Montreal do not even dream how the other half live, nor where they live. It would be a good lesson to some of us to visit a few of the "yards" off the bye-streets and lanes of this city, hidden away from the general public and scarcely noticed by the transient passer-by, where the poorest of the poor live; to witness the poverty, privation, want and filth in which thousands of the lower classes drag out their existence—living it can scarcely be called—would tend to make many an one content with his lot, who now grumbles at his position, and thinks himself thoroughly wretched because he cannot command some of the higher and daintier luxuries of life. To witness the abject destitution, the utter absence of even what are usually considered the necessities of life, the squalid filth and total want of comfort in which these people exist, would cause a feeling of astonishment that they can manage to subsist at all, and of thankfulness for our own place in the world. It is but a short time since the community was shocked by the recital in the newspapers of the terrible tragedy in Tabb's yard; and astonishment was expressed in the press that people could live in such a wretched place.[137] I have visited the spot and I say that bad as it is it is clean and comfortable as compared with some of the yards in Griffintown and in other portions of the city.

Briggs's Yard was far from being an exception to general rule of these yards, except that it might possibly be a little more dilapidated, a little more squalid and the inhabitants a little dirtier than most of the others. The entrance to it was from Kempt Street, and the yard itself was about a hundred feet long by thirty deep; on to this space, which served as a general repository for all the waste and garbage of the tenants, opened, on two sides, the fronts of the houses comprising the yard proper, while the third side was occupied by the wood sheds &c. of the yards, and the fourth side by the sinks and out-houses of the houses fronting on Kempt Street, whose noisome odors furnished the only perfume to be found in that locality. The yard itself was now ankle deep in mud and slush and half-melted snow which lay deep on the ground; and as the merciful covering which concealed the putrifying filth below slowly melted away, heaps of decaying animal and vegetable matter, offal, scraps, bones, rotten potatoes, and cabbage leaves, cats, and a dog far gone in the stages of decomposition, obtruded themselves on the eye and became obnoxiously palpable to the nose.

---

[137] Tabb's Yard was a tenement on Hermine Street (a short street connecting today's Viger and de la Gauchetière). On 28 November 1873 (Phillips's preface is dated 1 December 1873), a young man called Michael Flaherty found a bottle on Alexander Street and brought it to nearby Tabb's Yard, where he lived. About a dozen people drank from the bottle and six, including children, died. Although the liquid contained alcohol, it was actually a medical concoction based on colchicine (still used today to treat gout) which is lethal in large doses. Newspapers all over the world reported the story.

The houses were old, dilapidated, tumble-down shanties of two stories high, built of wood with shingle roofs which had been patched and mended in some places, and sagged down uncomfortably in others in a manner highly suggestive of a sudden collapse; they were innocent of paint but were black with age, and smoke, and mould, and mildew, and many of them were in so weak and worn-out a condition that they had had to be propped up in various places to induce them to retain something like an upright position; but no power short of pulling them down and building them over again could induce them to stand upright, and they all hung a little forward in a tired, worn-out way as if they had grown weary of remining so long in so wretched a place and longed to lie at length on the ground and be cut up as firewood and carried off to be burnt in stoves and so end their miserable existences. Around all these houses ran ricketty, old balconies which were reached by crazy, worm-eaten, slippery, foot-worn stairs, which creaked and groaned under the lightest footstep as if protesting against further ill-usage; and these stairs led to the upper parts of the houses, which were occupied by different families from the lower parts—the entrance to which were on the level of the yard—few residents of the yard being rich or exclusive enough to occupy an entire house.

About twenty families pigged it together in Briggs's yard, and the whole population turned out to witness the arrival of so distinguished a personage as "the pa'son" who had been sent for to visit "Billy the toad."

Crowding on the ricketty balconies, at the imminent risk of breaking them down, were dozens of shaggy-bearded, coatless, rough-looking men, and unkempt slatternly women, many of them with babes in their arms; while peering out from behind the dresses of the women, peeping between the frowsy pants of the men, and gazing through the bars of the balcony appeared the eager faces of scores of shock-headed children,[138] watching and listening with all their eyes and ears to catch every word and see every action of the visitor. Very quiet and respectful were the inhabitants of the yard, but very observant also; and remarks, not altogether complimentary, were passed on the visitor's legs—which one lady affirmed, *sotto voce*, "were bow-legged to that degree you could shove a wheelbarrow between 'em an' not touch his trousers;" on his spectacles, on his coat, on his heavy boots, and even on his umbrella, which one young female—whose hair was rather dishevelled, and whose shoes were considerably down at the heel—pronounced a "pokey" affair.[139] These remarks were not intended for the visitor's ears; but,

[138] "Shock-headed" means having shaggy or unkempt hair ("shock" can mean an untidy mass of bundle of things).
[139] Old slang word for shabby, pitiful.

nevertheless, some of them reached him as he inquired the way to "Mr. Taylor's," and was shown up a creaking stair which he was told led to the chamber where "Billy the toad" was.

It was the shabbiest and meanest of all the shabby and mean houses in the yard, into which the Rev. Charles Chessworth was ushered, and he had scarcely reached the balcony when a dirty little face was pushed out of the doorway and a sharp voice accosted him with,

"Come along, your rivirince, I'll show 'um to yer. He's took awful bad."

"Ah, there you are, my little woman, show me where the boy is."

At the rear of the room into which the balcony opened was a short ladder leading to a little cubby hole, or half attic in the roof, and there, lying on a dirty bed, was the boy who had been run over in the morning.

The Rev. Charles Chessworth was accustomed to visit the dwellings of the poor; he was not one of your kid-gloved clergymen who pay delicate and polite attention to the souls of the rich and endeavor to save them in a gentlemanly way, but leave the poor to take care of themselves; he believed in carrying hope and consolation to those who needed it most without any respect to persons; he was, therefore, prepared to find misery and poverty, but it appeared to him as he entered the room that he had never been in so wretched a hole before.

The room was small, scarce eight feet square, and the sloping roof came down to the floor making it difficult to stand erect anywhere except close to the door; the floor was rotten and creaked unpleasantly when trod on, while great gaps and seams in the shingle roof afforded glimpses of the heavy sky, and gave an opportunity for the rain to stream down in continuous little rivulets. The sides of the room were dank and mildewed, and the smell of decaying wood filled the place. Furniture there was scarce any; a broken down bedstead minus a leg, the place of which was supplied by an old box; a ricketty chair without a bottom; a few old boxes, a barrel, some blacking jugs[140] and a basket being all there was in the room, except two bundles of rags in corners which looked as if they may be used for beds, and gave the impression that three persons occupied this small room. Fire there was none, nor any place for making one, and the scantiness of the filthy covering of the bed caused one to wonder than any human being could sleep there during our long, cold winter nights and not freeze to death.

The boy was lying on the bed with his eyes closed as the clergyman entered, but he opened them on hearing a step, and tried to turn himself

[140] Jugs containing blacking paste were common in the 19th century. The paste was used for polishing boots and the black residue made the jugs or pots difficult to reuse, so they were usually thrown away.

a little so as to face his visitor, but the effort cost him a groan. There was no one in the room save the little girl who showed the way and Mr. Chessworth dispatched her on an errand, and drawing the bottomless chair to the bedside placed the head of the barrel across it and seated himself by the boy.

"How do you feel now, my boy?"

"Awful bad, sir; I'm broke all to pieces. Did they catch the murderin' thief, cuss him?" and then followed another string of oaths against the carter.

"My boy, do you know that you are in great danger; that your life is despaired of, and that in a few hours you may be in the presence of your Maker; are you not afraid to die with such sinful thoughts on your mind, such dreadful words on your lips?"

"I aint afraid of nothin'. What's the good of bein' a frighten' Friday."[141]

"Don't you fear God's anger?"

"Whose he? He never done nothin' fur me; what should I care fur him fur?"

"Do you know what day this is?"

"Yes, it's Christmas, an' there aint no papers to sell, worse luck."

"Do you know, why we commemorate Christmas Day?"

"I dunno; some of the boys said the first bull was killed Christmas Day, an' that's why people alwers eats roast beef an' plum puddin' that day, only I never gets none."

"Did you never hear of the Saviour who was born on this day to save sinners; were you never at Church?"

"No. Church ain't for the likes o' me; if I hang about the door for a little while an' thinks of goin' in, ther perlese alwers drives me off; church is fur rich folks as can wear clean closes and pay the pa'son, poor boys aint got no business there."

"Did your parents never send you to school?"

"I never had no parents; I was born by chance, an' me aunt bringed me up 'till I cud work fur misself, an' then I selled papers an' blacked boots opposite the Hall, only the perlese alwers a drivin' me off; they's drefful hard on a poor boy."

"And you never had any education?"

"Dunno what that is."

"Did you never learn to read or write?"

---

[141] A "frighten-Friday" is someone who is always afraid and lacks confidence (a "scaredy-cat"). The term is used mostly in Caribbean English, especially in Barbados.

"I learn'd to read, me an' Spotty can spell out some of the big letters in the papers; Spotty went to school at nights, he did, but they licked him[142] too much an' he don't go no more now."

"Who is Spotty?"

"He's me brother; his name's Jim, but the boys calls him Spotty. He's two years younger nor me, but he's partners with me now, he does the rounds an' I sells on the street."

"How do you live?"

"Me an' Spotty an' Snails keeps house here," the boy's voice had a touch of pride in it as he said this, "we pays Mrs. Mullins a dollar a month fur this room, an' we grubs ourselfs. We aint loafers, we aint, we pays our way. Say—" he added suddenly, "how long is I goin' to be laid up here? I aint got much money an' I must work perty soon, I aint goin' to loaf on Spotty an' Snails. I don't feel no pain now, I can't be very bad."

"You will be ill for some time, I am afraid; perhaps you may never recover."

"Well, I can't help that, it aint much use a poor boy living no how."

"You are very young, my boy, to have such opinions; how old are you?"

"I dunno; I 'spose I'm about a dozen."

Just then Dr. Homecraft, who had been for some splints, returned and set the broken leg. He represented the boy's case as dangerous, as he feared some internal injury, but said that with care he might recover, although it would be a long time before he would be able to work again.

Both men tried hard to induce the boy to allow himself to be taken to the hospital; he opposed the idea for a long time, but at last, having extracted a promise that he should not be "cut up" and have no "skilley" he consented, and arrangements were made for removing him at once.

The Rev. Charles gave up all idea of a pleasant Christmas dinner and sat down by the boy to read to him while Dr. Homecraft made the preparations for taking him to the hospital. Very gently, very lovingly, the rector read and talked to that boy, endeavouring to instil into his mind the truths of the Gospel. Very kindly and vey lovingly he tried to let in some light on that dark soul and expose to it some of the beauties of Christianity. Very tenderly and very feelingly he drew the picture of the birth of the Lamb of God on this day eighteen centuries ago, and unfolded the plan by which sinful man was to be reinstated in favor with his Creator. Very simply and very touchingly he spoke, and a prayer

---

[142] To be "licked" (that is, "beaten") was a term used especially by schoolboys.

went up from his own heart as the blessed words fell from his lips, that the light of truth may be shed on this dark mind, and that Christ might not have died in vain for this poor soul.

He used no flowers of speech, he tried none of the arts of oratory; he spoke plainly, feelingly, touchingly, and the boy listened; listlessly, unheedingly at first, but gradually becoming more interested as if he was hearing some pleasant tale, and something like a smile of hope, a flush of expectancy stole over his face as he asked:

"Do you think I'd have any chance? I ain't a very bad 'un; I never stole nothin', an' I don't lie much nor swear 'cept when I'm mad, an' I never was took up fur loafin' but on'st. Do yer think there's any chance fur me?"

"No one can be so wicked; no one can be so lost or depraved but what there is a chance for him in God's mercy, if he will only try to avail himself of it."

"I'd like to be respect'ble," said the boy, half musingly, "I'd like to wear good clothes, an' wash clean, an' be like some other boys I sees; not them as blacks boots an' sells papers, but them as goes to school an' goes to church, an' gets rich when they grows up. Do you think I'se got a chance?"

"There is a chance of success in this world for all who are honest and sober, and who are willing to work hard to deserve success. Will you try?"

"Yes, I'll try. I ain't afraid or work, an' I ken keep sober if I likes."

"Then we'll make a bargain. You go to the hospital and try to get well, I will come to see you, and when you are strong again I will see if I cannot help you to 'a chance' for a better life in the future. If God in his mercy spares your life I will try to afford you the 'chance' you ask to make that life good and useful; will you try to make good use of that 'chance'?"

"I'll do the best I can, boss; I'll try as hard as I know how."

Chapter III. Many Years After.

It was a long and desperate fight between life and death before "Billy the toad" was pronounce out of danger; and the long winter had passed away and the first breath of spring was perfuming the earth ere he was strong enough to leave the hospital, and even then he was very pale and weak and not able to do any work.

A great change had come over the boy; during his illness Dr. Chessworth had been unremitting in his kindness and attention, paid him frequent visits, loaned him books to read which he was capable of understanding, and gradually laid the foundation for training the mind at the same time that the body was slowly recovering. When Billy left the hospital his good friend, the rector, got him a place on a farm in the Eastern Townships, and the country air and exercise soon restored him to health; but he never went back on the streets to earn a living; the good seed which had been planted that Christmas Day that seemed the darkest in his life bore good fruit, and Briggs's yard knew him no more.

Years of quiet, patient, earnest plodding, and of hard honest labor in a country village gave him, by the time he reached manhood, a good position in the business he was engaged in, and his employer talked of giving him a share in the business; but he had set his heart on other things, and at the age of twenty-two, having saved money enough to pay his expenses, he resigned his position, and entered college to study for the church.

He was a quick and ready scholar and progressed rapidly, for the acquirement of learning had been the one pleasure of his life, and he had for years devoted all his spare time to study, so that when he entered college he knew more than most men do when they leave. The same energy and spirit of independence which has characterised him as a boy clung to him as a man, and he soon became noticed as one who would make his mark in the world. How true that prophecy will prove remains yet to be seen; but he bids fair to fulfill it.

Last Christmas morning there was a larger attendance than usual at Dr. Chessworth's church to hear the preaching of a young missionary who had just returned from the Hudson Bay Territory, where he had been two years; and it was well understood that he would probably be offered the position of assistant to Dr. Chessworth, whose age and declining health rendered him scarcely able to do the work of the parish alone. From the moment he began to preach the attention of the congregation was seized and never flagged to the end; but long ere that point was reached it was settled in the minds of his hearers that he was a man worthy to assist, and possibly, in the course of time, to succeed the good pastor who had for so many years presided over them.

It was a very pleasant party which assembled at the good rector's house that night, and not the least brilliant among the throng was the Reverend William Taylor, the "Billy the toad" of former years, and hanging on his arm was a beautiful and modest young woman whose slight blush at being addressed as "Mrs. Taylor," showed that matrimony was still new to her, and in whom I afterwards discovered—when this story was told me by the rector—the little crossings-sweeper of years gone by.

"And where is your brother Jim?" I asked of the Rev. Taylor, who was present.

"There, I hope and believe," he answered, reverently pointing upwards, "Jim has been called away early," he continued, "but we have the consolation of knowing that there is every reasonable belief that he was called to a better life than this. Ah, doctor," he went on, turning on Dr. Chessworth and speaking with great feeling, "What do I not owe you; what might I not have been but for your kindness and goodness to me when you took me out of the gutter."

JONES, THE LAWYER

CHAPTER I.

MR. JONES.

Plain "Jones, the lawyer," had his office in one of the buildings situate on St. James Street, between St. Gabriel Street and Place d'Armes Hill[143] on the right side of the street, going east.

I call him "Plain" Jones, not because he is plain; nor because that is his proper and peculiar Christian cognomen; nor because it is a nickname he has acquired; nor because he is so recorded in the directory; nor because he is ever so addressed. I call him Plain Jones because he is always alluded to as "Jones, the lawyer," without any special reference to any particular Christian name; and as any definite appropriation of a Christian name to him is at present unnecessary, I will call him, for a while, "Plain" Jones.

Plain Jones had an office in one of those queer looking houses on what used to be called "Little" St. James Street,[144] which now present so curious an appearance since the sidewalk on that side of the street has been lowered, and look as if they were ashamed of themselves for allowing a part of their foundations to be exposed, and were quite shocked at the idea of three or four little wooden steps being tacked on to them to enable people to reach their entrance doors; somewhat resembling the little flight of moveable steps which formed the means of access to the lofty four-post bedsteads of our boyhood's days.

Plain Jones was a lawyer; but you must not suppose he had any such plebeian word exposed on the outer part of his office door: no, there he was described as an "Advocate."

[143] All three streets still exist in Old Montreal, but St. James (St. Jacques today) no longer reaches St. Gabriel. It ends, after one block, in front of the new courthouse (Palais de Justice de Montréal). "Situate" is an old adjective, replaced today by the past participle "situated."

[144] Little St. James Street (la petite rue St-Jacques) was the portion east of Place d'Armes. Much of this portion does not exist anymore, the area it crossed east of St-Laurent being torn down in the late 1960s (see note 143).

It is a curiously noticeable fact that although there are about one hundred or more persons who have offices on the two blocks between St. Gabriel Street and Place d'Armes Hill, who get their living by "the study and practice of the law," there is not a single sign showing that there is a lawyer on the street. You will find "Advocates," "Notaries," "Commissioners," without number, but not a sign with the word "Lawyer" on it. Now why is this? I have looked up the two words, lawyer and advocate, in Webster's dictionary with the following result:

LAWYER, *n.* [that is *lawer*, contracted from *law-wer*, *law-man*.] One versed in the laws, or a practitioner of law; one whose profession is to institute suits in courts of law, and to prosecute or defend the cause of clients.

ADVOCATE, *n.* [L. *advocatus*.] One who pleads the cause of another before any tribunal or judicial court.

Now the only practical difference I can see between the two definitions is that a lawyer is "one *versed* in the laws," and an advocate is "one who pleads the cause for another before any tribunal or judicial court." Perhaps that may be the reason why there are so many advocates and so few lawyers. And that is the reason I have called my hero, "Jones, the lawyer," for although he had "advocate" over his door he was a "lawyer," and a good one, too, for he was "one versed in the laws."

Plain Jones had his office on the second floor, just at the head of the stairs, at the back, and the door, from which the paint had long ago peeled off, butted out at you in an offensive sort of way as you reached the top step. It was an antagonistic sort of door which seemed on the face of it to say, "You'll find it a pretty hard matter to get the better of me." And so it proved, if you tried to open it; for it was a difficult door to open and deceived you on the start, the knob turning round and round in your hand without causing any perceptible effect on the latch. After you had pulled two or three times you discovered that the latch was an entirely independent affair from the knob, and was controlled by a little iron flange, just big enough to accommodate your thumb, which protruded in a cautious sort of way, only a few inches from the door, a little below the knob. When you got your thumb on the little iron flange and tried to raise the hatch, you would find that your difficulties were not over; for the flange was worn very smooth and your thumb would slide off, unless you were very careful; and when you had a good purchase on it you would have to pull the door a little to you by the knob with the other hand, for the latch was stiff and would not come up without a struggle; and then some one would probably call out from inside "pull hard." After a tug or two the door would open in a sullen way, as much as to say, "Very well, my friend, you *would* get in, mind, it is not my fault if you find it harder to get out."

Some people did say it was harder to get out of Plain Jones' hands than to get into them, for he bore the reputation of being rather harder to deal with even than his door was; as a good many people had found out during the twenty odd years he had practised at the bar.

But Plain Jones was not a dry, musty old lawyer at all. He was plump and round-faced and oily-looking, with a fine high forehead, slightly bald about the temples, a wide head of kinky hair, almost white, which he wore well brushed back, a merry, twinkling blue eye, and a jolly, good-natured expression. He had full whiskers shaved all round, leaving the mouth and chin quite clean, which disclosed the fact that he had a slight double chin, with a merry little dimple on it which winked roguishly at you. His whiskers had once been red—auburn, I suppose I ought to say—but were now so sprinkled with white that they looked a light straw color, and gave the appearance of a fringe around his face. Taken altogether he was as pleasant-looking as a middle-aged gentleman, a little on the right side of fifty, as could be found in a day's search; and generally wore a quiet, cheerful little smile which was very refreshing to see. He was scrupulously neat and particular about his dress, and always had a clean, polished-up look, like a thorough-bred horse after being properly groomed.

Plain Jones was a bachelor—of his own free will, he would take pains to inform you, and not through any obduracy of the fair sex—and openly boasted that he was happy in his condition, and did not intend to change it; but he was not a musty old bachelor, nor a crusty one, nor a misanthropical one; and he avowed no antipathy to the fair sex, not he; far from it, he pretended—the sly, old fox—that his admiration for the whole sex in general had been the cause of his never centering his affection on one member of it in particular.

He was quite a lady's man, was Plain Jones, and on any fine summer's day he could be seen between four and five o'clock, dressed in faultless style, with a gay little flower in his button-hole, promenading St. James' or Notre Dame Streets, bowing and smiling at his many lady acquaintances in a style which put some of the younger beaux to the blush; and he has even been seen to give a sly wink as some particularly handsome woman has passed him, and has been known to make use of such expressions as "very fine girl"—somehow he had a way of calling all women not grey-headed or ugly, "girls"—"remarkably neat figure;" "an uncommonly well-turned ankle;" "what a perfectly beautiful face," and other similar phrases which showed that he considered himself quite a judge of the various phases of female beauty. But there was nothing of the libertine about Plain Jones, and although he frequently had lady clients, young and pretty ones too, sometimes, not a name stood higher amongst the advocates, and others who did not call themselves "lawyers"—although other people did—for morality and respectability, than did his.

It was a warm day in September, about four years ago, and Plain Jones was endeavoring to keep as cool as circumstances and the weather would permit in his close, stuffy office, when there came a modest rap, as from a parasol on the antagonistic door. Now be it known that Plain Jones had two offices, an outer one into which the antagonistic door opened, and which was occupied by his two clerks and his boy; and an inner one used by himself, and in which he received his clients. On this particular September day both clerks happened to be out and the boy was left in charge of the outer office.

Jones' boy was scrubby.

It seems to me that most lawyers' boys have a tendency to scrubbiness; but Jones' boy had more than the usual amount. He was short; but he was not fat. Not that he had any particular disposition towards unusual leanness, he was simply not fat; and his bones seemed to be of that kind which develop themselves faster than flesh could form to cover them, and gave that general appearance known, with reference usually to horses, as "high in bone, but low in flesh." He was not a pretty boy. His face was large and flat; with high cheek bones, a dirty yellow-brownish skin—sadly in need of soap and water—a short flat nose with extravagantly wide nostrils; and a mouth capable of biting a full-sized pippin in half at one snap, a feat he was very fond of performing when he could possess himself of the necessary two cents. He had too many teeth, had Jones' boy. Nature had been too bountiful to him in this respect; teeth grew out in all sorts of unexpected places in his mouth, and when he yawned and opened a chasm in his head something like twelve inches in circumference, he had the appearance of having another's boy mouth inside his with the teeth trying to escape. His eyes were round and saucer-like, of a nondescript color; and his hair was of a brick-red hue, worn close-cropped, and with a propensity to stick up unpleasantly at the crown. But the strong point about Jones' boy was his ears. I have heard the terms "clam shells," "flappers," &c., applied to ears, but in shape, size and general appearance the ears of Jones' boy more resembled a couple of those substantial articles of food known as "slap-jacks" than anything else. He seemed proud of his ears too, did Jones' boy, and had a way of working them up and down, back and forth, making horrible grimaces the while, which was fearful and wonderful to see. His clothes were not new, indeed they looked as if they never had been new and were most ridiculously short at the wrists and ankles, the bottoms of his trousers disclaiming the slightest connection with the tops of his boots and the sleeves of his jacket displaying an affection for his elbows which left several inches of remarkably dirty wristband constantly exposed to view. His wristbands were always dirty; just as his clothes seemed never to have been new, and although there is reason to believe that he sometimes changed his shirt, there was never any very perceptible change in its color, which led to the belief amongst the frequenters of the office that one of his bigger brothers wore it for a month or so first, and then transferred it to him when it had reached a stage where he could not get it much dirtier.

He was of a playful disposition, was Jones' boy. Most lawyers' boys have always appeared to me to possess playful dispositions, and give vent to it in various ways such as lolling out of windows, dropping pillets of paper on the heads of passers by; tormenting the caretaker's cat if they are so fortunate that she possesses one; whistling popular negro minstrel airs in a very loud key; practising clog dances in passages; performing daring and perilous feats on the bannisters; playing at "tag" in the corridors and on the stairs; singing little snatches of songs in very discordant tones; and in other equally pleasant ways conducting themselves in a manner calculated as much as possible to be agreeable and amusing to the busy clerks—for they generally take care to see that their employers are out before they begin to display their accomplishments—and frequently causing the sudden propulsion of a book or other missile at their heads, which causes them much merriment; for they are quick dodgers, are lawyers' boys, and as difficult to hit as a bat, unless you can be fortunate enough to steal on them in an unguarded moment from the rear.

Jones' boy was an adept at all these accomplishments except looking out of the window, which, occupying as he did a back office with only one window presenting a view of twenty feet of blank wall surmounted by a dilapidated chimney, and the sides of two neighboring houses, he was unable to practise to any advantage. This often depressed the spirits of Jones' boy, and time frequently hung heavy on his hands when his employer was in, so he invented a new amusement to while away his spare moments. He killed flies.

Not in the usual manner with his hand or handkerchief. He was too much of a sportsman for that. He took one of the office files and sharpened the end of it to needle-like fineness; then he procured five cents worth of molasses, and pouring a little on a blotting pad he would poise his spear and wait for game. At first he used to wait for flocks and take his chance out of the lot; but so adroit had he now become by long practice, that he could bring down his single fly with unerring precision, just as soon as it alighted near the seductive but ensnaring sweet. He was very busy on the September morning I have already referred to, and as flies were numerous was having good sport, so that the rap previously mentioned was thrice repeated before he condescended to take any notice of it and cry out,

"Come in!"

Then ensued a struggle with the door, which so much amused Jones' boy that he forsook his favorite amusement for a while, leaving the molasses to be devoured by the flies, and regaled himself with the uneffectual efforts of the party outside to conquer the antagonistic door.

"Pull it, stoopid," he said in a low voice, so that Plain Jones in the inner office might not hear him, "A long pull, and a strong pull and a pull altogether."

"Please open it for me," said a soft, sweet voice outside.

"My eyes," exclaimed Jones' boy, "it's a woman," and he instantly dropped on his knees and applied his eye to the keyhole. "Ain't she a pretty one, oh no, not at all!" he continued, as he hastily rose, licked the palm of his hand, passed it several times over the crown of his head to plaster down the hair that would stand up, and lifted the latch for the lady to enter.

A young girl, apparently not more than seventeen or eighteen, exquisitely beautiful, with great masses of golden hair flowing loose over her shoulders, and dressed in the height of fashion, stepped into the room; and, after bestowing a glance almost of terror Jones' boy— who was smiling in a sweet seductive way as only a gorilla or a lawyer's boy can smile—asked,

"Is Mr. Jones in?"

"Yes'um; right in here, m'um: lady to see you, sir," he said quite briskly, showing the way and bowing politely as she passed him; but the effect was somewhat marred a moment after by his putting his thumb into one of the pits which did duty with him as nostrils, almost up to the first joint, and meditatively digging away as he walked slowly over to his desk to resume his pleasant crusade against the flies.

Plain Jones rose as the young lady entered, bowed in his politest style, smiled his blandest smile, and offered her a chair with a gallant sweep of his right arm towards it, inviting her to be seated.

"Mamma asked me to give you this note and say she was too unwell to come to you herself, and would take it as a favor if you could make it convenient to call on her sometime to-day, or to-morrow; she thinks the business is important."

"Certainly, certainly, my dear, pray be seated;" somehow Plain Jones had a habit of addressing young ladies as "my dear," but he did it in a fatherly sort of way, and they didn't seem to mind it.

"Mamma is very sorry to trouble you; but we only returned from the seaside yesterday, and mamma found a letter waiting for her which annoyed her so much she is not able to leave the house to-day. It is too bad to have to trouble you."

"No trouble at all, my dear; your mamma"—but then Plain Jones stopped, puzzled; for he had not opened the letter and he did not know her mamma's name. So with old-fashioned politeness, which the youth of the present day don't know, or don't practise, he asked permission to break the seal; which being granted with a smile, he opened the envelope, and extracting a tiny sheet of rose-colored paper, very slightly scented, read the following:—

ALASKA VILLA,
15th September, 1869.
DEAR MR. JONES, —I only returned home yesterday and my nerves are so *terribly* shaken by a *dreadful* letter I found awaiting me, that I am *utterly unable* to leave the house to-day. May I ask you as a *great favor* to call on me at your *earliest convenience*. I know I am imposing a *serious tax* on your valuable time, but the letter says the business is *very* urgent, and I must consult my lawyer *at once*, so pray forgive me.
Apologising for the inconvenience I feel I am putting you to,
Believe me, Yours sincerely,
LOUIS TRYSON.
P.S.—Tilly will show you the *horrid* letter I received.

Plain Jones sat for a moment with the letter in his hand considering, and while he is doing so I will explain who the writer of the letter was.

Mrs. Tryson was the widow of an old business friend who had died some two years ago, leaving a wife, and one child by a former marriage, and a comfortable little property of about $5,000 a year, the management of which was in Jones' hands.

Plain Jones had had very little trouble in managing the property; for it was all invested in the city and left to Mrs. Tryson entire until Tilly was twenty-one, when the estate was to be evenly divided between the two ladies. The only provisos were that, in the event of Mrs. Tryson marrying again before her step-daughter, she should forfeit half of her portion, which then went to Jones; and should Miss Tryson marry under the age of twenty-one she forfeited half of her portion which in that event also went to Jones; with the further proviso that if Mrs. Tryson married first Tilly should not forfeit any portion of her fortune for marrying before she was twenty-one.

Now Jones was well acquainted with Mrs. Tryson, who frequently called at his office on business; but he rarely visited her; and, from the fact of Miss Tryson having been at school in England for seven or eight years past, and only returning during the present summer, Jones had not seen her since she was a little girl.

"Dear me, Miss—Miss Tilly," exclaimed Jones after his pause, "I declare I should never have recognized you. You've—you've—grown so much," he continued, quite ignoring the fact that girls usually do grow between the ages of ten and eighteen. "When I saw you last you were in short—that is, you were only so high," and he held his hand about a couple of inches above the desk to illustrate his meaning.

"Taller than that, I think," replied Tilly, smiling and displaying such pretty rows of small sparkling white teeth that Jones could not help feeling he would like her to bite him. "I know I have grown a great deal and changed very much, so I could not expect you to recognize me; but I knew you in a moment, you haven't changed a bit,"—Jones thought she need not have said that—"unless you have been getting younger while I have been away." Jones thought that very neat of her, altho' he tried to say something about being "an old man."

"Oh, you're not an old may yet," rattled on Miss Tilly, "although I can remember you ever since I was a baby, almost"—Jones thought she was rather too fond of ancient history—"and used to toss me in your arms and ride me to Banbury Cross."[145]—Jones thought he would like to do it now, but only smiled at the reminiscence. "You used to be a good, kind friend to me when I was a little girl, you must not be a cross old guardian to me now I am a woman; although Papa's will does not recognize me as a woman for three years to come," she added a little petulantly.

"Oh, that is on only one point, you know; and I am sure you will not want to run away from us before then. Three years is not long to wait."

Tilly said nothing, but looked as if she thought it was altogether too long.

"I am forgetting all about mamma's commission; will you go to see her?"

"Certainly; I have an appointment at twelve, I will go immediately after that. You may say I will be there by two."

"Oh, then, if you like, I will call for you at half-past one with the carriage, and we can go up together. I have some shopping to do which will occupy me until that time."

---

[145] "Ride a cock-horse to Banbury Cross" is a nursery rhyme. A "cock horse" means a hobby horse or anything a child can ride, including an adult's knee.

Jones thought how pleasant it would be to enjoy a drive of a couple of miles with such a charming young creature, and consented; then he asked for the letter Mrs. Tryson referred to in her note.

Now Miss Tilly had left the letter on her dressing-table, and she knew it; but she went through a most elaborate search of her pockets and reticule,[146] and at last, after Jones had several times assured her it was of no consequence as he could see it when he called, declared she must have left it at home.

"No mater at all, my dear, don't distress yourself about it; I daresay it is not very serious, ladies are so easily frightened by letters they do not clearly understand the meaning of."

"I know you men think women cannot understand any letters except love-letters, but I have a higher opinion of my sex than that."

"Oh, you wrong us, at least as far as I am personally concerned; although I do not deny that love-letters are very pleasant things to receive."

"Do you get many?" she asked archly, with that wining smile of hers.

"Not now, my dear. Young ladies do not think it worth while to favor an old man like me."

"Perhaps you do not try them," she retorted still in that arch manner.

"Well, to own the truth, my dear, I don't suppose I do; I have lived too long alone to think of changing my condition now, and no man has any right to pay particular attention to any lady when he has not 'serious intentions,' as the saying is."

Something very like a frown crossed Miss Tilly's face for an instant; but she chased it away with a smile and rose to go.

Jones insisted upon escorting her down stairs to the carriage, although she assured him she could find her way alone very well, or with the assistance of that "pretty" boy of his; which latter remark being overheard by Jones' boy, that young gentleman acknowledged the compliment by kissing his hand several times to her as she went down the stairs, and then turned a couple of handsprings in the passage, and stood himself up on his head in a corner in honor of the occasion.

---

[146] A small handbag made of velvet or other fabric, which could be closed with the help of a drawstring at the top. It was very popular at the beginning of the 19th century, but it was making a comeback in the 1860s and 1870s.

CHAPTER II.

MRS. TRYSON.

Mrs. Tryson lived in a very pretty cottage on the mountain side, and managed to enjoy life as much as a fascinating widow of thirty-five with a comfortable jointure,[147] and no small encumbrances possibly could. She married Tryson, who was twenty years her senior, when she was nineteen, and as none of her own children lived, she had grown to look on Tilly quite as her own child, and loved her quite as much as if she really had been. But Tilly as a child and Tilly as a beautiful young woman of eighteen were two very different persons, as Mrs. Tryson found when she took her step-daughter to Cacouna[148] with her immediately after the latter's return to Canada. Miss Tilly attracted rather the lion's share of attention, and, altho' Mrs. Tryson was far from being jealous of her step-daughter, she could not avoid feeling a little pique at the sudden desertion of some of her most devoted admirers to worship at a younger and fairer shrine.

Not much fairer though, for Mrs. Tryson was as rosy-cheeked, buxom, fascinating a little widow as any in the city, and more than one or two had tried to induce her to change her state, but without success. Not that Mrs. Tryson was particularly enamoured of widowhood, and intended to pass the remainder of her days in mourning; but, in the first place she had not met anyone since Tryson's death who had made any great impression on her heart; and next, she had no idea of forfeiting half her fortune by such a step as matrimony before Tilly was of the age prescribed in her father's will.

Of course, Mrs. Tryson did not think the provision of the will a wise one, which she declared "only put it into the girl's head to want to get married," but as the provision was there and could not be got over very well, she had almost reconciled herself to the idea that they must both wait three years. Mrs. Tryson was in the parlor when Jones and Tilly arrived, and looked an exceedingly interesting invalid as she

[147] An estate jointly used by both spouses and that is settled on the surviving one in the event of the death of a spouse (typically the husband).
[148] A small town in eastern Quebec (about 440 km north-east of Montreal), where several wealthy Montrealers built summer houses in the late 19th century.

lay half reclining on a sofa with a becoming morning wrapper pulled around her so as to display to advantage the general contour of a very pretty figure.

"Oh, Mr. Jones, how kind of you to come at once," she exclaimed, extending her hand, which was particularly small and soft, as Plain Jones advanced towards her. "I would never have troubled you only that letter frightened me so. What do you think of the dreadful business?"

"Well,—really—humph! The fact is, Miss Tilly forgot to take it with her and I have not seen it yet; but do not let it annoy you, it cannot be very serious."

"Oh, but it is dreadful. It threatens to deprive me of all my property; to turn me out of house and home. What shall I do? You'll help me, Mr. Jones, won't you?" and in her excitement she extended both hands towards him in an imploring way.

"Certainly, certainly," said Jones, taking the extended hands and pressing them gently—I said they were soft hands and pleasant to squeeze. "You are exciting yourself unnecessarily, where is this terrible letter?"

"Here it is," said Tilly, who had entered the room just in time to see Jones take Mrs. Tryson's hands; but, of course, she did not notice the squeeze.

"Now let me see what this wonderful document amounts to," said Plain Jones, spreading the letters open, and placing a gold double eyeglass on his nose; for Jones used glasses, occasionally, not altogether because he needed them, but partly because he looked well in them; and then, everybody will admit that a lawyer looks more imposing with a formidable pair of double eyeglasses astraddle of his nose than without them.

Plain Jones adjusted his glasses, and read:

Montreal, 12th September, 1869.

MADAM,

I am instructed by my client S. C. Tryson, Esq., to enter suit against you for the recovery of the property now illegally in your possession, under a, so-called, will of your late husband; and have to request that you will favor me with the address of your solicitor, at your earliest convenience, that I may consult with him. Mr. Tryson claims to be the eldest son of your late husband by a marriage contracted prior to his acquaintance with you; I regret to say that his claims appear to be exceedingly well founded and would advise you to lose no time in consulting your solicitor.

Madam,
I have the honor to be
Your very obedient servant,
PETER SNAP,
Solicitor.
TO MRS. L. TRYSON.

Mrs. Tryson watched Jones closely while he read the letter and her fears were not at all allayed by the look of astonishment which crept over his face as he read. Tilly turned to the window so that her own face was partly in the shade and she could watch the others unobserved.

"When did you get this letter?" asked Jones when he had finished reading it.

"I found it here when I came home yesterday. Oh, Mr. Jones, isn't it terrible? And to think that James should have—"

"It's all nonsense," cried Plain Jones quite hotly, "this letter was never written by a lawyer. There is no such solicitor in Montral as Peter Snap. There never was a lawyer called Snap, except in *Ten Thousand a Year*, and that's all gammon.[149] My dear madam, this is some miserable hoax some unprincipled scamp has had the audacity to perpetrate on you. The rascal; I'll find him out and teach him what it is to send threatening letters to a lady;" and Jones became quite excited and gave the letter a vicious sort of slap as if he wished it was somebody's head.

"Not true! a hoax! Oh, Mr. Jones, are you quite sure?" and the small, white hands were again impulsively extended; and again Plain Jones took them in his and pressed them gently.

"Perfectly certain. It is the work of some villain who has been trying to frighten you."

"I am afraid he succeeded then," said the widow, trembling violently, and looking very much as if she would like to put her head on Jones' shoulder and have a good cry; but just then a little sound came from Tilly, which sounded half like an hysterical sob, and half like a suppressed laugh, which made them both start; and Mrs. Tryson resumed her seat on the sofa, while Plain Jones returned his gold eyeglasses to the pocket in which he usually carried them, and turned to Tilly who advanced towards him.

"A hoax!" exclaimed that young lady, "who could have been so wicked?"

---

[149] *Ten Thousand a-Year* was a very popular novel by English lawyer and author Samuel Warren (1807-1877). It was first serialized in the *Edinburgh Magazine* from October 1839 to August 1841. Plain Jones uses a play on words, as "gammon" is an old term for a joke and the fictional lawyer he mentions is a partner in the firm "Quirk, Gammon, and Snap."

Ah! That was the question. Who could have been so wicked? The three sat near together and discussed this curious letter. Who could have written it? What was the object? What did it mean?

"Are you quite sure, Mr. Jones," said Mrs. Tryson, "that James,—"

"Nonsense, my dear madam, nonsense. I knew James Tryson from boyhood. He was married, as you know, before he met you; but as for his entering into any clandestine marriage before that, it is ridiculous. I knew the man too well for that; it was not the sort of man to trifle with solemn matters."

"But that man says he is heir-at-law?"

"Heir at fiddlesticks, ma'am! What is the good of his being heir-at-law when we have an incontestable will to fall back on."

"Does that make any difference?" asked Tilly, quite innocently.

"All the difference in the world, my dear," replied Plain Jones, rising to go.

"Won't you stay and take lunch, Mr. Jones?" asked Mrs. Tryson, hospitably, "I have unintentionally spoiled your own lunch, stay and share ours;" and she accompanied the invitation with a winning smile which quite captivated Jones.

Tilly turned away again, and there was no doubt this time that she laughed, but very softly to herself.

Jones hesitated. Some wise man has said, "who hesitates is lost,"[150] and as far as there could be said to be any winning or losing in this case, Jones' hesitation was certainly fatal to him, for at that moment the servant entered and announced lunch, and Jones consented to remain.

Now, altho' Jones had occasionally called on Mrs. Tryson during her widowhood on matters of business, he had never partaken of a meal in the house since his old friend died, and, even during his lifetime, Jones had only dined with him occasionally on special occasions, for their intimacy was more of a business than a social nature, and he was agreeably surprised to find the widow's taste so nearly agreed with his own.

The lunch was a light one; a cold duck; a cool, refreshing salad; a fruit stand filled with grapes, peaches, &c.; a tart and a bottle of sherry comprised its main features; and if Jones had been requested to order a lunch exactly to his taste he could not have suited himself better; for Jones was something of an epicure in his way and liked good living. He strongly maintained, however, that dining in the middle of the day was a barbarity, and could on no account have been induced to partake

---

[150] Often mentioned as a proverb, it seems to have originated in a misquoted line from Joseph Addison's play *Cato*.

of a hearty meal later than breakfast, until his own proper dinner hour at six; the widow's lunch was, therefore, just the thing to suit Jones. Still there was a drawback; no earthly happiness can be perfect and a sudden damper was put on Jones' pleasure by a thought which crossed his mind.

He would have to carve the duck.

Carving is one of the lost arts; and Jones' education had been sadly neglected in this particular branch. He had no idea of the anatomy of a duck than a duck had of his; what little carving he had been obliged to do, he had always done on general principles; he would place the fork firmly in the most available spot of the bird to be carved, and hew and hack about until, by main strength, he had reduced it to a mass of mangled remains. He knew that by great exertion he could tear the toughest chicken, or the most ancient duck to pieces, and even come off partially successful after an encounter with an obstinate old goose; but his carving never satisfied him, it was one of the few things he did that did badly; and he sighed gently as he took his seat at the little round table on which the repast was spread.

But the widow soon put him at his ease by insisting on carving the duck herself, altho' Jones made a desperate effort to appear very anxious to save her the trouble. The widow was obstinate. She was one of those few women who really carve well, and at small parties in her own house she was fond of displaying her accomplishment.

Carving is like everything else, very easy when you know how. The widow knew how; and Jones sat in silent admiration, watching her, as she puled her loose sleeves out of the way, thereby displaying part of a very plump, white forearm; gently impaled the duck with the fork and gracefully and dexterously carved it. It looked like magic the way the legs, wings, side-bones, breast, neck-bone, and merry-thought[151] came apart as the fair white hands fluttered for an instant over them; and as Jones gazed in wonder he felt that he almost wished he was a duck to be so quickly and scientifically dissected by those fair hands. But I fear if Jones had been a duck he would have proved rather a tough one.

Now there was nothing in the fact of Mrs. Tryson's carving a duck to cause laughter, nor in any way to account for the merry little peal which suddenly burst from Tilly's lips; nor was there any apparent cause for her blushing so vividly and hiding her face in her handkerchief and declaring that "something tickled her." Yet she did it; and several times during the meal some amusing thought seemed to recur to her, and she appeared on the point of laughing out again.

---

[151] Also, "merrythought;" another (archaic) name for the wishbone.

A round table is *par excellence* the table for a small party; everything is within easy reach so that very little waiting on is needed; and everybody is within sight and hearing of everybody else. It is certainly conducive to jollity and our little party of three were very merry, especially Tilly, who was the merriest of the three, and laughed longest and loudest at some of Plain Jones' jokes, for he could joke, could Plain Jones, and tell very good stories too when he pleased, and to use a common expression, "he came out strong" on this occasion, and kept his two fair auditors thoroughly amused. Mrs. Tryson had recovered her health and spirits wonderfully after the sudden disposal of the threatening letter by Plain Jones, and now appeared as the merry, jovial little soul she usually was.

After lunch they returned to the parlor, and Mrs. Tryson having excused herself for a few minutes, Tilly played some selection from Offenbach,[152] and sang a merry little French song, in a style which perfectly charmed Plain Jones, who was a great lover of music, and in his enthusiasm he made a confession which he rarely made.

He admitted that he performed on the violin. "Only a little," he said modestly; but Tilly went into ecstacies, and engaged him in such a lively conversation on musical matters until Mrs. Tryson's return, that Plain Jones had no opportunity of suggesting the propriety of retiring, which he had for some time been meditating.

"Oh, mamma!" exclaimed Tilly, enthusiastically as Mrs. Tryson entered. "Only think, Mr. Jones plays the fiddle!" but, seeing a slight shade pass over the usually serene face of Jones, she colored up and the next time she mentioned that noble instrument she did not forget to call it a violin.

"Does he! how nice; why you can play duetts together; if Mr. Jones will take pity on two lone women and spend an evening with us," she added with a smile.

Of course, Jones could only express the pleasure it would give him; and made a general statement about "some evening," but Tilly immediately cut in:

"Come next Thursday," she said, "and be sure to bring *the violin*."

Plain Jones promised he would come and went away smiling.

Now there was nothing particularly strange or amusing in Mrs. Tryson's inviting an old friend and legal adviser to spend an evening at her house; but it appeared to act with wonderful force on Miss Tilly's risibilities; for as soon as Jones had gone she ran up to her own room, locked the door, threw herself on the sofa and laughed until she seemed to be going into hysterics; then she danced about the room like a mad

---

[152] French composer Jacques Offenbach (1819-1880) was at the height of his fame, thanks largely to his numerous operettas.

thing, singing and laughing; and every now and then crying out "Oh, it's too good," "Oh, it's too funny," and then she sat down and wrote a long letter beginning, "My dearest, dearest darling" and ending—well never mind the ending, we haven't quite got to that yet.

Plain Jones drove away—for Mrs. Tryon insisted on his taking the carriage—in the most enjoyable frame of mind he had been in for some time; and he frequently confessed to himself that he had seldom spent so pleasant an afternoon. But the prominent idea in his mind seemed to be Tilly's growth, and several times he repeated to himself, "how she has grown;" as if the fact of her having changed from girlhood to womanhood in eight years, was quite a remarkable one, and evinced an unusual degree of smartness on her part. And by and by his thoughts changed a little in form, and he added to his thought, "and what a nice girl she is," and in this frame of mind he reached his office.

Jones' boy had had a happy afternoon in his master's absence, and in the various developments of his happiness had been twice kicked, once cuffed on the ear until he bellowed again, and at last summarily ejected from the office by the two clerks who had been trying hard to copy some deeds. He was just amusing himself singing "Good bye, Charlie"[153] through a keyhole for the benefit of the clerks inside when Jones returned; that brought him to his senses in a moment and he announced quickly, "Mr. Chops has been waiting for you for over an hour, sir, and he says he will call again to-morrow as he couldn't wait no longer."

"Bless me!" exclaimed Jones, consulting his watch, "half-past four, and I promised to cook up Chops' case for him at three; dear, dear, what a pleasant afternoon I must have spent, that I never once thought of Chops," and he passed into the office.

But Jones' boy did not immediately follow his master. He stood watching his retreating figure until the door was closed; then he shook his head in a deprecatory manner as if he wished it to be distinctly understood that he highly disapproved of Jones' conduct; and he solemnly shook his finger in a menacing way as if to warn Jones that he really would not be able to overlook such gross inattention to business. Then a brilliant idea seemed to occur to him. He smartened himself up a bit; smiled that bewitching smile of his; went through a pantomime of gracefully tucking a lady's arm under his, and bending low as if whispering soft nothings to his imaginary companion, proudly promenaded the passage-way for the next five minutes. What his exact

[153] A sentimental song ("Good Bye Charlie, or Do Not Forget Your Nelly Darling"), with music and lyrics by G. W. Hunt (1837-1904), a British composer of music hall songs.

thoughts were I am unable to say; but I have reason to believe he was imitating what he supposed Jones had been doing when he ought to have been attending to the case of Chops.

CHAPTER III.

MR. STEDMAN.

Plain Jones kept his appointment for Thursday evening, and took his violin with him. He was a mild and inoffensive performer on that noble instrument, and scraped up and down in a very correctly mechanical sort of way, throwing no feeling whatever into his playing. Just as I have heard some young ladies, with good voices, sing "Home, Sweet Home," or *Ah, che la Morte,*[154] or some other equally touching melody with an almost painfully mechanical and mathematical correctness, but without one atom of feeling. The fact is, Jones had a superabundance of music in his soul, but he could not succeed in drawing much of it out of his violin.

Still Tilly was greatly charmed with his playing and the widow said it was "sweet," and they managed to get up some very pleasant little musical parties to themselves. Tilly' singing was far above the average, and the widow had a rich, sweet contralto which harmonised with Tilly's soprano as well as any two women's voices can harmonize; so they sang duets with violin and piano acompanyment, and Jones even tried once to take the bass, but his chin was so firmly closed on the tail piece of the violin that he breathed most of it through the openings in the sound-board into the body of the violin and the effect was not harmonious. He did not try it again.

Of course, it must be understood that the first visit was only the forerunner of many others, and indeed it soon began to be looked on as a settled thing that Jones should spend at least one evening a week at Alaska Villa; and although he did not, as the saying is, "hang up his hat in the hall," he certainly did his violin case and left it there.

[154] "Ah, che la morte ognora" is an aria from Verdi's *Il Trovatore* ("The Troubadour"), first staged in 1853. "Home! Sweet Home!" (lyrics by John Howard Payne) is from the 1823 opera *Clari, or the Maid of Milan* by Henry Bishop.

Nor was music the only amusement. Tilly soon discovered that amongst his various accomplishments Plain Jones could play chess, and as she was a fair player she at one challenged him, and they had several pleasant games together. But Tilly quickly admitted that she was no match for Plain Jones and handed him over to her step-mother who was a much better player, and he and the widow had many mimic battles with varying success; for the widow was skilful in attack, and Plain Jones was often hard pressed to prevent a quick and disgraceful checkmate. Tilly would sit by and look on, but after a little while she usually strayed off to the piano and played and sung softly to herself, or brought out her writing desk and began another letter to "my dearest, &c.": it was surprising what an extensive correspondence this young lady had just about this time. It was noticeable, however, that Jones' attention was always distracted from his game when Tilly was not near; and he always endeavoured to avoid chess and substitute music so that they could all be together. But Tilly was obstinate and managed in some way or other to contrive that he should have his dose of chess very nearly as regularly as his music.

Very quiet and happy were those evenings at Alaska Villa, and Plain Jones began to find a home-like feeling come over him there, which he had not experienced since he was a boy. The change in his feeling was very gradual, and the Fall had slipped away and Christmas was close at hand before Jones himself began to be at all conscious that any feeling stronger than that of pleasure at being in the company of his old friend's widow and daughter, had anything to do with his visits at Alaska Villa.

But it was not at Alaska Villa alone that Plain Jones met the Trysons. They had many mutual friends, and he frequently encountered them at their houses. On these occasions Plain Jones balanced his attentions so nicely between mother and daughter that no one could say he was paying particular attention to either; only, he generally managed to escort Tilly to the carriage, greatly to the chagrin of many aspiring youths, who petulantly observed to each other, "Why don't the old fool stick to the widow?"

Nor was it at friends' houses only that they met either; for Tilly took a great passion for the theatre, and became a great patroness of that noble old barn in Cotté Street;[155] and it so happened that he usually

[155] Rue Côté, initially named Cotté, after Gabriel Cotté (1742-1795), a merchant and fur trader who was the original owner of the land on which the street was built, is today a short street one block west of Saint-Urbain. Much of the old street, including the area on which the Theatre Royal (founded in 1825 in a different spot) was located from 1852 to 1913, was demolished to make room for today's Palais des Congrès. In 1873, the building in Cotté Street could accommodate 2,000 theatregoers (Chisholm 19). At the time the story was written, the manager of the Theatre Royal was Kate Horn, an Irish-born Canadian actress (c.1826-1896).

managed so that Jones either accompanied them, or came into their box during the performance. For Jones was quite a patron of the drama, and sat out the very mediocre entertainment given, with a perseverance worthy of a better cause. Tilly too always evinced great interest in the play, and usually insisted on staying until the finish; but the widow was sometimes a little bored, and yawned slightly behind her fan.

Now it happened, quite by accident, that on the first occasion of their visiting the theatre, a young man, with whom Jones was well acquainted, chanced to be standing in the lobby of the dress circle, and, not noticing that Jones had ladies with him, stopped him to say "good evening;" this caused the whole party to halt for an instant, and that instant sufficed for Mrs. Tryson to recognize in the young gentleman a Cacouna acquaintance who had been very attentive to both Tilly and herself during the past summer.

"Oh, Mr. Stedman! How have you been since you left Cacouna?"

"Quite well, thanks. You and Miss Tryson have been quite well, I hope."

"Quite, thanks. Shall we see you in the box by and by?"

"Yes, with pleasure."

And so Mr. Stedman "dropped in" for a few minutes, and his few minutes proved to be pretty long ones, for they lasted until the end of the second act; and after that, Mr. Stedman managed, by accident, to be at the theatre every evening that Mrs. Tryson was, and, of course, he always dropped into her box for a few minutes; he seemed to be a lucky fellow, too, for it happened, by chance of course, that on the evenings he did not go to the theatre Mrs. Tryson was not there.

He was a very nice young fellow, Mr. Henry Stedman, and Jones, who knew his family well, spoke very highly of him. He was very attentive to Mrs. Tryson, and very polite to Tilly; and, after a while, the former invited him to visit her at Alaska Villa. After that the trio became a quartette, and Mr. Stedman was soon very nearly as constant a visitor at the villa as Jones.

The amusements became a little more regular after Stedman's appearance; for Jones almost always paired off with Tilly at the piano, and Stedman played chess with the widow.

The only one of the quartette who did not seem perfectly satisfied with this new arrangement was Tilly; and she made several attempts to get Jones back to chess with the widow, but met with but little success, as Jones did not second her efforts very warmly, and Stedman showed pretty plainly that he did not intend to be robbed of his pleasant little *tete-a-tetes* with the widow across the chess table; so Tilly had no recourse but to confide in her "dearest, dearest, &c.," which she did at considerable length.

Then Tilly changed her tactics a little, and visited Jones frequently at his office, sometimes inducing him to go out driving with her step-mother and herself. At first Jones felt a little delicacy about driving out with the ladies, but he soon got over that, and Miss Tilly congratulated herself that she had out-generalled Mr. Stedman. Not too fast, Miss Tilly; perhaps you have not taken the whole game into account.

Now Tilly's visits to Jones' office had an effect of which that young lady little dreamed.

Jones' boy fell in love with her.

It must be borne in mind that Jones' boy was about twelve years old, a very susceptible age; that he was scrubby, a state which tends to precocity; and that he was red-headed, and it is generally said—for what reason, or on what grounds I do not know—that persons having red hair are more easily overcome by the God of Love than those who boast of hair of any other hue. It was about the third or fourth visit of Tilly's to the office when this passion of Jones' boy first showed itself in visible form; but the first sign was a tremendous one.

He put on a clean shirt.

Never before had Jones' boy been known to commit such an act, and his appearance at the office created quite a sensation; but he cared nothing for that; he waited anxiously for *her*, and when she came he threw open his waistcoat in a careless sort of way and smiled so markedly that you could not only see all his teeth, but nearly half way down his throat. But she was in a hurry that day and passed him without looking at him. Then the heart of Jones' boy sank within him, and in the extreme bitterness of his spirit he speared every unfortunate fly which made its appearance in the office that day.

But the heart of youth if buoyant, and by the next morning Jones' boy was himself again, and had hit on a new idea. He washed himself perfectly clean for the first time in may months, and invested all his capital in a pot of Castor oil pomatum, which he had heard somebody say would turn red hair black; but the only effect produced by that was that the chief clerk, who had a particular antipathy to the smell of Castor oil, forcibly carried him to the nearest barber's shop and had him shampooed, an operation which Jones' boy did not at all relish; for, never having been shampooed before, he kept his eyes open when the water was turned on his head and both eyes got pretty well filled with soap suds. A day or two elapsed before he could pick up courage for another attempt to attract Tilly's attention; but when he did it was a great one.

He got a new suit of clothes.

You must not suppose that Jones' boy had the clothes made to order. Not at all. After a desperate effort he induced his mother to give him three dollars, and with that he purchased an entire suit from a pawnbroker—who had advanced fifty cents on them—and felt happy. Now, all the clothes Jones' boy had ever worn before were manifestly too small for him; this suit was just as palpably too large. The trousers were so long that he had to turn up about eight inches at the bottoms, and the jacket was so full that he could easily have carried a week's provisions in it without inconvenience. The chief clerk declared it "a good deal of a fit," and he probably was right. But Jones' boy cared little for the remarks of jealous clerks—he was sure they were jealous of his good looks—and having washed his face again and recklessly put on another clean shirt, impatiently waited Tilly's arrival.

She came; and the moment she saw him a peal of silvery laughter rand out such as that dingy old building had seldom heard within its walls; and when he grinned in delight, she almost went into hysterics and ran into Jones' office to ask who that funny boy was. Jones' boy heard her and his heart grew so big in his bosom that he was forced to go down to the street door and give vent to his feelings; which he did by whistling "Rule Britannia" in so loud and shrill a key that an excitable horse across the street ran away, smashed the carriage he was attached to all to pieces against a lamp post, and so furnished an item for the evening papers.

After this little episode the current of Jones' boy's love took another turn. The summer was quite gone now and with it the flies, and he found it difficult to amuse himself while Jones was in the office; so he became epistolatory, and used to amuse himself writing love-letters to Tilly, which he never delivered. He even went so far as to endeavor to soar forth in poetry, and after a whole afternoon spent in the throes of composition he produced the following:

> butiFul gurl of mI sole
> smile oN the 1 who Adoors the

But there his muse suddenly deserted him, and no amount of persuasion could induce her to return. Not being able to succeed at poetry, he next tried his hand at art and spoiled all the paper he could get from the clerks, endeavoring to draw Tilly's likeness.

This passion of Jones' boy was innocently fed by Tilly, who would sometimes say a few kind words to him if Jones happened to be out when she called; and this little encouragement so elated Jones' boy that he began to argue to himself that Tilly did not come to the office really to see Jones, but to see him. Then he determined to make known his passion, and in order that he might gain all the advantage which his most imposing appearance could give him, he plastered his head again with the Castor oil pomatum which led to his expulsion from the office by the chief clerk the moment he made his appearance.

This occurred just a week before Christmas. The snow was down, winter fairly closed in, and Jones' boy, expelled from the office on account of the unpleasant odor of his head, found refuge in the lower hall-way, and amused himself peeping through one of the little side windows at the sleighs going by. He had not been at his post more than five minutes when a covered sleigh with a lady and gentleman in it drew up at a short distance from the office, and before the lady alighted Jones' boy distinctly saw the gentleman kiss her and she seemed to like it too.

The lady was Tilly.

To say that the hair of Jones' boy's head stood on end would be to state an inaccuracy, it was too tightly plastered down with Castor oil pomatum for that; but it made the best effort it could to rise, and deadly and dangerous thoughts darkly flitted across his mind. Oh, that he had now the spear in his hand with which he has been used to impale flies, how gladly he would have plunged it into the heart of that base miscreant who had dared to press the lips of his beloved! And to think of her, the deceitful thing coming to the office to see him and allowing another to kiss her on the way, when even he had never dared to take such a liberty! It was terrible to think of; and in his jealous rage Jones' boy scowled darkly at Tilly as she passed him at the door, which made her laugh even more than his smile had frightened her; for as his smile was terrible so his scowl was irresistibly funny.

That smile decided Jones' boy on a scheme of vengeance. He determined that if he could not have Tilly himself, that black-moustached stranger should not have her, so he went to his desk and penned the following unique note to Jones:

Thare is a feLla makin luv tu yur Gurl   i seed him Kiss er luk out
a Fren

This epistle he addressed to Jones at his private residence, stamped it with an office stamp and posted it with his own hand while Tilly was talking to Jones in the inner office.

Now a little change had taken place in the arrangement of the quartette of late, and the change was owing to the widow's suddenly and unexpectedly giving the cold shoulder to Stedman and bestowing all her blandishments on Jones. Neither Tilly nor Stedman seemed to object very much to being thrown more together; but Jones scarcely appeared to relish the arrangement as much as when he was more in Tilly's society.

So matters stood on the day when Jones' boy wrote his anonymous note to Jones.

On that same evening Jones received the note and it angered him more than such a trifle ought to have angered a staid, middle-aged bachelor. He fumed over it, and delayed himself dressing to think of it; and the more he thought of it, the more it seemed to annoy him. At last, his mind was made up and he hastily finished dressing for the party he was going to, and where he expected to meet Mrs. Tryson and Tilly. All that evening he devoted himself to Tilly, so that the widow was quite tiffed, and when he asked permission to call on her next morning, she answered rather pettishly, which somewhat surprised Jones.

Jones handed Tilly to the carriage, as usual; and as he stood for a moment on the door-step he overheard young Trimmins say to Potts:

"What does old Jonse run after that girl so for, if he wants to marry here why don't he do it, I'm sure he is old enough; and if he don't mean to marry her he has no business to pay her so much attention."

"Of course not," replied Potts, "confounded selfish, he can't marry them both; he ought to stick to the widow and give us young men a chance at the girl."

"Certainly," responded Trimmins.

Jones said nothing, but walked thoughtfully away; and as he drew on his overcoat he murmured to himself,

"I'll do it to-morrow."

CHAPTER IV.

HOW IT ENDED.

Jones dressed himself with more than usual care next morning, and appeared at the office in all the glory of a white waistcoat, although it was nearly mid-winter. Jones had great confidence in white waistcoats; he said there was "a finish" about them which no other style of waistcoat possessed, and he always wore one on important occasions.

Jones' boy was fairly overpowered by his appearance, and immediately drew a caricature of him, adopting the easy plan of displaying the white waistcoat to proper advantage by filling up all the rest of the figure with ink.

Jones sat for a while in his office and seriously thought over the step he was about to take. The anonymous letter he had received, and he words he had overheard on the previous evening had decided him. A great change had come over him since his visits to Alaska Villa commenced. The glimpses of domestic happiness which had been disclosed to him had entirely changed his views, and he now began to think he had made a mistake in not marrying earlier in life.

Was it too late?

Jones had asked himself this question several times, but had not arrived at a satisfactory answer. The conversation he had overheard had raised a new question in his mind. Had he been too particular in his attentions to one of these ladies? Had he gone beyond the bounds of friendship and led others to suppose that he had other intentions? Jones asked himself these questions, and his conscience did not quite acquit him. Then Jones asked himself: Shall I get married? and his conscience answered, yes.

Then Jones put on his overcoat and gloves, pulled his cap well down over his ears, and started for Alaska Villa.

Mrs. Tryson had not passed a very happy night; in fact that estimable little widow had not been in quite as good spirits as usual for some days past. She had made a discovery. She had found out that she was not quite as contented in her present condition as she had thought she was. The widow was past the age of girlish sentimentality, and was not likely to be caught merely by a good figure or a handsome face. The three months that she had been thrown into frequent association with Jones had given her an opportunity of studying his character, and the more she studied him, the more she found to admire in him; in a word the widow discovered that she cared more about Jones than she would have liked to confess without a proposal from him; and, therefore, his sudden devotion to Tilly the previous evening, and consequent neglect of her had somewhat nettled her, and caused her to answer petulantly when he had asked permission to call on her.

But the morning brought with it cooler reflection; and calm consideration told her that it must be something of importance which Jones wished to speak to her about, or why should he make a special appointment when he had been in her company all the evening and could easily have spoken to her then about any ordinary business.

Could he intend to propose?

The thought made the widow blush a little, and she glanced anxiously in the glass several times while she was dressing, to be sure that she was looking well; and she dressed with more than usual care, so that she should look as attractive as possible.

And very pretty and charming she did look as Jones entered the room and advanced towards her; and Jones evidently thought so as he took her hand, for he looked admiringly at her, and bowed with even more than his usual *empressement*.[156]

"It is very kind of you to admit me at such an unusual hour," began Jones, in the manner of a man who has learned a speech by heart and means to say it before he can possibly forget it; "and nothing but the importance of what I have to say could have induced me to intrude on you at such an hour."

The widow interrupted him with an assurance that she was always charmed to see him at any time; but instead of putting him at his ease, this assurance seemed to confuse him, for he appeared to have forgotten the connecting link in his speech and to be unable to proceed.

"You cannot be surprised, after what I have said," continued Jones, getting into the middle of his speech and forgetting that he had said nothing yet, "that I should have become weary of my present mode of life." The widow said nothing, but discreetly turned her head away, leaving her hand, however, lying carelessly on her lap so that Jones could take it easily if he felt so disposed.

"It is rather late in life, perhaps," he went on, "for me to think of matrimony; but I am not a very old man—"

"Oh, certainly not," breathed the widow in a scarcely audible voice.

"And you know the common saying, 'It is better to be an old man's darling than a young man's slave.'"[157]

The widow did not exactly see the point of this argument, and therefore contented herself with a non-committal sigh.

"I can scarcely expect a very warm affection at my time of life," continued Jones, gently taking the hand which lay so invitingly before him in his, "but I flatter myself that I can command that feeling of respect which is often more lasting, and more conducive to true happiness than a mere girlish passion for a man of fewer years than myself."

The widow gave the slightest nod of assent and turned the least bit toward him.

[156] Obsolete term for "cordiality" (from a French word that means "eagerness").
[157] An old proverb, attested as early as the 16th century. Until the 19th century, the last word was "warling," i.e., someone you often quarrel with.

"It is curious," continued Jones, abstractedly squeezing the hand he held in his, "but I have sometimes thought that this was what my old friend intended when he put that curious provision in his will."

The widow bowed her head in acknowledgement that the same thought had occurred to her.

"For in this case the forfeiture will be a mere nominal one."

Again the widow bowed in assent, and a thought crossed her mind that he was rather longer in coming to the point than there was any necessity for.

"The arrangement will not be distasteful to you, I hope?" continued Jones insinuatingly, with another little pressure of the hand he held.

The widow sighed gently, and faintly articulated,

"No."

"And I may count on your consent?"

"Yes."

"Why then," said Jones, "we may consider it settled."

"Yes," returned the widow, speaking very low and turning on him a face radiant with happiness and covered with blushes.

Jones was a little astonished at this, but he went on apparently unmoved, "I am more than ever convinced I am following out the wishes of my old friend in this matter; and certain remarks I overheard last night have decided me in the opinion that it is time Tilly should have a male protector; and if her affections are not already engaged—"

"Tilly!" interrupted the widow. "What has she to do with it?"

"Why, as the person most interested, her inclinations must certainly be consulted. I shall see her at once and——"

But Jones did not finish that sentence; for the widow suddenly withdrew her hand from his and turning on him a look in which rage, contempt, surprise and shame were curiously blended, left the room without a word, her handkerchief going quickly to her eyes as she got near the door.

Jones could not understand this strange conduct, and severely blamed himself for forgetting his prepared speech and precipitating the matter so. "I was too sudden in my announcement," he thought, "the prospect of losing her step-daughter so unexpectedly has overpowered her; I will await her return."

A full half hour did Jones wait but the widow did not return, so at last he grew impatient and ringing the bell sent a servant to enquire whether Mrs. Tryson would see him again before he left. The servant soon returned with a message that his mistress was suddenly indisposed and would be unable to return, and handed him a note which Jones opened in some surprise and read as follows:

DEAR SIR,

If you think it wise and expedient at your time of life to marry a girl young enough to be your daughter, and the young lady is willing, I have no opposition to offer.

Yours truly,

LOUISA TRYSON.

It struck Jones that the consent was not couched in very flattering terms, but he did not pause to consider that and at once asked for Tilly.

"Miss Tryson went out about an hour ago, sir, and said she would not return until lunch time," replied the servant.

As it wanted two good hours to that time Jones left a message for Tilly that he would call in the evening and returned to his office.

On his way to the office Jones seriously thought of the events of the morning, and finally decided that he would make his proposal to Tilly by letter, as he felt confident he would acquit himself better on paper than if he urged his suit verbally; he, therefore, set himself to his task as soon as he reached his desk: but had only written the words "my dear" when there was a little struggle with the antagonistic door, and Tilly herself entered his room looking quite flushed and excited.

"Oh, Mr. Jones," she said before he could utter a word, "I have been here once already this morning and you were out; I want to ask you," but then her eloquence suddenly deserted her and she became quite confused.

"I am very sorry, Miss Tilly, that we chanced to miss each other, for I desired to see you this morning and have just returned from your house."

"Wanted to see me?" she exclaimed, turning pale for an instant and then flushing up again. "That is singular. What is it about?"

Instead of answering, Jones rose and went to the door of the private office to see that it was properly closed, and it was only by the exercise of the greatest agility that Jones' boy escaped from the key-hole in time to avoid detection and seated himself at his desk where Jones found him industriously engaged in sticking an office file into a piece of paper. Little did Jones imagine that that paper bore a caricature of himself in his white vest and that the boy was engaged in imagination in stabbing him to the heart with the file with which he had formerly immolated flies.

Having satisfied himself that the door was closed and that they were safe from intrusion, Jones returned to his seat and asked what Tilly desired to see him about.

"Oh nothing—that is nothing important," said Tilly a little nervously. "Tell me what you wanted to see me about that was of so much consequence."

Thus urged, Jones in brief terms made a formal proposal for her hand. It must be confessed that he did it more in a fatherly than a lover-like way; he made no great protestations of affection, but merely said that in his opinion it was time she ought to be married; that if she married anyone but him for three years to come she would forfeit half her fortune to him, and that altho' should that happen he had intended to restore it to her in his will, yet he felt he would not be carrying out her father's wishes if he did not claim it during his own lifetime; then he alluded to the impression on his mind that this was just what her father intended by the curious provision in his will, and concluded with the usual promise that he would devote his life to her happiness.

Long before he had finished Tilly was hiding her face in her hands, crying softly; and Jones' boy, who had again applied his eye to the keyhole, but could hear nothing, was shaking his fist in impotent rage at his master—who he felt assured was scolding Tilly—in fancied security, the door being between them. But alas for the vanity of human expectations! The chief clerk, returning unexpectedly at this moment, caught him by the collar, conducted him to the door, and without further ceremony, kicked him down stairs.

Tilly recovered herself a little as soon as Jones ceased speaking, and half sobbed out:

"You don't—mean to say—you want to—marry—me!"

"That is what I proposed, my dear," said Jones, soothingly.

"You ought to be ashamed of yourself," she said, so suddenly and unexpectedly that Jones involuntarily started; "No, no! I don't mean that. Oh, Mr.—Jones," with another burst of tears, "what made you— think—of—such—a—thing? I don't want to get married." Then, after a little pause, during which Jones looked on in too much astonishment to interrupt, "Just as I thought—everything was so nicely arranged, too"— more sobs—"and I'm sure mamma expected it, too," Jones started at this; "and I'm sure Harry did," Jones started still more when he heard this announcement, "and all my fine plot—gone—for—nothing," and another burst of tears closed this very intelligible speech.

Jones sat and looked at her in a state of astonishment he had rarely experienced in his legal career; and it somehow occurred to him that he did not understand the female sex quite so well as he had always prided himself he did.

Now, you must remember that Jones was not violently in love with Tilly; it was a mild sort of determination on is part, arrived at from a sudden conclusion that he was not happy as a bachelor; and his selection of Tilly as the object of his affection was as much due to what he had overheard young Trimmins and Potts say, and to what he considered the intention of Tryson's will, as anything else; therefore, although he was somewhat astonished at Tilly's sudden outburst, and naturally felt a little chagrin at his rejection, he felt none of the "pangs of rejected love" which all authors are in duty bound to describe as so terrible.

In fact, I am rather inclined to think that Jones, after the first moment of surprise, was rather relieved than otherwise, and was disposed to be as kind as possible to Tilly in her apparent distress.

"Come, come, Miss Tilly," he said, kindly patting her on the head, "don't cry so; this is only a foolish fancy of a stupid old man, and I will soon get over it. Believe me, child, that the silly notion I had will make no difference in my feeling towards you. I should probably make a very poor husband for a lively young girl like you, and I was a fool ever to think of it; come, let me be a good friend to you instead. Judging from your manner I should say you have some little trouble of your own, tell me what it is, and let me see if I can help you."

He said this in so kind and fatherly a manner that Tilly just threw her arms around his neck and gave him a sounding kiss without any more ado, which proceeding so astonished Jones that he quietly submitted to be kissed without offering any resistance; and Jones' boy, who had returned to his desk, and who heard the sound, was so exasperated that he made a violent stab at the ink bottle, broke it, and was for the next few minutes busily engaged wiping up ink from the desk, papers and floor with the blotting pad, which proceeding quickly obliterated all traces of the caricature of Jones, white waistcoat included.

"Oh, you good, dear, kind, darling, old guardy,"[158] exclaimed Tilly, accompanying each adjective with a kiss, "now I can love you ever so much again."

"Yes, yes, certainly," said Jones, somewhat embarrassed; "but what did you want to consult me about?"

It was Tilly's turn to be confused now.

"I thought," she stammered, "that you—that is mamma—and Harry said—I mean if she—" and then she stopped short and looked at Jones so helplessly that he could not refrain from smiling goodhumoredly.

"Oh, ho!" he said with a roguish twinkle in his eye, "Harry is it; I begin to think your objections to matrimony are more to the object than to the state. Come, tell me who Harry is!"

"Oh, you know him," replied Tilly blushing violently, "Mr. Stedman."

"Phew!" whistled Jones in such a loud key that the boy in the next room, who was industriously swabbing up ink, involuntarily started,

[158] An old diminutive for "guardian."

and in so doing overturned a chair, which attracted Jones' attention to him and caused him to order the boy to go to dinner and bolt the outer door after him to prevent his return.

"Mr. Stedman, eh!" said Jones, again taking his seat by Tilly. "You sly puss; why I thought—" but he did not say what he thought, but stopped suddenly and looked very hard at the carpet as a new idea seemed to occur to him.

"Yes," said Tilly, interrupting what he thought, "I know; but you are wrong. I told Harry he would overdo it and spoil everything."

"Spoil what!"

"Why—why—our little plot."

"Your little plot; what was that?!"

Instead of answering directly, Tilly slipped off her chair and knelt on one knee by Jones' side, with one arm thrown over his shoulder and her face resting on the white waistcoat, so that he could not see it. Then she began to take all the starch out of that vest by crying on it, and it was a little while before Jones could get her to compose herself and answer his question. Then she said,

"Don't be angry with me—Harry and I loved each other so much—and that will make me lose half my fortune if I married for three years—unless mamma—and if she married you—fortune would remain—and so I got Harry to write that letter—and I brought you together and I thought that you two—and I never thought—oh, do don't be angry with me; I thought it would be so nice," and a fresh tap was turned on which threatened to wash the white waistcoat quite away.

"Dear me!" exclaimed Jones, "*That* never struck me before; of course, the will says—why perhaps *that* is what Tryson meant; if so—"

"Oh, I'm sure of it."

"Are you? Well; dear me, dear me, what a mess I have made of it. It certainly would be a better match in every respect for both parties; and I think—" but again Jones did not say what he thought, and only looked at the carpet.

"You're not angry!" said Tilly raising her head and looking slily at him.

"If the widow marries before Tilly," mused Jones abstractedly, "she forfeits half her fortune to me, so that if she marries me it is the same as no forfeiture. Ah, I see!"

"Yes," said Tilly, looking up archly at him; "and if mamma marries before I am twenty-one then I—"

"I see what you mean; then *you* can get married as soon as she does. Oh, Miss Sly-boots oughtn't you to be ashamed of yourself to plot against your old guardian this way."

"Don't scold; tell me you're not angry with me."

"No, no," replied he smiling, "now run away and leave me to see if I can't plot a little; but Tilly you needn't tell anyone, that is, it's not necessary for anybody to know what an old fool—"

"Don't you ever say another word about that again, and I never will, there," and she kissed him again and ran laughing out of the office.

Then Jones sat down and hatched his diabolical plot, and several times he laughed to himself as if it was quite a merry matter he was thinking of. At last he drew a sheet of paper towards him and commenced to write.

The letter was to the widow, and Jones told a lot of stories in it; for he said that he did not understand what she had written him about marrying Tilly; that he never had any such intention; that Tilly was engaged to Mr. Stedman; that she had confessed it to him and asked his help; that he had thought what an easy way out of the difficulty it would be if he could persuade her [Mrs. Tryson] to marry him [Jones]; and how in trying to tell her of his love and Tilly's engagement at the same time he got the two subjects mixed, and, probably created a wrong impression in her mind. He wound up with an offer of his hand and heart and an intimation that he would call in the evening for his answer.

It was an artfully written letter and put the widow a little at disadvantage as long as she did not know that he had actually proposed to Tilly; and so Jones thought after he had despatched the boy with it, and he laughed quietly at his own cleverness.

The widow did not prove obdurate, and Jones was made a happy man that evening. A double wedding took place the following February, the widow and Jones being the first couple united, so that by a legal fiction Tilly did not lose her fortune. The quartette spent the honeymoon in Europe, and then settled down at Alaska Villa where they now are with a couple of little Joneses and Stedmans making the house young again with their squalls.

Jones' boy is Jones' boy no longer. The four years which have elapsed since my story opened have transformed him into Jones' duly articled clerk, and he talks largely of what he will do when he is "called to the bar." He is quite a swell now, has all his clothes made by a fashionable tailor whom he "promises" to pay; smokes cheap cigars which generally make him sick; cultivates assiduously three or four red hairs under his nose which he pompously refers to as his "moustache," and boasts of taking his "girl" out driving and to the theatre. In short he sets up for a "fashionable" young man, and gives promise of coming to no good end unless he materially alters his mode of life.

A FAMILIAR FIEND

I know him; you know him; everybody who is a housekeeper, or who has lived for any length of time in a house with "modern improvements," knows him. He is indigenous to large cities which boast water works, but he maintains a foothold in every town or village embraced in the circle of civilization. He is one of the necessities of civilization; and is only totally unknown in barbarous countries or in those lone and neglected places where lead pipes are unknown, where bath tubs are not, where cisterns never have a chance of becoming demoralized—because there are no cisterns—and where man uses water as nature provides it, and does not require "modern improvements" to introduce it into various portions of his dwelling place. In short the familiar fiend is a plumber.

Now, in the abstract, I like plumbers, provided I do not have to pay their bills. There is a peculiar kind of enjoyment in watching a plumber work, by the hour; for a friend or a neighbour; but the pleasure is considerably alloyed if he is working for you, and you know that all the time he wastes will be charged in your bill—by the hour. Nature seems to have specially constructed a plumber to work by the hour, and he makes it a point of honour never to disappoint nature in her kind intentions. There is a calm quiet dignity about a plumber that is inspirative of respect; there is a repose about him, and a sense of self-sustained and quiescent power that no other mechanic possesses; and he appears to consider it a part of his mission in life to impress the rest and meaner portion of mankind with the greatness and importance of repairing dilapidated taps; reconstructing disorderly water pipes; filling up holes in ancient cisterns, and performing other duties in the plumbing line—by the hour.

He is a noble and stupendous creature; but, like most great luxuries, he is expensive. Great bodies move slowly, and the plumber is no exception to the general rule! He is slow and dignified in all his movements; no one ever heard of such a thing as a plumber in a hurry, he could not be in a hurry; and, therefore, he is expensive, for time veritably money with him, as he always works by the hour.

I had some experience lately with a knight of solder and hot irons, which did not improve my opinion of the familiar fiend—when he is working for me.

On arriving at home one morning about breakfast time I found the house in a state of confusion consequent on the cistern in the bath-room having overflowed, and a young Niagara was fast flooding the house.

"Turn off the water," said I to Seraphina Angelina, the sharer of my present sorrows and future hopes.

"Impossible," replied that most amiable of women, "the last plumber that was here fixed the water so that it cannot be turned off at the main."

That was a fact. A plumber had done some repairing a few weeks previous and had carefully turned the water on, but neglected to make any provision for turning it off again; I, therefore, set all the taps in the house running, and went for the plumber.

I went by the minute; he came by the hour.

He came slowly. He looked at the overflowing cistern so long and earnestly that I thought he had some new and mysterious method of mending dilapidated cisterns by mesmerism, or magnetic influence.

I was about inquiring what process he used, when he said, very calmly, gravely and deliberately,

"There's something wrong here!"

I agreed with him.

After another pause, and another steady look at the cistern, he said, "It's running over."

As the bath-room was about an inch deep in water, this fact was self-evident and I did not think it worth while to make any remark.

Once more he mesmerised the cistern, and then, with the emphasis which a great mind uses when announcing the discovery of a vast and momentous fact, he said,

"It wants to be turned off."

He had got it. That ponderous intellect had at last grasped the idea, in all its immensity, that the water should be turned off to stop the cistern from overflowing. Then he proceeded to carry out his great idea—by the hour.

Slowly, and with great deliberation, he took off his coat, carefully folded it up, and laid it on the side of the bath. This did not seem to suit him, for, after critically regarding it for a few minutes, he unfolded it and carefully hung it on a peg behind the door—by the hour.

Then he looked at the place under the bath-tub where the pipes connect with the main and—scratched his head.

It is an imposing sight to see a plumber scratch his head—by the hour. There is a well considered, methodical way about his doing it no one can equal.

By the way he slowly rumpled his hair, and gently agitated his scalp with his finger nails, I knew he was burning to get something out. I was right. After the four scratch the idea came out, and he said,

"It wants something to turn it off."

Ever since his entrance I had been trying to impress on his mind the fact that the last plumber had neglected to make any provision for turning off the water; but he had to arrive at the idea in his own slow way—by the hour. He next slowly put on his coat, after examining it carefully to see if it had been hurt by its contact with the door, and said:

"I must go to the shop to get something to turn it off with," and, very slowly and deliberately, walked up stairs. Before going out of the door he turned to me and said, quite mildly and confidentially,

"It's running over; you'd better bail it out[159] until I come back." Then he closed the door behind him, but paused on the top step to light his pipe. I watched him for about five minutes carefully examine every pocket without finding his pipe; which he finally produced from the first pocket he had examined, polished it with great care on his coat sleeve, and then commenced to hunt for his tobacco.

I could not stand that. I went down stairs and began bailing. I had taken out eleven buckets of water when the bell was rung, and, on going to the front door, I was joyfully surprised to see the plumber. I scarcely thought it possible he could have been so expeditious; and it was with a feeling of wonder that I opened the door to admit him. He did not offer to enter; but stood calm, dignified, impressive, with the unlighted pipe in his hand, and gravely said:

"Have you got a match?"

I handed him a box and rushed down stairs to resume bailing, leaving him serene and unruffled on the door step, striking matches— by the hour.

He did not return until after lunch, and then he brought another man with him, equally calm and dignified. Each man was provided with a bag of tools, from which he drew a package of putty and solemnly deposited it upon the nearest convenient place.

---

[159] To bail (out) means to remove water (usually from a boat) with the help of a "bail" (a bucket or a scoop).

Putty is an amiable weakness of plumbers, they can do nothing without it: and, I believe that if a plumber was sent to a funeral to solder a lead coffin together he would take a lump of putty with him and slowly knead it while all the mourners waited on him.

It would be tedious to follow my two plumbers through their afternoon's work—for they took the whole afternoon about it—or to describe the playful manner in which they dropped candle grease on the carpet, deposited dirty bits of pipe, bolts, &c, on the furniture, and "made a mess generally;" suffice it to say that at last they got through and were ready to depart. I escorted them to the door and, my fiend of the morning, gave me a parting shot ere he left. He looked at me calmly, and, as I thought, compassionately, and said,

"The next thing you'll want will be a ball-cock," then he went carefully down the steps and commenced a search for his pipe, &c.,—by the hour.

The *next* thing I would want! Then he had not finished? Oh, dear no; plumber never do finish, they always leave something to be done at a future time—by the hour.

I went down stairs and sat in the bath-room to think about it. The seat felt soft and damp, softer and damper than wooden bottom chairs usually do; I rose suddenly and brought up about three rounds of putty firmly attached to my coat-tails and inexpressibles.[160] I did not use bad language, but I wished a fervent and sincere wish; I wished that I had that plumber back in the bath-room, I would have basted his head with his own putty—by the hour.

I naturally supposed that my annoyance was over, except the annoyance of paying the bill; but that act developed a new feature in the plumbing business, this time in the proprietor of the shop.

A few days after the bill came in; and although I knew that bills made out "by the hour" always exceed one's anticipation, I was not prepared for the magnitude of mine. I examined it carefully and the first item which struck my attention and raised me ire was

"3 lbs. putty @ 15c.—45c.—"

That wretch of a plumber had actually charged me for the putty he left on the chair, not one ounce of which he had used; and the only thing which he had done was the spoiling of my new trousers and most presentable business coat. I made up my mind at once to contest that item, and proceeded with the bill. The charge for time I passed over, as I knew it would be useless to contest anything charged "by the hour;" but the next item irritated me again.

---

[160] "Inexpressibles" was a euphemism for trousers (just as "unmentionables" was a euphemism for underwear).

"1 ball-cock, $1.50."

"One ball-cock!" and that plumber had solemnly assured me "the next thing you will want will be a ball-cock." I determined to contest that item also; and the next day went to the plumber-shop to interview the proprietor.

He was a grave, slow man, very methodical in his movements, and kept me waiting fifteen minutes while he critically examined a tap to discover what was wrong with it, although any one except a plumber, could have told at a glance that the handle was broken. At last he condescended to ask, with a sigh, "What do *you* want" with an air of offence, as if I had interrupted him in an important calculation—by the hour.

"I want these two items taken off that bill," I said, pointing to them. "I don't want putty left about my house for me to sit on; and I never had a ball-cock."

The stupendousness of this request seemed to paralyse him for a moment, and he looked from the bill to me, and from me back to the bill in speechless astonishment. Then he read over to himself, "Three pounds of putty at fifteen cents, forty-five cents;" and "One ball-cock, one dollar fifty cents." Then he looked at me again, and began to think it over. At last a brilliant idea seemed to strike him, and he turned to a desk behind him and opened a book lying on it. It seemed to me that he read the whole book through with the forefinger of his right hand as well as his eyes—for he carefully kept his finger on the book and slowly rain it down each page—before he looked up at me and said:

"They are charged to you on the book," and he kept his finger on the entry and gazed at me, as much as to say, "You can't object *now!*"

"I don't care for that," I responded unawed; "I did not have the ball-cock, and I won't pay for putty which I don't want."

He reflected again, and then said, in an argumentative kind of way, as if quite sure he must convince me now.

"What is the use of our keeping books and charging things, if people come in and want them taken off? We'll never ger rich that way."

"I cannot help it," I said. "If you please to charge things I did not have, I will not pay for them, that is all. Call your man who was at my house, and ask him if he put a new ball-cock in my cistern."

"We'll never get rich that way," he repeated meditatively, and then called the man.

The man admitted that he had not put in a ball-cock "yet;" but added, "that will be the next thing you will want," and seemed to think it hardly fair of me to refuse to pay for it before I had it. So that item was struck off the bill; but both master and man stuck as persistently to the putty as the putty had stuck to my coat-tails; and finally, to avoid further loss of time, I paid for it, and am now the proud possessor of three pounds of putty which I do not want, and which anyone is welcome to who will endeavour to take it away on his coat-tails and inexpressibles. But even this concession scarcely seemed to satisfy the master, and the last thing I heard him say as I left the shop, was, "We'll never get rich this way."[161]

---

[161] The editors of *Belford's* inserted the following footnote here: "The idea which the writer has worked out in this paper is not new to him; it will be found in Charles Dudley Warner's 'My Summer in a Garden;' but he has elaborated it into such a telling sarcasm that we do not need to offer an apology to the reader for giving the article a place in these pages. — ED." Indeed, a few pages in Warner's *My Summer in a Garden* are also a (milder) satire of plumbers' behavior, and include the repetition of the phrase "by the hour" (Warner 102-105). Warner's is a work of nonfiction and may have been used by Phillips as a starting point for his short story.

A TERRIBLE CHRISTMAS.
A STORY IN TWO PARTS; BY TWO PERSONS.

PART THE FIRST.

THE MADMAN'S STORY.

When was it? Was it last Christmas, or next Christmas, or was it ages and ages ago?

I can't remember. I can't remember anything since that night. I can't even be sure, sometimes, that I really remember all that took place then, or that all I remember ever did take place.

Let me see, where was it? Was it in Montreal?

I can't remember. Sometimes I think it was, and sometimes I think it was far, far away in some country I have forgotten now. I know it was in a large city. I remember the great tall houses, and the wide streets, and the constant buzz buzz of trade, and the whirl and swirl of fast and fashionable life. I remember the gay equipages, the prancing steeds, the handsome women, the foolish, foppish men—Ah! one of the women was so beautiful; and one of the men was so foolish.

I remember the churches too; with great tall spires stretching up, up until they were lost in the clouds. I remember climbing one of the spires until I had reached the clouds and rolled over and over in them, and danced in them, and swung to and fro in their fleecy folds as in a hammock.

Oh, it was fine fun! To be tossed up and down; to be danced back and forth; to hang on the gossamer thread of a thought, far above struggling humanity, and laugh at man's puny efforts to peer into illimitable space, and lay down the path for the planets to follow in their orbits, while the faintest trace of a cloud could mar his vision and set all his calculations at variance. And I could roll in the clouds, and laugh at men—aye, and women too; and above all at that one woman who was so beautiful, and that one man who was so foolish.

Fool! The clouds got into my brain. I can feel them now, still rolling over and over, still dancing back and forth; now banking up dark and lowering; now breaking out bright and glorious sun-capped mountains of golden vapor as the orb of day shoots his slender rays over them, tinging and fringing them with gold.

Clouds, clouds, clouds. Always clouds now. Sometimes damp and heavy, and wet with the vast amount of aqueous matter suspended in them; sometimes hot and dry and parched, as the fiery sun eats them up and leaves only a thin transparent film, which I only can see, to tell where they have been.

Was it all a cloud? Did it all happen up in that steeple? Did it ever happen at all?

I do not know. Sometimes I think it did; and then again it seems as if it had got mixed up with something else and I cannot remember.

It commenced by the sea. It was a gorgeously bright and clear day. The ocean lay lazily stretching itself out, out, out until the clouds came down and joined it and you could not tell where the ocean ended and the clouds began. The sun shone brilliantly, changing the little ripples of the water into shining scales, until it appeared as if the water had been converted into a million suits of burnished scale armor, and the sunbeams were dancing dizzy, whirling, maddening waltzes on it. The waves rolled slowly upon the long white beach, chasing the gleaming pebbles, rolling them over and over, in mere wantonness, and then leaving them stranded, high and dry, and lazily drawing themselves back to the depths of ocean. Isn't that like life? Does not strength always thus play with weakness; and, when its momentary pleasure has grown satiated, draw away and leave weakness to regret its own folly in being so easily beguiled?

I cannot tell. The clouds have come again and I am rolling in them. Jolly clouds. There is fun in you; but even you are treacherous, and open suddenly and drop me from your dizzy heights of airy thought to the dullness of earth. Away, I want no more clouds! Let me think.

Ah! I remember again, I remember that the wind whispered softly to the waves—I heard it, although it thought no one was listening; and it kissed and caressed them, and they tossed themselves up in laughing little flakes and kissed back again, as the soft zephyr breathed gently over the face of the water. Here and there brilliantly gleaming fishes darted through the calm and shining water, and a boy on a neighboring jetty, armed with a rod and line, threw his seductive bait to them in vain. They were too happy in that glorious sea to be seduced by the false sham of a wriggling worm only half concealing a cruel hook. Are men as wise as fishes? Do they seize at the apparent worm without regarding the concealed barb which will stick into them and poison their lives? I cannot remember. The clouds have come again.

Yet she laughed—she! Ah, now the clouds have rolled away and I can remember again.

She was with me. We stood by the seashore together, on a high rock, and gazed at the beauties of the sea, the sky, the earth; but naught was so beautiful in sea, in sky, on earth, as she. In all the wondrous beauty of her budding womanhood she stood by me and we gazed into each other's eyes; and while we drank in full draughts of nature's loveliness spread before us, our glances reflected back the deep, pure love which burned within us, and we felt that our hearts were made to throb in unison, our lives to be mingled together, even as the brooklet trickling out at our feet mingled with the ocean and rejoiced in the union.

I felt it, and thought that she felt it. I felt the warm passionate love surge through my veins and pour itself out in a torrent of words; I saw her start back to throw herself into my arms and seal our love with a kiss, and then—then—then—what then? I can't remember. The clouds have come again and I am swallowed up in them.

Was it then, or was it afterwards that he came? I cannot tell now. Was it that day by the seashore, or was it years afterwards in another country, and in a different scene that I saw him throw himself at her feet, and heard him utter words of love which she listened to with longing ears? I cannot remember; the clouds come into my brain and swallow all the recollection up.

But one thing I can remember. I can see that night plainly before me now. I can recall all its great agony, all its grand triumph. Ha! ha! it was rare sport to hear his bones crackle in the warm, leaping flame. It was joy to see him writhe and twist when he was seized in the arms of the fiery bride he little affected. I was delirious—stop—stop; not delirious; no, no; blot that out. I am sane, perfectly sane, you can see that, can't you? I am quite calm now. Listen, I will tell you how I revenged myself on him for his perfidy in stealing my love. How I paid him back a life for a life. Oh, I am calm now. He stole my love and robbed me of my reason. I know, I know, you say I am mad; wait a minute; wait until the clouds get out of my brain, I will tell you how I took his life—aye, his life—to pay for my reason. But it could not pay for my love; no, no; a hundred lives like his could not have paid for the one love he robbed me of—but I killed him. Ah! ha! I killed him—killed him—killed him. Burnt him up, body and soul. I saw him burning. I lighted the fire. I watched him as his cheek grew pale; as his lip quivered; as his breath came short and his strong hands clutched helplessly at the cords with which I had bound him; I heard him shriek for help, and I laughed—

laughed long and loud—and then, and then, the clouds came and I rolled in them, and shouted at man's folly and woman's love, and when I awoke again they told me I was mad. Mad! Well, perhaps, I am. I have loved; all who have loved have been mad.

PART SECOND.

THE SANE MAN'S STORY.

My earliest ambition was to attain fame as a lawyer. I burned to achieve success at the bar; to force truth and "justice under the law" into the minds of the most unsympathetic and phlegmatic jury, and to rescue injured innocence from the attacks of wrong and injustice and show it pure and spotless before the world.

I know there is a popular prejudice against lawyers; that the word is often misconstrued "liars," and that the main component part of a lawyer's soul (if he has one, which some people will not admit) is generally believed to be "costs;" but I think that there are rather more law students who enter on the "practice of the law" with honest intentions than can be found in any other profession. How long these "honest intentions" last I am not prepared to say; but, in the majority of cases, I really believe that they last as long as life does.

I was brimful of "honest intentions" when I received my degree of B.C.L. from McGill College,[162] Montreal, some ten years ago, and determined to enjoy a vacation, extending over the whole summer, before I settled down to the "practice of the law." Yet before that summer was over I had broken what was more than an implied promise, and had greatly failed in my "honest intentions."

My story, up to this period, may be briefly told as follows: I am the orphan son of a farmer in a small township (which I do not care to particularize) near the border of the United States. Both my parents died while I was quite young, too young indeed to know anything of their love or care. I was left to the guardianship of a bachelor uncle, who lived "across the line," and who carefully nursed for me, during my minority, my small estate. Uncle Bill was and is—for I am glad to say

---

[162] Bachelor of Civil Law, still offered at McGill University (which, until 1885, was better known as "McGill College and University" or "University of McGill College").

he is still alive—as genial, whole-souled and kindly a man as I have ever met. He is a strict observer of the obligations of honor, and has never been known to break his word.

My boyish days with Uncle Bill passed very pleasantly, and, having never known the love of either father or mother, both seemed to be made up to me in him. So time slipped away until I was fifteen years of age when, having graduated at our village school, Uncle Bill decided that I should pass the next three years in the high school, Montreal,[163] and then study for a degree in law at McGill. My first term at the high school passed about as pleasantly as such terms pass. I was not "the light of the school," neither was I the dullard, and I returned to Briardell, my uncle's homestead, not much better or worse than I had left it. But Briardell had undergone a great change since I had left it; my aunt Bella (Mrs. Isabella Stewart, widow of George Washington Stewart, who had lately gone to some other world, whether better or worse no one knew) had taken up her residence for the summer with Uncle Bill, and brought with her her only daughter Ettie, a pink skinned, blonde-haired little fairy of twelve.

George Washington Stewart, whose status in "the unknown world" was rather apocryphal, had had a pretty well-defined position in this world; he had for many years enjoyed a position of trust and emolument under the benign sway of Uncle Sam's Treasury Department, and on his decease left some three hundred and odd thousand evidences, in the shape of dollars, that he had looked after his own interests well, if not after those of his country. Mrs. Stewart was, therefore, a "rich widow," and Ettie was, prospectively, "a great heiress;" but I do not think either she or I was aware of the fact when we first met at Briardell, and grew rapidly into that intimacy which so easily springs up between cousins.

I like cousins, that is, I like cousins in the abstract, but I like one cousin in particular. Ettie and I soon became friends, then "great friends;" and, as the summer vacation drew to a close, we advanced to the stage of boy and girl love so common to youths of fifteen and maidens of twelve; and there I think we should have halted had it not been for Uncle Bill.

That worthy gentleman, Heaven bless him! had viewed the growing intimacy of his rich niece and his poor nephew with disfavor, and

---

[163] The High School of Montreal, which functioned between 1843 and 1979. From 1853 to 1870 it was known as the High School of McGill College. Classes were held in Burnside Hall (not to be confused with the current building by the same name, part of the McGill University campus), which stood in downtown Montreal. at the corner of today's Robert Bourassa and René Lévesque.

thought it incumbent on him, as our mutual guardian, to admonish me, as the sterner animal, on the subject; therefore, he called me into his private room the evening before my return to school—Mrs. Stewart and Ettie were to remain a few days longer—and addressed me somewhat as follows:

"Look-a-here, The-o-fullus," (my mother's father was named Theophilus and I was given his name) "yer must git eny fullish noshins abut Tetter out uv yer hed."

Ettie's proper name was Henriette; she preferred to be known only by the four last letters, and so did her mother and I; but Uncle Bill, and others, insisted upon it that Tetter was the proper abbreviation for Henriette, and so called her; just as many people persisted in calling me "Foley" as an abbreviation of Theophilus, and my uncle always addressed me as The-o-fullus. Uncle Bill paused a few seconds and then continued:

"Yeou an' Tetter hes been prutty entimet this summer, but yer aint nothin but gal an' boy, an' yer aint to git no foolish noshins in yer heds; so I warn yer Tetter es a great lady with hundreds uv thousands uv dollars comin' to her, an' yer aint got a red cent over seventy-five akors of ground thet aint worth the cost uv as much salt es wud enduce hef a dozen sheep to graze on it. So, Foley, don't yer get no foolish noshins in yer hed; yer got to git livin' an' mak' yer way in the world; an', meybee, yer may be Presidint ef the States effore yer die—purvided yer live long enuf; but Tetter hes a diferunt kereer befur her an' yer two aint ment to hitch hosses. So jest yer look sharp an' mind what I tell yer." After which speech he walked off, quite satisfied with his explanation, and I went to bed thinking, for the first time, that I was in love with Ettie.

Next morning I was to return to school in Montreal, and before I left my uncle spoke to me again.

"The-o-fullus," said he, "hev yer thought uv what I said to yer last nite?"

"Yes, uncle, I have," said I; "and I promise you that I will follow your advice with regard to Ettie, as far as possible; and I will never marry for money, but work honestly for my own living."

"Thet's rite," said he, "stick to thet."

*   *   *   *   *   *   *

Six years had slipped away since that day when I graduated at McGill, and determined on a six months' trip through the States and West India islands before settling down in Montreal. My uncle had husbanded my seventy-five acres, which he said were not "worth the cost of as much salt as would induce half a dozen sheep to graze on it" so well that, not only had my college expenses been paid, but I had a sufficient surplus to warrant my proposed trip before commencing work. During these six years I had not met Ettie again, although I had often heard of her, and we had occasionally corresponded. Lately her letters had ceased, and for two years past I had not heard from her, and did not even know what part of the States she was living in. So runs my story up to the 15th of June, 1866, when I left Montreal for my six months trip.

It is unnecessary to dwell on the incidents of my visits to the various large cities of the Union, suffice it to say that I gradually made my way South until I reached New Orleans, from whence I crossed to Havana, and there took the steamer for St Thomas and the Windward West India islands.[164]

It was a charming afternoon in September when the steamer dropped anchor in Carlisle Bay, Barbadoes,[165] and I was pulled ashore by four stalwart blacks, who captured me and my baggage, and placed both in a rather dirty boat, before I quite understood what was being done to me. Bridgetown, the capital of the island, is a veritable bee-hive of industry, and presents a pretty, animated picture from the bay; but it possesses little or no architectural beauties, and about the only imposing-looking building in the place is the fine old cathedral of St. Michael with its great massive square tower, in which is a good chime of bells and a rather uncertain clock as far as correct time is concerned.[166] The strong point about the island is the garrison, where about a thousand or more English troops and a regiment of blacks are usually stationed.[167] The barracks are very large, well-built and substantial, situated on a bluff at the head of the bay, and are considered the finest and most healthy quarters for troops in the West Indies. The parade

---

[164] St Thomas is now one of the U.S. Virgin Islands (a treaty between the U.S. and Denmark allowing the U.S. to purchase the small archipelago was agreed upon in 1867, but it was ratified only in 1917). The capital of the U.S. Virgin Islands (Charlotte Amalie) is located on St. Thomas. Between 1833 and 1885, Barbados was part of the British Windward Islands. It is still usually grouped today with the Windward Islands (a strictly geographical term).

[165] A small bay in southwestern Barbados. The capital Bridgetown is located there.

[166] The Cathedral Church of Saint Michael and All Angels, in downtown Bridgetown, rebuilt in 1789.

[167] Today, the Garrison Historic Area. It includes a racetrack that dates back to the 18th century.

ground is large, very level, and well shaded, and it is usual for the troops to be "put under canvas" for a few weeks during the months of August and September, the "hot season" out there. This was the case when I arrived; and, as it chanced to be Thursday, I soon found out that the "correct thing" to do was to go up to the parade ground—about a mile from the town—to hear the band practice, which it did every Thursday afternoon. This is the fashionable assemblage of the island; there all the notables congregate, and there the girls delight to go and have half an-hour's chat or flirtation with the officers of the garrison, for the Barbadoes girls, like girls the world over, are fond of the red coats of the British Army. Beyond the garrison is the little village of Hastings, a favorite bathing place, and "the rocks" at Hastings are a great resort for those who love to inhale the salt sea breeze, or to enjoy a sentimental stroll along the sands.[168] I had been furnished with letters of introduction by some friends in New York, and one of my newly formed acquaintances, a young man named Henry Bergen, a clerk in a large commission house, accompanied me to the parade ground, and proposed that we should extend our drive to Hastings rocks, which of course I did. I had noticed that Bergen frequently looked anxiously around while we were on the parade ground, as if searching for some one he could not find; but on reaching the rocks his face lighted up with pleasure as he noticed a handsome landau,[169] drawn by a fine pair of piebald horses, come towards us down the Worthing road[170] and stop at the rocks. Four ladies were seated in the carriage, two of middle age, two just blooming into womanhood.

I have never seen any one who so thoroughly filled my idea of perfect beauty as one of the young ladies who sat on the front seat of the carriage. I shall not attempt to describe her for two reasons; first, I could not do thorough justice to her, and, secondly, men's ideas of beauty differ so much that, possibly, what I consider exquisitely lovely, you may think ordinary or even plain looking; suffice it to say that the face so attracted me that I involuntarily asked my companion who she was.

"Miss Stewart," he answered with a blush which showed me there was no doubt what his opinion on the subject of her beauty was. "She is a young lady from the States who, with her mother, is paying a visit to the Jones' while they get some law business settled. Isn't she pretty?"

[168] Hastings Rocks is an area with spectacular views of the ocean, in the immediate vicinity of Hastings Beach (just west of the garrison). Today, there is a boardwalk (with a bandstand) that leads to the beach.
[169] A four-wheel convertible luxury carriage.
[170] Worthing Main Road runs parallel to the coast.

I looked at the elder ladies and instantly recognized my aunt, who had changed very little in the six years which had elapsed since I had last seen her, but Ettie had "grown out of all knowledge," as the saying is,[171] and I should never have recognized her again as the golden-haired little beauty with whom I had been so desperately in love six years before at Briardell.

Bergen, who was acquainted with all the ladies, proposed that we should alight and speak to them, which we did, he kindly introducing me, as I did not tell him I was a relative of the Stewarts. My aunt did not recognize me, and the name, "Mr. Langdon, a gentleman from America," did not seem to help her recollection at all; but Ettie knew me almost instantly, and holding out both hands in her old, impulsive way cried out,

"Why, it's The!" Somehow no one ever gives me my whole name, I always get it in fragments; sometimes a piece of the beginning, sometimes a part of the end, usually a nickname.

"You dear old stupid," she continued, getting out of the carriage and slipping her arm through mine in the old familiar manner, "who would ever have thought of seeing you in this out-of-the-way place; and what a fright you look with those great whiskers and beard. You'll just shave all the hair off your face to-morrow, except your moustache, or I'll never speak to you again."

We walked away from the carriage, and in a few moments were back on the friendly footing of childhood, laughing and talking over old memories and telling each other something of our lives during the past six years. Bergen remained by the carriage moodily, and I noticed his eyes flash as Ettie and I walked away; I paid no attention to it at the time, but I remembered it afterwards.

Ettie told me how it was I had met her mother and herself in Barbadoes. It appears that amongst the other property George Washington Stewart had left, was a claim to a portion of a sugar plantation in Barbadoes; and as the agent in charge had not been working it satisfactorily of late years, Mrs. Stewart had determined to visit her possession and endeavor to sell the estate. This had taken longer than was expected, as Stewart's partner in the plantation had lately died and the property could not be sold until his son came of age, which would be about Christmas, and Mrs. Stewart had determined to wait until the sale was completed, a purchaser having been found. The heir whose majority they were awaiting was Mr. Henry Bergen, a very devoted admirer of Ettie's, who seemed to think it would be a far better

---

[171] The original saying is "grown out of everybody's knowledge."

arrangement than selling the estate if a new partner was admitted in the person of Miss Ettie. What the young lady thought on the subject it was difficult to say; when I laughingly tried to joke her about Bergen's very evident admiration, her cheeks flushed, and her eyes glanced half angrily at me as she said,

"Don't talk nonsense, The; Mr. Bergin and I are very good friends, that is all. You men are all so stupid; if a girl says a civil word to you, you immediately think she is in love with you. What has Mr. Bergen been saying to you?"

"Nothing. I have seen very little of him the past few days"—this conversation took place a few weeks after my arrival—"and then he has scarcely spoken to me. He seems out of sorts."

"The," she said very earnestly, "promise me you will not make an enemy of Harry Bergen. You don't know what he may do to you."

"I have no desire to make him an enemy," I replied lightly; "and I have no fear of anything he can do to me."

"But promise me," she insisted. "I do not want that man to be your enemy."

"I will promise anything to please *you*," I said, trying to be impressive; but, although she blushed slightly, she pretended not to notice the intonation of my voice, and continued,

"Try to avoid him, The. I know he does not like you, and you must remember that there is insanity in the family."

"Is. there?" I answered carelessly; "I was not aware of the fact. Now you mention it, I remember having noticed several times that he has a strange, wild expression at times. So he is mad?"

"No. I did not say that; but his father died in the lunatic asylum here, and he has been 'queer' two or three times as a boy; but the doctors think he will get over it as he grows older, if he lives a quiet, steady life."

"Gets married and settles down, eh?" I said, trying to catch her eye; but she rose hastily, glanced out of the window and said,

"I must go and dress for dinner now. Shall I see you at the rocks this evening?"

I replied in the affirmative and left the house. In the avenue I met Bergen, and I spoke to him. He glared savagely at me and passed on towards the house without returning my salutation.

"Mad as a March hare," I soliloquized, as I went back to my hotel to dinner.

When I landed in Barbadoes I had intended to remain there only a day or two, and as soon as I had visited "Hackleton's Cliff," "the Animal Flower Cave" and "The Boiling Spring," (the three "sights" of the island)[172] to have taken the first trading vessel for St. Vincent[173] and continue my tour through the beautiful islands of the Caribbean sea; but that chance meeting with Ettie changed my purpose, and indeed changed my whole life, and I lingered on from day to day, from week to week, falling more and more in love every time I saw my cousin. My "honest intention" on being admitted to "the practice of the law" was to earn a competency before I thought of marriage, and that I would never so demean myself as to owe fortune to my wife, but that resolve was gone, and I found myself hanging on every word Ettie uttered, and constantly trying to decide whether she really returned my love or whether she had only that cousinly feeling for me which sometimes comes so near to being love and yet is not. While at dinner I resolved, for the hundredth time, to "know my fate" that evening, and with that resolve went to keep my appointment with Ettie at the rocks.

It was "band" evening and the rocks were crowded. I saw the Jones' carriage with Mrs. Stewart in it, but Ettie was not there, she had doubtless alighted for a stroll along the beach as usual, and, after saluting my aunt, I turned to seek her. As I turned I saw her. She was standing on the highest point of the rock, leaning against a wall which bounded a private residence, and by her side was Henry Bergen. He was speaking rapidly and gesticulating violently, and she appeared terrified, and anxious to break from him. Suddenly he threw himself on his knees and his words poured forth in an almost unbroken torrent as he declared his love and pleaded his suit with her. By this time I was quite close, and as Ettie turned to leave him she saw me and sprang towards me. Bergen jumped to his feet and faced me. Never can I forget that wild, despairing look, nor the gleam of madness starting from his strained and glaring eyes.

"Ah," he shouted rather than spoke, "it is you. She leaves me to go to you; but it shall not be. You shall not have her, she is mine, mine, mine! We are going to be married beneath the sea," and with a wild laugh he sprung on Ettie, seized her in his arms and leaped off the rocks into the water below.

The movement was so quick that although I was within a yard of him I could not arrest him before he took the desperate leap, and

---

[172] Hackleton's Cliff is on the other side of the island and has scenic views. The Animal Flower Cave is a sea cave in the parish of Saint Lucy (at the northern edge of the island). The Boiling Spring was a mineral water spring in a forest called Turner's Hall Wood. Some of the gas it contained was flammable.

[173] An island west of Barbados (and, like Barbados, part of the British Windward Islands at the time). It is now the largest island of the country of Saint Vincent and the Grenadines.

Ettie's terrified scream of horror rang out on the calm air, startling the idle loungers into a knowledge of the tragedy attempted to be enacted before them.

In an instant I had plunged after them and seized the maniac. The rocks at this point are over twenty feet high, and the waves break under them into a cavern formed by the constant surging of the waters; fortunately, however, the tide was out and the water was not over two feet deep. Bergen turned as I touched him, and loosing his hold of Ettie allowed her to drop into the water while he turned on me. I am naturally powerful, and my athletic training at McGill had greatly developed my muscles; but I was no match for the raving lunatic who rushed on me like a demon and strove to throw me into the water. I struck him a heavy blow in the face, but he did not heed it, and in another second he had closed with me, and what I knew was a struggle for my life had commenced. Strong as I am I felt like a child in his grasp, and in less time than it takes to write it he had forced my feet from under me and we both fell into the water, he above me holding me down and endeavoring to keep my head under water. The struggle was brief but fierce, and I felt my strength failing me, when help arrived, in the shape of some gentlemen who had run down the rock to the beach and hastened to my assistance. Even with this assistance it was a difficult task to secure the madman and take him to the shore, which Ettie had already reached, and where I was speedily assisted, for I was too much exhausted to stand alone.

That night I told Ettie of my love and learned that I was loved in return. Mrs. Stewart, with whom I was a great favorite, willingly gave her consent. Indeed I think she was secretly very much obliged to me, for she was greatly afraid of Ettie's falling in love with one of the "red coats" and being separated from her.

My aunt's consent to my union with Ettie was, however, conditional. She approved of the marriage, but required that I should return at once to Montreal, commence practice, and the wedding should take place a year from the next Christmas. Of course I consented—I would have consented to any terms—and left Barbadoes about the middle of November, Mrs. Stewart promising to be in Canada early in the ensuing year. Harry Bergen was then in the lunatic asylum, apparently a confirmed lunatic.

I returned to Montreal, and at once secured an office on that portion of St. James Street then known as "Little" St. James Street,[174]

---

[174] The east end of Saint James (now Saint-Jacques; see notes 143-144), as opposed to the "Great Saint James Street," which ran west of Place d'Armes.

and entered on "the practice of the law." Everything went well with me. I got a large amount of business, for a young lawyer, and, before my first year had expired, I had gained some celebrity by winning two or three rather difficult cases. My aunt came on in the spring and, partly to please Ettie, bought a house in Montreal and decided to settle there. ·

So matters stood with me on the day before Christmas, and an eventful day it seemed to me, and so it proved to be, although not in the way I had expected, for I was to be married on Christmas day.

I spent Christmas Eve at my aunt's house and did not leave until nearly eleven o'clock, when I went to my room over my office in Little St James Street, which I was to occupy for the last time that night.

My office was one of five on the second flat of an old-fashioned brick building; and the third flat was divided into four rooms, with a bath room and a large roomy vault for storing books, papers, etc. The place was very convenient and suitable for bachelors, and the four rooms were occupied by young men, like myself, who were just starting in the world and had not yet made a name, or a home.

The vault was one of the "institutions"—to use an Americanism— of the house. Why it had ever been built on the third flat nobody knew, yet there it was; what use it could be put to no one could tell, until one day I invited a reporter to visit me; and, in showing him the conveniences of the place, he noticed the vault and said, "What a splendid place that is for you fellows to keep your beer. It is cool, all lined with iron, with an iron door—and has a gas jet in it, so that you can always get a light. By Jove, it is a handy place for beer!" and he looked about wistfully as if he wondered that no one had ever before thought of what a useful purpose the vault could be put to, and, therefore, stocked it with "Bass" or "Dawes,"[175] or some other brand congenial to his palate. That hint of the reporter's "took;" and from that time the vault was used as a receptacle for beer, the door being left unlocked so that the four of us living on the flat could have free access at any time.

When I reached my room that Christmas Eve after parting from Ettie, I found all the rooms on the "living" flat—as we used to call it—unoccupied. My fellow-lodgers had, evidently, not finished their Christmas Eve yet.

I lighted the gas, lit a pipe; and, having donned my slippers and dressing-gown, sat before the fire and took a look into the future. I

---

[175] Bass is a British brewery, the largest exporter of beer in the world in the 1870s. Dawes was a Montreal brewery (founded in 1811 by Thomas Dawes). It was absorbed by Canadian Breweries Limited (CBL) in the 20th century. CBL itself was first acquired by Rothmans and renamed Carling O'Keefe, then by Molson Coors.

thought of what a great change to-morrow would make in my life; how different it would be to have some one waiting for me at the door when I came home, not the scarred, blistered, and "unpainted for twenty years" door which now admitted me to my "home" (?); but to a real home, with a real wife and real additions in the prospective future.

It was a jolly train of thought, and I do not know which gave out first, the pipe or the "additions in the prospective future;" but the last thing I can remember distinctly was that my eldest son was appointed Governor General of Canada, and that, following the example of Mr. U. S. Grant, President of the United States, he had appointed me postmaster for Montreal.[176] I was just completing a scheme for building a new post office when I lost consciousness; and how long I slept I do not know.

My awakening was a rude one.

The first sensation I experienced, that I can remember, was one of suffocation. I struggled, and wrestled, like one in a nightmare; and finally, by a great effort, awoke.

Awoke to what? To find myself gagged and bound hand and foot to the chair I had been sitting in when I dropped to sleep; and standing between me and the fire was a form which at first I took to be only a remnant of my nightmare, but which I soon found to be a stern reality.

It was the form of Henry Bergen.

He was watching me with a fixed, steady gaze, as if noting every breath I drew; and as I opened my eyes and became conscious he changed his position, and seemed relieved to find that I was awake.

"You are surprised to see me," he said quite calmly, although the light of madness smouldered in his eyes. "You did not expect me? Ha! ha! never mind. You might have invited an old friend to your wedding, but you didn't and I have invited myself. It will be a jolly wedding; oh, such fun! A bride waiting for a bridegroom who will never come— never, never come. I have escaped from the prison you threw me into; I have crossed the seas; I have followed you like a sleuth hound until I have tracked you down. Oh, it is rare fun. You thought to have her; you thought you could outwit me—no, no; I am too clever for you, and to-morrow, while your bones are lying charred and blackened amongst the ruins of this house, I will console your bride for you—your bride? She shall be my bride. As for you I have prepared a bride for you, death; come and see how pleasant I will make it for you."

He lifted the chair in which I was bound and carried me with ease out of the room into the vault and deposited the chair in the centre of

[176] Jesse Root Grant (1794-1873) was appointed postmaster of Covington, Kentucky, by President Andrew Johnson in 1866. In 1870, President Ulysses S. Grant, Jesse's son, confirmed him for another term.

it. The gas was lighted, and I noticed that a bottle with a candle stuck in its mouth had been placed in one corner. There was nothing else in the vault except a few bottles of beer.

Bergen looked at me for a few moments and laughed; then he lit the candle which was in the bottle and placed it near my feet; he then crossed to the gas burner and turned the light out, still keeping his hand on it, however. He then laughed again and said:

"I've turned the gas off, but I am going to turn it on again, only this time *I shall not light it*." He turned on the gas and then continued, "I shall lock the vault door and leave you with the escaping gas and the burning light; when the vault is filled with gas there will be an explosion and you will be blown to atoms. Ha! ha! it's funny, isn't it! It needed a madman to think out such a fine revenge. You stole my love. I'll steal your life. Good night."

He stepped out of the vault, and I heard the door closed and locked.

My situation was truly terrible, and there seemed to be no possible escape from a horrible death. I was most securely bound to the chair, my hands being strapped behind its back and my feet firmly fastened to the lower rung in front, while two stout cords around my body held me securely to the back of the chair. I was gagged; but so gagged that I could breathe, although I could not cry out. To release myself was impossible, and there appeared to be no means of attracting attention to my condition, even had there been any one on the flat, which I knew there was not, as the three friends who occupied rooms there had gone into the country to spend Christmas, and would not be back for two days. The janitor lived in the basement, and there was no one else in the building.

I fully realized my position, and knew that my death was almost inevitable; but I did not quite despair. The gas burner, which was now open and fast filling the vault with noxious vapor, was very near the floor; and, if I could get to it, I might be able to reach up to it and turn it off with my teeth. Although I was only five or six feet from the side of the vault where the gas burner was, it took me a long time to jerk and twist my chair over to it, and the vault was now so filled with gas, that every moment I expected the fatal explosion to take place. At last I reached the burner and by a great effort stretched my neck up so that one end of the wooden gag which was in my mouth rested against the screw and in a few seconds more I had pushed it round and shut off the stream of poisonous vapor.

I was saved for the present; but was so exhausted and overpowered by the gas that I fell to the ground insensible, bringing the chair down with me.

When I recovered consciousness I found that almost all the gas had escaped out of the vault, and the air was comparatively pure, but intensely cold, and my limbs were so benumbed I could not move. Some hours must have elapsed, as the candle had burned almost out, and I supposed it must be nearly morning; but would morning bring relief? I scarcely hoped so. I should not be missed until near mid-day; and when I was missed, who would think of searching for me in the old vault? It was with a bitter pang that I resigned myself to the idea that I was doomed to pass many hours, perhaps days, in that gloomy vault unable to make myself heard. I was to have been married at eleven o'clock; but all chance of that was over now, for even should I be released in time, I was in too weak and exhausted a condition to do more than be put to bed.

Wearily the minutes dragged themselves away, and the candle went out, leaving me in darkness. Then a new fear came to me: suppose Bergen should return to see if his work was completed? There would be no hope for me then. The idea grew, and grew until my brain reeled and I again became unconscious.

When I awoke to reason again I found myself in bed in my own room with a doctor and some friends attending me.

I owed my deliverance to my reporting friend's weakness for beer. He had awoke very thirsty about ten o'clock on Christmas morning, and having no beer in his boarding house, had come to my rooms where he knew there was a supply, and so found me. There was no wedding that day, and it was several weeks before my system recovered from the severe shock it had received; then Ettie and I were married and spent our honeymoon where we had learned to love each other, in Barbadoes.

How Bergen found me out I do not know. He had been discharged from the asylum in Barbadoes some months after I left the island, and started on a pleasure trip to Europe; very little more was heard of him until he appeared in my room on that memorable Christmas Eve. He must have been in Montreal some days watching me; but I never discovered where he had been staying. After locking me in the vault he went to the St. Lawrence Hall and spoke and acted so strangely that a policeman was called who took him to the station house "for safe keeping," and he was shortly after sent down to Beauport,[177] where he now is a confirmed lunatic.

[177] The Beauport Lunatic Asylum, founded in 1845; today, the Institut universitaire en santé mentale de Québec.

LIST OF WORKS BY J. A. PHILLIPS

Stories and Sketches

"My Reporter. A Story of an Elopement." *The Hearthstone* 3: 5 (3 February 1872), 1-2. Reprinted in *Out of the Snow and Other Stories and Sketches* (1886).

"S. E. B. H. A Story of a Secret Society." *The Hearthstone* 3: 6 (10 February 1872), 1-2. Reprinted in *Out of the Snow and Other Stories and Sketches* (1886).

"A Perfect Fraud." *The Hearthstone* 3: 16 (20 April 1872), 1-2. Reprinted in *Out of the Snow and Other Stories and Sketches* (1886).

"From Bad to Worse. A Tale of Montreal Life." *The Hearthstone* 3: 18-26 (4 May-29 June 1872). Reprinted in *From Bad to Worse* (1877).

"How I Smashed a Ghost." *The Favorite* (Extra Christmas number) (28 December 1872), 8 [Signed J. A. P.].

"The Christmas Anthem." *The Favorite* (Extra Christmas number) (28 December 1872), 9-10. Reprinted in *Thompson's Turkey and Other Christmas Tales* (1873).

"Hard to Beat. A Dramatic Tale, in Five Acts, and a Prologue." *The Favorite* 1:1-13 (11 January-5 April 1873). Reprinted in *From Bad to Worse* (1877).

"Mr. Fitz-Boodle's First Masquerade." *The Favorite* 1:9 (8 March 1873), 140.

"Mr. Fitz-Boodle's Private Theatricals." *The Favorite* 1: 13 (5 April 1873), 198.

"A Familiar Fiend." *Belford's Monthly Magazine. A Magazine of Literature and Art* 1: 1 (December 1876), 78-82. Reprinted in *Out of the Snow and Other Stories and Sketches* (1886).

Thompson's Turkey and Other Christmas Tales, Poems, &c. Montreal: John Lovell, 1873.
> "Thompson's Turkey"
> "The Christmas Anthem" (reprint from *The Favorite*)
> "The Policeman's Christmas"
> "Out of the Gutter"
> "Jones, the Lawyer"
> "Out of the Snow." Reprinted in *Out of the Snow and Other Stories* (1886).
> "Christmas in the Flies"

From Bad to Worse; Hard to Beat; and a Terrible Christmas. Three Stories of Montreal Life. Montreal: Lovell, 1877.
> "Hard to Beat. A Dramatic Tale in a Prologue and Five Acts"
> "From Bad to Worse"
> "A Terrible Christmas." Reprinted in *Out of the Snow and Other Stories* (1886).

The Ghost of a Dog. A Christmas Story, in Four Acts; with a Prologue and Epilogue. Ottawa: A.S. Woodburn, Printer, 36 Elgin Street, 1885.
> "The Ghost of a Dog"
> "How I Was Mesmerised"

Out of the Snow and Other Stories and Sketches. Ottawa: Free Press, 1886.
    "Out of the Snow" (reprint from *Thompson's Turkey*)
    "A Familiar Fiend" (reprint from *Belford's*)
    "A Perfect Fraud" (reprint from *The Hearthstone*)
    "A Terrible Christmas" (reprint from *From Bad to Worse*)
    "My Reporter" (reprint from *The Hearthstone*)
    "The Ghost of a Coat"
    "S. E. B. H." (reprint from *The Hearthstone*)

Essays

[as James Bumpus." "Bumptown Papers. By James Bumpus. Paper I. Our Town." *The Hearthstone* 3: 12 (23 March 1872), 4.

[as James Bumpus." "Bumptown Papers. By James Bumpus. Paper II. Our Railway." *The Hearthstone* 3: 13 (30 March 1872), 4.

[as James Bumpus." "Bumptown Papers. By James Bumpus. Paper III. Our Press." *The Hearthstone* 3: 14 (6 April 1872), 4.

[as James Bumpus." "Bumptown Papers. By James Bumpus. Paper IV. On the Jew's-Harp." *The Hearthstone* 3: 15 (13 April 1872), 4.

[as James Bumpus." "Bumptown Papers. By James Bumpus. Paper V. On the Strike." *The Hearthstone* 3: 16 (20 April 1872), 4.

[as James Bumpus." "Bumptown Papers. By James Bumpus. Paper VI. The Nine Hour Movement." *The Hearthstone* 3: 17 (27 April 1872), 4.

[as James Bumpus]. "Our Christmas Dinner." *The Favorite* (Extra Christmas number) (28 December 1872), 10.

"Mr. Bumpus on Curiosity." *The Favorite* 1: 17 (3 May 1873), 269.

"A Dream of Life. An Allegory." *The Favorite* 1: 25 (28 June 1873), 395 [Signed J. A. P.].

Poetry

"Dreamland." *The Hearthstone* 3: 14 (6 April 1872), 1. Reprinted in *Thompson's Turkey*.

"The Silent Voice." *The Hearthstone* 3: 14 (6 April 1872), 5.

"In a Dream." *The Hearthstone* 3: 20 (18 May 1872), 5.

"God in Nature." *The Hearthstone* 3: 40 (5 October 1872), 6. Reprinted in *Thompson's Turkey*.

"The Factory Girl." *The Favorite* 1: 1 (11 January 1873), 9. Reprinted in *Thompson's Turkey*.

"Music." *The Favorite* 1: 9 (8 March 1873), 129. Reprinted in *Thompson's Turkey*.

"The Silent Voice." *The Favorite* 1: 14 (12 April 1873), 209.

"In the Fire." *Belford's Monthly Magazine. A Magazine of Literature and Art* 1: 1 (December 1876) 29.

"The Flag for Me." *The People's Almanac 1896* (Montreal: December 1895), 7.

CHRONOLOGY

1842 (25 February), John Arthur Phillips born in Liverpool

1854, cholera in Barbados, where Phillips spends his boyhood

1865 (January), Phillips starts working for the New York *Citizen*

1870, comes to Canada and joins the Montreal *Star*

1872, becomes editor of *The Hearthstone*; he publishes his first stories, essays, poems, and a novella

1873, he is editor of *The Favorite*; he publishes his second novella, a short story, essays and poems

1873 (December), his first volume is published: *Thompson's Turkey and Other Christmas Tales*

1873-1875, he works for the Montreal *Star*

1875, he marries Ivy Sarah Parson

1875-1876, he works for the Toronto *Sun* and maybe other publications

1875-1878, he compiles the *History of the Dominion of Canada* for C. R. Tuttle

1876 (December), he publishes a sketch and a poem in *Belford's Monthly Magazine*

1877, he publishes his second volume: *From Bad to Worse, Hard to Beat, and A Terrible Christmas. Three Stories of Montreal Life*

1878, he publishes occasional poetry on the departure and arrival of governors-general

1880, he begins Ottawa correspondences for the Winnipeg *Times*

1881, he is Ottawa correspondent for the Quebec *Chronicle*

1882-1905, he is Ottawa correspondent for many different newspapers, especially the Montreal *Gazette*

1885, he publishes his third volume: *The Ghost of a Dog*

1886, he publishes his fourth and last volume: *Out of the Snow and Other Stories and Sketches*

1890-1891, he works in the newsroom of the Ottawa *Citizen*

1895 (December), he publishes his poem "The Flag for Me"

1896, he is vice-president of the Ottawa Press Gallery

1897, he is president of the Ottawa Press Gallery

1899, his wife Ivy Sarah dies

1906-1907, he works for *Le Temps* in Ottawa

1907 (8 January), he dies in the press room of the House of Commons in Ottawa